GASTON LEROUX

The Phantom of the Opera

Translated and edited by
MIREILLE RIBIÈRE

With an introduction by
JANN MATLOCK

PENGUIN BOOKS

PENGUIN CLASSICS

Published by the Penguin Group
Penguin Books Ltd, 80 Strand, London WC2R ORL, England
Penguin Group (USA) Inc., 375 Hudson Street, New York, New York 10014, USA
Penguin Group (Canada), 90 Eglinton Avenue East, Suite 700, Toronto, Ontario, Canada M4P 2Y3
(a division of Pearson Penguin Canada Inc.)
Penguin Ireland, 25 St Stephen's Green, Dublin 2, Ireland (a division of Penguin Books Ltd)
Penguin Group (Australia), 250 Camberwell Road, Camberwell, Victoria 3124, Australia
(a division of Pearson Australia Group Pty Ltd)
Penguin Books India Pvt Ltd, 11 Community Centre, Panchsheel Park, New Delhi – 110 017, India
Penguin Group (NZ), 67 Apollo Drive, Rosedale, Auckland 0632, New Zealand
(a division of Pearson New Zealand Ltd)
Penguin Books (South Africa) (Pty) Ltd, Block D, Rosebank Office Park,
181 Jan Smuts Avenue, Parktown North, Gauteng 2193, South Africa

Penguin Books Ltd, Registered Offices: 80 Strand, London WC2R ORL, England

www.penguin.com

Le Fantôme de l'Opéra first published 1909–10
This translation first published in Pocket Penguin Classics 2009
This edition published 2012

010

Translation copyright © Mireille Ribière, 2009
Additional editorial material © Mireille Ribière, 2012
Introduction © Jann Matlock, 2012
Illustration (p. 2) copyright © The British Library Board, *Le Nouvel Opéra*, 1733.b.1.
All rights reserved

The moral right of the translator and author of the introduction has been asserted

Set in 10.25/12.25pt PostScript Adobe Sabon
Typeset by Jouve (UK), Milton Keynes
Printed in Great Britain by Clays Ltd, St Ives plc

ISBN: 978-0-141-19150-8

www.greenpenguin.co.uk

Contents

THE PHANTOM
OF THE OPERA

Chronology

(See Further Reading for Leroux's works translated into English)

1868 6 May: Born in Paris to Dominique Alfred Leroux, a building contractor from Le Mans, and Marie Bidault from Fécamp in Normandy.

13 June: His parents marry in Rouen and the family settles in Normandy, where three other children – Joseph, Henri and Hélène – will be born.

1880 Starts attending boarding school at Eu (Normandy).

1886 29 July: Passes his baccalauréat with honours.

October: Moves to Paris and begins Law School.

1887 First short story, 'Le Petit Marchand de pommes de terre frites', published in *La République française*.

1889 30 October: Graduates from Law School.

1890 22 January: Is sworn in as a trainee barrister.

1891 December [or January 1892]: Meets Adrien Lefort, the editor of the gossip column of *L'Écho de Paris* under the pseudonym of Robert Charvay. Becomes his secretary and is invited to contribute to the newspaper.

1894 January: Following his reports on the death sentence of anarchist bomber Auguste Vaillant in *Paris*, Leroux is invited to join *Le Matin*, a major daily newspaper, and subsequently leaves the bar.

August: Visits Italy to investigate the background of Sante Geronimo Caserio, an anarchist sentenced to death for the fatal stabbing of French president Sadi Carnot, and then witnesses Caserio's execution.

1897 17 April: *Le Turc au Mans*, a one-act musical co-written with his brother Joseph, opens in Paris with little success.

17 August–5 September: Covers President Félix Faure's visit to Russia.

5 December–14 March 1898: First novel, *L'Homme de la nuit*, serialized in *Le Matin* under the pseudonym of Gaston-Georges Larive.

1899 10 May: Marries Marie Lefranc in Paris. Soon separates from her, but she refuses divorce.

June–August: Covers the retrial of Alfred Dreyfus, a French officer of the Jewish faith wrongly convicted of treason in 1895, who became a cause célèbre thanks to novelist Émile Zola.

1900 Writes an autobiographical novel, *Ton maître*, which remains unpublished until 1997. Visits Sweden.

1901 Becomes international correspondent for *Le Matin* and *Le Français*.

1902 January: Writes against capital punishment in *Le Matin*. Is made Chevalier de la Légion d'honneur by the French government for his distinguished services as a journalist.

March: Meets Jeanne Cayatte (born 1878) in Leysin (Switzerland) and starts a lifelong relationship with her.

1903 5 October–22 November: *Le Chercheur de trésors* serialized (published as *La Double Vie de Théophraste Longuet* by Flammarion in 1904).

1904 Reports from Madeira, Port Said (Egypt), Rome and St Petersburg.

1905 February: Leaves with Jeanne Cayatte for a year-long visit to Tsarist Russia.

15 March–10 March 1906: Writes a series of articles for *Le Matin* published posthumously as *L'Agonie de la Russie blanche* in 1928.

31 July: Jeanne Cayatte gives birth to a son, André-Gaston (nicknamed Miki), in St Petersburg.

1907 26 January: First of only ten performances in Paris of Leroux's play *La Maison des juges*.

April: Following a short-lived dispute with the general editor of *Le Matin*, decides to devote himself entirely to writing fiction.

7 September–30 November: *Le Mystère de la chambre jaune* (vol. 1 of the adventures of Joseph Rouletabille, reporter) serialized.

1908 Moves with Jeanne Cayatte and their son to Menton on the French Riviera.

January: *Le Mystère de la chambre jaune* is published in book form by Éditions Pierre Lafitte.

30 June: Jeanne Cayatte gives birth to a daughter, Madeleine.

26 September–2 January 1909: *Le Parfum de la dame en noir* (vol. 2 of the adventures of Rouletabille) serialized (published by Lafitte in 1908).

24 October–9 February 1909: *Le Roi Mystère* serialized (published by Fayard in 1910).

18 December: First of eighty-five performances of *Le Lys*, a play co-written with Pierre Wolff.

1909 Moves to Mont-Boron, a suburb of Nice.

23 September 1909–8 January 1910: *Le Fantôme de l'Opéra* serialized (published by Lafitte in 1910).

November 1909–November 1910: *Le Fauteuil hanté* serialized (published by Lafitte in 1911).

1910 20 March–29 June: *Un Homme dans la nuit* serialized (published by Lafitte in 1911).

18 August–31 January 1911: *La Reine du Sabbat* serialized (published by Lafitte in 1913).

1911 Settles down with his family in Cimiez, above Nice.

9 October–18 December: *Balaoo* serialized (published by Tallandier in 1912).

17 December: His play *L'Homme qui a vu le diable* opens in Paris, proving highly successful.

1912 March–August: *L'Épouse du soleil* serialized (published by Lafitte in 1913).

1913 10 January: First of the 160 performances in Paris of *Alsace*, a patriotic play co-written with Lucien Camille.

7 March: Release of *Balaoo*, a film based on Leroux's serialized novel of 1911.

7 April–4 August: *Chéri-Bibi* serialized (published as 2 vols., *Les Cages flottantes* and *Chéri-Bibi et Cécily*, by Lafitte in 1921).

3 August–19 October: *Rouletabille chez le Tsar* (vol. 3 of the adventures of Rouletabille) serialized (published by Lafitte later that year).

1914 August: Outbreak of First World War.

28 March–2 August and 18–24 October: *Rouletabille à la guerre* (vols. 4 and 5 of the adventures of Rouletabille) serialized (published as 2 vols., *Le Château noir* and *Les Étranges Noces de Rouletabille*, by Lafitte in 1916).

23 December: Declared unfit for military service because of his weak heart.

1916 16 January–15 February: First 'war novel', *Confitou*, serialized (published by Lafitte in 1917).

29 April–8 September: *La Colonne infernale* serialized (published as 2 vols. by Fayard in 1917).

June–January 1917: *L'Homme qui revient de loin* serialized (published by Lafitte in 1917).

November: Release of Leroux's film adaptation of his *L'Homme qui revient de loin*.

1917 1 March: Divorces his estranged wife, who has finally agreed to a settlement.

14 June: Marries Jeanne Cayatte.

7 September–12 February 1918: *Les Aventures effroyables de M. Herbert de Renich* serialized (published as 2 vols., *Le Capitaine Hyx* and *La Bataille invisible*, by Lafitte in 1920).

September–March 1918: *Rouletabille chez Krupp* (vol. 6 of the adventures of Rouletabille) serialized (published by Lafitte in 1918).

1918 Writes the screenplay for *La Nouvelle Aurore*, a film in sixteen 30-minute parts.

11 November: Armistice ending First World War.

1919 Moves with his family to central Nice.

18 April–7 August: *La Nouvelle Aurore* is serialized daily in *Le Matin* (published as *Nouvelles Aventures de Chéri-Bibi* in 2 vols., *Palas et Chéri-Bibi* and *Fatalitas!*, by Lafitte in 1921); also released as a 16-part film from 25 April.

September: Helps set up La Société des Ciné-romans, which will produce novels and films simultaneously.

1920 15 January: *Le Cœur cambriolé*, a novella, serialized (published in a collection by Lafitte in 1922).

July: Writes in defence of the adventure story in *Le Petit Niçois*.

7 October–30 December: *Tue-la-mort* serialized daily in *Le Matin* (published as 2 vols. by Lafitte in 1923); and as a 12-part film from 15 October.

1921 9 September–1 December: *Le Sept de trèfle* serialized daily in *Le Matin* (published as 2 vols. by Lafitte in 1923); also released as a 12-part film from 16 September.

October–November: *Le Crime de Rouletabille* serialized (vol. 7 of the adventures of Rouletabille, published by Lafitte in 1922).

1922 March: Release of the film *Il était deux petits enfants* to a screenplay by Gaston Leroux.

4 October–14 December 1922: *Rouletabille chez les bohémiens* serialized daily in *Le Matin* (published as vols. 8 and 9 of the adventures of Rouletabille by Lafitte in 1923). Also released from 13 October as a 10-part serial film, which marks the end of Leroux's collaboration with La Société des Ciné-romans.

1923 1 July–9 August: *La Poupée sanglante* serialized (published by Tallandier in 1924).

10 August–19 September: *La Machine à assassiner* serialized (published by Tallandier in 1924).

December: The publication of *Tue-la-mort* marks the end of Leroux's association with Éditions Pierre Lafitte.

1924 12 April–20 July: *Les Ténébreuses* serialized (published as 2 vols. by Tallandier in 1925).

25 July–13 September: *La Coquette punie* serialized (published as *La Farouche Aventure* by Gallimard in 1925).

1925 19 February–18 May: *Hardi Gras* serialized (published as *Le Fils de trois pères (Hardi Gras)* by Baudinière in 1926).

2 May: Lengthy interview with Leroux appears in *Les Nouvelles littéraires*.

16 July–4 October: *Chéri-Bibi, le marchand de cacahouètes* serialized (published as *Le Coup d'état de Chéri-Bibi* by Baudinière in 1926).

11 December–21 January 1926: *La Mansarde en* or serialized (published by Laffont in 1984).

1926 29 January: Universal Pictures' silent film adaptation of *The Phantom of the Opera* (USA, 1925) opens in Nice to great acclaim (20,000 tickets sold).

17 July–19 September: *Les Mohicans de Babel* serialized (published by Baudinière in 1928).

1927 12 January–25 February: *La Véritable Histoire du célèbre Mister Flow* serialized (published as *Mister Flow* by Baudinière later that year).

20 January: First instalment of Leroux's last serialized novel *Les Chasseurs de danses* (later completed by Charles de Richter, but unpublished as a novel).

15 April: Dies of an embolism, the day after surgery for a urinary disorder. Buried in Nice.

Mireille Ribière, 2011

Introduction

*New readers are advised that this Introduction makes
details of the plot explicit*

The Opéra Ghost

They don't tell you about the Phantom unless someone asks.
And even then, the guides for the Paris Opéra tours work very
hard to keep that aspect of the building's lore to a minimum.
There is no copy of Gaston Leroux's novel in the Palais Garnier
gift shop either, though the staff insist this is only because it is
currently out of print in French. The only mask you can find
there is a decorative one, resembling the full mask of comedy,
too large to fit a human face; it is more reminiscent of Verdi's
opera about Venice than of the tortured figure whose half-mask
haunted the fantasies of the twentieth century.

We start the tour in the Grande Salle, the neo-Baroque auditorium fitted out in scarlet and gold, with its undulating sculpted
figures and vertiginous circles of balconies. The guide waits
patiently as we file into several rows of plush velvety seats
facing the immense, deep stage. For a split second, as voices
echo in the distance and a few musicians tune their instruments
in preparation for the evening's event, the space collapses into
time. We could be in 1875, the year that Charles Garnier's
Opéra was inaugurated with stupendous fanfare. Except for
the electric lights and the Chagall ceiling painting, the room
seems frozen in the early Third Republic, as if still waiting for
Swedish soprano Christine Nilsson to charm its audience with
her rendition of Marguerite in Gounod's *Faust*.[1] One almost
expects to see a dark figure lurking in 'Loge 5' – three boxes
over from the left of the stage and one floor above the orchestra – from which, on the night of the Grand Opening, Anselme
de Batbie, a government minister and prominent legal figure,

surveyed the spectacle. Only sketchy information remains about the occupants of that box in 1880–81, the years serving as a backdrop for the events in *The Phantom of the Opera*.[2] Nonetheless, a hundred years after Erik's story concluded its run in the Paris daily *Le Gaulois*,[3] it is still possible to return to the imaginary space of Leroux's novel, the opera house that commands three acres in central Paris and has as many floors – seventeen in all, five of them underground – as the Eiffel Tower. Amidst its nooks and crannies, its swirling staircases and its shadowy private boxes have multiplied more mysteries and surely as many ghosts as in any public monument of the nineteenth century. In the basement vestibule before the tour, for a brief moment there was no one in sight, just the low light, shadows, echoing footsteps. It is easy to imagine that Belle Époque journalists whispered as much as 'the ushers, the cloakroom attendants and the concierge'(5) that there were secrets kept by the marble of the Palais Garnier.

So did the Phantom of the Opera exist? That is what, even today, visitors to the Opéra and fan websites repeatedly ask – the latter often weaving chains of circumstances as baroque as the Palais Garnier itself. They speculate on what real-life personalities and events inspired those depicted in the novel. More strikingly, they imagine where the novel's hero 'really' came from and what became of him after his story appears to end. They do so because the novel invites them to ask about the reality behind the scenes of the opera house.

The novel begins, in fact, with a declaration that seems to foreclose debate on this question: 'The Phantom of the Opera did exist . . . Yes, he did exist in flesh and blood' (5). But look carefully at the workings of this Prologue. There was a ghost, we are told, but he wasn't a ghost. There was a Phantom but he was far more real than anyone wants to admit. The narrator evokes mythical 'mishaps attributed to the *ghost*' in order to connect the creature – reputed to lurk only in the 'overexcited brains' of the Opéra's female population – with a 'tragedy' that occurred thirty years earlier (5). That tragedy – which, according to the Prologue, entailed the disappearance of a beautiful soprano and a wealthy young aristocrat at the same time as that man's brother was found dead below the opera house – is reported here as a well-known set of facts in the recent past of the famous theatre. The first-person narrator's evocation of these events as remembered history thrusts us as readers head-long into his search for archival documentation and eyewitness testimony. Before we learn what befell these individuals, we are told to believe they were real, and that their plight resulted from their connections to the rumoured Opéra ghost.

But novels are fiction, and fiction is by its very nature a lie. No documents have ever emerged to construct a history of the Vicomte de Chagny, Count Philippe and Christine Daaé. Fur-thermore, no evidence exists of strange phenomena afoot in the new opera house whether due to supernatural causes or to a vengeful genius with a preternatural ability to move around in the darkness. *The Phantom of the Opera* nonetheless lures us into its search for proof as surely as if it were a journalistic exposé of corruption in high society. For that is, indeed, what the novel remains, even if not a word of the central story is true. As an acclaimed reporter, Leroux knew intimately the world he placed in the background of his novel. He also had the skills to narrate an investigation that leads the reader smack into a fantasy of plausible truths while spinning an account of improbable, even outlandish 'events'. The novel's opening line, 'The Phantom of the Opera did exist', thus resonates as the answer to a question that its readers should ask: 'Was there really a Phantom?' The novel will go on answering that ques-tion in the affirmative for centuries to come until it no longer really matters if a man like the one at the centre of this tale existed. What will matter is why people wanted to believe in him and what they projected onto his lonely, deformed body.

The Novelistic Investigation and the Investigative Journalist

'My intention here is not to revive the memory of that momen-tous event, for the curious reader can easily consult the accounts that appeared in the press at the time,' writes Leroux's narrator of the spectacular moment (in French, *'une heure historique'*) when the chandelier crashes into the auditorium (92). 'Five hundred kilos on the head of a concierge!' was the real headline in *Le Matin* about a similar event in 1896 when Leroux was that paper's senior courtroom reporter. Once the excitement about the accident had calmed, the press admitted that what had killed an audience member – in the middle of a performance of Duvernoy's *Hellé* – weighed barely ten kilos.[4] The chandelier of the central auditorium weighed over seven tons and would have killed dozens more, had it actually fallen, than did the piece of the ceiling counterweight that really landed on a working-class woman on her first visit to the Opéra. Parodying the exaggerations of sensational French journalism, the novel pretends that, after the incident that ended Carlotta's Opéra career, the chandelier was evoked by a fictional newspaper as being twenty-seven times its real weight: '*Two hundred thousand kilos hit concierge!*' (92).

This moment is instructive in how *The Phantom of the Opera* plays on expectations of the historical and the real. For all of the narrator's claims that he does not plan to reproduce a time out of the past, he nonetheless draws our attention to how much this work is preoccupied with just that kind of reconstruction, even if it makes up 'facts' as it goes along and twists other perfectly accurate historical details to flatter a completely fantasmatic tale. Paradoxically, Leroux's novel reproduces in astonishing ways exactly that '*heure historique*' of the opera house of the Third Republic (1870–1940). Just how much it does so is most apparent when one reads the novel through its details, both its descriptions of the building and its account of the musical performances that occurred there. *The Phantom of the Opera* is not a compendium of the life of the Opéra Garnier as it sometimes pretends to be. Nonetheless, it is an extraordinary evocation of the fantasies that surrounded that space and that population of thousands of spectators, performers and workers who came together every day in central Paris to fabricate jointly a dream world of spectacle.

Ironically, too, by evoking the 'press at the time' (92), the novel suggests that it is grounding its story in an everyday reality of the late nineteenth century. Its depiction of press reporting recalls how often newspapers operated in a world of hyperbole and even fantasy. Not only did the mass press after 1881 frequently draw on the over-the-top modes of sensationalism and melodrama that we associate with turn-of-the-century pulp fiction, but it increasingly embraced the newspaper serial novel and, after the First World War, the cinematic serial novel (called *Ciné-roman*) in order to sell issues and attract subscribers. But lest we let the anecdote about the chandelier suggest that the press was all sensation and little news, we should remember that this novel's story – bookended by the dates 1880–81, when its central events transpire, and 1909–10, when it was published – also coincides with the rise of the modern mass press.

Gaston Leroux (1868–1927) made his career as a journalist with several of the most prominent papers of his day. We can see the strategies he adopted as a reporter in the workings of this novel: the investigative frame that gives credence to the narrator's discovery of a 'hidden reality' amidst modern urban Paris; the anchoring of the text in details plucked from contemporary accounts of the opera house and its musical repertory; the accumulation of textual archives that suggest our savvy narrator is sharing private as well as police documents. Leroux's background as a lawyer – a profession, chosen by his family, that he abandoned as soon as he had an alternative – served him well in his journalistic career. Starting out as a writer for *Le Lutèce*, a short-lived weekly, he joined *L'Écho de Paris*, a prominent daily known for its political as well as cultural analyses, before reporting on the anarchist bombings and trials of 1893–4 for the small daily *Paris*. From 1894, he worked for one of the four leading French papers: *Le Matin* called itself the first 'modern' French daily, using catchy headlines to trumpet reports wired in by correspondents around the world. There Leroux covered major international events such as Dreyfus's second trial in 1899 and the first Russian revolution in 1905. Sadly, only one notebook remains from his fourteen years as a reporter. What we know of his approach to reporting comes, therefore, from the articles themselves, three collections of which have been published.[5] In his articles, Leroux works quickly, offering cogent details about the scenes he confronts and the individuals whose circumstances – often tragic if not also bloody – he investigates. He does not shy from pronouncements about the implications of what he is reporting, such as his assertion in 1899 that the date of the trial verdict about Dreyfus would one day be as crucial for French schoolchildren to learn as the crowning of Charlemagne.[6] His journalism brings together the best of the nineteenth century's insights into criminal psychology and the twentieth century's embrace of on-location reporting. It likewise foregrounds an insistence on unique testimonial perspectives backed by careful documentation. This is not the work of a scandalmonger but that of a careful journalist collecting deep background evidence and exploring the scene of current events. 'The reporter is looking on behalf of society,' commented Leroux. 'What could be better than to run all around the globe in order to write about the deeds of men?'[7]

One of the inventions of the modern press, as historian Dominique Kalifa has demonstrated, is the marriage of the police investigation with the journalistic investigation.[8] Nowhere in the early years of the twentieth century does this become more apparent – or more acclaimed by popular opinion – than in the novelistic series that marked Leroux's departure from reporting: in 1907, he published his second serial novel under his own name, rejuvenating the genre of the *roman-feuilleton* made popular in the July Monarchy (1830–48) by Honoré de Balzac, Eugène Sue and Alexandre Dumas *père*.[9] *Le Mystère de la chambre jaune*, along with the eight other adventures of Joseph Rouletabille that followed between 1907 and 1922, told the story of a quirky young journalist who joins forces with the police, sometimes operating in rivalry and occasionally even outside the law, to solve crimes that seem to have no solution. Explicitly invoking Sherlock Holmes as a model, the Rouletabille novels also veer into the dark regions made famous by Edgar Allan Poe (1809–49) and exploit the legacy of Sue's *Mystères de Paris* with its anxious depiction of political conspiracies and social injustice.[10]

We know that Leroux's understanding of journalism influenced the novel. Between 1907 and his death in 1927, when his fiction was a mainstay in the mass press, his understanding of the novel in turn had constitutive effects on the newspapers of

the era. Equally intriguing is how much Leroux's special brand
of novelistic investigations participated in the making of French
national cinema in the crucial years between the end of the
First World War and the coming of sound in the late 1920s.
The collaboration of the press and the police reached its apogee
in the early 1920s, in the very period when Leroux sought ways
to exploit the rich cinematic technologies of the Seventh Art.
His contemporaries, Marcel Allain and Pierre Souvestre, had
already brought their 1911–13 Fantômas novels to the screen
in 1913–14 with the help of director Louis Feuillade.[11] The
First World War brought a screeching halt to the French film
industry, leaving most theatres showing American productions
like *The Exploits of Elaine* (1914–15), marketed as *Les Mystères de New York* (1915). In the war's aftermath, Leroux
formed a company with *Fantômas* star René Navarre and began
producing serialized films and newspaper novels called *Ciné-
romans*, designed to launch quality French co-productions
between the press and the cinema whose weekly instalments
complemented one another. Leroux's job was to create a serialized novel as well as a film screenplay. Beginning with the now-lost
Nouvelle Aurore of 1919, he used this format to revivify a popular character he had invented at the war's onset, Chéri-Bibi, a
former *bagnard* or military prisoner, whose personal battles
intersected with contemporary political issues. *Rouletabille chez
les bohémiens* (1922), Leroux's final work of a half dozen *Ciné-
romans* – two of them starring his daughter Madeleine – would
return to the detective whose exploits first made him famous.[12]

French Culture in Hollywood

Leroux's decision in 1922 to sell *The Phantom of the Opera* to
an American production company might seem all the more surprising given his own active involvement with French cinema.
The story goes that Carl Laemmle, the head of Universal Studios, was visiting France on a scouting expedition for his
production of the Lon Chaney[13] *Hunchback of Notre Dame*
(1923) when he happened to meet Leroux, who gave him his
novel and a tour of the Paris Opéra.[14] Universal initially

planned to shoot *The Phantom of the Opera* in Paris using the
Palais Garnier as a stage, but this proved too costly. Instead,
Laemmle spent a fortune constructing in California a steel and
cement facsimile of the Paris Opéra – known as the first major
Hollywood film soundstage.[15] The production expenses for this
film 'jewel' of Universal Studios in 1925 could very well have
bankrupted the company, especially in light of problematic
responses to two versions screened in Los Angeles and San
Francisco early that year. Costs rose further as Laemmle
ordered rewrites and reshoots for Rupert Julian's clunky directorial effort before its delayed New York premiere in September.
Luckily for Universal, a crowd 'partial to thrills and creepy suspense', in the words of *The New York Times*, raced to see the
Phantom unmasked. 'New York "Got the Spirit",' announced
the ad that boasted: 'Thousands thrilled – gasped – laughed –
applauded – cheered – acclaimed the extraordinary fantastic
romantic thriller.' Sold-out crowds gave Universal its most
successful year in the decade.[16] In addition to the expressive
character actor Chaney, the star of the film was the set, especially the ominous cellars and the extravagantly furnished
lake-house, which featured a real courtesan's 'boat bed', shipped
from Paris. This was one of many ways that the film gave its
own twist to the story – in this case, making the underground
gothic boudoir a stark contrast to the staid bourgeois living-
room decorated by Leroux's Phantom (266–7). The film
ultimately bears little resemblance to the novel, particularly in
its conclusion, which mobilizes a revolutionary mob and cul-
minates – in the words of film historian Scott MacQueen – in
'bathos, bashed brains, and bubbles'.[17] However, even if the
entire set was made in Hollywood, the Paris subterranean represented there may not be far from the truth of the early years
of the Opéra (minus Erik's lair, of course). Artistic adviser Ben
Carré's drawings of the opera-house underground, based on
his recollections of working on set designs there at the turn of
the century, bear a marked resemblance to engravings of these
areas dating from the late nineteenth century.[18] Although the
film inspired mixed reviews in France, in part due to ambiva-
lence about whether a French novel made in America was a

good thing for the French film industry,[19] the cinematic *Phantom of the Opera* nonetheless was massively popular on both sides of the Atlantic. By contrast, because of a scandal in 1925 when Laemmle's British marketing company hoaxed the military into providing armed escorts from the film's landing at Southampton to London, Universal's *Phantom of the Opera* was banned in the UK until the sound-synchronized reissue of 1930.[20]

The world receipts for the 1925 film – $2 million for a $632,000 cost – made it the most successful movie of its era as well as the first major horror film on a list, including *Dracula* and *Frankenstein*, for which Universal would become famous in the interwar years. Although a (lost) 1916 German film preceded Laemmle's and more than a dozen other adaptations followed it,[21] it is the Universal version, which included over six minutes of revolutionary Technicolor, that made film history and ensured that the *Phantom* continues haunting to this day. Published serially in a newspaper with a relatively small pressrun of under 30,000, and with only one book edition before the film opened in 1926 in Leroux's adopted city of Nice, the novel might have been forgotten. Leroux's sale to Laemmle brought about the triumph of French culture in Hollywood even if it paradoxically let an American cinematic production colonize that culture. Grand opera, ballet, the gothic tale, the realist novel and even avant-garde visual experiments all permeated what one French cinema magazine praised as the American contribution to the 'expansion of French art in the entire world'.[22] *The Phantom* put the Paris Opéra at the centre of Hollywood and, in turn, of the American imagination at a moment when European culture no longer seemed as sure an anchor for a changing world. From its reconstruction of the Grand Escalier (Grand Staircase) for the Red Death masked ball sequence to the panoramic views of Paris seen from a rooftop perch below Apollo's statue, the film adaptation promotes the Garnier Opéra as a beacon of French national pride.[23] While Abel Gance's attempts, in *J'accuse* and *Napoléon*, to write and direct cinematic epic for France actually premiered at the Garnier Opéra in 1919 and 1927 respectively, the 1925 film had that monumentality at its core. The set may well have been built in Universal City, but the cinematic *Phantom* could not forget its space was Paris – and not just any Paris but the very concrete and spectacular Paris of the new Opéra inaugurated in 1875. What was it about the Paris Opéra that fuelled all these fantasies?

The New Opéra and Its Legends

The Palais Garnier was built between 1863 and 1875 after designs by the man who gave it his name, Charles Garnier (1825–98). Garnier, who studied at the national French art school in the 1840s, was remarkably young, just thirty-five years of age, when he won in 1861 the competition for the new opera over the favourite, rationalist Viollet-le-Duc. Garnier's plans achieved a blending of styles that included current taste in classicism along with romantic excess, Italianate mosaics recalling the Renaissance, and Baroque splendour reminiscent of Versailles. This Opéra owes much to the designs of architect Victor Louis (1731–1800), who in 1791–3 built the Théâtre des Arts (called the Salle Montansier) where the French national opera made its home until 1820. Tragedy struck that year when the heir to the throne was assassinated leaving the opera, leading the king to order that the building be torn down and the productions moved to the Salle Le Peletier. That opera house was doomed in its turn by an assassination attempt (a bombing that targeted Napoleon III in 1858) and finally destroyed by fire in 1873. Gas lighting, used in theatres through the turn of the century, was often the source of the disastrous fires that ravaged nine theatres in Paris between 1826 and 1849; 350 theatre fires occurred in Europe between 1850 and 1880, with 28 fires in the year 1881 alone.[24]

Built to protect the head of state from danger and to withstand catastrophe, Garnier's Opéra is most remarkable in its embrace of spectacle. It uses mirrors, some of which create endless reflections, to transform the space into plays of light and form. Its central staircase makes an actor of everyone who goes to see an opera there. The sweeping heights of the ceilings in the Grand Foyer, in the main staircase area and in the auditorium itself, draw the gaze upward and into the illusions to come. The 'Nouvel Opéra' – as it was called by Garnier and his contemporaries – opens onto a fantasy world. 'Look into my dream and judge for yourselves!' writes Garnier of his architectural achievement.[25] The 33 million franc cost of the building let the architect bring ninety painters and sculptors together with the best artisans of crystal, gilding, bronze, ornamental woodwork and stonemasonry.[26] Modernity was conjugated with traditional skills and materials in every aspect of the project. Such a spectacular space was possible, for example, thanks to new mining technologies and the colonial exploitation of Algerian onyx. But it depended, too, on Garnier's vast knowledge of the historical use of marble in Greek and Italian architecture.[27] Despite its Baroque and Orientalist evidence, the Opéra was extraordinarily modern in its use of cast iron, not unlike the structures exemplified by Gustave Eiffel's 1889 Tower. The Nouvel Opéra was also socially modern in its opening of all the public spaces to every kind of spectator.[28] Perhaps most revolutionary of all was its transformation of the interactions in the opera house: women of high society now strolled through the entire building during intermissions whereas previously they stayed closed up in their boxes.[29] For all of the Nouvel Opéra serving as a palace of sound – voices, instruments, bells, human footsteps and rustling silk – it came to be the premier space of vision in the Third Republic. And it gave the gaze to anyone lucky enough to hold a ticket for one night's entry into the dream.

Opera houses were a source of fantasy from the early nineteenth century. According to Margaret Miner, opera-house mysteries were inspired by the author of the Nutcracker story, E. T. A. Hoffmann, whose tales were first translated into French in 1829. A series of thrill-mongering works published during the July Monarchy and Second Empire (1851–70) further encouraged speculation on the secret sites of the Opéra.[30] Opera houses had several appeals. They could nourish the fantasies of those who already knew a genre of Paris underworld texts such as *Les Mystères de Paris*. Like all theatres, they had a backstage where more happened than the audience suspected. Like museums, they provided a rich cultural setting where workers and spectators from all walks of life mingled daily with members of society's upper echelons. Like the cinema of the future, they launched performers around whom a new celebrity culture swirled; for instance, gossip speculated whether female performers might be purchased by wealthy patrons, for the right price. Like other nineteenth-century spaces of spectacle, from the boulevard street shows to the panorama and waxworks, opera houses offered an escape into fantasy but with connections to real political and social conflict. Like all these sites of spectacle, they reflected the rapid historical change of the modernizing world.[31] Miner points out that opera-house mysteries construct a reality of the theatrical spaces in order to exploit sensationalistic and sometimes supernatural fantasies.[32] The opera house was unique among nineteenth-century spectacular venues for both the extravagance of its public spaces and the luxuriousness of its stage decors. In the Opéra Garnier, this meant five floors beneath the stage, dressing rooms equipped for 538 artists, underground stables for a herd of white horses, 7,455 gas burners – later 6,333 Edison electrical lamps – and even a cistern full of water to help fight potential fires.[33]

For indeed, beneath the Opéra was a kind of lake, not unlike the one belonging to the fantasy of Leroux's novel. Built from an underground river, it fuelled intrigues even before the 1875 Grand Opening. During excavations in 1861–2, the Garnier construction team discovered a subterranean tributary of the Seine, twelve metres below ground level. Steam pumps were installed to evacuate the water which, according to architectural historian Christopher Mead, was collected into a concrete cuve with specially designed double foundations: the creation of this 'artificial lake' enabled builders 'to control the river's flow and protect the superstructure from direct contact with the moisture'.[34] After the completion of the Opéra, as its archivist Charles Nuitter explained in 1875, nine reservoirs were built to hold 100,000 litres of water in case of fire, but also to provide for hydraulic power and heating.[35] In 1906 the weekly

L'Illustration claimed to offer the first photograph of the cistern, entitled 'Under the Opéra'. The picture accompanied an article pretending to debunk legends about the famous monument:

> If one believes some of the stories, there is even a real river whose waves beat against the structure's foundation. A boat is said to be tied loosely to a jetty and sometimes it floats downstream, carrying young dancers who come there in the summer to enjoy in their own way the charm of deep waters or maniac fly-fishing lovers who hold out fallacious hooks for doubly blind fish.[36]

The photograph shows a low-hanging stone ceiling over a long, narrow 'room' full of water. Nothing in this image would encourage anyone to believe boats might float around in the Opéra's cellars, but the discussion of the myths in this widely read periodical must have sparked the imagination of readers who knew only the theatre's comfortable auditorium and gilded reception areas. Surely, in a building that had 1,942 keys,[37] there were people who knew how to get down to these cellars without the permission of the authorities. Perhaps there were even those who made these undergrounds their regular haunt.

Subterranean Paris has inspired fantasies since the late eighteenth century when overcrowded cemeteries were moved into tunnels called the Catacombs. While there are no official burial sites below ground on the right bank of the river, it is no secret to Parisians that a vast network of passageways exists beneath the entire city, not unlike that labyrinth to which thousands of remains were transported under today's thirteenth arrondissement. Rumours circulate to this day about interlopers, called *cataphiles*, who explore these regions, using their tunnels for secret purposes. A fully functional cinema was discovered in 2004, leading to speculation about the exploitation of this part of Paris by groups unknown even to the police. Soon after, a low-budget horror film (starring the rock singer Pink) imagined teenagers staging unsupervised raves down there – and stalked by a killer.[38] That Leroux's Phantom unrepentantly murders anyone who gets in his way seems to go with the territory. People who live in the undergrounds of Paris are either dead themselves or dangerous.

Ghost Tricks

While writers have speculated since the early nineteenth century about whether the undergrounds of Paris are haunted, it took Leroux's novel to put a face on that ghostliness and to claim that the rumours had become specific to the New Opéra itself. Despite a proliferation of illustrated publications celebrating the Opéra at the time of its inauguration, the novel's account of its managers' and players' superstitions seems to have no known sources. Financial crises in the wake of the Franco-Prussian war of 1870–71 and the devastating civil war ending the Paris Commune (also in 1871), meant that, in the period surrounding 1880, the Opéra struggled to break even. However, none of the gossip-mongering newspapers ever hinted that anyone bilked money from the management, let alone harassed players and staff, as the novel imagines Erik having done. Much of the novel revolves, nonetheless, around the narrator's amassing proof, such as Moncharmin's apocryphal memoirs, that eerie events in the opera house had their source in the acts of a real person. What is extraordinary, within the context of the era's fantastic literature, is how little *The Phantom of the Opera* bends in the direction of making Erik potentially supernatural. There was no ghost in the Opéra, states the narrator – and later Leroux himself: the Phantom materializes as a man of flesh and blood. In fact, *The New York Times* complained in 1911 that the story became boring when 'the Phantom ceased to be a phantom'.[39] So what does a novel of the fantastic get out of closing off the ghostly realm? Or is this novel fantastic at all?

Literary theorist Tzvetan Todorov describes the 'fantastic' as hesitating between a rational and a supernatural explanation, distinguishing the subgenre from the 'marvellous' (with its supernatural explanations) and the '*étrange*' (the bizarre or uncanny, with rational explanations always ultimately emerging for whatever seemed out of the ordinary). 'The fantastic,' he writes, '. . . leads a life full of dangers and may evaporate at any moment.'[40] Unlike Hoffmann's short story 'The Sandman' (1816), which leaves characters and the reader alike uncertain as to whether a mysterious stranger is only in the protagonist's imagination or a real threat, *The Phantom of the Opera* explains away nearly every aspect of Erik's bizarre appearances in the Opéra. He is neither dead nor supernatural. He has no magical powers over the space – instead he is a master stonemason who learned all there is to know about the building in the 1860s while participating in its construction. His control over the actors has no supernatural basis; rather, he is a skilled ventriloquist who took over Carlotta's performance from a hiding place the day she sang to '*bring down the chandelier*' (92) and covertly provided singing lessons through the walls of Christine's dressing room. Erik is not even magically hideous. While film adaptations, both those projected and those completed, have often sought new rational explanations for his disfigured face – making him, for instance, a shell-shocked soldier wounded in the Great War, or the victim of torture by those whom he betrayed – the original novel has him simply born that way. And yet, despite the horror that ostensibly lurks beneath his mask, this is a character who has quite literally haunted the last decades of the twentieth century through his depiction in the most popular stage musical comedy of all time.[41] Women swoon when the Phantom appears during performances of the Andrew Lloyd Webber stage productions, aficionados write fan fiction about him, dozens of websites debate his motives in the novel, film and stage versions – to such an extent that on one website, amidst discussions of how to locate Erik's birth certificate in Rouen, a contributor cautioned: 'He's fiction, people!'[42] For all of Erik's fictionality, this character has escaped not only the Opéra but the novel, into a world that gives him a life of his own.

Erik's novelistic backstory is so outlandish as to invite us to suspend disbelief. We come to know his magic through his acts and his inventions, then get explanations that only barely make sense of what we have experienced as marvellous phenomena.

According to the exiled police investigator called 'the Persian' (whose writings are quoted as authoritative by the narrator for five chapters before being completed by paraphrased oral testimony), Erik is not just a talented mason but a brilliant architect. He is not only a masterful ventriloquist and vocalist but a genius composer. His years in Persia and Turkey have given him skills at torture (such as the Punjab cord that he uses on stagehand Joseph Buquet) in addition to transforming him into a trapdoor expert, what the novel calls '*l'amateur de trappes*'. He has built trick entrances and hidden passages modelled on the workings of magic boxes (280–82). And he has created secret spaces in the Opéra based on what his 'artistic, *illusionist* bent' inclined him to do: 'to hide his genius' *and* to '*squander it on tricks*' (282).

The pivoting mirror of Christine's dressing room serves as a remarkable metaphor for the genius of the novel's hero – and for his tricks. By throwing his voice from behind her mirror, he has convinced Christine that he was sent by her dead father. He has posed as 'the Angel of Music' to offer her singing lessons while she stares at her own image. He lures her through that very mirror and down into the labyrinth to his abode where she spends the first evening complacently enraptured, listening to him sing. Although the second day of her imprisonment finds her confronted with the masked man's designs to keep her captive, she continues not to press him to show his face. In this cellar dining-room next to a chamber where he sleeps in his own casket, she even enjoys a large meal after more music and a remarkably calm chat about his plans for her stay. Only later during their operatic sing-along does she finally work up the courage to tear off his mask. It is at this point that the novel declares Erik to attain something of the 'superhuman': he does this not through his acts and even less through his ability to outlive a mortal existence, but through his grief expressed in a '*clameur surhumaine*'. As Christine testifies, 'Were I to live to be a hundred . . . I shall never forget the infernal, howling cry of agony and rage he uttered' (144). It is the extent of this passion that again captivates Christine despite her pledge to the handsome aristocrat Raoul de Chagny, whom she has loved since their childhood in Brittany. She claims she can take no risks with Erik's 'vindictive soul' (145) and, in order to preserve her boyfriend from harm, she opts to wear the Phantom's ring and visit him regularly.

Raoul's response on the Opéra rooftop to the confession of his betrothed does not inspire confidence. Jealousy, hatred, mistrust of her motives and swaggering vows to slay Erik – a mixture of pettiness and overreaction marks the Viscount's discovery of the implausible interactions in which Christine has been caught up for the previous weeks. Raoul answers his girlfriend's self-sacrificing concern to protect him with a demand that she proclaim her hatred for his rival. While Raoul's less-than-heroic characterization may be one of the ways that the novel chastises the ruling classes, it leaves most readers today more sympathetic to murderous, twisted, hideous but pathetic Erik than to the often clueless beau. The young woman's honourable refusal to give Raoul the key to a shortcut into the cellars may not seem very wise on her part, but it nonetheless demonstrates her moral mettle despite pressures weighing on her from every angle. Raoul remains profoundly feckless, not even capable of managing his own brother's dismay at a union that promises neither title nor fortune. When Christine disappears again, as if by magic, this time through a stage trapdoor while singing *Faust*'s Marguerite, the police blame Raoul's overprotective sibling – and would have convinced the baffled Viscount of his guilt had the Persian not offered to help him find Erik's 'secret retreat' by the lake (195, 198). Together the Persian and Raoul return to the scene not just of the crime (of kidnapping) but of Christine's seduction by the Voice – and to the magical properties of the dressing-room mirror (201). And soon they will discover the further ways that Erik has prepared a world in which he can hide his genius and play tricks with it.

The 'torture chamber' of the Opéra cellars emerges as the pinnacle of both that genius and that trickery. But it is also one of the sites of the novel where Erik's mastery seems to change into something like magic. The hexagonal room replicates 'the most horrendous invention' (233) that Erik produced during his stint as architect, assassin and entertainer for the Persian emperor and his favourite daughter. That the Persian, who once served as the emperor's police chief, fears this room so much suggests how horrible its prototype must have been. Erik is depicted as the designer of this space rigged with tortures set to begin without a human hand; he is likewise given credit for inventing its mirror illusions, which have since been imitated in the mirage houses of nineteenth-century exhibitions (247).[43] Overwhelmed by the illusions projected on endlessly reflecting walls, the Persian and the Viscount nevertheless find a trapdoor leading into a cellar where they discover that Erik has been plotting to blow up central Paris. This plot is again linked to his architectural genius as well as his tricks. In short, he has created a system designed either to flood the cellars or to blow the building sky high. With the turn of one tiny bronze creature, a scorpion or a grasshopper, the world could change for tens of thousands of innocent Parisians. And their fate rests on Christine's decision – and on whether she can believe the man who tells her what choice each beast represents. If she'll marry him, he says, turn the scorpion. Should her answer be no, then turn the grasshopper. The eavesdropping Persian expects Erik to have been lying from the start, not even playing fair with the information that would let her consent honourably to self-sacrifice. For a few moments, as readers, we hesitate with Christine. The future of both the Opéra and Paris hangs in the balance. The novel pushes its melodrama to the hilt, leaving us doubting whether anything the masked genius would say now might extend hope for a future, for himself or anyone else. But Erik has not lied and though the flood nearly drowns both would-be rescuers, a quasi-magical intervention saves everyone's life. The Persian returns home safely. And although he knows of the Viscount's safety only from Erik's words, by this point we have no reason to doubt the dying Phantom. The Viscount has escaped with Christine – as if in a fairy tale by Hans Christian Andersen – on a train to the north of the world (274).

The magic boxes of the layers of narrative fold in upon one another to such an extent that it is hard to know where truth might lie. For a work so obsessed with achieving a proper investigation, arriving at the actual truth proves at best illusory.

Believing the narrator requires giving credence to each nuance offered by the Persian – details that have been treated by the Paris police as nothing more than the ravings of a madman (269). Trusting the Persian's story depends on believing Erik. That diabolical illusionist is, finally, the only source for Christine's promise to return to bury Erik with the ring he gave her – in a dying monologue whose truth is supposedly guaranteed by the Phantom's 'genuine emotion' (272–3). Ultimately, we only know that Christine made it out alive – and with Raoul – from the lips of the Phantom, whose story is told to the Persian – whose oral history is shared with the narrator who writes it down for us. There are, in short, a lot of places where the truth might go missing as do the Phantom, the soprano, the charming Viscount, or even the Persian who conveniently perishes before the writing of the text we have been reading. If we believe one, we can believe them all, up to a point. But what if we start to doubt one?

Subterranean Hauntings

Holding up the foundation for the entire architecture of this hall of mirages of a novel is one concrete detail that the text tenders as the overwhelming evidence for the truth of its investigation: a skeleton with a ring on its finger. Erik is real, we have been told from the outset, with the narrator using the French expression '*en chair et en os*', literally 'in flesh and bones'. And indeed, it is the 'real' of a skeleton that the novel submits as its ultimate guarantee of that reality. Bones found, no less, while voices were being buried. '[L]atterly workmen, digging in the vaults of the Opera House where phonographic recordings of singers' performances were to be buried, came upon a corpse; I had immediate proof that it was the body of the Phantom of the Opera,' writes the narrator in the Prologue (8). Until recently, the account of this time capsule of gramophone records entombed below the Opéra appeared as far-fetched as the fantasy of a luxuriously furnished private dwelling on a lake underneath the Palais Garnier. The plot device seemed ingenious, the perfect exchange of a cadaver for a permanently living voice. What a sublime figure for the obsessions of the novel: voices like those coveted by the Phantom captured on disks and preserved like bodies underground!

But the story about the phonograph records was not made up. In 1989, men working on the Opéra ventilation system found a locked room deep in its sub-basements. Four time capsules of phonograph records were discovered within – which were turned over to the Bibliothèque nationale for safe-keeping.[44] A century after they were 'buried', as promised, the voices were in 2008 unleashed from those discs. The model for Leroux's soprano, Christine Nilsson, was not one of them since she had stopped singing long before technology was able to share her voice with the future. The discovery of the recordings put a ghost into the novel that worked so hard at demonstrating the only person haunting the Opéra was a man. The spectral voices of modernity singing from these very real buried discs raised the question of what else might yet be learned about the underworld of the Opéra.

While the press of 1907 and 1912 covered amply the burial of these phonograph recordings, one finds no mention of any skeletons, whether 'a victim of the Commune' (as journalists supposedly dubbed the one taken by Leroux's narrator to be the Phantom (8)) – or any other.[45] By making so much ado about how the skeleton cannot possibly be linked to the Commune, the novel draws our attention to the conditions that would have led to such confusion. Who were 'the poor wretches who were massacred during the Commune' (8) and why would the press – or this novel – have been concerned with them? The Commune – the revolutionary utopian government established by popular insurgent forces who, in protest at France's turn to the right after its humiliating defeat to Prussia, seized Paris for two months in 1871 – does provide a fascinating thread throughout *The Phantom of the Opera*. We are constantly led down the 'Communards' passage' (226–8, 230, 232, 278), reminded of the underground dungeon where the Commune kept its prisoners (205, 225, 278), even told that the Opéra rooftop once launched Communard balloons (205). Once again here, the novel changes history to suit its whims. While the yet-unfinished Garnier monument served during the Prussian siege of Paris as a storehouse for food and ammunition, and probably also as a bomb shelter, it never became a prison. The Communards held those charged with crimes like spying in places that had already been prisons before the war. The opera house was nowhere near the locales where several dozen hostages were killed by the Communards in response to the attack by 130,000 Versailles troops. It would not have been the least bit surprising, however, for the Opéra to shield the body of one of those 'wretches' massacred during the *Semaine sanglante* (Bloody Week) between 21 and 28 May 1871, when an estimated 25,000 Parisians met their deaths.[46] Indeed, at the turn of the century, theirs were the bones turning up amidst new urban developments, just as they were the very real phantoms haunting Paris. Evoking a relationship between Erik, in death, and those dead at the time of the Commune, the novel invites reflections on another tragedy that haunts Paris, this time all too realistically.

The Face of the Voice

It is a gold ring that underwrites our narrator's claim to have found the Phantom's skeleton. That ring, he asserts, proves Christine kept her promise to bury Erik and it suggests she has delayed her idyll with Raoul until her pledge was honoured. The ring differentiates Erik from those skeletons connected to the Commune and enables the narrator to argue that these bones should lie in 'the archives of the National Academy of Music' rather than in a mass grave. '[T]hese are no ordinary bones' (282), he maintains, evoking the talent of the one who once animated them. Erik's genius musicality and his voice merit a special resting place. But this all-too-significant piece of evidence has disappeared into thin air.

In this 'Epilogue', where most ends are tied up in the interest of pretending 'The reader knows what followed or can guess the rest of this incredible yet true story' (282), we should consider what else escapes the text. Two things, at least: that face and that voice. Surprisingly, in the final moment of the novel, the Phantom no longer seems deformed: 'I did not recognize the skeleton by his hideous head,' remarks the narrator, 'for all men who have been long dead are the same' (282). It might be easy to dismiss this statement as believable enough within the framework of the novel's often fantastic logic. It nonetheless reminds us how often, in the course of this text, we have been asked to imagine the 'horror' of the Phantom's face.

Much depends on this novel's depiction of Erik as a 'monster' (148): Christine must be sufficiently horrified by what she sees beneath his mask to trade her ecstatic admiration, developed over months of sharing music through his 'lessons', for disgust and terror. The text must manage to convey something piteous about Erik's traditional aspirations to a marriage in the Madeleine Church as well as something tragic in his withdrawal from society into the Opéra cellars. His face must be imagined by readers to be so horrible that not even a sublime voice and genius talent could render it innocuous. In this respect, the novel is itself hideously intolerant of physical disability. It subscribes disturbingly to nineteenth-century eugenic philosophies, which conceived of anything other than 'perfect' northern European features as denoting a potentially criminal, atavistic or degenerate character. Critics and film participants alike have given much thought to the implications of this fantasy of masked facial horror. In a 1925 review, poet Carl Sandburg remarked that the entire film builds suspense towards the 'sometime' when we'll see 'just what it is he's hiding'.[47] Medical historian Sander Gilman has suggested that Erik's damaged face evokes the ravages of hereditary syphilis, while for psychoanalytic theorist Slavoj Žižek, Erik represents a walking phallus.[48] Taking his cue from the novel's description of the role of ' "living corpse" ' (280) that Erik was forced to play in freak shows, actor Chaney asked make-up artists for the 1925 film to liken his face to a skull with piercing eyes. Only late in the Lloyd Webber rehearsals did the mask metamorphose from one covering the upper half of Erik's face (similar to the one in the novel) to a half-mask exposing on one side a handsome face while leaving the other side to the imagination.[49] Leroux's narrator declares Erik as ugly as any other man in death, but the work depends on the shock value of his horrible looks in life.

'I wanted to see the *face of the Voice*,' says Christine, explaining the unmasking at the heart of the novel (145). Erik's face undoes whatever desire his angelic music inspires. But it is perhaps no less sublime – terrible and beautiful at the same time – than the crazy singer's 'cries' predict (145). Unlike Bram Stoker's Dracula, who never has much heart and certainly has no soul, Erik aspires in novels,[50] films and stage versions to love, art and beauty. His longings are noble preoccupations that would be hard to hold against him were he not also a stalker, a blackmailer, a kidnapper, a torturer, a murderer and a would-be terrorist potentially responsible for the deaths of thousands. Although his bad behaviour and perverse world-view may be excused, considering the ordeal inflicted upon him in his youth by an intolerant society, the thrill of Erik's 'point of no return'[51] is hard to reconcile with the very real crimes for which he is accountable. At some level, however, he is at one with other criminals and madmen of the opera, which in nineteenth-century France pursues a long Western tradition of giving the most sublime roles to those who are the most out of control – with Don Giovanni as a prime example. It is perhaps not surprising that Erik aspires to write his own *Don Juan triomphant* and obsesses about the female love interest in that tale of bargains with the devil that is *Faust*. Erik's voice, imagined as passionate, magical, supernatural even, is what somehow redeems this character, even amidst his crimes. Or maybe it is one with those crimes. Disembodied, the ventriloquist's voice floats through the pipes, pierces doors, seems to emanate from mirrors, flies out of nowhere to become something angelic. It seduces and enraptures both characters and readers. The 'face of the voice' can never match what the ears imagine.

The word *'fantôme'* in French means simply 'ghost'. The novel is perhaps most accurately called 'The Opera Ghost'. In the 1911 English translation and subsequent adaptations, Erik became, by chance or luck, not just a run-of-the-mill spook but a 'phantom': the epithet retains his Frenchness as well as a certain chic. Rising up from the underworld of high culture and high society, Erik haunts even if he is 'flesh and blood'. Mixing genres, playing with truth and fiction, thwarting audience expectations for serial literature by infusing it with the lyric fantasies of grand opera, reconstructing the physical space of the Palais Garnier from the Grand Escalier to the rooftop and down again to the fifth sub-basement, this novel masquerades as many things. It throws its own voice like a genius ventriloquist into so many spheres that as readers we are hard-pressed to harmonize the many directions at play. It ultimately asks us to see in our mind's eye something so terrible it is beyond imagining and to hear something so sublime it is beyond knowing. And in that space, the novel's very real 'Phantom' goes on haunting.

But what perhaps haunts the most are the very real obsessions, anxieties, spectacular pleasures and even voices from the nineteenth century that the novel invites to go on residing in the Paris Opéra. The Phantom has done much to keep the music and the architecture of a nineteenth-century monument alive.

Jann Matlock, 2011

NOTES

1. Nilsson (1843–1921), who is evoked in the background and roles of the character Christine Daaé in *The Phantom of the Opera*, never actually sang at the new Opéra. Although she was scheduled to sing Marguerite at the Grand Opening, she cancelled at the last minute, claiming she had a cold, and never appeared on the Garnier stage (Martine Kahane, *L'Ouverture du Nouvel Opéra: 5 janvier 1875*, Paris: Réunion des musées nationaux, 1986, pp. 24–5). Just how eagerly the Opéra awaited her voice may be seen from the engraving, 'Inauguration du Nouvel Opéra: La Salle vue de la scène', *Le Monde illustré*, 9 January 1875, which shows the anticipated scene from *Faust* (Kahane, p. 25).

2. Kahane, *L'Ouverture du Nouvel Opéra*, p. 20. For the Opéra's seating arrangements, which show 'Loge 5' as belonging to 'les premières loges côté jardin' (grand tier, stage right), see Charles

Nuitter, *Le Nouvel Opéra*, Paris: Hachette, 1875, p. 138. We know who held the subscription for *Loge 5* in the early 1880s thanks to the microfilmed archives of the Bibliothèque de l'Opéra, but we do not know who actually sat in that box. The ageing countess who paid to use *Loges 5* and 7 three nights a week surely invited friends and relatives. Unlike the Phantom, who claims Box 5 as a courtesy and pays nothing, Madame la Comtesse de Béhague was charged nearly 25,000 francs to keep the box in her family (Registre des Comptes courants, CO 232, 1880, p. 445).

3.   *Le Gaulois*, a small but influential conservative daily with an average print run of 30,000 in 1910, published *Le Fantôme de l'Opéra* in daily instalments between 23 September 1909 and 8 January 1910. For comparison, in the same year the fourth largest newspaper in France, *Le Matin*, for which Leroux worked as a journalist for fifteen years and in whose pages he published several serial novels, had a circulation of 670,000. The first three, *Le Petit Parisien*, *Le Petit Journal* and *Le Journal*, had circulations of 1,400,000, 835,000, and 810,000 respectively. See Claude Bellanger, et al., *Histoire générale de la presse française*, Paris: PUF, 1972, vol. 3, p. 296; and Christophe Charle, *Le Siècle de la presse*, Paris: Seuil, 2004, pp. 155–67.

4.   *Le Gaulois* provides accounts in 'Une Alerte à l'Opéra', 21 May 1896, pp. 1–2 (including the real weight of what fell, p. 2) and 'Le Lustre', 22 May 1896, p. 1. The sensational headline is from *Le Matin*, 21 May 1896, p. 1.

5.   Gaston Leroux, *Sur mon chemin*, Paris: Flammarion, 1901; *L'Agonie de la Russie blanche* (1928), Paris: Le Serpent à plumes, 1998; *Du capitaine Dreyfus au pôle Sud*, ed. Francis Lacassin, Paris: UGE, coll. 10/18, 1985. On Leroux's journalism, see Guillaume Fau, 'Rouletabille à la Bibliothèque', in Fau, ed., *Gaston Leroux, De Rouletabille à Chéri-Bibi*, Paris: Bibliothèque nationale de France [BNF], 2008, p. 19; and Pierre Assouline, 'La Contrebande Invisible: Gaston Leroux et le journalisme', in Fau, *Gaston Leroux*, pp. 12–17.

6.   Leroux, 'La Cour révise', *Le Matin*, 4 June 1899, p. 1, collected in *Du capitaine Dreyfus*, p. 294. After 23 August 1899, *Le Matin* replaced Leroux on this case because of his support for Dreyfus (Fau, *Gaston Leroux*, p. 38).

7.   Leroux, *Cahiers semestriels du Cercle Gaston Leroux*, no. 5, p. 8, cited in Fau, *Gaston Leroux*, p. 44.

8.   Dominique Kalifa, *L'Encre et le sang: Récits de crimes et société à la Belle Époque*, Paris: Fayard, 1995.

9. In 1897–8, Leroux published a first novel, *L'Homme de la nuit*, in his own paper *Le Matin*, using the pseudonym Gaston-Georges Larive; his second serial novel appeared there as *Le Chercheur de trésors* in 1903, this time under his own name. Leroux broke with *Le Matin* in 1907 for his first Rouletabille novel, *Le Mystère de la chambre jaune*; along with its sequel, *Le Parfum de la dame en noir* (1909), it appeared in *L'Illustration*. Published in France in 1836, Balzac's *La Vieille Fille* was one of the first *romans-feuilletons* to appear in daily instalments in the national press. Sue contributed the century's runaway bestsellers with *Les Mystères de Paris* (1842–3) and *Le Juif errant* (1844–5). Dumas reinvented himself as a *feuilletoniste* with *Les Trois Mousquetaires* (1844) and *Le Comte de Monte Cristo* (1844–6). Following Second Empire restrictions on the publication of serials, the newspaper novel thrived again only with the Third Republic liberalization of the press after 1881. Leroux's works in the 1910s attained a popularity that rivalled the July Monarchy masters. For an historical overview of the genre, see Lise Queffélec, *Le Roman-feuilleton français au XIXe siècle*, Paris: PUF, 1989.

10. Leroux promoted the myth that Rouletabille was his alter ego: 'When I was a reporter, that is to say when I was Rouletabille, we engaged, among special correspondents of every country, in courteous but ferocious battles in the field of the news,' he writes in *Une heure de ma carrière* (Paris: Baudinière, 1926), excerpted in Leroux, *Oeuvres*, *Vol. 1*, ed. Francis Lacassin, Paris: Robert Laffont, 1984, p. 1003.

11. Marcel Allain (1885–1969) and Pierre Souvestre (1874–1914) jointly created the mysterious criminal who struck the homes of the wealthy bourgeoisie of pre-war Paris and repeatedly escaped thanks to masterful disguises. In the thirty-two novels written by the two authors (and eleven more penned by Allain alone after Souvestre's death), as well as in the five serial films directed by Louis Feuillade (1873–1925), journalists and the police joined forces to chase Fantômas – a character whose name seems to recall Leroux's protagonist of 1909–10. See Tom Gunning, 'A Tale of Two Prologues: Actors and Roles, Detectives and Disguises in *Fantômas*, Film and Novel', *Velvet Light Trap*, 37 (1996), pp. 30–36.

12. Of Leroux's *Ciné-romans*, only *Le Sept de trèfle* and *Rouletabille chez les bohémiens* exist today, both preserved in the Centre National du Cinéma film archive. Stills from *La Nouvelle Aurore*

are in Fau, *Gaston Leroux*. On serial cinema, see Richard Abel, *French Cinema: The First Wave, 1915–1929*, Princeton, NJ: Princeton University Press, 1984, pp. 72–3, 77–85, 119.

13. Lon Chaney (1883–1930) played the lead in Universal's *Hunchback of Notre Dame* (1923) and in its subsequent *Phantom of the Opera*. His mythical facial plasticity brought him fame as a silent film actor between 1912 and his death in 1930. He is known to have been the uncredited director of major portions of the 1925 *Phantom*, replacing Rupert Julian, whose incompetent direction Chaney reportedly refused to accept.

14. A photograph shows the two standing together in front of the Opéra (Philip Riley, *The Making of The Phantom of the Opera*, Absecon, NJ: MagicImage Filmbooks, 1996, p. 28).

15. 'Notre Opéra reconstitué à Universal City', *Ciné-Miroir*, 15 October 1924, p. 326; 'Le Fantôme de l'Opéra, Paris reconstitué en Californie', *Mon Ciné*, 18 June 1925, pp. 12–13. This structure, called 'The Phantom Stage', still exists today (though its chandelier disappeared in the 1960s) and has frequently transported American films to fantasmatic Paris. Websites on haunted places report sightings of a figure in black, reputedly Chaney's ghost, on the set. The documentary *The Opera Ghost: A Phantom Unmasked*, on the DVD of *Phantom of the Opera* (1943), cites a number of films shot on Stage 28, including *Torn Curtain* (1966) and *Thoroughly Modern Millie* (1967). By contrast, Audrey Hepburn's turn on the Opéra Grand Escalier in *Funny Face* (1957), featured on the cover of *Charles Garnier: Un architecte pour un empire* (Paris: ENSBA, 2010), was shot on site in Paris.

16. Mordaunt Hall, 'A Fantastic Melodrama', *The New York Times*, 7 September 1925, p. 15. Also see the advertisement for the film on the same page. *The Phantom of the Opera* was the fifth most popular US attraction in 1925, according to Richard Koszarski, *An Evening's Entertainment: The Age of the Silent Feature Picture, 1915–28* (Berkeley: University of California Press, 1990), p. 33.

17. Scott MacQueen, Audio Commentary, *The Phantom of the Opera*, Milestone Collection, DVD (2003).

18. For contemporary engravings of the cellars, see Nuitter, *Le Nouvel Opéra*. On Carré, see Larry Langman, *Destination Hollywood: The Influence of Europeans on American Filmmaking*, Jefferson, NC: McFarland, 2000, pp. 50–51; and MacQueen, Audio Commentary. For further background on the 1925 film,

see Jerrold Hogle, *The Undergrounds of the Phantom of the Opera*, New York: Palgrave, 2002, pp. 136–52.

19. A popular cinema journal claimed Leroux would have been 'stupid' not to have accepted Universal's remarkable offer. The editor, Sylvio Pelliculo, further argues that France is well served by the enterprise because 'the initial work is ours and the reconstitution of the Opéra over there is remarkable' ('Tout pour la France', in 'Vous avez la parole', *Mon Ciné*, 20 August 1925, p. 2).

20. See 'The Escorted Film: A Clever and Humiliating Hoax', *Manchester Guardian*, 30 June 1925, p. 13; 'Escorted Film Withdrawn', *The Times of London*, 14 August 1925, p. 7; 'British Ban Holds', *The New York Times*, 14 October 1926, p. 22; 'British May Lift Laemmle Film Ban', *The New York Times*, 15 November 1928, p. 27.

21. Hogle gives an overview of the film versions in *The Undergrounds of the Phantom of the Opera*, pp. 135–204. Of special interest are Arthur Lubin, dir., *Phantom of the Opera* (1943), starring Claude Rains; Terence Fisher, dir., *The Phantom of the Opera* (Hammer Films, 1962); Brian De Palma, dir., *Phantom of the Paradise* (1974); Dwight Little, dir., *Phantom of the Opera* (1989), starring Robert Englund. The only version filmed on location in the Paris Opéra is the television *The Phantom of the Opera* (1990), dir. Tony Richardson, with Burt Lancaster as the Opéra director.

22. 'Un Hommage de l'Amérique à l'Art français', *Cinémagazine*, 25 September 1925, p. 514.

23. The French premiere incited Leroux to rearticulate his narrator's words – speaking this time under his own name: 'The Phantom of the Opéra existed,' he wrote in an unpublished text, 'En Marge du Fantôme de l'Opéra', in Leroux, *Oeuvres*, p. 1000.

24. Anselm Gerhard, *The Urbanization of Opera*, trans. Mary Whittall, Chicago: University of Chicago Press, 1998, p. 302; Gérard Fontaine, *Palais Garnier: Le Fantasme de l'Opéra*, Paris: Noesis, 1999, p. 241. On the transition from gas to electrical lighting, see F. W. J. Hemmings, 'Fires and Fire Precautions in the French Theatre', *Theatre Research Journal*, 16: 3 (1991), pp. 237–49. The most catastrophic Paris opera fire occurred at the Opéra-Comique in 1887, killing 170. In 1936, the Palais Garnier confronted tragedy: a fire destroyed its original stage but spared the main public spaces (Gérard Fontaine, *Charles Garnier's Opéra: Architecture and Interior Decor*, trans. Charles Penwarden, Paris: Éditions du Patrimoine, 2004, p. 98). On building the Opéra, see François Loyer, ed., *Autour de l'Opéra: Naissance de la ville moderne*, Paris: Délégation à l'action artistique de la

Ville de Paris, 1995; and Christopher Curtis Mead, *Charles Garnier's Paris Opéra: Architectural Empathy and the Renaissance of French Classicism*, Cambridge, MA: MIT Press, 1991.

25. Charles Garnier, *Le Nouvel Opéra* (1878–81), repr. Paris: Linteau, 2001, vol. 1, p. 327. Note Garnier's emphasis on the sense of sight: 'What a feast for the eyes!' (vol. 1, p. 328).

26. Mead, *Charles Garnier's Paris Opéra*, p. 4. Including furniture and theatrical machinery, the Opéra cost 36 million francs, a cost overrun of 3 million francs (Mead, p. 197).

27. Details may be found in Fontaine, *Charles Garnier's Opéra*, pp. 50–57.

28. Fontaine, *Charles Garnier's Opéra*, p. 120. Even the uppermost *loges* have their own private salons, suggesting that Garnier thought anyone with an opera ticket ought to have a chance to entertain in a private space behind the part of the box visible from the auditorium.

29. *La Vie parisienne* noted of this promenade: 'Decidedly, we don't need masks at all' ('Invitation à la Valse', 13 November 1875, pp. 86–8, cited in Kahane, *L'Ouverture du Nouvel Opéra*, p. 9).

30. Margaret Miner, 'Phantoms of Genius: Women and the Fantastic in the Opera-House Mystery', *19th-Century Music*, 18:2 (Fall 1994), pp. 121–35, offers several antecedents to Leroux's tale that evoke the Le Peletier Opera House. Miner's writings in progress, 'Opera Under Water: The Siren Improvises' and 'Auditions: From Propriety to Performance in Nineteenth-Century France', promise further insights on both Paris opera and *The Phantom* (mss. given to me by the author).

31. See Vanessa Schwartz, *Spectacular Realities: Early Mass Culture in Fin-de-Siècle Paris*, Berkeley: University of California Press, 1998; and Maurice Samuels, *The Spectacular Past*, Ithaca, NY: Cornell University Press, 2004.

32. Miner argues that these mid-century texts imagine the Opéra as the 'site of musical and fantastic danger to women' ('Phantoms of Genius', p. 124), a feature shared by Leroux's *Phantom of the Opera*.

33. See Fontaine, *Charles Garnier's Opéra*, pp. 97–8. Electricity came to the Opéra on 15 October 1881, and was fully implemented in November 1885 (Fontaine, pp. 98–102).

34. Mead, *Charles Garnier's Paris Opéra*, p. 147. One reason for the substantial overrun of building costs was the extra time and expense required by the unexpected subterranean waters.

35. Nuitter, *Le Nouvel Opéra*, pp. 232–6.

36. Serge Basset, 'L'Opéra', in *L'Illustration*, 29 December 1906, p. 433. In this and a later article, Basset explores 'The Unknown Corners of the Opéra', describing those who work backstage alongside photos of the cellars (*L'Illustration*, 29 December 1906, p. 441; 6 January 1907, p. 14). Recent photographs of the reservoir appear in Jacques Moatti, et al., *L'Opéra de Paris: Palais Garnier*, Paris: Adam Biro, 1987.

37. Kahane, *L'Ouverture du Nouvel Opéra*, p. 16.

38. See John Henley, 'In a Secret Paris Cavern, the Real Underground Cinema', *Guardian*, 8 September 2004; Martine Valo and Jean-François Pantaloni, 'Les Visiteurs du noir', *Le Monde* 2, 16 October 2004, pp. 40–43; Christopher Ketchum, 'Spelunking the Empire of the Dead', *Salon*, 19 June 2002; and the classic anthropological study by Barbara Glowczewski, prefaced by Félix Guattari, *La Cité des Cataphiles* (1983), re-ed. Paris: Éditions associatives ACP, 2008. For the film, see *Catacombs*, FearNet 2007, DVD 2008 (dir. Tomm Coker). On the haunting of the Paris Catacombs, see Jann Matlock, 'Phantom Undergrounds', forthcoming in *Dix-Neuf*. David L. Pike explores the dangers of underground Paris in '*Paris Souterrain*: Before and After the Revolution', *Dix-Neuf*, 15:2 (October 2011), pp. 177–97.

39. 'An Opera-house Phantom', *The New York Times Book Review*, 19 February 1911, p. 90.

40. Tzvetan Torodov, *The Fantastic*, trans. Richard Howard, Ithaca, NY: Cornell University Press, 1975, pp. 25, 41.

41. Hogle surveys the backstories given to Erik's face in various adaptations in *The Undergrounds of the Phantom of the Opera*, pp. 135–231. The Andrew Lloyd Webber musical, *The Phantom of the Opera*, premiered in London in 1986. 'High Notes: The Rise and Rise of the Phantom', *Guardian*, 10 March 2010, counted 9,500 performances in London, 100 million viewers worldwide and 40 million records sold. Since its 1988 New York opening, the musical has exceeded 9,000 performances (Joe Brescia, 'Longest-Running Show on Broadway is Usher at "Phantom" Theater', *The New York Times*, 12 October 2009).

42. Hathor, comment #698, 'Erik, phact or phiction', *Phantom of the Opera.com* at http://www.phantomoftheopera.com/modules/newbb/viewtopic.php?topic_id=131&forum=2&post_id=534852. See also http:/www.phantomoftheopera.ro/a_existat_erik_covezi_chagny.php, both consulted 10 December 2010.

43. Spectacular mirror halls were a Persian specialty from the twelfth century, culminating in the nineteenth-century Isfahan palaces of

Shiraz. See Sergio Jaretti, et al., *Palazzi di Specchio/Mirror Palaces: Iran and India*, Turin: Celid, 2008, pp. 106, 159.

44. For the September 2008 opening of two containers, see Elizabeth Giuliani, '1907–2008: Le Long Sommeil des urnes de l'Opéra', in *Les Voix ensevelies*, BNF, http://expositions.bnf.fr/voix/arret. 01.htm, which includes recordings as well as a film of the event. Michael Walsh claims he 'found' the urns in 1988 while writing a biography of Lloyd Webber ('Phantoms of the Opera', *France Today*, April 2008, at www.francetoday.com/features/phantoms. php, consulted 4 May 2008).

45. An extensive set of press clippings was compiled by the BNF: 'Les Urnes de l'Opéra: Revue de presse', Département de l'audiovisuel de la BNF (mss. shared by film curator Alain Carou).

46. The novel's expression, *'les malheureux qui ont été massacrés, lors de la Commune'* ('the poor wretches who were massacred during the Commune' (8)), does not pinpoint the Communards themselves as those who killed: the reference to skeletons under the Opéra expands to encompass any of the dead of that moment. For an overview of this period, see Robert Tombs, *The Paris Commune, 1871*, New York: Longman, 1999. On the difficulty of knowing the numbers killed during the *Semaine sanglante*, see Gay Gullickson, who reports that 'most historians subscribe to a figure of twenty thousand to thirty thousand, frequently settling on twenty-five thousand' (*Unruly Women of Paris: Images of the Commune*, Ithaca, NY: Cornell University Press, 1996, pp. 165–6). Jean Braire, *Sur les Traces des Communards* (Paris: Éditions des Amis de la Commune, 1988, p. 181), reports the discovery, during work in January 1897 on a reservoir in north-east Paris, of 800 skeletons still dressed in their Communard *fédéré* uniforms. Discoveries of makeshift burial grounds – the result of summary executions of thousands by government troops – were in all likelihood underreported in the Belle Époque.

47. Carl Sandburg, *Chicago Daily News*, 7 December 1925, in Sandburg, *'The Movies Are'*, Chicago: Lake Claremont Press, 2000, p. 286.

48. Sander Gilman, 'The Phantom of the Opéra's Nose', in Gilman, *Health and Illness: Images of Difference*, London: Reaktion, 1995, pp. 67–92. Slavoj Žižek, 'Grimaces of the Real, or When the Phallus Appears', *October*, 58 (October 1991), pp. 44–68.

49. Related in the documentary *Behind the Mask* (dir. Jamie Crichton, 2005), included with the DVD of the 2004 *Phantom of the Opera* (dir. Joel Schumacher).

50. Examples include Susan Kay, *Phantom* (1990) and Frederick Forsyth, *The Phantom of Manhattan* (1999). Forsyth was an early collaborator on the stage musical *Love Never Dies* (2010), Andrew Lloyd Webber's sequel to his *Phantom of the Opera* (1986).
51. I allude here to the song entitled 'Past the Point of No Return', in Lloyd Webber's stage production. (See George Perry, *The Complete Phantom*, New York: Henry Holt, 1988, pp. 163–4.)

Further Reading

WORKS BY GASTON LEROUX
TRANSLATED INTO ENGLISH

Only a few of the titles listed below have been reissued or retranslated since they first appeared in English.

Novels

The Adventures of a Coquette, trans. Hannaford Bennett (London: T. Werner Laurie, 1926). Original titles: *La Coquette punie* (serial, 1924); *La Farouche Aventure* (book, 1925).

The Amazing Adventures of Carolus Herbert, trans. Hannaford Bennett (London: Mills & Boon, 1922). Original title: *Le Capitaine Hyx* (vol. 1 of *Les Aventures effroyables de M. Herbert de Renich*, 1920).

Balaoo, trans. Alexander Teixeira de Mattos (London: Hurst & Blackett, 1913). Original title: *Balaoo* (1912).

The Bride of the Sun, trans. uncredited (New York: McBride, Nast, 1915; London: Hodder & Stoughton, 1916). Original title: *L'Épouse du soleil* (1913).

The Burgled Heart, trans. Hannaford Bennett (London: John Long, 1925); also published as *The New Terror* (New York: Macaulay & Co., 1926). Original title: *Le Cœur cambriolé* (1922).

Chéri-Bibi and Cecily, trans. Hannaford Bennett (London: T. Werner Laurie, 1923); also published as *The Missing*

Men: The Return of Chéri-Bibi (New York: Caldwell, 1923). Original title: *Chéri-Bibi et Cécily* (1921).

Chéri-Bibi, Mystery Man, trans. Hannaford Bennett (London: John Long, 1924). Original title: *Palas et Chéri-Bibi* (1921).

The Double Life, trans. Edgar Jepson (New York: J. E. Kearney, 1909); also published as *The Man with the Black Feather* (Boston: Small, Maynard & Co., 1912; London: Hurst & Blackett, 1912). Original title: *La Double Vie de Théophraste Longuet* (1904).

The Floating Prison, trans. Hannaford Bennett (London: T. Werner Laurie, 1922); also published as *Wolves of the Sea* (New York: Macaulay & Co., 1923). Original title: *Les Cages flottantes* (1921).

The Haunted Chair, trans. uncredited (New York: E. P. Dutton & Co., 1931). Original title: *Le Fauteuil hanté* (1911).

The Kiss that Killed, trans. uncredited (New York: Macaulay & Co., 1934). Original title: *La Poupée sanglante* (1924).

The Machine to Kill [sequel to *The Kiss that Killed*], trans. uncredited (New York: Macaulay & Co., 1935). Original title: *La Machine à assassiner* (1924).

The Man of a Hundred Masks, trans. uncredited (London: Cassel & Co., 1930); also published as *The Man of a Hundred Faces* (New York: Macaulay & Co., 1930). Original title: *Mister Flow* (1927).

The Man who came back from the Dead, trans. Geoffrey Garrod (London: Eveleigh Nash & Co., 1916). Original title: *L'Homme qui revient de loin* (1917).

The Masked Man, trans. Hannaford Bennett (London: John Long, 1927). Original title: *Tue-la-mort* (1923).

The Midnight Lady, trans. Hannaford Bennett (London: John Long, 1930). First part of *La Reine du Sabbat* (1913).

The Missing Archduke, trans. Hannaford Bennett (London: John Long, 1931). Second part of *La Reine du Sabbat* (1913).

The Mystery of the Yellow Room, trans. uncredited (New York: Brentano's, 1908). Original title: *Le Mystère de la chambre jaune* (1908).

The New Idol, trans. Hannaford Bennett (London: John Long, 1928). Original title: *Le Coup d'état de Chéri-Bibi* (1926).

Nomads of the Night: The Latest Adventures of Chéri-Bibi, trans. Hannaford Bennett (New York: Macaulay & Co., 1925); also published as *The Dancing Girl* (London: John Long, 1926). Original title: *Fatalitas!* (1921).

The Perfume of the Lady in Black, trans. uncredited (New York: Brentano's, 1909). Original title: *Le Parfum de la dame en noir* (1908).

The Phantom of the Opera, trans. Alexander Teixeira de Mattos (London: Mills & Boon, 1911); trans. Lowell Bair (New York: Bantam, 1990); trans. Leonard Wolf (New York: Plume, 1996). Original title: *Le Fantôme de l'Opéra* (1910).

The Secret of the Night: Further Adventures of Rouletabille, trans. uncredited (London: Everleigh Nash, 1914). Original title: *Rouletabille chez le Tsar* (1913).

The Slave Bangle, trans. Hannaford Bennett (London: John Long, 1925); also published as *The Phantom Clue* (New York: The Macaulay Company, 1926). Original title: *Le Crime de Rouletabille* (1922).

The Sleuth Hound, trans. Hannaford Bennett (London: John Long, 1926); also published as *The Octopus of Paris* (New York: Macaulay & Co., 1927). Original title: *Rouletabille chez les bohémiens* (1923).

The Son of Three Fathers, trans. Hannaford Bennett (London: John Long, 1927). Original title: *Le Fils de trois pères (Hardi Gras)* (1926).

The Veiled Prisoner, trans. Hannaford Bennett (London: Mills & Boon, 1923). Original title: *La Bataille invisible* (vol. 2 of *Les Aventures effroyables de M. Herbert de Renich*, 1920).

Short Stories

All the titles mentioned below are published in *The Gaston Leroux Bedside Companion*, ed. Peter Haining (London: Victor Gollancz Ltd, 1980).

'The Crime on Christmas Night', trans. Mildred Gleason

Prochet and Morris Bentinck, pp. 100–15. Original title: 'Le Noël du petit Vincent-Vincent' (1924).

'The Gold Axe', trans. Hannaford Bennett, pp. 136–47. Original title: 'La Hache d'or' (1912).

'In Letters of Fire', trans. uncredited, pp. 116–35. Original title: 'L'Homme qui a vu le diable' (1908).

'The Inn of Terror', trans. Mildred Gleason Prochet and Morris Bentinck, pp. 59–83. Original title: 'L'Auberge épouvantable' (1925).

'The Mystery of the Four Husbands', trans. Mildred Gleason Prochet and Morris Bentinck, pp. 36–58. Original title: 'Not' Olympe' (1924).

'A Terrible Tale', trans. Hannaford Bennett, pp. 17–35. Original title: 'Le Dîner des bustes' (1911).

'The Woman with the Velvet Collar', trans. Mildred Gleason Prochet and Morris Bentinck, pp. 84–99. Original title: 'La Femme au collier de velours' (1924).

Plays

The Man Who Saw the Devil: A Play in Two Acts, trans. Frank J. Morlock (Rockville, MD: Borgo Press, 2009). Original title: *L'Homme qui a vu le diable* (first performed in 1911).

WORKS WRONGLY ATTRIBUTED TO GASTON LEROUX

Lady Helena or The Mysterious Lady [sequel to *The Man of a Hundred Masks* aka *The Man of a Hundred Faces*], trans. uncredited (London: T. Werner Laurie, 1931). Original title: *Le Collier de Lady Helena*, written by Louis Latzarus (perhaps from notes Leroux donated to Charles de Richter). The novel was serialized under the title *Lady Hélèna* in *Le Journal* (1 February–22 March 1929) and published in book form as *Le Collier de Lady Helena* (Paris: Miro, 1946).

'The Waxwork Museum', trans. Alexander Peters, in *The Gaston Leroux Bedside Companion*, ed. Peter Haining (London: Victor Gollancz Ltd, 1980), pp. 148–56. Scholars do not recognize this as a genuine short story by Gaston Leroux.

Critical Studies

There are very few in-depth and well-documented studies of *The Phantom of the Opera* in the English language.

Fau, Guillaume (ed.), *Gaston Leroux: de Rouletabille à Chéri-Bibi* (Paris: Bibliothèque nationale de France, 2008). Of interest because of the numerous illustrations.

Haining, Peter, 'Foreword to *The Phantom of the Opera*' (London: W. H. Allen, 1986). Interesting collection of anecdotes about the Paris Opera House, Gaston Leroux and the various film adaptations of the book. Unfortunately perpetuates the myth of the lake.

Hogle, Jerrold E., 'The Gothic and the "Otherings" of Ascendant Culture: The Original *Phantom of the Opera*', *South Atlantic Quarterly*, 95 (1996), 821–46.

Hogle, Jerrold E., *The Undergrounds of* The Phantom of the Opera. *Sublimation and the Gothic in Leroux's Novel and Its Progeny* (Basingstoke: Palgrave MacMillan, 2002). This academic study of the novel and its major film and stage adaptations is overall well informed and (despite its title) quite accessible. One does not need to agree with M. Hogle's conclusions to appreciate his insights.

Husson-Casta, Isabelle, *Le Travail de l'obscure clarté' dans* Le Fantôme de l'Opéra *de Gaston Leroux* (Paris: Lettres Modernes, 1997). A key study by a leading Leroux specialist.

Newark, Cormac, ' "Vous qui faites l'endormie": The Phantom and the Buried Voices of the Paris Opera', *19th-Century Music*, 33: 1 (2009), pp. 62–78.

Shah, Raj, ' "L'Effroi du masque": Masks, Identity and Death in Three Works by Jean Lorrain, Marcel Schwob and Gaston Leroux' (dissertation, University of Cambridge, 2008, 42 pages). Includes a most perceptive study of *The Phantom of the Opera*.

Žižek, Slavoj, 'Grimaces of the Real, or When the Phallus Appears', *October*, 58 (1991), pp. 44–68.

Mireille Ribière, 2011

Translator's Note

This new, unabridged translation is based on the 1910 edition of *Le Fantôme de l'Opéra* published in Paris by Éditions Pierre Lafitte.

As befits a work of popular fiction, the issue of readability has been uppermost in my mind, particularly with regard to sentence structure. However, it seemed appropriate to mark the centenary of the first publication of the novel with a translation that also seeks to convey the flavour of the original, which is why I have aimed for historical accuracy in terms of usage. Translating the book into the English language afforded a unique opportunity to evoke the prose of the English and American writers that Leroux admired: first and foremost Dickens for his humour and vivid descriptions, but also Kipling and Wells for the poetic lyricism of some of their stories, as well as Conan Doyle and Edgar Allan Poe. This I hope to have achieved through particular attention to sentence flow and the use of distinctive phrases.

The titles of the musical works and operas cited have generally been kept in French. So have the names of the characters of the operas performed, not only as a reminder that the action takes place inside the Paris Opera House, but also because all works staged at the Paris Opera House had to be in French: Verdi's opera *Les Vêpres siciliennes* (1855), for example, was premiered in French, and later translated into Italian. The lyrics of the arias, however, are quoted in English, where possible using the translations that were available at the beginning of the 1880s – when the story is supposed to take place – or as near as possible to the time of writing. When the English wording was somewhat distant from the original French, my translation of the surrounding text had to be adjusted to achieve a seamless flow.

This translation differs significantly from previous translations of the novel on a number of points relating, for the most part, to the descriptions of the Paris Opera House. Gaston Leroux, who was a journalist and a theatre critic, not only had first-hand knowledge of the building but also used sources such as Charles Nuitter's *Le Nouvel Opéra* (1875) and the two volumes of Charles Garnier's *Le Nouvel Opéra de Paris* (1876–81). My rendition of descriptive passages therefore is based on the English terminology put forward by Edwin O. Sachs and Ernest A. E. Woodrow, who clearly consulted the same reference material as the novelist for their chapters on the Palais Garnier in *Modern Opera Houses and Theatres* (1896–8). Leroux referred to the mezzanine floors housing the scenery and complex theatre machinery underneath the stage as *les dessous*, a neutral term whose meaning can be expressed with 'down' or 'below'; he reserved the word *cave* (i.e. 'cellar') for the lowest area. Similarly I have used 'cellar' sparingly. Where Leroux departs from reality, he remains coherent: Erik built his dwelling within the double watertight shell around the lower part of the building; there is no suggestion in French that it stands *on* the lake. So as to convey the mysterious grandeur of *la demeure du lac* without altering its position on the inside of the retaining wall of the imaginary lake, it has been translated as 'the lake-side retreat', instead of the usual 'house on the lake'.

Throughout, I have aimed for clarity and accuracy. Thus I have faithfully reproduced Leroux's unusual and idiosyncratic use of italics, which serve not only to render emphasis in reported speech, but also to highlight the significance of particular phrases within the narrative. Likewise I have kept the dotted lines that appear here and there as text breaks within chapters. However, this translation deviates from the French on one occasion: at the very end of Chapter XXVI, 'The Scorpion or the Grasshopper?', which marks the climax of the book. Any close rendition of the onomatopoeia used in this passage tended to weaken its dramatic import – given a choice, readers of the manuscript opted for my edited version.

My warm thanks to Thalia Marriott, Ros Schwartz, Derek Scott and Catherine Warner for their comments on the manuscript, and to Isabelle Husson-Casta and Paulette Perec for helping me clarify a few obscure references. I am greatly indebted to Tim Warner for his unwavering support, and valuable comments and suggestions from start to finish.

Mireille Ribière, 2011

THE PHANTOM
OF THE OPERA

The New Opera House (1875), by Alphonse Royer

TO MY GOOD OLD BROTHER JO[1]
Who has nothing of a ghost, but definitely something of an Angel of Music like Erik

Ever affectionately,
Gaston LEROUX.

PROLOGUE

*In which the author of this singular account tells
the reader how he came to ascertain that the
Phantom of the Opera really existed*

The Phantom of the Opera did exist. He was not, as was long
believed, born out of the fertile imagination of the artists, the
credulity of the directors, or the ludicrous fancy and overexcited brains of the young ladies of the *corps de ballet*,[1] their
mothers, the ushers, the cloakroom attendants and the concierge. Yes, he did exist in flesh and blood, although he assumed
in every respect the appearance of a ghost – that is, of a shadow.

When I consulted the archives of the National Academy of
Music,[2] I was immediately struck by the curious coincidence
between the mishaps attributed to the *ghost* and an exceedingly
mysterious and extraordinary tragedy that occurred at the
same time; I soon conceived the idea that the former might provide a rational explanation for the latter. The events in question
took place no more than thirty years ago.[3] Even today, it would
not be difficult to meet, in the Ballet Room,[4] elderly gentlemen
whose words are not to be doubted and who can remember, as
if it were only yesterday, the mysterious and dramatic circumstances that surrounded the abduction of Christine Daaé, the
disappearance of Viscount Raoul de Chagny and the death of
his elder brother, Count Philippe, whose body was found on
the shore of the underground lake that lies beneath the Paris
Opera House where it borders the Rue Scribe.[5] However, until
now, it would not have occurred to any of these witnesses that
the somewhat mythical character of the Phantom of the Opera
might have something to do with that dreadful affair.

The truth dawned upon me slowly. In my investigations I
was constantly coming across events that appeared, at first, to
be not of this world; and more than once I was very close to

giving up, for I was exhausting myself vainly chasing an elusive image. At last, I found proof that my intuitions were not unfounded, and all my efforts were rewarded the day I finally ascertained that the Phantom of the Opera was more than a mere shadow.

That day, I had spent long hours poring over the light-hearted *Memoirs of a Theatre Director*, whose author, the all too sceptical Moncharmin, had understood nothing, during his term at the Opera, of the mysterious behaviour of the Phantom. In fact, he was deriding it over-much even as he was becoming the first victim of the curious financial operation that took place inside the 'magic envelope'.

I had just left the library and was in poor spirits when I met the charming administrator of our National Academy on a landing; he was chatting with a spry old man of smart appearance, to whom he cheerfully introduced me. The administrator knew all about my investigations and how frustrated I had been in my search for the whereabouts of the examining magistrate[6] for the famous de Chagny case, M. Faure. No one knew what had become of him, whether alive or dead. But then, upon his return from Canada where he had just spent fifteen years, he had come at once to the secretarial office of the Opera to apply for complimentary tickets: the little old man before me was M. Faure himself.

We spent much of the evening together and he told me all he knew, and had understood at the time, about the de Chagny case. Given the lack of evidence, he was bound to conclude that the Viscount had lost his sanity and that his elder brother's death was accidental; he was nevertheless convinced that something terrible had happened between the two brothers in connection with Christine Daaé. He was unable to say what had become of Christine and the Viscount. And, of course, when I mentioned the Phantom, he simply laughed. He too had been told of the curious occurrences that seemed to point to the existence of an extraordinary being, residing in one of the most shadowy corners of the Opera House; he had also heard about the 'envelope'. In all this, however, he saw nothing worthy of note as examining magistrate in charge of the de Chagny case;

and he paid little attention to the testimony of a witness who came forward of his own accord to say that he had met the Phantom. The witness in question was none other than the man whom everybody in Paris at the time called 'the Persian' – a figure well known to the subscribers of the Opera.[7] The magistrate took him for a crank.

As you can guess, this story about the Persian aroused my keenest interest. Hoping that it would not be too late and that he still lived at the same address, I immediately set out in search of so unique and invaluable a witness. Good fortune was on my side again, and I managed to track him down to the small apartment that he still occupied in the Rue de Rivoli, and where he was to die five months later.

I was wary at first; but then he told me, with the ingenuousness of a child, all that he personally knew about the Phantom. And once he had handed over to me proof of the latter's existence, as well as a bundle of letters written by Christine Daaé that shed significant light on her dreadful fate, there was no more room for doubt. None whatsoever! The Phantom was not a myth.

Yes, I know, there was the suggestion from some quarters that this correspondence might not be authentic and had perhaps been forged from start to finish by a man whose imagination had surely been fired by wondrous tales; but fortunately, I was able to find a sample of Christine's handwriting elsewhere, and the comparison between the two laid to rest any lingering suspicions I might have had.

I also looked into the Persian's past and found that he was an honourable man, incapable of inventing a story that might mislead the Law.

My opinion in this matter was, moreover, shared by the prominent figures who were directly or indirectly concerned with the de Chagny case, by friends of the de Chagny family, and by those to whom I showed all the documents in my possession and disclosed my conclusions. I received the noblest encouragements from them. In this respect, allow me to reproduce here some of the lines that were sent to me by General D—:

MONSIEUR, – I cannot urge you too strongly to publish the results of your investigation. I remember perfectly well that in the Ballet Room, a few weeks before the disappearance of the great singer Christine Daaé and the tragedy that afflicted the whole of the Faubourg Saint-Germain,[8] there was much talk of the ghost; and I am certain that it only stopped once the whole dreadful affair had ceased to occupy our minds. However, were it possible – as your revelations have led me to believe – to explain this great tragedy by the existence of the ghost, then I beg you, monsieur, revive the ghost. However mysterious he may appear at first, his existence will always be more easily explained than the grim story, as malicious rumour would have it, of two ever-loving brothers tearing each other apart to the death . . .

   Yours, etc.

Clutching the case file and checking that all I had seen and all I had uncovered corroborated every detail of the Persian's revelations, I once more wandered through the Phantom's vast domain, the mighty edifice of which he had made himself ruler; and then came the wonderful discovery that put an end to my enquiry and crowned my labours.

Some of you may remember that latterly workmen, digging in the vaults of the Opera House where phonographic recordings of singers' performances were to be buried,[9] came upon a corpse; I had immediate proof that it was the body of the Phantom of the Opera. Thanks to me, the administrator himself saw the evidence at first hand, and the present claim by the press that the body was that of a victim of the Commune[10] is a matter of utter indifference to me.

The poor wretches who were massacred during the Commune in the vaults of the Opera House were not buried on this side of the building; their skeletons are to be found, I can confidently assert, at a considerable distance from the vast crypt that was stocked with all sorts of provisions during the siege. I found their burial place while looking for the remains of the Phantom, whose corpse I would never have discovered had it not been for the extraordinary accident of chance described above.

We shall return in due course to the issue of the corpse and of what ought to be done with it. For now, I must bring this much needed prologue to its conclusion by expressing my gratitude to all those whose generous assistance proved invaluable to me: Inspector Mifroid (who was first on the scene when Christine Daaé vanished); M. Rémy, the former secretary; M. Mercier, the former administrator; M. Gabriel, the former chorus-master; and, above all, Baroness de Castelot-Barbezac, once known as 'Little Meg' (for which she feels no shame), the most charming prima ballerina of our admirable *corps de ballet* and the eldest daughter of the late Mme Giry, herself the worthy attendant in charge of the Phantom's box. Thanks to them, I am now able to recount in every detail those moments of intense love and terror.*

---

* It would be churlish on my part, on the threshold of this awe-inspiring and true story, not to thank the present management of the Paris Opera House, who so kindly helped me with my enquiries, and M. Messager[11] in particular; I should also like to thank the present administrator, the charming M. Gabion, as well as the amiable architect entrusted with the preservation of the building, who did not hesitate to lend me the works of Charles Garnier,[12] though he guessed that I would probably never return them to him. Finally, I must pay public tribute to my friend and former colleague, M. J.-L. Croze,[13] who allowed me to search his splendid collection of theatre books and borrow rare editions that he greatly valued. – G.L.

I

The Ghost!

That evening, Messrs Debienne and Poligny, the directors of the Paris Opera House, were giving a last gala performance to mark their joint departure. Suddenly the dressing-room of Sorelli, one of the ballerinas, was invaded by half-a-dozen young ladies of the *corps de ballet*, just back from dancing *Polyeucte*.[1] They burst into the room in a state of great agitation, some of them laughing excessively and unnaturally, others uttering cries of terror.

Sorelli, who wished to be alone for a moment to 'run through' the little speech that she was to give to the resigning directors, was upset at the sight of them thoughtlessly crowding in. She turned round and glared enquiringly at the frantic girls. It was Little Jammes – with her snub nose, her forget-me-not eyes, her rose-red cheeks and lily-white throat – who explained the situation in a trembling, fearful voice: 'The ghost!' she cried before locking the door.

Sorelli's dressing-room had a formal, bland elegance. The furniture was basic and consisted of a swing mirror, a sofa, a dressing-table and a number of wardrobes. On the walls there were several engravings, relics from her mother dating back to the glorious days of the old Opera House in the Rue Le Peletier,[2] as well as portraits of Vestris, Gardel, Dupont and Bigottini.[3] To the girls of the *corps de ballet*, Sorelli's room was like a palace. They themselves had to share dressing-rooms, where they spent their time singing, arguing with each other, quarrelling with the dressers and hairdressers, and treating themselves to small glasses of *cassis*,[4] beer, or even rum, until the first call came through.

Sorelli was very superstitious and shuddered when she heard Little Jammes mention the ghost. 'Silly little fool,' she cried. But, as she was the first to believe in ghosts in general, and in the Opera's own ghost in particular, she was eager to know more. 'Have you seen him?' she enquired.

'As plainly as I see you now!' answered Little Jammes, collapsing on a chair with a groan.

'If that was him, then he's very ugly!' quickly added Little Giry, a girl with dark eyes, jet-black hair, a swarthy complexion and taut skin over her puny little frame.

'Oh, yes!' cried the ballet-girls in unison. And they all began to talk at once. The ghost had appeared to them as a gentleman dressed in black. He had loomed out of the dark in a corridor. They had no idea where from. It had all occurred very suddenly, as if he had come straight out of the wall.

'Well, really!' said a girl who had kept a cooler head. 'You see the ghost everywhere!' And it was true. For several months, there had been talk of nothing else at the Opera but the ghost dressed in black who stalked the building like a shadow. He spoke to nobody, nobody dared speak to him and should anyone see him, he would vanish at once, without trace or clue. As became a real ghost, he walked silently. At first, people had scoffed and made light of this spectre dressed like a gentleman or an undertaker; but the story of the ghost had soon grown to monumental proportions among the members of the *corps de ballet*. All the girls claimed to have come across this supernatural being in one way or another, and to have suffered at his hands. And those who laughed loudest were not best reassured. When he did not actually show himself, he signalled his presence or his passage with disastrous or comic occurrences for which he was more often than not blamed, so rife were the feelings of superstition. Had there been some accident, had one of the girls been the butt of a practical joke by a friend, or lost a powder-puff, the culprit must be the ghost, the Phantom of the Opera!

Ultimately though, who had actually seen him? One meets so many men in black coats at the Opera who are not ghosts. But this coat was like no other. It clothed a skeleton. Or so the ballet-girls said. Not to mention, of course, the cadaverous head.

Was there any truth in all this? The image of the skeleton originated with the description of the ghost given by Joseph Buquet, the chief stage machinist.[5] He had found himself face to face – in a manner of speaking, for it could hardly be called a face – with the mysterious figure on the little staircase by the footlights that leads directly down to the mezzanine floors below the stage. He had only caught a glimpse of it – for the ghost had fled – but that sight had made an indelible impression upon him.

Here is what Joseph Buquet said about the ghost to anyone who cared to listen: 'He is extraordinarily thin and his black coat hangs loosely off his skeletal frame. His eyes are so deep-set that you cannot make out his pupils: all you can see are two big black holes, as in a skull. His skin is stretched over his bone structure like a drumhead, and is not white but an ugly yellow. His nose is almost non-existent when seen sideways; and this *absence* is a horrible thing to *behold*. As for his hair, it consists of no more than three or four long dark strands on his forehead and behind his ears.' The chief machinist had pursued this strange apparition but without success. It had vanished as if by magic, leaving no trace.

Now Joseph Buquet was a reliable, sober, steady man, not prone to flights of fancy. His words aroused interest and amazement; and soon there were other people claiming that they too had met a man dressed in black with a skeletal head. Sensible people, who had heard the story, began by suggesting that one of his assistants must have played a prank on the machinist; but, when a series of curious and inexplicable incidents occurred in quick succession, even the most incredulous began to wonder.

We are all agreed that firemen are brave! Nothing frightens them, least of all fire! Well, one day,* the fireman on duty, who had apparently ventured a little further down into the

---

* This is again a true story, which was related to me by M. Pedro Gailhard himself, a former director of the Opera House.[6]

mezzanines than usual while on his rounds below stage, came back up suddenly looking pale, bewildered and trembling, with his eyes popping out of his head; indeed, he had practically fainted in the arms of the proud mother of Little Jammes. What had happened? He had seen *a head of fire floating in the air at a man's height* coming towards him. As I said before, firemen are not usually afraid of fire.

The fireman in question was called Papin.

The *corps de ballet* were alarmed. This blazing head did not tally with Joseph Buquet's description of the ghost. The fireman and the machinist were cross-questioned; whereupon the young ladies were convinced that the ghost had several heads, which he changed at will. And, of course, they thought themselves in the gravest danger. If a fireman saw fit to faint, then the dancers had reasons a-plenty to be frightened, and henceforth quickened their pace whenever they passed some dark recess in an ill-lit corridor.

On the day after Papin's misadventure, Sorelli herself, followed by all the dancers, including the little ones from the ballet school in their leotards, walked over to the administrative wing and deposited a horseshoe[7] on the table outside the concierge's lodge. Anyone who entered the building, other than as a patron, was meant to touch the horseshoe before setting foot on the first step of the staircase, so as to be protected from the occult forces that had taken over the entire Opera House. Like all else that is recounted here, this anecdote is not – alas! – an invention of mine; the horseshoe is still there, on that very table, as anyone entering the Opera House via the courtyard of the administrative wing can confirm.

This should give you some idea of the state of mind of the young ladies of the *corps de ballet* on the evening when they had rushed into Sorelli's dressing-room and Little Jammes had cried: 'The ghost!'

The dancers' nervousness had all but diminished. An agonized silence now filled the dressing-room. The only sound was that of the gasping girls. Presently Little Jammes, who had hastily retreated to the farthest corner of the room, whispered: 'Listen!' They all thought they heard a rustling outside the door. But no sound of footsteps. It was like silk brushing ever so lightly against the panel. Then it stopped.

Determined to show more nerve than the others, Sorelli walked towards the door and asked in a wan voice: 'Who's there?' Nobody answered. Aware that her slightest movements were being watched intently by all around her, she mustered her courage and shouted: 'Is there anyone behind this door?'

'Oh, yes, yes! There must be somebody behind the door!' cried dark little Meg Giry, heroically holding Sorelli back by her tulle skirt. 'Whatever you do, don't open the door! Oh, Lord, don't open the door!'

However, Sorelli, armed with a dagger that never left her side, dared turn the key and open the door, while the ballet-girls drew back towards the dressing-closet at the rear of the room.

'Oh, my word!' breathed Meg Giry.

Sorelli bravely looked into the corridor. It was empty; a fluttering flame trapped in glass cast a red and dubious light upon the surrounding darkness, yet could not quite dispel it. The ballerina quickly closed the door, with a heavy sigh. 'No,' she said, 'there is no one there.'

'But we did see him!' declared Little Jammes, timidly resuming her place beside Sorelli. 'He must be prowling somewhere out there. I shan't go back to dress. We had better all go down together to the Ballet Room for your little "speech", and then come back here together.' Thereupon the child reverently touched the little coral amulet that she wore as protection against bad luck,[8] while Sorelli surreptitiously traced, with the rosy tip of her right thumb, a St Andrew's cross on the wooden ring[9] that adorned a finger of her left hand.

'Sorelli,' wrote a famous critic, 'is a tall, handsome, willow-waisted ballerina, with a grave, sensuous face, who is often described as a "classic beauty". Emerald-green eyes sparkle in her pale face, framed by rich, golden hair. Her head sways gently, feather-like, on her long, elegant and proud neck. At times, when she dances, a particular, indescribable movement of her hips sets her whole body a-quiver with an ineffable sensuality. When she raises her arms and bends forward at the start of a pirouette, with her corsage pressed tightly to her figure and her hip bone thrust forward, she is a sight, some say, to die for.' As for brains, there is strong evidence that she had none. But no one held it against her.

'Come now, girls, pull yourselves together!' she said to her young companions. 'Perhaps none of you has really seen the ghost.'

'Yes, yes, we have seen him! We saw him just a moment ago!' they cried.

'With his skull head and his frock-coat, just as when he appeared to Joseph Buquet!'

'And Gabriel saw him too!' Little Jammes added. 'Only yesterday! Yesterday afternoon – in broad daylight.'

'Gabriel? The chorus-master?'

'Why, yes. Didn't you hear?'

'And he was wearing his black coat, in broad daylight?'

'Who? Gabriel?'

'No! The ghost!'

'Yes, he was!' asserted Little Jammes. 'Gabriel told me so himself. That's how he recognized him. It all started with a visit from the Persian. Gabriel was in the stage manager's office when suddenly the door opened and the Persian entered. He has the "Evil Eye",[10] as you know.'

'Oh, yes,' chorused the ballet-girls, conjuring him up in their minds and making the gesture of the 'horned hand' by extending their index and little fingers outwards while holding down their middle and ring fingers by their thumbs.[11]

'And you know too how superstitious Gabriel is,' Little Jammes continued. 'All the same, he's never rude. When he meets the Persian, he gently slips his hand into his pocket and fingers his keys.[12] Well, the moment the Persian appeared in the doorway, Gabriel leaped from his chair and reached out for the cupboard lock, so as to touch metal! In so doing, he ripped the tail of his jacket on a nail. Rushing out of the room, he bumped his forehead against a coat rack and, recoiling, grazed his arm on the screen by the piano; he leaned forward on to the piano to try and steady himself, but the lid fell and caught his fingers; then, he ran out of his room like a madman, tripped at the top of the first flight of stairs and tumbled down to the bottom. I was just passing by with Mother. We helped him up. He was badly bruised, with blood all over his face. What a frightful sight! Yet he grinned at us and sighed: "Thank God, I escaped so lightly." And as we pressed him to explain himself, he told us of his terror at seeing the ghost appear *behind* the Persian – *the ghost with his skull head* just as Joseph Buquet has described him.'

Little Jammes raced through her story as if the ghost was at her heels and was quite out of breath when she reached the end. Her listeners murmured among themselves, aghast, and then fell again into a silence while Sorelli, visibly moved, continued polishing her nails.

'Joseph Buquet should hold his tongue,' remarked Meg.

'Why should he hold his tongue?' someone asked.

'Because Mother says so,' replied Meg, lowering her voice lest other ears than those present might overhear her words.

'And why does she say so?'

'Hush! Mother says the ghost wants to be left in peace.'

'And how does she know?'

'Because . . . because . . . nothing . . .'

Her knowing reticence only served to arouse further the curiosity of the dancers who crowded round her, begging her to explain herself. They were close together, all leaning forward in a gesture of entreaty and fear, communicating their terror to one another and yet exhilarated by it.

'I swore not to tell!' gasped Meg. But they insisted, and promised so earnestly to keep her secret that Meg, burning to tell all that she knew, began, with her eyes fixed on the door: 'Well, it's because of the private box.'

'What private box?'

'The ghost's box!'

'The ghost has a box?' At the thought that the ghost might have his own box in the theatre, the girls could not contain their fearful feelings of anticipation. 'Oh, do tell us, do tell us!' they said.

'Not so loud!' said Meg. 'It's Box Five. You know, the box on the grand tier, next to stage box, on the left.'

'Really?'

'Yes, I am telling you. Mother is attendant of that box. But promise not to say a word!'

'I promise!'

'Well, that's the ghost's box. No one has had it for over a month, save the ghost of course. And orders have been given at the box-office that it is no longer available.'

'And does the ghost really make use of it?'

'Yes.'

'So there *is* somebody in there?'

'Why, no! *The ghost makes use of it, but there is nobody in there.*'

The girls exchanged glances. If the ghost did make use of the box, why had no one seen him with his black coat and his skull head?

'That's just it!' Meg replied. 'The ghost cannot be seen! There is neither coat nor head to see! All that talk about his different heads is nonsense! There's nothing in it. You can only hear him when he is in the box. Mother has never seen him, but she has heard him. She knows all this because she gives him his programme.'

At this point, Sorelli thought it best to intervene. 'Meg Giry, you are teasing us!' she said.

Whereupon the girl began to cry: 'I should have kept quiet – if Mother ever knew! But all the same, Joseph Buquet should have stayed out of it ... He'll suffer the consequences ... Mother was saying so last night.'

At that very moment, there was a sound of heavy, hurried footsteps in the corridor and a breathless voice called: 'Cécile! Cécile! Are you there?'

'Mother!' said Little Jammes. 'What's the matter?'

She opened the door. A respectable lady, as sturdy as a Pomeranian grenadier,[13] burst into the dressing-room and sank into an empty chair with a groan. Her eyes rolled madly in her gloomy ruddy face. 'What a tragedy!' she exclaimed. 'What a tragedy!'

'What's happened? What's happened?'

'Joseph Buquet ...'

'What about him?'

'Joseph Buquet is dead!'

The room filled at once with exclamations of shock and disbelief, and anxious requests for an explanation.

'He was found hanging below stage, down on the third mezzanine! . . . *But the worst thing about it,*' the poor lady went on in gasping tones, '*the worst thing about it is that the machinists who found the body claim that, close by, they heard something that sounded like music for the Dead.*'

Little Giry seemed unable to hold back her cry of 'The ghost!' but she quickly checked herself, pressing her hands to her mouth: 'No, no! I said nothing! Nothing!'

Her companions were panic-stricken. 'It must be the ghost!' they repeated under their breaths.

Sorelli was very pale. 'I shall never be able to give my little speech now,' she murmured.

Little Jammes's mother, downing a glass of liqueur that happened to be on a table nearby, declared that the ghost must have something to do with it.

The truth is that no one has ever really explained how Joseph Buquet met his death. The verdict at the inquest was 'suicide under natural circumstances'. In his *Memoirs of a Theatre Director*, Armand Moncharmin, one of the co-directors who succeeded Messrs Debienne and Poligny, relates the incident as follows:

A most unfortunate accident ruined the little party that Messrs Debienne and Poligny were giving to mark their departure. I was in the directors' office when Mercier, the administrator, suddenly came in. He was most agitated and he told me that the body of a machinist had been found hanging on the third mezzanine below the stage, between a flat and a scene[14] from *Le Roi de Lahore*.[15] I cried: 'Let's go and cut him down!' But by the time we had climbed down the stairs and the Jacob's ladder,[16] the man was no longer hanging and the rope was gone!

This is what M. Moncharmin termed 'natural' circumstances: a man is swinging at the end of a rope; they rush to cut him down; the rope has disappeared. Oh, Moncharmin's explanation was straightforward enough! Listen to him: '*The dancers were performing that night and took immediate precautions to procure a charm to ward off the Evil Eye.*' That was it! Picture the dancers scampering down the ladder, cutting up the deadly rope and sharing the pieces among themselves in less time than it took me to write about it! Nonsense! Personally, pondering on the event and the particular spot where the body was discovered – down on the third mezzanine – I believe that the vanishing of the rope, after it had done its murderous job, served *some purpose*; and time will show whether I am right.

The dreadful news soon spread to the whole of the Opera House, where Joseph Buquet was very popular. The dressing-rooms emptied and the ballet-girls, surrounding Sorelli like timorous sheep around their shepherdess, made for the Ballet Room through the ill-lit corridors and staircases, scuttling along as fast as their little legs could carry them.

II

The New Marguerite

On the first landing, Sorelli ran into the Count de Chagny, who was ascending. The Count, usually so calm, appeared in a state of rapturous emotion. 'I was just coming up to see you,' he said, greeting her with the utmost gallantry. 'Ah! What a wonderful evening, my dear! And Christine Daaé . . . What a triumph!'

'Unbelievable!' countered Meg Giry. 'Only six months ago, she squawked like a parrot! But we must be on our way, Count,' said the sprightly girl, dropping a brisk curtsey. 'We're off to see about a poor man who was found hanging by his neck.'

On hearing this remark, the administrator of the Opera House, who was hurrying by, stopped dead in his tracks. 'What! Have you heard already?' he said with some asperity. 'Well, keep it to yourselves. Please, not a word to Messrs Debienne and Poligny! It would be just too upsetting for them on their last evening.'

They all went on to the Ballet Room, which was already crowded.

The Count de Chagny was right. There was something unique about that gala performance;[1] those fortunate enough to be there still speak of it with emotion to their children and grandchildren. Imagine: Gounod, Reyer, Saint-Saëns, Massenet, Guiraud and Delibes took turns to conduct their own compositions; Faure and Krauss sang;[2] and, that very evening, Parisian society was astounded and thrilled by the young woman whose mysterious fate is the subject of this book.

Gounod had conducted his *Marche funèbre d'une marionnette*;[3] Reyer, the beautiful overture to *Sigurd*;[4] Saint-Saëns, his *Danse macabre* and *Rêverie orientale*;[5] Massenet, an unpublished

Marche hongroise;[6] Guiraud, his *Carnaval*;[7] Delibes, the *Valse lente* from *Sylvia* and the pizzicato from *Coppélia*.[8] Mlle Krauss had sung the bolero from *Les Vêpres siciliennes*,[9] and Mlle Denise Bloch the drinking song from *Lucrezia Borgia*.[10]

All the same, it was Christine Daaé who triumphed. Her performance had begun with arias from Gounod's *Roméo et Juliette*[11] that she had never sung before, as the work was yet to be staged at the Opera House; it had only just been revived by the Opéra-Comique, some years after it was first performed at the old Théâtre Lyrique by Mme Carvalho.[12] Ah! How we must pity those who did not have the good fortune to hear Christine Daaé as Juliette, admire her graceful candour, be touched to the quick by her seraphic voice and feel their spirits soar with her own above the tombs of the Verona lovers in the final 'O Lord! Lord! Lord! Forgive us!'[13]

Yet nothing compared to the unearthly power of her singing in the prison scene and the final trio of *Faust*[14] that she performed in place of Carlotta, who was indisposed that night. Nothing quite like this had ever been heard or seen before! Daaé revealed a new Marguerite, a Marguerite of a splendour and radiance hitherto unimagined. Moved beyond words, the whole house cheered and clapped ecstatically, while Christine sobbed, fainting in the arms of her fellow-performers. She had to be carried to her dressing-room and looked as if she had breathed her last.

The great critic P. de St-V. preserved the memory of those wonderful moments in a piece appropriately entitled: *The New Marguerite*. With the sensitivity of a great artist, he understood that this beautiful, sweet creature had brought to the stage rather more than her art on that occasion, that she had indeed brought her *heart*. All those closely associated with the Paris Opera knew that Christine's heart remained as pure as that of a child; which is why P. de St-V. felt that in order to understand what had happened to Daaé, he 'could only imagine that, for the first time in her life, she had fallen in love!' He added:

I have no wish to be indiscreet, but only love could have worked such a miracle and brought about such a stupendous transform-

ation. Two years ago, when we heard Christine Daaé at the competition of the Paris Conservatoire,[15] we found charming promise
in her voice. *But today it is sublime! From whence does this
come? If not down from Heaven on the wings of love, then up
from Hell; and Christine, like the minstrel Ofterdingen, must
have made a pact with the Devil.*[16] One must have heard Christine sing the final trio to truly know *Faust*: the exaltation in her
voice and the mystic elation of her pure soul are unsurpassable.

A number of subscribers protested: why had such a treasure
been kept away from them for so long? Until now Christine
Daaé had played an acceptable Siébel[17] to Carlotta's all too
splendidly physical Marguerite. It was only owing to Carlotta's
unexpected and unexplained absence that Daaé had been able
to show, at a moment's notice, the full measure of her genius in
a part of the programme usually reserved for the Spanish diva.
When Carlotta withdrew, what made Messrs Debienne and
Poligny think of Daaé? Had they known all along of her hidden
talent? If so, why keep it hidden? Indeed, why had she chosen
to conceal it? More baffling yet, she had, for all they knew, no
singing master, having declared on several occasions that she
had determined to work alone. The whole thing was a mystery.

The Count de Chagny, standing in his box, had watched as
the audience erupted into a delirious ovation and joined in with
his own bravos.

Philippe-Georges-Marie, Count de Chagny, was precisely
forty-one years of age. He was from the highest nobility and a
handsome man to boot. He was taller than average, with a
pleasant face despite his strong forehead and his rather cold
eyes. He was exquisitely polite to women and a little haughty
to men, who did not always forgive him his many social successes. He also possessed excellent qualities of heart and a
flawless conscience. On the death of old Count Philibert,
Philippe de Chagny had become the head of one of the oldest
and most illustrious French families, whose lineage could be
traced back to King Louis X the Stubborn in the fourteenth
century.[18] The family's wealth was substantial and, as the old
Count had died a widower, it was on Philippe's shoulders that

the heavy burden of managing the estate had fallen. His two sisters and his brother Raoul would not hear of it being divided. They provisionally waived their claims, putting everything into Philippe's trust as if the right of primogeniture had never ceased to exist. When the two sisters were married – on the same day – their respective shares were handed over to them by their brother, not so much as something that was theirs by right, but more as a dowry that they gratefully received.

The Countess de Chagny, née de Moerogis de La Martynière, had died giving birth to Raoul, twenty years after Philippe was born. At the time of the old Count's death, Raoul was twelve years of age. Philippe himself took charge of the education of the child. He was admirably assisted in this task, first by his sisters and later by an elderly aunt, the widow of a naval officer, who lived in Brest[19] and gave young Raoul his love of the sea. The young man joined the navy, finished his training on board the *Borda*[20] with honours and subsequently completed, as a matter of course, his first voyage around the world. Thanks to the support of powerful friends, he had just been invited to join the *Requin* on her official mission to the North Pole in search of survivors of the *D'Artois* expedition, from whom nothing had been heard for three years.[21] As he was not to set sail for another six months, Raoul was enjoying a long leave of absence; but the dowagers of the Faubourg Saint-Germain were already lamenting the hardships awaiting this beautiful and seemingly frail youth.

Raoul was remarkably shy and, one might be tempted to say, pure. It was as if he had only just left the care of his loving sisters and aunt. This exclusively female upbringing had given him candid manners stamped with a charm hitherto unblemished. He was a little over twenty-one, yet appeared no more than eighteen. He had a small, fair moustache, fine blue eyes and the complexion of a girl.

Philippe doted upon Raoul. He was proud of him and anticipated with great joy that he would have an illustrious naval career, following in the footsteps of one of their ancestors, the great de Chagny de La Roche, who had risen to the rank of admiral. The Count was making the most of his brother's

extended leave, showing him Paris with all its luxurious pleasures and artistic delights. He felt that Raoul had reached an age
when one could be too good for one's own good. Philippe, for
his part, had a well-balanced character; he was measured in his
approach to work and pleasure alike, perfectly mannered and
quite incapable of setting a bad example to his brother. He took
Raoul with him wherever he went. He even introduced him to
the Ballet Room. I know that Philippe was said to be on 'best
terms' with Sorelli. But what of it? He was a bachelor with
plenty of time on his hands, especially now that his sisters were
settled. Surely no one could reproach him for spending an hour
or two after dinner in the company of a dancer who, though
hardly noted for her sparkling wit, had the most beautiful eyes!
Besides, there are places where a true Parisian of such great
standing as the Count is duty bound to make an appearance;
and, at that time, the Ballet Room was such a place. Philippe
might not have taken the young man backstage, however, had
Raoul not suggested it. In fact, he did so repeatedly with a gentle obstinacy that the Count would later recollect.

On the evening of the gala performance, Philippe, having
applauded Daaé, turned to his brother and found him alarm-
ingly pale.

'Look!' said Raoul. 'She is unwell.'

And indeed, at that very moment, Christine Daaé had to be
supported.

'It seems that you are the one about to collapse,' said the
Count, leaning towards his brother. 'What's wrong?'

But Raoul had already recovered and was now standing up.
'Let's go,' he said with a tremor in his voice.

'Where do you want to go?' asked the Count, who was surprised at Raoul's agitation.

'Let's go and see! She has never sung like that before.'

The Count stared at him enquiringly and his lips curled up
in a slightly amused smile. 'If we must,' he said, adding quickly:
'Come then, let's go!' with delight in his face.

Soon they were at the crowded subscribers' door.[22] While
waiting to make their way through to the stage, Raoul pulled
at his gloves absently. Philippe was too good-natured a man to

make a jest of his impatience, but now he knew. He understood why Raoul looked distracted when he spoke to him, and why he seemed to take such a keen pleasure in bringing all their conversations around to the Opera House.

As the two brothers reached the stage, a black-coated throng was heading for the Ballet Room and the dressing-rooms. The shouts of the machinists mingled with the strident calls of the managers. The usual hustle and bustle of intermissions – supernumeraries hired for the last tableau on their way out; figurantes jostling past,[23] the frame of a scenery flat being carried through; a backdrop coming down from the flies; a 'practicable'[24] being hammered into place; the ubiquitous 'Make room!' warning of the impending threat to one's top hat or of a forceful thrust into one's back – never fails to unnerve the uninitiated, but not so the young man with the fair moustache, blue eyes and girlish complexion who was now crossing, as fast as the crush would allow, the stage where Christine Daaé had triumphed and beneath which Joseph Buquet had met his death.

Never had the theatre been in such turmoil, nor Raoul so bold. He purposefully shouldered his way forward, ignoring what was being said around him, not even trying to make sense of the machinists' startled comments. His desire to see the woman whose magic voice had captured his heart was his sole concern. He felt that his poor, pristine heart no longer belonged to him. Since Christine, whom he had known as a little girl, had reappeared, he had tried very hard, out of self-respect and faith, to defend himself against the tender feelings that she inspired in him; he had sworn to love only the woman that he would make his wife and, naturally, marrying a singer was out of the question. Now those tender feelings had given way to pain. Sensations? Sentiments? His response was at once physical and emotional. His chest hurt, as if it had been cut open and his heart removed. Inside he felt only a terrible hollowness, a genuine emptiness that could only be relieved by his winning the heart of the one he loved. The psychology of love is such that experiences of this kind can best be understood, it seems, by those to whom love, as the French *coup de foudre* suggests, has revealed itself with the unexpected abruptness of lightning.

Count Philippe had difficulty in keeping up with Raoul, but retained a knowing smile on his lips.

Backstage, past the double doors that opened on to the steps leading to the Ballet Room and those that led to the parterre boxes[25] on the left, Raoul had to stop as a small group of dancers, who had just descended from their attic dressing-rooms, blocked his way. Teasing remarks flew from more than one painted little mouth, but he did not respond; and when his path was finally clear, he disappeared into the darkness of a corridor ringing with the cheers of enthusiastic admirers and, above all, cries of 'Daaé! Daaé!' 'He certainly knows the way,' thought the Count, wondering how it was, since he had never taken Raoul to Christine's dressing-room. He must have gone there alone while the Count was, as usual, in the Ballet Room with Sorelli. She often asked him to stay with her until she went on stage, sometimes even handing him the little gaiters that she wore while descending the stairs to protect her shiny satin dancing-shoes and her immaculate flesh-coloured tights. We must indulge Sorelli for she had lost her mother.

Postponing his planned visit to Sorelli for a few moments, the Count followed his brother down the corridor that led to Daaé's dressing-room. He had never seen so many people gathered there before: the whole house seemed excited by both her success and her subsequent collapse. The beautiful girl had not yet come round, but medical help was at hand. The house doctor pushed his way through the crush and Raoul, hard on his heels, followed him into the dressing-room. Thus Christine received first aid from the former, while opening her eyes in the arms of the latter. The Count stood in the crowded doorway.

'Don't you think, Doctor, that all these gentlemen should clear the room?' asked Raoul with unbelievable audacity. 'One can hardly breathe in here.'

'You're quite right,' the doctor agreed.

Whereupon he sent everyone away save Raoul and the maid, who stared at the young man in absolute bewilderment. She had never seen him before, but dared not ask him questions. As for the doctor, he imagined that Raoul was acting as he did only because he was entitled to do so. The Viscount, therefore, remained in the room and watched Christine slowly return to life, while even the joint directors, Messrs Debienne and Poligny, who had come to congratulate her, were sent out of the room with all the other black coats.

Among them was the Count de Chagny, who could not help laughing to himself. 'Oh, the cunning little devil!' he murmured. 'One should never trust youths who look all too innocent!' Beaming with joy, he concluded: 'He's a Chagny after all!' and made for Sorelli's dressing-room. He met her as she was descending the stairs on her way to the Ballet Room with her little flock of timorous ballet-girls, as recounted earlier.

Meanwhile, in her dressing-room, Christine Daaé sighed deeply and was answered by a gentle moan. She turned her head, saw Raoul and started. She looked at the doctor and smiled, then at her maid, and then at Raoul again. 'Monsieur,' she finally said in a voice that was little more than a whisper, 'who are you?'

'Mademoiselle,' replied the young man, dropping on to one knee and pressing his lips fervently to the diva's hand, '*I am that little boy who went into the sea to retrieve your scarf.*'

Christine looked again at the doctor and the maid; and all three began to laugh.

Raoul stood up, blushing profusely. 'Mademoiselle,' he said, 'since it pleases you not to recognize me, may I have a word with you in private, about something very important?'

'Please, monsieur, when I am better.' And there was a trembling in her voice. 'You are very kind.'

'Yes, you must go now,' said the doctor with his most pleasant smile. 'Leave me to attend to mademoiselle.'

'But I am not ill,' cried Christine suddenly with an energy that was as strange as it was unexpected. She rose, brushing her fingers over her brow. 'Thank you, Doctor! I should like to be alone. Please go away, all of you. Let me be. I feel especially restless this evening.'

The doctor protested briefly, but the young woman was so agitated that he thought it best not to go against her wishes and left the room with Raoul.

'She is not herself tonight. She is usually so gentle,' said the doctor to a helpless Raoul before walking away.

The Viscount stood by himself outside her door in a part of the theatre that was now quite deserted. The farewell party must be in full swing. Thinking that Daaé might join the celebrations, he waited alone in the silence. He even shrank into the propitious shadow of a doorway. He still felt an excruciating pain in the place of his heart. And that was the very topic that he wanted to discuss so urgently with Daaé. Suddenly the dressing-room door opened and the maid came out by herself, carrying bundles. He stopped her to ask how her mistress was. She replied, laughing, that Christine was quite well, but wished to be alone and was not to be disturbed. In his feverish state, he thought: 'Of course, Daaé has sent everyone away so as to be left alone *for me!*' Had he not told her that he wanted to speak to her in private?

Hardly breathing, he walked up to her door, pressed his ear against it to catch her reply and prepared to knock. But his hand dropped. He had just heard, from inside the dressing-room, *a man's voice* say in a surprisingly commanding tone: 'Christine, you must love me!'

Christine, as if in tears, replied in a pained, trembling voice: 'How can you say that? *I sing only for you!*'

Raoul, reeling with pain, leaned against the door panel. His heart was back in his breast, where he could feel it and hear it thumping fiercely. It was loud to the point of deafening, and as if resonating in the corridor. Surely, if it kept pounding like a double-drum, someone would hear it, open the door and send him away. How humiliating for a de Chagny to be found eavesdropping. He clutched his chest with both hands, in an attempt to quieten his heart. But you cannot muzzle a heart as you would a hound. And even a hound muzzled with two hands – to prevent it from barking unbearably – can still be heard growling.

The voice spoke again: 'You must be very tired!'

'Oh, tonight I gave you my soul and I am dead!'

'Your soul is a beautiful thing, my child,' replied the deep voice, 'and I am grateful. No emperor ever received so great a gift. *The angels wept tonight.*'

Then all fell silent. Yet Raoul did not go away. Fearing that he might be discovered, he retreated back into his shadowy corner and determined to hide there until the man left the room. In a single moment, he had learned both to love and to hate. He knew that he was in love. He needed to know the object of his hatred. To his bewilderment, the door opened and Christine Daaé appeared alone, wrapped in furs, with her face hidden under a lace veil. She closed the door behind her, but without locking it, Raoul noticed.

As she walked past him, he did not even look after her. His eyes were fixed upon the door, which remained closed. The corridor was once more deserted. Raoul went over to the unlocked room, let himself in, shut the door quickly and pressed his back to it. He found himself in absolute darkness. The gas-light had been turned out.

'I know there is someone here!' said Raoul in a quivering voice. 'Why are you hiding?' The room was dark and silent. The sound of his own breathing was all he could hear. He was quite oblivious of the fact that his conduct exceeded all possible bounds of discretion. 'You shan't leave this room until I let you!' he cried. 'Show yourself, you coward! I'll expose you, no matter!' And he struck a match. The flame lit up the room. There was no one there!

Raoul was mindful to lock the door before lighting the gas globes and lamps. He went into the dressing-closet, opened the wardrobes, searched inside, felt the walls with clammy hands. Nothing! 'How can this be?' he said, aloud. 'Am I going mad?' He stood for several minutes in the peaceful, empty room, listening to the hissing of the gas; the thought of stealing a ribbon so as to take away with him the perfume of the woman he cherished never even entered his mind. Finally, he left the room, not knowing what he was doing or where he was going.

At one point in his wanderings, as he was standing at the bottom of a narrow staircase, an icy draught of air struck his face. A procession of workmen was descending behind him just then, carrying a kind of stretcher covered with a white sheet. 'Can you show me the way out, please?' he asked.

'Can't you see! Just in front of you,' replied one of the men. 'The door's open. But let us through first.'

Pointing to the stretcher, Raoul asked offhandedly: 'What's that?'

' "That", monsieur, is Joseph Buquet, who was found hanging below stage on the third mezzanine, between a flat and a scene from *Le Roi de Lahore*.'

Raoul stepped back to let the procession pass, bowed his head and went out.

III

*In which, for the first time, Messrs Debienne and
Poligny disclose in confidence to the new directors
of the Opera House, Messrs Armand Moncharmin
and Firmin Richard, the true reason for their
departure from the National Academy of Music*

The farewell ceremony was in full swing.

As I have already said, this sumptuous celebration was held to mark the departure of the directors of the Paris Opera, Messrs Debienne and Poligny, who wished to end, as the phrase goes, on a high note.

All those who mattered in Parisian society and the arts had helped organize this superlative yet sombre programme. After the performance, everyone met in the Ballet Room, where Sorelli waited for the arrival of the resigning directors with a glass of champagne in her hand and the little speech she had prepared on the tip of her tongue. The other members of the *corps de ballet*, young and old, gathered closely behind her. Some of them discussed the events of the day in whispers; others discreetly signalled to their friends, who were already crowding noisily around the tables raised for the refreshments upon the sloping floor of the Ballet Room, in-between *La Danse guerrière* and *La Danse champêtre* painted by M. Boulanger.[1]

Several dancers had already changed; but most of them were still wearing their light tulle skirts, and all were mindful to adopt a demeanour appropriate for the occasion. All, that is, save Little Jammes. In her carefree, happy youthfulness, she seemed to have already forgotten the ghost and the death of Joseph Buquet. She never stopped chattering, jabbering, hopping about and playing practical jokes; so much so that when Messrs Debienne and Poligny appeared on the steps of the Ballet Room, she was sternly called to order by an impatient Sorelli.

Everyone noticed that the outgoing directors appeared

cheery. This would have seemed surprising in the provinces, but in Paris it was thought to be in the best possible taste: true Parisians have learned to wear a mask of gaiety over their sorrows, and conversely a façade of sadness, boredom or indifference over their inward joy. Thus if you know that one of your friends is aggrieved, do not try to comfort him, for he will tell you that he has already recovered; on the other hand, when he meets with good fortune, take care not to congratulate him, for he finds his situation so very natural that he will be surprised that you should remark upon it. To the Parisian, life is but a masked ball, and the Ballet Room was the last place where two men as socially aware as Messrs Debienne and Poligny would make the mistake of betraying their grief, however genuine it might be. In fact, they were smiling a little too broadly as Sorelli began her speech. Then a cry from that little madcap Jammes suddenly erased their smiles, and the dismay and fear that lay hidden beneath became at once all too apparent: 'Aaah! The ghost!'

Jammes had uttered those words in a tone of indescribable terror and now pointed her finger among the crowd, to a face so pallid, so gloomy, so horrid, and with such deep, black, hollow eyes, that the skull head, thus singled out, instantly scored a huge success.

'The ghost! The ghost!' The company laughed, jostling and keen to toast the ghost; but he was gone. He had slipped through the crowd. They searched for him in vain, while two old gentlemen endeavoured to calm Little Jammes, and young Giry screeched like a peacock.

Sorelli was furious: before she could finish her speech, Messrs Debienne and Poligny had kissed her, thanked her and vanished as fast as the ghost himself. No one thought it amiss as they were expected to go through a similar ceremony on the floor above, in the Music Room. Later their personal friends would join them for a last time in the lobby of the directorial office, where a full supper was awaiting them.

This is precisely where we find them now, in the company of the new directors, Messrs Armand Moncharmin and Firmin Richard. The outgoing directors hardly knew their successors, but made abundant professions of friendship and received myriad compliments in return; upon which, those of the guests who had dreaded the prospect of a somewhat tedious evening began to perk up. The supper was little short of lively and, when glasses were raised, the government representative proposed a toast to the glories of the past and the successes of the future with such consummate skill that the utmost cordiality soon reigned among the guests.

The handing over of responsibilities had taken place informally the day before. Outstanding issues had been settled under the watchful eye of the government representative and in such a spirit of mutual understanding that, in truth, it seemed entirely natural that the four directors should now be smiling so profusely.

The two tiny master-keys, which opened all the doors – literally, thousands of doors – of the Opera House had also been handed over. These were being passed quickly around the supper table as objects of general curiosity, when some of the guests suddenly noticed the extraordinarily wan, gaunt face and sunken eyes that had already appeared in the Ballet Room and been greeted by Little Jammes's cry of: 'Aaah! The ghost!'

And there he sat, at the end of the table, like any other guest, except that he neither ate nor drank. Those who had first stared at him with amusement soon turned away from a sight that evoked nothing but darkness and gloom. No one tried to make light of him as before, and no one cried: 'Aaah! The ghost!'

He had not uttered a word and even those sitting on either side of him were at a loss to say at what precise moment he had appeared; everyone felt nevertheless that had Death come and sat at the table of the living, he would not cut a more macabre figure. Richard and Moncharmin's friends assumed that this spectre was one of Debienne and Poligny's guests, while Debienne and Poligny's friends thought that the cadaverous figure was there at the invitation of Richard and Moncharmin. Therefore no questions were asked, no disagreeable comments passed, nor jokes in poor taste made, that might offend the visitor from beyond the grave. Some of those who knew the story of the ghost and the description of him given by the chief machinist – Joseph Buquet's death was still unknown to them – thought privately that the man at the end of the table might easily pass for the incarnation of the character whom they thought to be a figment of the staff's incorrigible imagination. If their story were to be believed, the ghost had no nose; yet the character seated at the table had one. In his *Memoirs*, Armand Moncharmin claims that the nose of the guest in question was 'long, thin and transparent'. Personally, I am inclined to suggest that it was false, and that Moncharmin mistook mere shininess for transparency. Thanks to the advances of science, as everyone knows, remarkably believable false noses can now be made for those people who have lost their own as a result of natural causes or an operation. Did the ghost really invite himself to the directors' table that night? And can we be sure that the figure they described was indeed the Phantom of the Opera himself? Who can really know? I venture to mention the incident not because I have the slightest wish to make the reader believe that the Phantom was capable of such a magnificently bold move, but because, when all is said and done, it is quite possible.

I find some justification for this in Chapter XI of Moncharmin's *Memoirs*: 'When I think back to that first evening, I cannot dissociate what Messrs Debienne and Poligny disclosed to us in confidence in their office from the presence at our supper table of a *ghostly* figure that not one of us knew.'

This is what happened:

Debienne and Poligny were seated halfway down the table. They did not notice the man with the skull head until he suddenly spoke.

'The ballet-girls are right,' he said. 'The death of poor Buquet may not be so natural as people think.'

Debienne and Poligny started. 'Is Buquet dead?' they cried.

'Yes,' replied the man, or the shadow of a man, quietly. 'He was found hanging between a flat and a scene from *Le Roi de Lahore* down on the third mezzanine.'

The two directors, or rather ex-directors, rose at once to their feet and stared strangely at their interlocutor. They were

more agitated than might have been expected of men in their
position on hearing about the death of a machinist. They
looked at each other. They had both turned whiter than the
tablecloth. Finally, Debienne gestured to Richard and Moncharmin, Poligny offered a few words of apology to the guests,
and all four went into the directors' office. I leave the remainder of the story to Armand Moncharmin, who writes in his
Memoirs:

Messrs Debienne and Poligny were increasingly agitated and
manifestly ready to disclose something of great embarrassment to
them. First, they asked us if we knew the man seated at the end
of the table who had broken the news of Joseph Buquet's death;
and, when we answered in the negative, they seemed more upset
still. They took the master-keys from our hands, stared at them
for a moment, nodded their heads and advised us to have new
locks made, with the greatest secrecy, for any room, closet and
press that we might wish to keep secure. They looked so funny as
they spoke that we laughed and asked if there were thieves at the
Opera. They replied that there was something worse: the *ghost*.
We began to laugh again, and assumed that this was some sort of
joke meant to crown our friendly little gathering. Then, at their
request, we composed ourselves and resolved to indulge them by
entering into the spirit of the game. They told us that they only
mentioned the existence of this ghost because they had received
formal instructions from him to the effect that they should urge
us to cooperate and grant him whatever he might request. Being
exceedingly relieved at the prospect of leaving a house that had
fallen prey to a tyrannical shadow, they had delayed to the very
last moment the disclosure of certain curious happenings to which
our sceptical minds were surely not prepared. The announcement
of Joseph Buquet's death was, however, a brutal reminder that,
whenever they had chosen to ignore the ghost's demands, some
fantastic or dreadful occurrence would reawaken their sense of
impotence.

This astonishing account was made in the strictest confidence
and in a tone of the most profound seriousness. All the while my
eyes were on Richard. In his student days, Richard had estab-

lished a reputation as a consummate practical joker and knew of a thousand and one pranks that could be played on all and sundry, as the concierges of the Latin Quarter quickly learned to their cost. He seemed to be relishing the dish that was now being served up to him. He did not miss a morsel of it, though the seasoning was a little grisly for his taste because of Buquet's death. He nodded his head sadly while Messrs Debienne and Poligny spoke, and he assumed the air of someone who bitterly regretted any involvement with the Opera House, now that he knew about the ghost. As for me, I could think of nothing better than to mimic his dismay. However, in spite of all our efforts, we could not stifle our laughter for much longer. Seeing us pass abruptly from the darkest gloom to a most insolent merriment, Debienne and Poligny acted as if they thought that we had gone mad.

Feeling that the joke was being stretched overmuch, Richard asked half in jest, half in earnest: 'Come now, what does this ghost of yours want?' M. Poligny went to his desk and returned with a copy of the memorandum of terms of the Opera House.[2] The document began with the words: 'The directors of the Paris Opera shall ensure that the representations of the National Academy of Music exhibit the splendour that befits the foremost lyric theatre in France'; and ended with: 'Clause 98. The appointments may be revoked for failure to abide by the conditions stipulated therein.' Those conditions followed.

The copy that Poligny showed us was written in black ink and identical to our own, except that it ended with an additional paragraph in red ink and in a bizarre, disjointed handwriting. It was as if the words had been traced with the tip of a matchstick dipped in ink, and the writing resembled that of a child who is still at the stage of making strokes and has not yet learned to join up the letters. This curious addition ran as follows (I copy it verbatim):

Or should the directors delay for more than a fortnight in any month the payment of the allowance owed to the Phantom of the Opera and set until further notice at twenty thousand francs per month – that is two hundred and forty thousand francs per year.

Poligny pointed timidly to this last condition, which we did not in the least expect.

'Is that all? Does he not want anything else?' asked Richard, with supreme self-control.

'Oh yes, he does,' replied Poligny.

And he leafed through the memorandum until he came to Clause 63 and read it aloud:

> Stage Box One on the grand tier, on the right-hand side, shall be reserved for the head of state at all performances.

> Parterre Box 20 and Box 30 on the grand tier shall be placed at the disposal of the prime minister on Wednesdays and Fridays.

> Box 27 on the second tier shall be made available daily to the prefect of the Seine *département* and the chief commissioner of the Paris police.

And then came, as before, an additional paragraph in red ink: '*Box Five on the grand tier shall be placed at the disposal of the Phantom of the Opera at all performances.*'

Upon hearing this, we rose to our feet, warmly shook our predecessors' hands and congratulated them on their charming little mystification, which proved that the old French sense of humour was not on the wane. Richard even added that he now understood why Debienne and Poligny were resigning their positions at the National Academy of Music. 'Business as usual' was clearly impossible with so demanding a ghost.

'Two hundred and forty thousand francs are no small pickings, of course,' added Poligny, unperturbed. 'And you have no idea of how much the loss of Box Five alone is costing us at every performance! Not only that, but we had to reimburse those who had rented it for the season. It's terrifying! Really! We are not in this business to keep ghosts! Better to leave!'

'Yes,' echoed Debienne. 'Better to leave! Come, let's go.' And he stood up.

Richard said: 'It seems to me that you have been much too kind to this ghost. If I had such a troublesome ghost, I should have him arrested.'

'But how? Where?' they cried in a single voice. 'We have never seen him!'

'But when he comes to his box!'

'*We have never seen him in his box.*'

'Then, rent it.'

'Rent the Phantom's box? Well, gentlemen, you try it.'

Thereupon we all four left the office. Never before had Richard and I laughed so much.

IV

Box Five

Armand Moncharmin wrote such voluminous *Memoirs* that we may well ask whether, during his years as co-director of the Paris Opera House, he ever found the time to discharge his duties other than by keeping a chronicle of events there. He had no knowledge of music; but he was on friendly terms with the Minister for Public Education and Fine Arts, had tried his hand as a theatre critic and enjoyed the advantages of a substantial private income. He was a charming fellow who, having decided to delegate some of his responsibilities at the Opera House, demonstrated a good deal of intelligence by choosing Firmin Richard as the most capable man to act as co-director.

Richard was a distinguished composer and a man of honour. I leave the *Revue des théâtres* to describe him at the time of his appointment:

M. Firmin Richard is about fifty years of age. He is a tall man of sturdy but lean build with a fine presence and a distinguished bearing. His face is ruddy and his thick hair, growing rather low on his brow, worn short like his beard. There is a touch of sadness in his face, tempered at once by the frank and straightforward look in his eyes and his charming smile.

M. Firmin Richard is a distinguished musician. An able harmonist and an accomplished contrapuntalist, he has composed essentially lofty pieces. In addition to his chamber music, greatly appreciated by connoisseurs, he has published scores for piano – sonatas and highly original fugitive pieces[1] – as well as a collection of songs without words. Finally his *Mort d'Hercule*,[2] performed in concert at the Conservatoire, has an epic breadth reminiscent of Gluck, who is one of his acknowledged masters. His love of Gluck, however, does not preclude him from admiring Piccinni;[3] M. Richard takes his pleasure where he finds it. While revering Piccinni, he bows to Meyerbeer, relishes Cimarosa, and no one is known to appreciate Weber[4] more wholeheartedly than he does. As for Wagner, M. Richard is close to claiming that he, Firmin Richard, is the first and perhaps the only person in France who understands him.[5]

I need not quote further from this review, which already makes abundantly clear, I would think, that since Firmin Richard loved virtually all music and all musicians, so all musicians were duty bound to love Firmin Richard in return. Let me add, to complete this hasty portrait of him, that he had what some would euphemistically call an 'authoritarian character', and others a 'foul temper'.

During their first few days at the Opera, the new co-directors[6] basked in the joy of finding themselves at the head of such a great and magnificent enterprise. They had definitely forgotten all about the intriguing and uncanny business of the ghost until an incident occurred that proved to them that the joke – if a joke it were – was far from over.

That morning, Richard arrived at his office at eleven o'clock. His secretary, M. Rémy, showed him half a dozen letters that had been left unopened as they were marked 'personal'. One of these letters caught Richard's eye at once, not so much on account of the address on the envelope being written in red ink, but because he thought that he recognized the handwriting. It soon came to him that it was written in the same clumsy, child-like hand and red ink as the strange additions to the memorandum of terms of service. He broke the seal and read:

DEAR DIRECTOR, – *Please excuse my troubling you at perhaps one of those precious moments when you are deciding the fate of the most accomplished artists of the Opera House: extending important contracts, signing new ones and displaying in all this a sureness of judgement, a knowledge of the theatre, an understanding of the public and their taste, and an authority that – experienced as I am in these matters – I find almost astonishing. I know what you have just done for Carlotta, Sorelli and Little Jammes, as well as a few others whose admirable qualities, talent or genius you have divined. (You know perfectly well what this is about: I am not referring to Carlotta who cannot sing for toffee, and should have stayed at the Théâtre des Ambassadeurs and the Café Jacquin;[7] nor to Sorelli whose success largely lies in the chassis department; nor to Little Jammes who dances like a heifer in a meadow; neither am I referring to Christine Daaé whose talent is unquestionable, but whom you invidiously prevent from singing new roles.) You are, after all, free to conduct your little business as you think fit, are you not? All the same, before you are minded to sack Christine Daaé, I should like to have the opportunity to hear her sing Siebel, as the role of Marguerite has been denied to her since her triumph of the other day. Please ensure that my box is placed at my disposal today and every day henceforth for, lately, on my arrival at the Opera I have had the disagreeable surprise to learn from the box-office that, on your orders, it was let for rent.*

I did not protest, first because I have no taste for scandal and, second, because I thought that your predecessors, Messrs Debienne and Poligny, who were always charming to me, had perhaps neglected to mention my little peculiarities to you before leaving. It is, however, clear from their reply to my request for an explanation that you know all about my memorandum of terms and that you are therefore trifling with me in a most outrageous manner. If you want peace, start by not denying me my box.

With these small reservations, I remain, dear Director, your most humble and obedient servant,

Signed: P. of the Opera

The letter was accompanied by the following advertisement cut out of the *Revue théâtrale*: '*Dear P. of the O. – R. and M. have no excuse. We warned them and left your memorandum of terms in their hands. Regards.*'

Richard had barely finished reading this letter when Moncharmin came into the office, holding a letter that was identical to the one addressed to his co-director. They looked at each other and burst out laughing.

'They are keeping up the charade,' said Richard, 'but this is beyond a joke.'

'What does it all mean?' asked Moncharmin. 'Do *they* think that we'll allow them, as former directors of the Opera House, to claim a box indefinitely?'

There was no doubt in their minds that these letters were the fruit of their predecessors' mischief.

'I am not in the mood to let them make a fool of me for much longer!' said Richard.

'They mean no harm,' declared Moncharmin. 'All they want is a box for tonight!'

Firmin Richard told his secretary to reserve Box Five on the grand tier for Messrs Debienne and Poligny, assuming it was still available. As it was, the ex-directors were immediately informed that it was theirs for the evening. Debienne lived at the corner of the Rue Scribe and the Boulevard des Capucines; Poligny, in the Rue Auber. The two letters from the Phantom of the Opera bore the stamp of the Boulevard des Capucines post-office, Moncharmin noticed after examining the envelopes.

'You see!' said Richard.

They shrugged their shoulders and lamented the fact that supposedly mature men should take such pleasure in childish pranks.

'And furthermore, one would have at least expected them to be civil!' remarked Moncharmin. 'Did you notice their comments about us as regards Carlotta, Sorelli and Little Jammes?'

'Why, my dear fellow, those two are simply mad with envy! To think that they went to the expense of placing an advertisement in the *Revue théâtrale*! Have they nothing better to do?'

'By the way,' added Moncharmin, 'they seem to show great interest in our little Christine Daaé.'

'You know as well as I do that she has the reputation of being virtuous,' said Richard.

'This reputation may be untrue,' replied Moncharmin. 'Do I not have the reputation of a man who knows music while, in fact, I cannot tell the difference between a *bass* and a *treble* clef?'

'Fear not!' Richard said. 'You have no such reputation.'

Thereupon he asked the doorman to show in the artists who had just spent two hours pacing up and down the spacious lobby of the administrative wing, waiting for the directors' door – behind which lay fame, fortune or dismissal – to open.

Throughout that day contracts were discussed, negotiated, signed or cancelled; and, that evening – the evening of January 25th – the two directors went to bed early. As you can imagine, after so many exhausting hours of angry exchanges, intrigue, recommendations, threats and professions of love or hatred, they retired without so much as a cursory glance at Box Five to see whether Debienne and Poligny were enjoying the performance. The Opera House had not stood idle since their departure, for although essential work had been carried out on Richard's orders, it had not interfered with the scheduled performances.

Next morning, the directors each received a note of thanks from the Phantom:

DEAR DIRECTOR, – *Thank you. Charming evening. Daaé exquisite. Choruses still need some work. Carlotta, a splendid but not unique talent. Will write to you soon about the 240,000 francs, or to be precise the 233,424 francs and 70 centimes that you owe me now that Messrs Debienne and Poligny have sent me 6,575 francs and 30 centimes for the first ten days of this year – their appointments ended on the evening of the tenth. Your obedient servant,*
     P. of the O.

That morning, they also received a letter from Debienne and Poligny:

MESSIEURS, – *We are much obliged for your kind attention; but you will readily understand that, pleasant as the prospect of hearing* Faust *again might be to the former directors of the Opera, we cannot accept your offer. We have no right to occupy Box Five on the grand tier, for it belongs exclusively to him of*

whom we spoke when we went through the memorandum of
terms with you last time. See Clause 63, final paragraph.
We remain, gentlemen, etc.

'Oh, those two are really beginning to annoy me!' barked Richard, snatching up the letter from their predecessors.

That evening Box Five was made available to the public.

The next morning, on arriving at their office, Richard and Moncharmin found a report from the house manager relating an incident that had happened in Box Five the previous evening. The most telling part of his brief report, written on the evening in question, ran as follows:

> I was compelled to call in a constable on two occasions – at the beginning and in the middle of the second act – to clear Box Five of its occupants. Having arrived as the curtain rose on the second act, they caused an uproar by their laughter and their foolish remarks. There were cries of 'Hush!' from all around them and the whole house was beginning to protest when the box attendant came to fetch me. I walked into the box and made all necessary admonitions. Judging by their stupid comments, the occupants of the box were not in their right minds. I told them that I should have to ask them to vacate the box, should the disturbance persist. Yet, no sooner had I left than I heard fresh laughter from them and renewed protests from the house. I fetched a constable, who turned them out. They complained, still laughing, and refused to leave unless a refund was paid. When they finally calmed down, I allowed them back into the box. But the laughter resumed at once; and, this time, I had them turned out for good.

'Send for the house manager,' said Richard to his secretary, who had already read the report and added notes in blue pencil.

M. Rémy, the secretary, was an intelligent, elegant and distinguished young man of twenty-four with a delicate moustache, who dressed and behaved formally. He wore a frock-coat by day, as was the custom at the time, and showed due deference towards M. Richard, who paid him 2,400 francs a year out of

his own purse to check the daily newspapers, deal with correspondence, send complimentary boxes and tickets, arrange
appointments, make small talk with those who were kept waiting, visit artists who were indisposed, find understudies and
exchange notes with the managers, and altogether act as a gate-
keeper to the directors' office. M. Rémy could nevertheless be
dismissed at a day's notice, since he was not part of the official
establishment.

The secretary, who had already sent for the house manager,
had him shown in. The house manager looked slightly worried
as he entered.

'Tell us what happened,' said Richard sharply.

The manager faltered and mentioned the report.

'But, why were those people laughing?' asked Moncharmin.

'They must have dined well, and felt more inclined to fool
about than to listen to good music. No sooner had they entered
the box than they came out and called the attendant. When she
enquired what the matter was, they replied: "Look inside the
box: can you see anyone in there? Anyone at all?" "No one,"
said the woman. "Well," they declared, "when we went in, we
heard a voice saying that the box was already occupied."'

Moncharmin could not help smiling as he looked at Richard; but Richard did not smile. He remembered his student
days too well not to recognize, in the ingenuous account of the
house manager, the hallmark of one of those practical jokes
which their intended victims find at first amusing and then
infuriating.

To curry favour with Moncharmin, who was smiling, the
house manager felt that he should smile too. But this was a mistake! Richard glared at his subordinate, who immediately
assumed an expression of utter dismay.

'So when those people arrived,' roared Richard, 'there was
nobody in the box?'

'Not a soul, monsieur, not a soul! And no one on either side,
left or right. No one! Believe me, monsieur! I swear! Which
proves that it was no more than a practical joke.'

'And the attendant? What does she say about it?'

'Ah, as far as she's concerned, it's obvious: she says *it's the ghost!* And there's no arguing with her.'

The house manager guffawed but realized again that this was a mistake. For he had barely uttered the words: 'she says it's the ghost!' than Firmin Richard's despondency turned to rage.

'Send for her!' he demanded. 'Now! Have her brought here and throw everyone else out!'

The manager tried to protest, but Richard shut him up with a fierce: 'Be quiet!' And then as the lips of the wretched underling seemed to be forever sealed, the director ordered him to speak again.

'What is this ghost?' he finally asked with a disgruntled air.

But by now the house manager was quite incapable of opening his mouth. He made a despairing gesture suggesting that he knew nothing, or rather that he wished to know nothing.

'This ghost: have you ever seen him?'

The house manager shook his head vigorously, denying ever seeing him.

'All the worse for you,' retorted Richard coldly.

Upon hearing these ominous words, the house manager stared at the director enquiringly with eyes popping.

'Because I'm going to dismiss anyone who has not seen him!' explained the director. 'Since he appears to be everywhere, I'm not having people tell me they have not seen him. I expect my staff to earn their wages!'

V

Continuation of 'Box Five'

Having uttered these words, M. Firmin Richard ignored the house manager and proceeded to discuss various matters of business with the administrator, who had just arrived. The house manager, assuming that he could go, was edging back towards the door slowly, slowly – oh, so slowly! – when suddenly M. Richard noticed his manoeuvre and nailed him to the spot with a cracking: 'Stay where you are!'

The box attendant, who worked as a concierge in the Rue de Provence, not far from the Opera House, and had been fetched at M. Rémy's request, soon made her appearance.

'What's your name?'

'Mme Giry. We have met before, monsieur. I'm the mother of Little Giry! You know, Little Meg!'

This was said in a direct and earnest tone that disconcerted M. Richard for a moment. He stared at Mme Giry, standing there in her faded shawl, worn shoes, old taffeta dress and dingy hat. It was quite clear from the director's demeanour that he neither knew nor could remember ever having met this Giry woman, even less Little Giry, and less still Little Meg! But such was the attendant's pride and reputation (I believe that the French word *giries*, meaning gossip, tittle-tattle in backstage parlance, was derived from her name. For instance, one might hear a singer reproach another for her idle talk with a 'This is nothing but *giries*!'), that the said attendant assumed everybody had heard of her.

'No idea who she is,' the director finally declared. 'But no matter, Mme Giry, I need to know what happened last night. What made you and the house manager call in a constable?'

'Well, that's exactly what I wanted to tell you, monsieur, so that you don't suffer the same unpleasantness as Messrs Debienne and Poligny. They wouldn't listen to me at first.'

'I'm not asking you about that. I'm asking you what happened last night.'

Mme Giry turned purple with indignation. No one had ever spoken to her like that! The feathers on her dingy hat shook with righteous anger as she gathered her skirts and made to leave; but then she thought better of it, sat herself down again and said haughtily: 'I'll tell you what happened! Someone has upset the ghost again!'

At this, realizing that Richard was about to erupt, Moncharmin intervened and took charge of the questioning. Thus, he learned that the attendant found it quite natural that one should hear a voice claiming that a box was occupied when there was clearly nobody there. This had happened before, and as far as she was concerned the only explanation was the ghost. No one saw him in the box, but everyone heard him. She had often heard him herself, and they could trust her because she never lied. Ask Messrs Debienne and Poligny and everyone who knew her, not to mention M. Isidore Saack, whose leg the ghost had broken!

'Yes, yes!' interrupted Moncharmin. 'So poor Isidore Saack even had his leg broken by the ghost?'

Mme Giry's eyes widened in disbelief at such ignorance. She consented, however, to enlighten these two pitiable innocents. It had happened in Messrs Debienne and Poligny's time, in Box Five and during a performance of Gounod's *Faust*, as on the previous evening. Mme Giry cleared her throat, took a deep breath and began, as if she was about to sing the whole opera: 'It was like this, monsieur. That evening, M. Maniera, the jeweller from the Rue Mogador, and his wife were seated at the front of the box, with their old friend, M. Isidore Saack, sitting just behind Mme Maniera. Méphistophélès sang (*Mme Giry singing*) "While you play at sleeping",[1] and M. Maniera heard in his right ear – his wife sat on his left – a voice saying "Oho! Julie doesn't play at sleeping!" – his wife is called Julie. He turned to his right to see who had spoken. No one! He scratched his ear and thought: "I'm imagining things!" Meanwhile

Méphistophélès kept singing ... Stop me if I'm boring you, gentlemen!'

'No, no, go on!'

'You're too kind, gentlemen! (*Smirking*) As I said, Méphistophélès kept singing his serenade. (*Resuming*) "Beloved Catherine – Accord the bliss – To a mortal bending lowly – Of a kiss",[2] and just then the jeweller heard a voice in his right ear saying: "Oho! Julie wouldn't deny Isidore a kiss!" So he turned to his wife, on his left, and what did he see? Isidore holding Mme Maniera's hand from behind and kissing it feverishly through the little opening on the inside of her glove – like this, gentlemen (*greedily kissing the patch of skin on the palm of her hand not covered by her glove*). You can imagine that M. Maniera was not going to let it pass! Slap! Slap! So the jeweller, who was big and strong like you, M. Richard, repeatedly cuffed Isidore Saack, who was, saving your presence, small and puny like M. Moncharmin. The house was in uproar with people shouting: "Stop him! Stop him! He'll kill him!" And then, at last, Isidore Saack managed to escape.'

'But you said that the ghost broke M. Saack's leg!' interposed Moncharmin, a little vexed that his physique had made so poor an impression upon Mme Giry.

'Oh yes, but he did, monsieur,' replied the attendant on her high horse (for she had noticed his patronizing tone). 'It happened on the great staircase as M. Saack was rushing down, monsieur! And I dare say it will be a long time before the poor gentleman is able to climb those stairs again!'

'Was it the ghost who told you what he whispered into M. Maniera's right ear?' probed Moncharmin, with a gravity that he thought exceedingly humorous.

'No, monsieur, it was M. Maniera himself who told me. He ...'

'All I'm asking is if you, my good lady, have ever spoken to the ghost?'

'As I'm speaking to you now, my good sir!'

'And, when the ghost speaks to you, what does he say?'

'Well, he asks me to bring him a footstool!' replied Mme Giry earnestly.

Thereupon her face froze, assuming the coldness of the yellow marble with red veins – known as Sarrancolin marble – of the columns supporting the great staircase of the Opera House. She stared at Richard who, together with Moncharmin and Rémy, the secretary, was laughing again. Only the house manager, seasoned by experience, was careful not to laugh. He was leaning against the wall, anxiously fumbling with the keys in his pocket and wondering where all this was going. And the more arrogant Mme Giry became, the more he feared some fresh outburst of directorial anger. In the face of the co-directors' mirth, her tone became positively threatening. 'Instead of scoffing,' she cried indignantly, 'you'd better do as M. Poligny did! He found out for himself.'

'Found out about what?' asked Moncharmin, who had never enjoyed himself so much.

'About the ghost, of course! You must believe me! Listen!' (*Sensing the gravity of the moment*) 'Listen! I remember it as if it were yesterday. This time, it was a performance of *La Juive*.[3] M. Poligny thought he would watch it on his own from the ghost's box. Mme Krauss had received a standing ovation. She had just sung, you know, that aria in the second act. (*Singing softly:*)

> 'Close to the one I love,
> I want to live and die,
> And Death itself
> Shall not tear us apart.'[4]

'Yes, yes, I know the piece,' interjected Moncharmin, with a disparaging smile.

But Mme Giry continued softly, the feathers on her dingy hat swaying to the tune of:

> 'Let us flee! Let us flee! On this earth and in the heavens,
> The same fate henceforth awaits us both.'[5]

'Fine! Fine! We know!' repeated Richard, becoming impatient again. 'And then? And then?'

'And then just as Léopold cried: "Let us flee!" and Éléazar

stopped them with his: "Whither go you?" . . . well, just then I
saw M. Poligny – I was watching him from the back of the next
box, which was empty – I saw him get up and walk out as stiff
as a statue. I barely had time to ask: "Whither go you?" like
Éléazar. But he did not reply. He was paler than a corpse. He
descended the staircase – without breaking his leg although he
walked as if in a dream, a bad dream. And he seemed utterly
lost – strange for someone who is paid to know his way round
the Opera House.'

Thus spoke Mme Giry, who then paused to gauge the effect
of the Poligny story upon her audience.

Moncharmin nodded. 'Still, that does not tell me how and in
what circumstances the ghost came to ask you for a footstool,'
he insisted with his eyes fixed on the doughty matriarch.

'Well, from that evening onward – because from then on, we
left the ghost alone – the box was his to keep. Messrs Debienne
and Poligny gave orders that it should be placed at his disposal
for all performances. And when he came, he'd ask for his footstool.'

'H'm! H'm! A ghost asking for a footstool? Are we to think
that this ghost of yours is a woman?'

'No, the ghost is a man.'

'How do you know?'

'He has a man's voice! Oh, a lovely man's voice! Let me tell
you: he usually arrives in the middle of the first act. He raps
three times at the door of Box Five. The first time I heard it –
when I knew perfectly well there was no one in there – I was
puzzled, as you can imagine! I opened the door, listened and
looked in: no one! And then I heard a voice say, "Mme Jules" –
my poor husband's name was Jules – "a footstool, please."
With all due respect, gentlemen, I must confess that I blushed.
Then the voice went on, "Do not be frightened, Mme Jules, I
am the Phantom of the Opera!" It was such a benevolent,
friendly greeting that I was hardly frightened at all. The voice
came *from the front of the box, over on the right-hand side*;
except that I did not see anyone in that particular seat. All the
same, monsieur, I could have sworn that there was someone
there speaking, and very politely too.'

'What about the next box on the right?' asked Moncharmin. 'Was there anyone there?'

'No. Box Seven on the right and Box Three on the left were still empty. The curtain had only just gone up.'

'So what did you do?'

'Well, I brought him a footstool. Of course, it wasn't for himself that he wanted it, but for his lady! But I've never heard or seen her.'

What? The ghost now had a wife! The eyes of the two directors went from Mme Giry up to the house manager standing behind her and waving his arms to draw their attention. He put his finger to his temple and made a dismissive gesture suggesting that she was surely unhinged – which confirmed Richard in his opinion that a house manager who keeps a lunatic on his staff ought to be dismissed.

Meanwhile, the dear lady kept talking about her ghost, now waxing eloquent about his generosity: 'At the end of each performance, he gives me two francs, now and again five, and up to ten sometimes, when he has not come for several days. Except that now that people have begun to upset him again, I get nothing at all.'

'My good lady . . .' (*whereupon the feathers on Mme Giry's dingy hat visibly quivered with dismay at so persistently patronizing a manner*) 'forgive me, but how does the ghost manage to deliver the two francs?' asked the naturally inquisitive Moncharmin.

'Why, he leaves the money in the box, of course. I find it under the ledge with the programme I always bring him. Some evenings, I even find flowers there, such as a rose that must have dropped from his lady's dress . . . I am sure he comes with a lady sometimes because one day they left a fan behind.'

'Aha! The ghost left a fan behind, did he? And what did you do with it?'

'Well, I returned it to him the next time.'

Here the house manager intervened: 'You've broken the rules, Mme Giry, I shall have to fine you.'

'Hold your tongue, you fool!' growled M. Richard (*basso profundo*).

'You returned the fan. And then?'

'Well, then, they took it away with them, monsieur. It was not there at the end of the performance; and in its place there was a tin of boiled sweets, the ones I like best, monsieur. That was one of the ghost's little treats.'

'Thank you, Mme Giry. You can go now.'

After Mme Giry had respectfully taken her leave, with the dignity that never failed her, the two directors told the house manager that they had decided to dispense with the services of the old bat and bade him good day. And after he had gone too – not without having first protested his devotion to the Opera House – the directors instructed the administrator to make up the manager's accounts. When they were finally alone, they discussed an idea that had occurred to both of them simultaneously: they would take a look at Box Five for themselves.

And that is where we shall soon join them.

VI

The Magic Fiddle[1]

Owing to various intrigues – of which more anon – Christine Daaé did not immediately repeat her famous gala evening triumph at the Paris Opera. She had, however, occasion to sing in town at the invitation of the Duchess of Zurich, when she performed the most beautiful pieces in her repertoire. The distinguished critic X.Y.Z., who was among the honoured guests that evening, gave the following account:

> Listening to her Ophélie, one wondered if Shakespeare had left his resting place in the Elysian Fields to help her rehearse *Hamlet*[2] . . . And when she assumed the star-studded crown of the Queen of the Night in *The Magic Flute*,[3] Mozart must have left the heavens to come and listen to her. Unless, of course, the enthralling singer reached up to him with her powerful, vibrant voice, just as effortlessly as she passed from her parents' cottage in the village of Skotelof to the palace of gold and marble that M. Garnier designed for the Paris Opera.

The Duchess of Zurich's *soirée* was Christine Daaé's last society engagement. Henceforth she refused all invitations. With no credible excuse, she cancelled her appearance at a charity concert at which she had pledged to sing. Altogether, she acted as if she were no longer the mistress of her own destiny, almost as if she feared that she might triumph again.

When she learned that, to please his brother, the Count de Chagny had diligently pleaded her cause with M. Richard, she wrote to thank him, but also asked him not to mention her again to the directors of the Opera House. What might be the reason for such curious behaviour? Some claimed that it was a mark of immeasurable pride; others spoke of her saint-like modesty. Yet, as a rule, artists are rarely so modest; in truth I am rather tempted to ascribe her actions to sheer dread. Yes, I believe that Christine Daaé was frightened by what had just happened to her, and was as taken aback by it as everybody else around her. I have here with me one of her letters (from the Persian's collection) relating the events of that time. To suggest that Christine was taken aback or even frightened by her triumph is in fact an understatement: having reread the letter, I would say that she was *terrified*. Yes, yes, terrified. 'I am no longer myself when I sing,' she wrote.

Poor, sweet, innocent child!

She was nowhere to be seen and the Viscount de Chagny tried in vain to cross her path. He sent her a letter asking permission to call upon her and was despairing of ever receiving a reply when, one morning, the following note was delivered to him:

MONSIEUR, – I have not forgotten the young child who fetched my scarf from the sea. I feel compelled to write to you on the day when I go to Perros[4] to perform a sacred duty. Tomorrow is the anniversary of my poor father's death. You knew him and he was very fond of you. He is buried in Perros, with his violin, in the graveyard of the little church; the one that stands at the foot of the hill where we played so often as children, and beside the track where, when we were a little older, we bade each other adieu for the last time.

Having read her note, the Viscount de Chagny rushed to consult a railway guide, dressed hurriedly, scribbled a few lines to his brother and jumped into a cab. Unfortunately, he reached the Gare Montparnasse[5] too late to board the morning train, which he had hoped to catch. He spent a dismal day in town and his spirits only recovered when he settled in his compartment that evening on the train bound for Brittany. In the course of the journey he read Christine's note over and over again, savouring its fragrance and recalling the sweet images of his childhood. During that agonized night, his feverish dreams all began or ended with Christine. Day was breaking when he alighted at Lannion and hurried on to the stage-coach bound for Perros-Guirec. He was the only passenger. He questioned the driver and learned that, on the previous evening, a young lady who looked like a Parisian had gone to Perros and put up at the Auberge du Soleil-Couchant.[6] It could only be Christine. She had come alone. Raoul let out a deep sigh: he would be able to speak with her at leisure, without their being disturbed. His love for her was so overwhelming that it took his breath away. This young man, who had sailed round the world, was as pure as a virgin who had never left home.

As he drew nearer to his destination, he recalled with pious fervour the story of the young Swedish singer,[7] which has hitherto remained largely confidential:

Once upon a time, there lived a peasant farmer with his family in a small market town near Uppsala. He tilled his land on weekdays and sang bass in the choir on Sundays. He taught his little girl to read music even before she knew her alphabet. Perhaps unbeknown to him, Christine Daaé's father was a great musician. He played the violin and was regarded as the best fiddler in all Scandinavia. His reputation spread far and wide and he was often invited to set the couples spinning at weddings and other celebrations. His wife, an invalid, died as Christine reached her sixth year. Soon afterwards her father, who loved only his daughter and music, sold his smallholding and went to Uppsala in search of fame and fortune. Sadly, he only met with failure.

And so he returned to the countryside, travelling from fair to fair, scraping on his violin, while his child, who never left his side, listened to him in rapture or sang to his playing. One day, at Ljimby Fair, a certain Professor Valerius happened to hear them and immediately took them with him to Gothenburg. He maintained that the father was the best fiddler in the world and that the daughter had the makings of a great artist. He provided for her education and training. She made rapid progress, charming all who met her with her beauty, her graceful deportment and her eagerness to better herself. When Valerius and his wife went to live in France, they took Daaé and Christine with them. Mme Valerius treated Christine as her own daughter. Daaé, however, was so homesick that his health began to decline. When in Paris, he always remained indoors. He lived in a kind of dream, which he sustained with the help of his violin. For hours at a time, he shut himself away in his room with his daughter, playing and singing softly, all too softly. Sometimes Mme Valerius would come and listen behind the door, let out a heavy sigh, wipe a few tears from her eyes and then tiptoe away. For she too pined for the old country.

Daaé only seemed to recover his strength when, in summer, the whole family went to Brittany, staying at Perros-Guirec, a remote fishing village little known to Parisians. He loved the Atlantic Ocean, whose colour, he said, reminded him of home; he would often play his most plaintive tunes on the beach, and claimed that the sea stopped to listen to him. One year, he pleaded so compellingly with Mme Valerius to allow him a further indulgence that she let herself be persuaded.

Henceforth for a whole week during the religious festivals known as 'pardons' and other village celebrations and dances, he would go off with his fiddle as in the olden days, taking his daughter along with him. The villagers never tired of listening to them. Daaé and his daughter gave even the smallest of hamlets a cornucopia of musical delights to last them for a whole year. At night, having turned down the offer of a bed at the local inn, they slept in barns, lying close together on the straw as they had done in Sweden when they were very poor. Now, however, they were neatly dressed, made no collection and refused to take the coins offered to them. The people they met did not understand why the rustic fiddler tramped the roads with the pretty child who sang like an angel. Some followed them from village to village.

A young gentleman was so captivated by the pure, sweet voice of the little girl that one day he took his governess on a long detour. Thus they came to the shore of an inlet – still known as Trestraou – which was nothing but sky, sea and a stretch of golden sand. The wind was high and blew Christine's scarf out to sea. Christine gave a cry and reached out for it, but the scarf was already floating away. Then she heard a voice saying: 'Don't worry, mademoiselle, I'll go and fetch your scarf from the sea.'

And she saw a young boy running as fast as he could towards the sea, despite the screams and indignant protests of a good lady in black. He ran into the water, fully clothed, and brought back the scarf; both were thoroughly soaked. The lady in black would not calm down, but Christine laughed wholeheartedly and kissed the boy. He was none other than Viscount Raoul de Chagny and was staying at Lannion with his aunt at the time. During the remainder of the season, he saw the girl and played with her almost every day. At the request of the boy's aunt and the insistence of Professor Valerius, Daaé consented to give the young aristocrat some violin lessons. Thus Raoul came to love those tunes that had charmed the young Christine.

Both children were calm, imaginative little souls. They delighted in folk tales and old Breton legends, and would often go knocking on doors to beg for stories: 'Madame,' or 'Mon bon monsieur, would you have a story for us?' they asked. And more often than not, they were given one. Nearly every Breton grandmother has, at least once in her life, seen fairies frolic upon the heath by moonlight.

But their greatest treat was when, later in the day, Daaé came and sat with them by the roadside, in the peaceful twilight, after the sun had dropped below the watery horizon. Then, in a low voice, lest he should frighten the ghosts he evoked, he would recount ancient legends, enchanting or terrifying, from his homeland in the North. Some were as beautiful as Andersen's tales, others as gloomy as the Great Runeberg's verse.[8] And the moment the old man stopped, the children would say: 'Tell us more.'

There was one story that began: 'A king sat in a small boat on one of those deep, still lakes that open like bright eyes amidst the Norwegian mountains ...'[9] And another: 'Little Lotte thought of everything and nothing. With her fair locks crowned with flowers, she was like a summer bird caught in the golden rays of the sun. Her soul was as pure and limpid as her blue eyes. She was devoted to her mother, hugged her doll and took great care of her frock, her little red shoes and her fiddle; but, most of all, she enjoyed[10] listening to the Angel of Music as she went to sleep.'

While the old man told this story, Raoul gazed at Christine's blue eyes and golden hair; and Christine felt that Lotte was very fortunate to hear the Angel of Music as she went to sleep. In fact, the Angel of Music featured in all but a few of the stories, and the children asked about him endlessly. Daaé maintained that all great musicians, all great performers were visited by the Angel of Music at least once in their lives. Sometimes the Angel leaned over their cradle, as happened to Lotte, which was why some child prodigies as young as six could play the violin better than men of fifty – and that, admittedly, was astounding. Sometimes the Angel came much later, because the children had been naughty and had not learned their lessons or practised their scales. And sometimes the Angel did not come at all because the children lacked a pure heart and a clear conscience. The Angel was never seen but could be heard by those who were meant to hear. This often happened when you least expected it, when you were sad and down-hearted. Then your ears would suddenly hear celestial harmonies, a divine voice, which you would remember for ever. Those who had been visited by the Angel were stirred. They experienced a thrill unknown to other mortals and henceforth could not touch an instrument or open their mouths to sing without producing sounds that put all other musicians to shame. The people who knew nothing about the angelic visitation called them geniuses.

Little Christine asked her father if he had heard the Angel of Music. He shook his head sadly, but his eyes lit up and he added: 'You will hear him some day, my child! When I am in Heaven, I will send the Angel to you, I promise!'

Around this time the old fiddler developed a cough.

At the onset of autumn Raoul and Christine had to part. When they saw each other again, three years later at Perros, they were no longer children; and their meeting made such an impression on Raoul that it remained with him for the rest of his life. By then, Professor Valerius had died, but his widow stayed in France, where she was settled, together with Daaé

and his daughter. As before, they would sing and play the violin, taking their beloved benefactress along with them into their
melodious world, so that she now seemed to live on music
alone. Having come to Perros in the hope of finding them,
Raoul entered the cottage where Christine used to stay. He first
saw her father, who got to his feet with tears in his eyes and
embraced him. They remembered him fondly, said the old man;
in fact, hardly a day had passed without Christine mentioning
his name. Daaé was still talking when the door opened and his
delightful, caring daughter appeared, carrying a pot of steaming tea. She recognized Raoul and put the tray down, blushing
a little at the sight of him. She stood there hesitantly and said
nothing while her father gazed at the two of them. Then Raoul
went up to her and gave her a kiss, which she made no attempt
to resist. She asked him a few questions, graciously attended to
her duties as hostess, took up the tea-tray and left the room.
She went out to seek comfort in the solitude of the garden and
sat on a bench. Feelings that she had never known before now
stirred in her young heart. Raoul joined her and they talked
until evening – with much bashfulness on both sides. They
were quite changed: they hardly recognized the characters they
had become and seemed to have gained stature in each other's
eyes. They were as cautious as two diplomats and their conversation did not touch on their budding sentiments. When they
took leave of each other by the roadside, Raoul pressed a kiss
on Christine's trembling hand and said: 'Mademoiselle, I shall
never forget you!'

But as he went away, he regretted his bold statement, for he
knew that Christine could never be the wife of the Viscount de
Chagny.

As for Christine, she went back to her father and said to
him: 'Didn't you find that Raoul is not as nice as he used to be?
I don't think I like him any more!' And she tried to forget him.
It proved rather difficult, so she fell back on her art, to which
she devoted every moment of her life. She made wonderful progress, and those who heard her claimed that she would become
the greatest singer in the world. But sadly her father died and,
all of a sudden, her voice, her soul and her genius seemed to

have died with him. She retained just enough of those gifts to gain a place at the Paris Conservatoire. Her studies there were altogether undistinguished: she attended the classes without enthusiasm and only secured a prize to please Mme Valerius, with whom she continued to live.

The first time Raoul saw Christine at the Opera he was charmed by her beauty, which conjured up enchanting memories of the past; yet to his surprise he found that there was something wanting in her performance. She seemed detached from all around her. He came back to listen to her. He went backstage. He waited for her behind a scenery flat. He tried to catch her eye and, more than once, he followed her all the way to the door of her dressing-room; but she did not see him. As a matter of fact, she seemed to see no one. She was indifference itself. Raoul felt hurt for she was beautiful; and, shy as he was, he dared not admit to himself that he loved her. Then came the shock, the revelation of the gala performance: the heavens opened, and an angel's voice was heard upon this earth to the sheer delight of mankind and the utter surrender of Raoul's heart.

And afterwards, there was that voice behind the door saying: 'You must love me!' though there was no one in the room . . .

Why had she laughed on opening her eyes when he had said: '*I am that little boy who went into the sea to retrieve your scarf*'? Why had she not recognized him? Why had she written to him?

Oh! The road to Perros went on and on, up and up. Here was the crucifix at the crossroads, the deserted moor, the frozen heath, the still landscape under the colourless sky. The coach windows rattled relentlessly, filling his ears with their sound. The coach was so noisy and its progress so slow! He recognized the thatched cottages, the enclosures, the embankments, the trees along the road. Then, at last, they went around the final bend in the road and the coach clattered all the way down to the sea and the bay of Perros.

So she had put up at the Auberge du Soleil-Couchant. Of course! It was the only inn, and a good one. And he recalled that, once upon time, they had heard beautiful stories there. His heart beat faster! What would she say when she saw him?

The first person he saw when he walked into the smoky dining-room of the inn was the landlady, Mme Tricard. She recognized him, greeted him warmly and asked him what brought him to these parts. He blushed and replied that having travelled to Lannion on business, he had 'come over to pay his respects'. She wanted to serve him breakfast, but he said: 'Later.' He seemed to be expecting someone or something. Then the door opened and he leaped to his feet. He had guessed right: here she was! He tried to speak but was dumbstruck. She was standing before him, smiling and not showing the least surprise. Her fresh-looking face was the colour of a wild strawberry grown in the shade.[11] She was slightly out of breath as if from a brisk walk. Her bosom, which held a kind heart, gently rose and fell. Her clear blue eyes were the colour of the still, dreamy waters of the far Northern lakes and offered a tranquil reflection of her candid soul. Her fur coat was open, revealing her slender waist and the pleasing outline of her young, graceful body. Raoul and Christine looked at each other for a long time. Mme Tricard smiled and discreetly slipped away. Then, at last, Christine spoke: 'So you have come. I am not surprised. I knew I should find you here, at the inn, when I came back from Mass. *Someone* told me.'

'Who told you?' he asked. He took her small hand into his and she did not pull away.

'Why, my poor dead father.'

There was a silence, and then Raoul asked: 'Did your father also tell you that I love you, Christine, and that I cannot live without you?'

Christine blushed and turned her head away. In a trembling voice, she said: 'You love me? But this is madness, Raoul.' And she burst out laughing to conceal her true feelings.

'Do not laugh, Christine! I am serious,' Raoul retorted.

And she replied gravely: 'It was not to hear such things that I wanted you to come.'

'But you *wanted me to come*, Christine. You knew that your letter would make me come, that I should hasten to Perros. How could that be, if you did not think I loved you?'

'I thought you would remember our childhood games, and

how my father would often join in. To tell you the truth, I hardly know what I thought . . . Perhaps it was wrong of me to write . . . Your sudden appearance in my dressing-room at the Opera, the other evening, brought back memories of our distant past, and the girl I then was wrote to you: at a time of sadness and solitude, she longed to have her friend by her side.'

They kept silent for a few moments. Raoul felt that there was, in Christine's demeanour, something unnatural, which he could not quite pin down. He did not feel that she was hostile towards him; far from it: the tender look in her eyes told him as much. But why was that tenderness tinged with sorrow? That was perhaps what he needed to ascertain, and what already troubled him.

'Did you notice me before you saw me in your dressing-room, Christine?'

She could not tell a lie. 'Yes,' she said, 'I had seen you several times in your brother's box. And also backstage.'

'I thought so!' exclaimed Raoul, pursing his lips. 'Then tell me: when you saw me in your room, at your feet, reminding you that I had retrieved your scarf from the sea, why did you answer as if you did not know me? Why did you laugh?'

The harshness in his voice, as he put those questions to her, startled Christine. She stared at him without replying. As for Raoul, he was aghast, finding himself suddenly quarrelling with her at the very moment when he should have been murmuring tender loving words. He sounded like an offended husband or lover with righteous claims on his wife's or mistress's affections. He knew he had spoken out of turn and felt foolish but, in his anger with himself, he saw no better way out of this absurd situation than to behave in a resolutely odious manner.

'You don't answer!' he said, in exasperation and dismay. 'Well, I will tell you why. It was because in that room there was someone else, whose presence made you feel uneasy, Christine; and you did not want him to know that you could be interested in another!'

'If anyone made me feel uneasy, Raoul,' Christine replied icily, 'if anyone made me feel uneasy that evening, it must have been you, since you are the one I threw out!'

'Yes! So that you could remain with *him*!'

'What are you saying, monsieur?' gasped the young woman. 'Whom do you mean?'

'I mean the man to whom you said: "*I sing only for you! Tonight I gave you my soul and I am dead!*"'

Christine clasped Raoul's arm, gripping it with a strength quite unimaginable in so frail a creature. 'So you were listening behind the door?'

'Yes, because I love you. And I heard everything.'

'You heard what?' Strangely regaining her composure, the young woman released Raoul's arm.

'He said to you: "Christine, *you must love me!*"'

At these words, a deathly pallor spread over Christine's face and dark shadows appeared around her eyes. She reeled and was about to collapse. Raoul reached out for her, but Christine had already overcome her passing faintness and said in a low, almost dying voice: 'Go on! Go on! Tell me everything you heard.'

Raoul looked at her hesitantly, unable to understand her distress.

'Go on! I want to know! This is killing me!'

'I also heard his reply to you when you said you had given him your soul: "*Your soul is a beautiful thing, my child*," he said, "*and I am grateful. No emperor ever received so great a gift. The angels wept tonight.*"'

Christine raised her hand to her breast and looked at Raoul with indescribable emotion. She had an intense, fixed stare, as if she had lost her mind. Raoul was awestruck. Then suddenly her eyes moistened and two heavy tears rolled, like two pearls, down her ivory cheeks.

'Christine!'

'Raoul!'

The young man tried to take her in his arms, but she eluded him and fled in alarm and confusion.

While Christine remained locked in her room, Raoul bitterly regretted his rashness; all the same, burning jealousy coursed through his veins. For the young woman to be so upset on learning that he had discovered her secret, it must be important.

Raoul did not doubt the purity of her heart in spite of what he had overheard. He knew that she had a great reputation for virtue and he was not so naive as to be unaware that such an artist was bound sometimes to hear declarations of love. True, she had answered by saying that she had given her soul; but it was all clearly to do with singing and music. Or was it? And if indeed it was, why had she been so distressed earlier on? Oh, Raoul felt wretched! Had he confronted that man – *that voice* – he would have demanded a full explanation.

Why had Christine fled from him? Why did she remain in her room?

He declined lunch. He was utterly wretched and grieved that the hours he had hoped to spend in the sweet company of the beautiful Swedish girl were now slipping away. Why did she not join him? They could have revisited the places that evoked so many shared memories. And since she seemed to have nothing more to do in Perros – and indeed was, at present, unoccupied – why did she not leave for Paris at once? He had heard that she had had a Mass said, that morning, for the repose of her father's soul and that she had spent many hours praying in the little church and at the old musician's grave.

Sad and disheartened, Raoul took himself to the graveyard. He wandered alone among the graves, reading the inscriptions. When he came upon the area behind the church, he saw a dazzling array of flowers laid out over a granite tombstone and spilling on to the frozen ground; and he knew at once that this was her father's grave. The air of this wintry corner of Brittany was filled with the fragrance of the flowers, glorious red roses that seemed to have blossomed that very morning in the snow, bringing a breath of life to the dead. For death was all around and had even spilled out above ground. Skeletons and skulls by the hundred were piled up against the wall of the church and held there by flimsy wire netting, which left the macabre edifice entirely exposed. The skulls, lined up and stacked like bricks with carefully weathered bones inserted in the gaps, almost seemed to provide the footing upon which the walls of the sacristy had been built. A door was placed in the middle of this grisly repository so typical of Breton churchyards.

Raoul said a prayer for M. Daaé and then, deeply unsettled by the eternal smiles of the skulls, left the graveyard. He climbed to the top of the hill and sat down at the edge of the heath overlooking the sea. A vicious wind raced along the shore, baying at the poor, timid light of day, which surrendered and fled until only a pale streak showed on the horizon. Then the wind fell silent. Night came. Raoul was shrouded in icy shadows. In his imagination he wandered across the deserted and desolate heath, and remembered that he had often come to this very spot with little Christine to watch for fairies frolicking under the rising moon. However good his eyesight, he had never even glimpsed any; whereas Christine, who was a little short-sighted, claimed to have seen fairies many a time. He smiled at the thought and then suddenly gave a start. A figure had appeared without his noticing the slightest movement or sound – a familiar figure who now stood next to him.

'Do you think the fairies will come tonight?' she asked. It was Christine. When he tried to speak, she placed her gloved hand over his mouth. 'Listen, Raoul, I must tell you something, something very serious!' she said in a trembling voice.

He remained silent, waiting.

'Do you remember the story of the Angel of Music?' she continued, clearly distressed.

'Yes, I do!' he replied. 'It was here, I believe, that we first heard it from your father.'

'And it was here that he said: "When I am in Heaven, I will send the Angel to you." Well, Raoul, my father is in Heaven and I have been visited by the Angel of Music.'

'I do not doubt it,' replied the young man gravely. He assumed that she connected the pious memory of her late father with her triumphant gala performance.

Christine seemed slightly surprised by the calm manner in which the Viscount de Chagny had responded to her announcement. 'Do you understand what I am saying?' she asked, bringing her pale face so close to his that he might have thought that she was going to kiss him; but she only wanted to read the expression in his eyes, despite the darkness.

'I understand,' he said, 'that no human being can sing as you sang the other evening without some miracle, or some heavenly intervention. No teacher on earth could have taught you to sing so divinely. You have indeed heard the Angel of Music, Christine.'

'Yes,' she said solemnly, '*in my dressing-room*, where he comes every day to teach me.'

She spoke with such conviction and so strangely that Raoul looked at her, alarmed, as one might look at someone who had just uttered an absurdity or was the victim of a delusion to which she clung with all the strength of her poor, sick mind. She had stepped back from him and remained motionless, a mere shadow in the night.

'In your dressing-room?' Raoul echoed uncomprehendingly.

'Yes, that's where I heard him; and I am not the only one who heard him.'

'Who else heard him, Christine?'

'You, Raoul.'

'I? I heard the Angel of Music?'

'Yes, the other evening, it was his voice you heard when you listened behind the door. It was his voice saying: "You must love me." But, at that time, I thought that I was the only one who could hear him. Imagine my surprise when you told me, this morning, that you had heard him too.'

Raoul burst out laughing. Just then the darkness lifted and the moon rose above the desolate heath, bathing the two young people with its light.

Christine turned to Raoul. Her eyes, usually so gentle, flashed with anger: 'Why are you laughing? Perhaps you think you heard the voice of a man!'

'Why, yes!' replied the young man, puzzled and confused in the face of Christine's intense hostility.

'Raoul, is that what you really think? You, my childhood friend, whom my father loved so! You have changed! I no longer recognize you. How can you think that? I am an honourable woman, Viscount, and I do not lock myself up in my dressing-room with men. Had you opened the door, you would have seen for yourself that there was no one in the room!'

'That's true! I opened the door when you were gone, and I found no one there.'

'You see ... Well then?'

The Viscount summoned up all his courage: 'Well, Christine, I think that someone is playing a trick on you.'

She gave a cry and fled. He ran after her, but she turned on him, wild with anger: 'Leave me alone! Leave me alone!' And she disappeared.

Raoul returned to the inn feeling weary, dispirited and desperately sad. He learned that Christine had just retired to her room saying that she would not be down for dinner. The young man enquired if she was unwell from Mme Tricard, who replied ambiguously that if the young lady was sick, her sickness could not be very serious. Putting the whole thing down to a lovers' tiff, she walked away, shrugging her shoulders and muttering that it was a pity that young people should vainly waste the hours the Good Lord had given them on this earth. Raoul dined alone next to the fireplace and, as the reader might imagine, in a melancholy mood. Finally he went up to his room, where he tried to read; then to bed, where he tried to sleep. He did not hear a sound from the adjoining room. What was Christine doing? Was she asleep? And if she was awake, what was she thinking? And what about him? What was he thinking? Could he even tell? His bizarre conversation with Christine had thoroughly unsettled him. He was thinking less about Christine herself than about *her situation*, which seemed to him so vague, so hazy and so elusive that he felt a strange unease and anguish.

The hours passed very slowly. It was about half-past eleven when he distinctly heard light, furtive footsteps in the room next to his. Christine was not in her bed, then! Without thinking, Raoul dressed, taking care not to make a sound. And then he waited expectantly. What did he expect? He had no idea. His heart leaped when he heard Christine's door slowly turn on its hinges. Where could she be going at this hour, when the whole of Perros was asleep? He quietly opened his door and glimpsed her white figure cautiously slipping down the corridor in the moonlight. She reached the staircase and, as she descended, Raoul leaned over the banister. He heard two hurried voices. He only caught one sentence: 'Don't lose the key.' It was the landlady's voice. Someone opened the door that gave on to the waterfront and locked it again. All went quiet. Raoul rushed back to his room and quickly opened the window. The white figure of Christine stood on the deserted quayside.

The inn was not a tall building. A tree growing against the wall held out its branches to Raoul's impatient arms, enabling him to climb down and leave the inn unbeknown to the landlady. Hence her astonishment, the next morning, when the young man was brought back to her half frozen and more dead than alive, and she learned that he had been found lying on the steps of the altar of the little church. She ran at once to tell Christine, who hurried down and, aided by the landlady, lavished care and attention on him. He soon came to and quickly revived on seeing the charming face of his beloved leaning over him.

What had happened to him? A few weeks later, following the tragic events at the Opera House that led to the involvement of the Public Prosecutor's Office, Inspector Mifroid[12] was able to question the Viscount de Chagny about what happened that night at Perros. I reproduce here the transcription of the interview included in the official report (Ref. no. 150):

Question: 'Did Mlle Daaé see you climb down from your room by the unusual route you had chosen?'

Answer: 'No, inspector, she did not, although I made no effort to deaden the sound of my footsteps when I caught up with her. In fact, I was only too anxious that she should look back, see me and acknowledge my presence. I realized that my following her was quite wrong – spying on her in such a fashion was unworthy of me; but she seemed not to hear me and acted as if I were not there. She left the quayside at a leisurely pace and then suddenly hurried up the road. The church clock had just struck a quarter to twelve. I thought this might be the reason for her sudden haste, for she began almost to run and continued in this fashion until she reached the graveyard.'

Q.: 'Was the gate open?'

A.: 'Yes. I thought it odd, but Mlle Daaé did not seem at all surprised.'

Q.: 'Was there anyone in the churchyard?'

A.: 'I did not see anyone. If there had been someone, I would have noticed. There was a brilliant moon whose light was reflected by the snow on the ground, making the night even brighter.'

Q.: 'Was it possible for anyone to hide behind the tombstones?'

A.: 'No, inspector. There were only small, modest tombstones, lying under a layer of snow, with their crosses rising just above the ground. The only shadows were ours and those of the crosses. The church was resplendent in the moonlight. I have never seen such brightness at night. It was very beautiful, remarkably clear and very cold. I had never found myself in a graveyard at night before and I did not expect such light there – I can only describe it as "weightless".'

Q.: 'Are you superstitious?'

A.: 'I believe in God, inspector.'

Q.: 'Can you describe your state of mind at that time?'

A.: 'Sound and self-assured, I would say. True, at first I was deeply troubled by Mlle Daaé's curious nocturnal sortie; but as soon as I saw her enter the churchyard, I thought that she meant to fulfil some pious duty at her father's grave and it seemed so natural to me that I felt reassured. I was still surprised, however, that she had not heard me walking behind her, for the hard snow crunched under my feet. Thinking that she must be absorbed in her own pious thoughts, I decided not to disturb her; and, when she reached her father's grave, I held back. She knelt down in the snow, made the sign of the cross and began to pray. At that moment, the church clock struck midnight. The twelfth stroke was still ringing in my ears when suddenly I saw her raise her eyes to the heavens and her arms to the moon, as if in a state of rapture. I was wondering what the cause might be when I myself raised my head, cast a distracted look around me and felt the whole of my being drawn towards the Unknown, towards *the disembodied music now playing for us*. And what music! It was

music Christine and I had heard as children. But never before had
it been played so divinely on Daaé's violin. At that moment, all I
could do was remember all that Christine had said about the
Angel of Music. I scarcely knew what to think of the unforget-
table sound we heard and which – were it not coming down from
the heavens – revealed nothing of its earthly origins. No instrument nor hand holding the bow was anywhere to be seen. Oh! I
will never forget that sublime melody. It was *Lazarus*,[13] which the
old fiddler used to play for us at times of sadness and pious con-
templation. Had Christine's Angel existed, he could not have
played better on her father's fiddle, that night. We were so
entranced by Jesus' Invocation that I almost expected to see his
grave open. The idea also came to me that the old man had been
buried with his violin, and, in all truth, I cannot say how far, during those doleful, yet glorious moments in this small, remote pro-
vincial graveyard, standing beside those skulls grinning with their
motionless jaws ... no, I cannot say how far my imagination
wandered and where it stopped.

'When the music ceased, I recovered my senses. I thought I
heard a noise coming from where the skulls were stacked.'

Q.: 'So you heard a noise coming from the bone repository?'

A.: 'Yes, inspector, it was as if the skulls chortled, and I could
not help shuddering.'

Q.: 'Did it not immediately occur to you that the repository
might conceal the celestial musician who had charmed you so?'

A.: 'Yes, the thought did occur to me; and it being foremost in
my mind, I did not follow Mlle Daaé when she stood up and
slowly made her way out. She was so self-absorbed I am not surprised she did not see me.'

Q.: 'And what happened then? How was it that you were
found in the morning lying half-dead on the steps of the altar?'

A.: 'Oh! It all happened very quickly ... First a skull rolled to
my feet ... then another ... then another still ... as if I were the
jack in some grisly game of bowls. I assumed that the delicate
balance of the edifice concealing our fiddler had been accidentally
disturbed. It seemed all the more plausible when all of a sudden a
shadow slid across the brightly moonlit wall of the sacristy.

'I chased after it. The shadow had already pushed open the

door and was entering the church. I rushed in pursuit and saw that the shadow wore a hooded cloak. Quick as a flash, I grabbed hold of it. At that moment, we were both standing right in front of the altar; and the moonlight coming through the main stained-glass window fell straight upon the ground before us. As I would not let go of the cloak, the shadow turned round and beneath the hood I saw a terrifying skull, whose staring eyes burned with the fire of Hell. I thought I was face to face with Satan himself. It was like a vision from beyond the grave. I felt so helpless that I lost consciousness ... and I remember nothing more until I came round at the Auberge du Soleil-Couchant.'

VII

A Visit to Box Five

We left Messrs Firmin Richard and Armand Moncharmin as they were about to visit Box Five and take a look for themselves.

Turning their backs on the broad staircase that led from the lobby of the administrative wing to the stage and adjoining areas, they crossed the stage, went through the subscribers' door and along the first corridor on the left, thereby gaining access to the stalls. Then they made their way through the first few rows so as to look up into Box Five. They could not see it well, for it was in semi-darkness and the red velvet ledge was hidden under huge dust-covers.

They found themselves virtually alone in the vast and gloomy theatre; all was silent around them. This was the tranquil hour when the machinists went for a drink,[1] deserting the stage for a while, half-way through raising a set. A few rays of light – a wan, sinister light that seemed to issue from a dying sun – fell from somewhere upon an old tower whose pasteboard crenellations rose above the stage; in this fake darkness – or deceptive light, rather – everything took on a fantastic appearance. The dust-covers thrown over the surrounding seats suggested an angry sea, whose dull, grey-green waves had been suddenly stilled by secret order of the Phantom of the Sea – or Adamastor, as we all know.[2] Moncharmin and Richard were as if shipwrecked amid the motionless turbulence of a cloth sea. Like sailors who have abandoned ship desperately trying to swim ashore, they made for the boxes on the left. There, in shadow, stood the eight great polished columns supporting,

like so many stone pillars, the threatening bulk of the pot-
bellied, jagged cliff rising from the sagging strata of the boxes
that bulged out of the grand, first and second tiers. Further up,
at the very top of the cliff, the usually solemn figures lost in
Lenepveu's copper ceiling[3] now peered down at Richard and
Moncharmin, laughing, jeering and scoffing at their anguish.
These figures[4] were Isis, Amphitrite, Hebe, Flora, Pandora, Psyche, Thetis, Pomona, Daphne, Clytie, Galatea and Arethusa.[5]
Yes, Arethusa herself, and even Pandora, whom we all know
because of her box,[6] watched the new joint directors of the
Opera House who, finally clinging to some wreckage, looked
up silently at Box Five on the grand tier.

I suggested just now that they were anxious; at least I
assumed so. Armand Moncharmin, at any rate, admitted in his
Memoirs that he was bewildered. To quote his own words:

> All that 'humbug' about the ghost (*what magnificent style!*)
> which had been so kindly rammed down our throats since we
> had taken over from Messrs Poligny and Debienne, must have
> eventually disturbed our imaginative as well as our visual facul-
> ties. Was it the exceptional setting in which we found ourselves
> and the fantastic silence all around us that made such a strong
> impression on us? Were we the victims of some hallucination due
> to the dimness of the house and the semi-darkness shrouding Box
> Five? All I can say is that both Richard and I saw at the same time
> a vague *form* in Box Five. Richard did not say a word and nor did
> I. But we instinctively clutched each other's hand. We stood still
> for a moment, seeking to identify it; but it had already vanished.
> We left the theatre and, having reached the corridor, exchanged
> our impressions, talking about what we had seen. Unfortunately,
> my description was completely at odds with Richard's. I had
> glimpsed something resembling a skull resting on the ledge of the
> box, whereas Richard had seen the shape of an old woman who
> reminded him of Mme Giry. Thus we came to the conclusion that
> we had, in fact, been the victims of some illusion. Without further
> delay, and laughing hysterically, we ran up to Box Five, went
> inside and found nothing unusual there in any shape or form.

Box Five, where they now stood, was like any other box on the grand tier. In truth, there was nothing to distinguish it from any of the others.

Moncharmin and Richard, ostensibly enjoying themselves and joking with each other, moved the furniture around, lifted the dust-covers and the seats. They examined with particular care the chair from whence *the voice spoke*; but all they saw was a respectable chair with no magic about it. All in all, there was nothing exceptional about the box with its red hangings, its chairs, its carpet and its ledge covered in red velvet. Having purposefully felt along the carpet and discovered nothing special there or anywhere else, they went down into the box directly below the Phantom's box and to the left of the first rows of stalls. There, they found nothing worthy of note either.

'Those people are all making fools of us!' Richard eventually exclaimed. 'There is a performance of *Faust* on Saturday: we shall both watch it from Box Five!'

VIII

In which Firmin Richard and Armand Moncharmin
have the audacity to allow Faust *to be performed in a*
'cursed' theatre and the terrible events that ensued

That Saturday morning, on reaching their office, the two directors each found a letter from the Phantom, which ran as
follows:

MY DEAR DIRECTORS, – Is it to be war?

If not, then these are my conditions:

1. My box must be freely available to me again – as of today.

*2. The part of Marguerite will be sung this evening by Christine
Daaé. Do not worry about Carlotta: she will be indisposed.*

*3. Mme Giry must be allowed to resume her duties forthwith,
for I greatly value her good and loyal services.*

*4. As regards my monthly allowance, let me know in writing
that you agree, as your predecessors did, to my terms; and hand
your letter to Mme Giry, who will ensure that it reaches me. I will
inform you later how the monies are to be delivered.*

Should you refuse, tonight's performance of Faust *will be
cursed.*

This is my ultimatum! Be warned!

P. of the O.

'Well, I'm thoroughly sick and tired of him!' Richard roared,
angrily raising his fists in the air and banging them down on to
the top of his desk.

At that moment Mercier, the administrator, appeared. 'Messieurs, Lachenal needs to talk to one of you,' he said. 'The
matter is clearly urgent and he seems quite upset.'

'Who's Lachenal?' asked Richard.

'He's your chief groom.'

'What do you mean, my chief groom?'

'There are several grooms at the Opera,'[1] explained Mercier, 'and they work under Lachenal.'

'And what does this chief groom do?'

'He has charge of the stables.'

'What stables?'

'Why, yours, monsieur – the stables of the Opera House.'

'Are there stables here, at the Opera? Upon my word, I never knew that! And where are they?'

'In the basement on the Rotunda side, they are very important: we have twelve horses.'

'Twelve horses! And what for, in Heaven's name?'

'Why, we need trained horses for the processions in *La Juive*, *Le Prophète* and so on – horses accustomed to the stage. The grooms' job is to train them. Lachenal is very good at it. He used to manage Franconi's stables.'[2]

'Very well . . . but what does he want?'

'I don't know, but I never saw him in such a state.'

'Then show him in.'

M. Lachenal strode into the office and stood there, nervously beating one of his boots with the riding-crop he held in his hand.

'Good morning, M. Lachenal,' said Richard, somewhat impressed. 'To what do we owe the honour of this visit?'

'Monsieur, I have come to ask you to get rid of the lot.'

'What, you want to get rid of the horses?'

'Not the horses! The stablemen.'

'How many of them are there, M. Lachenal?'

'Six! And that's at least two too many.'

'These positions,' Mercier interposed, 'were created and forced upon us by the under-secretary for Fine Arts. They are filled by protégés of the government and, if I may . . .'

'I don't care a jot about the government!' roared Richard. 'We don't need more than four stablemen for twelve horses.'

'Eleven,' said the chief groom correcting him.

'Twelve,' repeated Richard.

'Eleven,' repeated Lachenal.

'But the administrator told me that you had twelve horses!'

'I did have twelve, but there are only eleven left since César was stolen.'

And at this M. Lachenal thwacked his boot with his crop for emphasis.

'César has been stolen?' cried the administrator. 'César, the white horse in *Le Prophète*?'

'Yes, the one and only César,' said the chief groom curtly. 'I was ten years at Franconi's and I have seen many horses in my time. But there is only one César. And now he has been stolen.'

'How?'

'I cannot say. Nobody knows. That's why I have come to ask you to sack the stablemen.'

'And what do they say?'

'All sorts of nonsense. Some of them accuse the supers. Others claim that it is the concierge of the administrative wing . . .'

'My concierge? I'll answer for him. I would trust him with my life!' protested Mercier.

'All the same, M. Lachenal,' cried Richard, 'you must have some idea.'

'Yes indeed, I have,' came Lachenal's brisk reply. 'I have an idea and I'll tell you. There's no doubt in my mind that . . .' and, having drawn closer to the two managers, he whispered: '. . . *the ghost did it!*'

Richard started: 'What! You too? You too?'

'How do you mean, I too? It's only natural . . .'

'Why, of course, M. Lachenal! Of course!'

'. . . that I should tell you my thoughts,' continued Lachenal, 'after what I saw!'

'What did you see?'

'I saw, as plainly as I can see you now, a black shadow riding a white horse that looked just like César!'

'And did you run after them?'

'Yes, monsieur, I ran after them and I called out, but they vanished at tremendous speed into the darkness of the underground gallery.'

Richard rose. 'That will do, M. Lachenal. You can go. We will lodge a complaint against the *ghost*.'

'And sack the lot?'

'Oh, of course! Good morning to you.'

Lachenal bowed and withdrew.

Richard fumed: 'Settle that idiot's accounts at once, please!'

'But he is a friend of the government representative!' Mercier ventured.

'And he drinks with Lagréné, Scholl and Pertuiset, the lion-hunter, at Tortoni's,'[3] added Moncharmin. 'The whole press will be against us! They'll hear about the ghost and make us a laughing stock! This will be the end of us!'

'All right, say no more about it,' conceded Richard, his mind already on something else.

At that moment the door flew open. It had obviously been left unguarded by its usual Cerberus,[4] for Mme Giry came in unbidden, holding a letter in her hand. 'I beg your pardon, gentlemen, but this morning I received a letter from the Phantom of the Opera, saying that I should call at your office, that you have something . . .'

She did not complete her sentence. She saw Firmin Richard's face; and what a terrible sight it was! He seemed ready to explode. His fury showed in the crimson colour of his face and the mad glint in his eyes. He said nothing. He could not speak. But suddenly he sprang into action. He seized upon quaint Mme Giry with his left arm, and swung her back round so unexpectedly, so swiftly that she yelped in dismay. And then the honourable director raised his right foot and stamped his footprint upon the black taffeta of a skirt that had surely never suffered such merciless outrage.

It had all happened so fast that, finding herself back in the corridor, Mme Giry, in shock, looked uncomprehending. But then, suddenly, she realized what had happened, and the Opera rang with her indignant shrieks, virulent protests, and threats of death and retribution. It took three lads to hustle her down to the courtyard of the administrative wing and two constables to forcefully escort her off the premises.

At about the same time, Carlotta, who lived in a small town-house on the Rue du Faubourg-Saint-Honoré, rang for her maid, and had her letters brought to her bed. Among them she found an anonymous letter, which read:

> *Be warned that, should you sing tonight, a great misfortune may befall you during your performance . . . a misfortune worse than death.*

The threatening letter was written in red ink, in a clumsy, disjointed hand. Upon reading it, Carlotta lost all appetite for breakfast. She pushed away the tray on which stood a cup of steaming hot chocolate, sat on her bed and pondered. It was not the first letter of this kind that she had received, but none before had been so overtly threatening.

At the time, she imagined herself to be the victim of multifarious jealous scheming and readily spoke of a secret enemy intent on her ruin. She claimed that a wicked plot was being hatched against her, a conspiracy that would soon come to light; but, she added, she was not a woman to be intimidated.

The truth is that, if conspiracy there was, it emanated from Carlotta herself and was directed against poor Christine, who had no inkling of it. Carlotta had never forgiven Christine for her triumphant performance when she had stepped in at a moment's notice. When Carlotta heard of the extraordinary ovation that her understudy had received, she was instantly cured of her incipient bronchitis and recovered at once from her recent fit of sulking against the directors. Henceforth she evinced no further desire to leave the Opera. Thereafter, she tirelessly endeavoured to 'silence' her rival, enlisting the support of influential friends who pressed the directors not to give Christine another opportunity to triumph. Those newspapers which had begun to praise Christine's talent, now only showed interest in Carlotta's fame. Even at the Opera, the celebrated diva spoke about Christine in the most disparaging terms and tried to cause her an endless stream of petty troubles.

Carlotta possessed neither heart nor soul. She was merely an instrument – a wonderful instrument, but an instrument nevertheless! Her repertoire included everything that might befit an ambitious diva, be it the work of German, Italian or French masters. Until then she had never sung out of tune nor lacked the vocal strength demanded by any part in her vast repertoire. In short, the said instrument was wide-ranging, powerful and perfectly tuned. But no one could have said to Carlotta what Rossini told Krauss after she had sung 'Selva opaca'[5] in German for him: 'You sing with your soul, my child, and your soul is beautiful!'

Oh, where was your soul, Carlotta, when you danced in the brothels of Barcelona? Where was it later, in Paris, when you performed coarse, roistering songs in seedy music-halls? And again, where was your soul when you let that supple and extraordinary instrument of yours – which could sing, with equal perfection, of sublime love and orgiastic pleasure – demean itself by performing in the salon of one of your lovers? O Carlotta, if you had ever possessed a soul and come to lose it, you would have found it again when you became Juliette, when you sang Elvira, Ophélie or Marguerite! For others have risen from lower depths than you did and were purified by art, attended by love.

In truth, when I consider all the pettiness and wickedness that Christine Daaé suffered at Carlotta's hands during that time, I can barely contain my anger. It is no wonder that my indignation should be expressed in rather sweeping statements about art in general – and the art of singing in particular – which Carlotta's admirers are bound to find unwarranted.

Having pondered the threat contained in the strange letter that she had just received, Carlotta rose from her bed. 'We'll see!' she said resolutely, throwing in a few oaths in her native Spanish for good measure.

The first thing she saw, upon looking out of her window, was a hearse. The hearse and the letter convinced her that she ran the gravest danger that evening. She summoned all her friends, and the friends of her friends, to her house and told them that a conspiracy, hatched by Christine Daaé, threatened the success of her performance. She insisted they must thwart that upstart of a girl by filling the house with her own – that is Carlotta's – admirers. Surely they were numerous enough? She relied on them to be ready for any eventuality and to suppress the enemy should they, as she feared, create any disturbance.

M. Richard's private secretary called on the diva to ask after her health and returned with the assurance that she was perfectly well and that, 'were she staring death in the face', she would still sing the part of Marguerite tonight. As the secretary had urged her, on behalf of the director, to take good care of herself, stay at home and avoid any draughts, Carlotta could not help wondering, after he had left, about a possible connection between these unusual and unexpected recommendations and the threats contained in the letter.

It was five o'clock when the post brought a second anonymous letter in the same hand as the first. It was short and simply said:

> You have a bad cold. You ought to be sensible enough to understand that it would be madness to sing this evening.

Shrugging her magnificent shoulders, Carlotta scoffed and sang two or three notes to reassure herself.

Her friends kept to their promise. They were all at the Opera that night, but looked round in vain for those fierce conspirators whom they were meant to silence. Except for a few outsiders – fine, upstanding citizens whose placid faces betrayed no more than the desire to hear again music which had earned their approval long ago – they found themselves as usual among patrons whose elegant, quiet and respectable manners ruled out any possibility of a riot. Unexpectedly, however, Box Five was occupied by Messrs Richard and Moncharmin. Carlotta's friends assumed that, having perchance heard about the planned disturbance, the directors had decided to attend so as to intervene at once if need be; but, as the reader knows, this was not the true reason for their presence. Richard and Moncharmin were thinking only of their ghost.

> 'Vain! In vain do I call, through my vigil weary,
> On creation and its Lord!
> Never reply will break the silence dreary!
> No sign! No single word!'[6]

The famous tenor Carolus Fonta had barely launched into Doctor Faust's first appeal to the powers of darkness, when Firmin Richard, who was sitting in the ghost's own chair – the chair at the front on the right – leaned over to his partner and enquired cheerily: 'Tell me, has the ghost whispered a word in your ear yet?'

'Let's wait! Let's not rush to conclusions,' replied Armand Moncharmin, in an equally cheery tone. 'The performance has only just begun and, as you know, the ghost usually only comes in towards the middle of the first act.'

The first act passed without incident. This was no surprise to Carlotta's friends since Marguerite does not appear before the second act. As for the directors, they grinned at each other when the curtain fell.

'That's the first one over!' exclaimed Moncharmin.

'Yes, the ghost is late,' added Richard.

'Not an undistinguished audience,' suggested Moncharmin, light-heartedly, '*for a house with a curse upon it.*'

Richard gave a condescending smile. He pointed to a big, healthy, common-looking woman dressed in black and flanked by two rather coarse men clad in broadcloth coats. They were sitting in the middle of the stalls.

'Who on earth are these people?' asked Moncharmin.

'They are my concierge, her husband and her brother.'

'And you gave them tickets?'

'Yes, I did. My concierge had never been to the Opera. This is her first time; but not the last since henceforth she'll be here every evening. I wanted her to have a good seat before she spent her time showing other people to theirs.'

Moncharmin asked what he meant and Richard explained that he had persuaded his concierge, in whom he had the greatest confidence, to act as a replacement for Mme Giry.

'By the way,' said Moncharmin, 'did you know that Mme Giry is going to lodge a complaint against you?'

'With whom? The ghost?'

The ghost! Moncharmin had almost forgotten about him. True enough, the mysterious character had done nothing as yet to remind the directors of his existence.

Suddenly the door of the box flew open to admit the stage manager, who was visibly distraught.

'What's the matter?' they asked, surprised at seeing him standing there at such an unexpected moment.

'It seems that Christine Daaé's friends are plotting against Carlotta. Carlotta's furious.'

'What on earth is this all about?' said Richard, frowning.

But just then the curtain rose on the second act and he waved the stage manager away. When the co-directors were alone again, Moncharmin leaned over to Richard.

'Daaé has friends, then?' he enquired.

'Yes, she has.'

'Who are they?'

Richard glanced across at a box on the grand tier with only two occupants. 'The Count de Chagny?'

'Yes, he commended her to me with such warmth that, if I had not known him to be Sorelli's friend . . .'

'Really? And who is that pale young man beside him?' asked Moncharmin.

'That's his brother, the Viscount.'

'He ought to be home and in bed. He looks unwell.'

The stage echoed with merry songs, intoxicating music in praise of the vine:

> 'Red or white liquor,
> Coarse or fine!
> What can it matter,
> So long as we have wine?'[7]

Jubilant students, burghers, soldiers, girls and matrons danced outside an inn, under the auspices of Bacchus. And then Siebel entered. Christine Daaé looked charming in her male attire.[8] There was something instantly appealing in her fresh youthfulness and melancholy grace. Carlotta's supporters assumed that Christine's friends would greet her with an ovation that would give away their intentions as well as constitute an unfortunate gaffe. But nothing happened.

On the other hand, when Carlotta crossed the stage to sing Marguerite's only two lines in the second act:

> 'No, my lord, not a lady am I, nor yet a beauty;
> And do not need an arm, to help me on my way!'[9]

she was met with enthusiastic applause. This was so unexpected, so uncalled-for that those who were not in the know exchanged puzzled glances. Even so, the second act too passed without incident. Now the expectation was that something must surely happen in the course of the next act. Some, supposedly better informed than the rest, declared that the 'racket' would begin with the ballad of the King of Thulé[10] and rushed to the subscribers' door to warn Carlotta.

The directors left the box during the interval to find out more about the conspiracy that the stage manager had mentioned; but they soon returned to their seats, shrugging their shoulders and treating the whole affair as an absurdity. The first thing they saw, on entering the box, was a tin of boiled sweets on the little shelf under the ledge. Who had put it there? They asked the attendants: no one knew. Glancing back at the shelf, they now saw, next to the tin of sweets, a pair of opera glasses. They looked at each other. They were in no mood for laughter. They remembered all that Mme Giry had told them, and felt a curious kind of draught around them. They sat down in silence, bewildered.

It was the garden scene:

> 'Gentle flow'rs in the dew,
> Be message from me . . .'[11]

As she sang these first two lines with her bouquet of roses and lilac in her hand, Christine raised her head and saw the Viscount de Chagny in his box. Thereafter, her voice seemed to lose some of its usual confidence, purity and crystal clarity, as if her singing was dulled and muffled as the result of some unknown and mysterious agency. And underneath, there was alarm, dread.

'How odd!' remarked one of Carlotta's friends in the stalls. 'The other night she was divine and now she is bleating. No experience, no method!'

> 'Gentle flow'rs, lie ye there,
> And tell her from me . . .'[12]

The Viscount held his head in his hands and wept. Seated behind him, the Count chewed fiercely on the tip of his moustache, shrugged his shoulders and frowned. For him to betray his feelings in such a fashion, the Count – usually so formal and restrained – must have been truly upset. And indeed he was. He had seen his brother return from his short and mysterious trip in a worrying state of health. Their ensuing conversations had clearly done nothing to reassure the Count, for such was his anxiety that he had asked Christine Daaé to meet him. She had had the audacity to reply that she could see neither him nor his brother. He suspected some unspeakable scheme. He resented Christine for making Raoul suffer; but, above all, he resented Raoul for suffering because of Christine. Ah, how wrong of him to take a brief interest in a girl whose one-night triumph no one could comprehend.

> 'Would she but deign to hear me,
> And with one smile to cheer me . . .'[13]

'The conniving little minx!' growled the Count to himself. And he wondered what she expected, what hopes she could possibly entertain. She was a virtuous girl, she was said to have no friends, nor protectors of any kind. That Scandinavian maiden must be very cunning indeed!

Raoul hid his boyish tears behind the curtain of his hands and thought only of the letter that he had received on his return to Paris – Christine was already there, having fled from Perros like a thief in the night.

MY DEAR FRIEND AND CHILDHOOD COMPANION, –
Be brave and agree never to see me or speak to me again . . . If

you love me just a little, please do this for me and trust that I
shall never forget you, my dear Raoul. I am begging you, do not
return to my dressing-room *ever again. My life depends upon it.*
Yours depends upon it, too.
   YOUR LITTLE CHRISTINE

Carlotta entered to thunderous applause. The garden act
unfolded as usual. Marguerite sang the ballad of the King of
Thulé to great acclaim; the 'Jewel Song' too.

> 'Ah, the joy past compare,
> These jewels bright to wear! . . .'[14]

By now, sure of herself, of her friends in the audience, of her
voice and of her success, Carlotta felt supremely confident. She
gave her all, with fervour, enthusiasm and sheer exhilaration.
Reserve and modesty were cast aside. No longer Marguerite,
she became Carmen.[15] The audience rewarded her with renewed
applause and her ensuing duet with Faust promised still more,
when suddenly something terrible happened.

Faust was now on his knees:

> 'Let me gaze on the form before me.
> While from yonder ether blue
> Look how the star of eve, bright and tender, lingers o'er me,
> To love thy beauty too!'[16]

And Marguerite replied:

> 'Oh, how strange!
> Like a spell does the evening bind me!
> And a deep languid charm
> I feel without alarm
> With its melody enwind me
> And all my heart subdue.'[17]

At that moment . . . At that very moment, something happened, something terrible, as I said, happened.

The whole house rose to its feet as one. In Box Five, the directors could not suppress their cries of horror. Men and women in the audience, baffled by such a turn of events, exchanged startled looks as Carlotta's face contorted in agony. There was madness in her haunted eyes. The wretched woman drew herself up, with her mouth still half-open, having just sung: 'With its melody enwind me . . .' But she was singing no longer. *She dared not utter another word, nor make another sound.*

For her harmonious voice – that agile instrument which had never failed her; that magnificent organ which could create the most beautiful sounds and deliver the most demanding melodies, the most subtle modulations, the most passionate rhythms; that sublime human machine which, to be divine, lacked only the heavenly fire which alone can convey true emotion and lift the soul – had just produced . . . For her very mouth had just produced . . . *a toad!* And what an awful, hideous, scummy, slimy, venomous, hoarse toad it was!

How did it find its way there? How did it come to crouch on her tongue, with its hind legs folded so as to spring higher and further? It had surreptitiously issued from her larynx and . . . croak! Croak! Croak! Oh! What a dreadful sound!

The toad in question was, of course, a metaphorical one. It could not be seen, but, in Hell's name, it could be heard! The house felt as if besmirched by the sound of it. Never was such a raucous croak heard, by the side of a noisy pond, ripping through the nocturnal air.

No one could have predicted anything like this. Carlotta was still unable to believe what her throat and her ears had told her. The crack of a thunderbolt would not have startled her as much as that hoarse croak springing out of her mouth; and thunder would not have caused her downfall. Whereas a toad crouched on a singer's tongue will inevitably ruin her. Some have even died from it.

Dear God! Who would have believed it? She had been singing 'With its melody enwind me . . .' so fluently. She had been singing it, as ever, with the calm confidence and ease of a casual 'how do you do?'

There are, no doubt, those presumptuous singers who over-estimate their powers and who, out of sheer conceit, want to stretch the weak voice that God gave them to extraordinary effect and reach heights that were denied them from birth. And this is the very moment when, by way of punishment, the Almighty unexpectedly places a croaking toad into their mouths. Everyone knew that, but no one believed that Carlotta's voice, which had two octaves within its range, could also harbour a toad.

Many still recalled her piercing *high Fs* and superb *staccati* in *The Magic Flute*. People also remembered her resounding triumph in *Don Giovanni*, when, as Elvira, she sang the high B flat that her fellow-singer, as Donna Anna, could not quite reach.[18] So what was the meaning of that croak at the end of her serene and tranquil little phrase: 'With its melody enwind me'? There was something unnatural about all this. Some dark magic must be at work here. There was a whiff of brimstone about that toad. Poor, wretched Carlotta was hopelessly defeated!

The clamour from the audience was growing. Had a similar misfortune befallen any singer other than Carlotta, she would have been booed. But as Carlotta's voice was known for its perfection, there was no display of anger, only horror and dis-may – the sort of dismay that must have been felt by those who witnessed the dismemberment of the Venus de Milo.[19] And even then, they would have seen disaster strike, and under-stood. But this! This was incomprehensible!

So much so that Carlotta wondered for a few seconds whether she had actually heard that note coming out of her own mouth – and could you call that sound a note? was it even a sound? A sound may still be music. She tried to convince her-self that the infernal noise had never happened, that she had momentarily been deceived by her ears, not betrayed by her voice. She anxiously looked about her, as if in search of some refuge, some protection, or rather a spontaneous assurance that her voice was not at fault. She clutched her throat in a ges-ture of self-defence and denial. No, no! That croak did not come from her! Carolus Fonta himself seemed to share her sentiment: he was staring at her with a child-like expression of immense bewilderment. As he had witnessed the event and remained by her side, perhaps he could explain how such a thing had happened! No, he could not! He gaped at her mouth as children gape at a magician's bountiful top hat. How could such an enormous croak come out of such a small mouth?

The croak, the emotion, the horror and uproar of the house, the confusion on stage – as well as the befuddled faces in the wings – all that I have described at length happened within seconds.

These few terrible seconds seemed to last for ever, particularly to the co-directors watching from Box Five on the grand tier. Moncharmin and Richard were both very pale. This unprecedented and inexplicable incident filled them with dread, with a sense of foreboding that was all the more potent since they had been, for a few moments now, in the immediate presence of the ghost. They had felt his breath. Moncharmin's hair stood on end. Richard wiped the perspiration from his forehead. Yes, the ghost was there . . . around them . . . behind them . . . beside them . . . They sensed his presence without seeing him! They heard him breathe – so close, so very close to them! *You know when someone is there!* They knew! They were sure that *there were three people in the box*. They trembled. They thought of fleeing, but dared not. They dared not move nor say anything that might tell the ghost that they knew he was there! And what now? What could possibly happen next?

Carlotta's croak! That is what happened! The directors' cry of horror was heard above the hullabaloo of the house. *They smarted under the Phantom's attack*. Leaning over the ledge of Box Five, they stared at Carlotta as if they no longer recognized her. That infernal creature must, with her croak, unleash doom. Ah, disaster would strike soon, they knew it! The ghost had warned them! The house had a curse upon it! The looming disaster already weighed heavily on these directorial chests. Richard's gasping voice was heard calling to Carlotta: 'Continue!'

But Carlotta did not continue. Instead, bravely, heroically, she returned to the beginning of the verse that had ended in the croak. The house now settled into a terrifying silence. The vast theatre was filled again by the lone voice of Carlotta:

'Like a spell does the evening bind me!'

(The spectators were spellbound too.)

'And a deep languid charm . . . croak!
I feel without alarm . . . croak!
With its . . . croak!'

The toad was still there.

The whole house erupted in pandemonium. Having slumped back into their chairs, all strength drained from their bodies, the two directors dared not even turn round. The ghost was chuckling behind their backs! And, finally, they distinctly heard, from their right, his voice, his impossible disembodied voice saying:

'*Her singing tonight is enough to bring down the chandelier.*'

They looked up as one to the ceiling and let out a terrible cry. The chandelier, the enormous mass of the chandelier, was moving, slipping downwards in response to that fiendish voice. Unhooked, it plummeted down from the very top of the house, crashing into the middle of the stalls, amidst a thousand screams. Terror struck, followed by a general stampede. My intention here is not to revive the memory of that momentous event, for the curious reader can easily consult the accounts that appeared in the press at the time. Suffice it to say that many people were wounded and one died.

The chandelier had crashed upon the head of a poor woman who had come to the Opera that evening for the very first time in her life, and killed her instantly.[20] She was the concierge whom Richard had chosen to replace Mme Giry, the Phantom's preferred attendant. The next day, one of the headlines read: '*Two hundred thousand kilos hit concierge!*' That was her sole obituary!

IX

The Mysterious Brougham

That tragic evening affected everyone. Carlotta fell ill. As for Christine Daaé, she vanished after the performance; two weeks later, she was still nowhere to be seen, neither at the Opera nor elsewhere. This first disappearance, which went largely unnoticed, is not to be confused with the famous abduction, which occurred some time later in the strangest and most dramatic circumstances.

Raoul was naturally the first to be baffled by the young diva's absence. He wrote to her, care of Mme Valerius, but received no reply. Initially, he was not overly surprised for he knew her state of mind and her resolve to break off with him, even though her reasons remained a mystery. These uncertainties added to his grief and he eventually became quite concerned when her name never appeared on any programme. Even *Faust* was performed without her. At about five o'clock one afternoon, he went into the directors' office to enquire about Christine and found Messrs Richard and Moncharmin both extremely anxious. Even their own friends did not recognize them: their cheerfulness and high spirits had gone. They were seen crossing the stage, heads down, brows knitted with worry and looking pale, as if they were being pursued by terrible thoughts or prey to some malicious fate.

With the fall of the chandelier, they had incurred many liabilities, which they were unwilling to discuss publicly. The inquest had delivered a verdict of accidental death, the result of wear and tear of the chandelier's fixing; nevertheless, both the former and the new directors ought to have been aware of the fault and remedied it before the catastrophe occurred.

It must be said that Firmin Richard and Armand Mon-charmin appeared so changed, so remote, so strange, so unfathomable at this time that many of the subscribers imagined that their spirits had been affected by some other event, more horrific still than the fall of the chandelier. In everyday matters they were exceedingly impatient, except when dealing with Mme Giry, who had been reinstated. The manner in which the Viscount was received when he came to enquire about Christine might be imagined. They merely told him that she was on leave. And when he asked how long that leave was expected to last, they replied curtly that it was for an unspecified period of time, as requested by Mlle Daaé for reasons of health.

'So is she ill?' he cried. 'What is wrong with her?'

'We have no idea!'

'Didn't you send for the house doctor?'

'No, she didn't ask for him and, as we trust her, we did not doubt her word.'

There was something odd about all this. Raoul's mind was besieged by gloomy thoughts as he left the Opera House. He resolved, come what may, to find out more by visiting the good Mme Valerius. He had not forgotten Christine's letter and her admonishment to make no attempt to see her; but his experiences at Perros, the voice he had heard through the door of her dressing-room and his conversation with Christine at the edge of the moor made him suspect some machination which, evil though it might be, was none the less human. The girl's excitable imagination, her loving and trusting soul, the countless stories she had learned as a child, her constant thoughts of her dead father and, most of all, the sublime ecstasy which overwhelmed her whenever music was played in particular circumstances – had he not witnessed it in the churchyard at Perros? – all this must constitute, Raoul thought, an ideal moral ground for the malevolent designs of some mysterious and unscrupulous agent.

Of whom was Christine Daaé the victim? Such was the reasonable, common-sense question that Raoul put to himself as he hurried off to see Mme Valerius. For the Viscount's judgement was remarkably sound. Of course he was a poet, he loved music at its most lofty, relished those old Breton tales about fairies dancing in the moonlight and, more than anything, was in love with Christine Daaé, his sweet little maiden from the North. All the same, he only believed in the supernatural with regard to religion, and even the most fantastical story could not convince him that two and two are five.

What would Mme Valerius tell him? He trembled as he rang the bell of her small apartment in the Rue Notre-Dame-des-Victoires. The door was opened by the maid whom he had seen coming out of Christine's dressing-room one evening. He asked if he could talk to Mme Valerius and was told that she was ill in bed and unable to receive any visitors.

'Just present my card, please,' he said.

He did not have to wait for long. The maid soon returned and showed him into a small, sparsely furnished drawing-room, in which portraits of Professor Valerius and old Daaé hung on opposite walls.

'Madame begs monsieur to excuse her,' said the maid. 'She can only see him in her bedroom because her poor legs are now too weak to support her.'

Five minutes later, Raoul was ushered into a dimly lit room where he recognized at once the kindly face of Christine's benefactress in the semi-darkness of an alcove. Mme Valerius's hair had turned completely white, but her eyes were as young as ever, even more so, in fact: never before had he seen them so clear, so pure, so childlike.

'M. de Chagny!' she cried merrily, holding out both her hands to her visitor. 'Ah, you are Heaven-sent! We can talk of *her*.'

This last sentence sounded quite ominous to him. 'Madame, where is Christine?' he hastened to ask.

'She is with her guardian spirit!' the old lady replied calmly.

'What guardian spirit?' exclaimed Raoul.

'Why, the *Angel of Music*!'

The Viscount dropped into a chair in dismay. Really? So Christine was with the *Angel of Music*! Meanwhile Mme Valerius lay in bed, smiling at him as she raised one finger to her lips to urge discretion: 'You must not tell anyone!'

'You can trust me!' said Raoul. He hardly knew what he was

saying, for his thoughts of Christine, already greatly confused, were becoming increasingly muddled and he felt giddy: everything began to swim around him, around the room and around that extraordinarily kind lady with her white hair and her limpid sky-blue eyes. 'You can trust me,' he repeated.

'I know! I know I can!' she laughed merrily. 'But come closer, as you used to do when you were a little boy. Give me your hand as you once did when you recounted the story of little Lotte, which Christine's father had just told you. Ah, M. Raoul, I am very fond of you. And so is Christine!'

'She is fond of me?' sighed the young man. He had difficulty gathering his thoughts. His mind lurched from Mme Valerius's *guardian spirit* to the *Angel of Music* of whom Christine had spoken so strangely; from the nightmarish skull head, which he had glimpsed on the steps of the altar at Perros, to the macabre description of the *ghost* which he had overheard, as he lingered backstage at the Opera one evening, from some machinists who had themselves heard it from Joseph Buquet shortly before his mysterious death by hanging.

'What makes you think that Christine is fond of me, madame?' he asked softly.

'She would speak of you every day.'

'Really? And what did she say?'

'She did mention that you had made a declaration of love!'

And the dear old lady burst into hearty laughter, revealing her well-preserved teeth. Raoul sprang from his chair, flushing and in agony.

'What's this?' she cried. 'Where are you going? Sit down, please! Do you think I will let you go like this? If you're angry with me for laughing, please forgive me. After all, what happened was not your fault. You didn't know. You are so young, and you thought that Christine was free.'

'What? Is Christine engaged to be married?' gasped the distressed young man.

'Why no! No! You know as well as I do that Christine could not marry, even if she wanted to!'

'But I know nothing of the sort! Why may Christine not marry?'

'Because of the *Spirit of Music*,[1] of course!'

'Him again!'

'Yes, he forbids her to.'

'He forbids her? The Spirit of Music forbids her to marry?' Raoul leaned over to Mme Valerius with his jaw fiercely thrust forward. Had he wished to tear her to pieces, he could not have looked more ferocious. Sometimes excessive naivety can appear so outrageous that it becomes insufferable; such was Raoul's response to Mme Valerius at this moment.

Failing to notice the terrible gaze fixed upon her, she continued innocently: 'Oh, he forbids her . . . without forbidding her. He just tells her that if she were to marry, she would never hear him again. That's all! And that he would go away for ever! So, you understand, she does not want to lose the *Spirit of Music*. It's only natural.'

'Yes, yes,' Raoul acquiesced in a whisper, 'it's only natural.'

'I thought Christine had told you all that when she met you at Perros. She had gone there with her guardian spirit.'

'Oh, she went to Perros with her "guardian spirit", did she?'

'Rather, he arranged to meet her there in the churchyard, by her father's grave. He promised to play *Lazarus* for her on Daaé's violin!'

Raoul de Chagny rose to his feet and asked authoritatively: 'Madame, kindly tell me where this spirit resides.'

The old lady showed no surprise at his indiscreet demand. She looked up and replied: 'In Heaven!'

Her candour disconcerted him. He was stunned by her simple and unfaltering faith in a spirit that would descend from Heaven every evening to frequent the performers' dressing-rooms of the Opera House. Now he understood Christine's state of mind – a girl brought up by a superstitious fiddler and a deluded old lady – and shuddered at the consequences of it.

'Is Christine still pure?' he could not help but ask.

'I swear to it, as God is my witness!' exclaimed Mme Valerius, suddenly incensed. 'And, if you doubt it, monsieur, I don't know why you came here at all!'

Raoul pulled at his gloves nervously. 'How long has she known this "spirit"?' he enquired.

'About three months. Yes, it has been a good three months since she had her first lesson with him.'

The Viscount threw up his arms in utter despair and let them drop with a moan. 'The spirit gives her lessons! Where?'

'Now that she has gone away with him, I can't say; but, up to a fortnight ago, it was in Christine's dressing-room at the Opera. It would not be possible here. My apartment is too small and the whole house would be disturbed. Whereas, at the Opera, at eight o'clock in the morning, there is no one about, you see!'

'Yes, I do see!' cried the Viscount. And he took leave of Mme Valerius with such haste that she asked herself privately if the young nobleman was not a little off his head.

On his way out, he found himself face to face with the maid in the drawing-room and was about to question her; but he fancied he glimpsed the hint of a smile on her lips. He thought that she was mocking him and so he fled. Had he not learned enough? And now that all his questions had been answered, what more could he ask? He made his way back to his brother's house on foot and in a wretched state.

He was so angry with himself that he wanted to smash his head against the wall! To think that he had believed in her innocence, in her purity! That he had tried for a moment to explain everything by her naivety, her simplicity of mind and her extreme candour. The Spirit of Music! He knew him now! He saw him! Surely he was some minor singer at the Opera, some good-looking Lothario, some coxcomb all smiles and sweet talk. He felt ridiculous and pitiable. Ah, what a wretched, insignificant and foolish young man you are, Viscount de Chagny! he raged to himself. As for Christine, what a brazen, devilishly cunning creature!

All the same, his brisk walk along the streets did him good, and somewhat cooled down his feverish mind. He went into his bedroom, intent on throwing himself on to his bed to smother his sobbing. But his brother was there, waiting for him, and Raoul fell into his arms like a child. The Count consoled him paternally without asking for an explanation; and Raoul would certainly have been reluctant to tell him the story of the *Spirit*

of Music. While there are things about which one does not
boast, there are others for which to be pitied would be all too
humiliating.

The Count took his younger brother out to dinner that evening. Raoul's despair was so profound that he would probably
have declined the invitation if the Count had not told him, by
way of enticement, that the lady of his thoughts had been seen
at the Bois[2] the previous evening, in the company of a man. The
Viscount would not believe him at first, but was given so full
and detailed a description that he was finally convinced. After
all, was it not a commonplace occurrence? She had been seen
in a brougham,[3] with the window down, leisurely taking in the
cool night air, and in the clear moonlight had been easily recognized. As for her companion, he was no more than a vague
shadow glimpsed in the dark. The carriage moved at a walking
pace along a lonely lane behind the grandstand of the race-
course at Longchamp.[4]

Raoul dressed in frantic haste, eager to fling himself into a
'giddy round of pleasures', as the phrase goes, so as to forget
his distress. Alas, he cut a sorry figure and, having left his
brother early, found himself, by ten o'clock that evening, in a
hansom cab behind the race-course at Longchamp. It was bitterly cold. The deserted lane was bathed in bright moonlight.
He told the driver to wait for him patiently at the corner of a
narrow lane nearby and, concealing himself from view as best
he could, began to stamp his feet to keep warm. He had been
engaged in this worthy exercise for less than half an hour when
a carriage, coming from the direction of Paris, turned the corner ahead and ambled towards him at a leisurely pace.

He thought at once: 'It's Christine!' And his heart began to
race. He could feel it pounding in his chest as it had done when
he heard the voice through the door of her dressing-room. Dear
God, how he loved her!

The carriage continued to move towards him. He stood still
and waited. Should it be Christine, he was determined to jump
out ahead of the carriage and stop the horses. He would confront the Angel of Music at any cost! In a few moments, the
carriage would be level with him. He was certain that it was

she. He could see a woman's head leaning out of the window.
Her hair shone palely in the moonlight.

'Christine!' The hallowed name of his beloved sprang from
his lips. He was unable to stifle it. He leaped out as if to take it
back; but that name hurled into the night had already acted as
though it were an agreed signal for the horses to break into a
headlong gallop. The carriage flew past him before he had time
to attempt anything. The window had been shut. The face of
the young woman had disappeared. And the brougham, which
he was now chasing, was already no more than a black dot on
the white moonlit drive.

He called out again: 'Christine!' But there was no reply and
he stopped, surrounded by silence. He stared despairingly at
the sky, at the stars above; he beat his burning breast with his
clenched fist: he loved and was not loved in return. With a
weary look in his eyes, he gazed along the cold, desolate road
and into the pale, dead night. His heart was cold, frozen solid:
he had loved an angel and now he despised a woman!

How that sweet little maiden from the North has trifled with
your affections, Raoul! Did she really need to look so fresh, so
shy and so ready to wrap herself in the blushing mantle of
modesty only later to pass through the lonely night in a luxurious brougham in the company of a mysterious lover? Surely
there ought to be some sacrosanct limit to duplicity and deceit!
And one should not be allowed to conceal the soul of a courtesan behind the innocent eyes of a child.

She had passed by without answering his call.

But why had he attempted to bar her way? Why had he suddenly appeared before her like a living reproach, when all she
had asked was to be forgotten: 'Go away! Disappear! You
mean nothing to me!'

In his plight he thought of dying. He was only twenty years
old! His manservant found him the next morning sitting up,
fully dressed, on his bed and looking so shattered that, at the
sight of him, the servant feared some tragedy. He had brought
some letters, which Raoul snatched up, having recognized one
of them by the paper and handwriting. Christine had written:

MY FRIEND, – Meet me at the Opera on the night after tomor-row for the masked ball. At twelve o'clock, be in the small salon beyond the fireplace of the crush-room. Stand near the door lead-ing to the Rotunda. Do not mention this assignation to anyone. Wear a white domino[5] and hide your face carefully. You must not be recognized, my life depends upon it.
  CHRISTINE

X

The Masked Ball

The mud-spattered envelope had no stamp. It bore the words
'To be handed to Viscount Raoul de Chagny', written in pencil
along with the address. It must have been cast into the street in
the hope that a passer-by would pick it up and deliver it, which
was what had happened; it had been found on the pavement of
the Place de l'Opéra. Raoul feverishly read the note again.

It was enough to rekindle his hopes. The sombre picture of
a Christine losing her self-respect, which had formed in his
imagination, gave way to that earlier image of an unfortunate,
innocent child, the victim of her own imprudence and excita-
bility. But how much of a victim was she at this hour? Whose
sway had she fallen under? Into what abyss had she been lured?
Such were the agonized questions he now asked himself; but
his present anguish seemed bearable when compared to the
frenzy that had overwhelmed him at the thought of a duplici-
tous and deceitful Christine. What had happened? What undue
influence had been exercised upon her? What sort of a monster
had carried her off, and by what means?

By what means indeed, but those of music? The more he
pondered over this, the more he convinced himself that the
truth lay there. Had he forgotten the tone of her voice when
she told him, at Perros, that she had been visited by a heavenly
spirit? Was there some clue to the dark, prevailing mystery in
Christine's recent past? Had he given too little consideration to
her sorrow at her father's death and her ensuing disaffection
with everything, including her art? At the Conservatoire, she
had been but a poor, soulless, singing automaton. And then
suddenly she had come to life as if through divine intervention.

Visited by the Angel of Music! She sang Marguerite in *Faust* and triumphed! The Angel of Music! Who could make her believe that he was indeed this fabulous spirit? Who could know of the legend of Little Lotte and make use of it in such a way that Christine was, in his hands, no more than a helpless instrument to be played at will?

'This situation is not altogether without precedent,' thought Raoul as he recollected the story of Princess Belmonte, whose despair at having lost her husband had turned into a state of stupor: for a month, the princess could neither speak nor show any feelings. Her mental and physical apathy worsened by the day; her powers of reason deteriorated, leading to a gradual weakening of all life in her. Every evening, she was carried into the famously beautiful gardens of her palace, but she appeared to be unaware of her surroundings. The renowned German singer Raff,[1] passing through Naples, expressed the wish to visit those celebrated gardens and was asked to sing, out of sight, near the grove where the Princess was resting. Raff consented and sang a simple air that the Princess's husband had sung to her in the early days of their marriage. It was an expressive, moving song. The melody, the words, the singer's splendid voice, all combined to stir the soul of the Princess and revive her. Her eyes welled with tears; she wept. She was thus saved and remained convinced that her husband had come down from Heaven that evening to sing to her that half-forgotten melody from their past. Yes, that evening! Raoul thought. That particular evening! It had happened just once. For that enchanting moment would not have withstood repetition. Had the perfect, doleful Princess returned to the grove every night for three months, she would have eventually discovered Raff, hiding nearby.

The Angel of Music had given lessons to Christine for three months. What a diligent teacher he had been! And now at night he took her to the Bois in his carriage! Slipping his clenched fingers across his chest to the spot where he could feel his jealous heart beating, Raoul tore at his flesh. Inexperienced as he was, he wondered with dread what role Christine intended for him in the forthcoming masquerade. And how much of a fool would an actress from the Opera make of a meek young man, quite new to love! Oh, how wretched he was!

Thus Raoul's opinion of her swung from one extreme to the other. No longer did he know whether to pity Christine or to curse her, and so he pitied and cursed her by turns. Nevertheless, he bought a white domino.

The time of his assignation came at last. Clad from head to foot in white like a romantic pierrot, his face completely covered by a mask trimmed with heavy lace, the Viscount felt quite ridiculous. Gentlemen did not attend the ball of the Opera in fancy dress, for it would surely raise a smile. He was consoled by the thought that he would never be recognized. And his costume and mask had the added advantage of allowing him to move in society and yet be alone, somewhat comfortable with the distress of his soul and the sadness of his heart. He would not have to feign, he would not need to compose himself for his face was masked.

This annual ball was quite a magnificent affair. It was given some time before Shrovetide to celebrate the birthday of a famous illustrator whose pencil had immortalized, in the style of Gavarni, the extravagant carnival parade down La Courtille.[2] As such, the ball was an altogether merrier, noisier and more Bohemian occasion than was usual for a masked ball. Many artists had arranged to meet there; they arrived with an entourage of models and pupils, who, by midnight, had become quite boisterous.

Raoul climbed the grand staircase at five minutes to midnight. He did not linger to admire the many-coloured costumes on display all the way up the marble steps of one of the most luxurious settings in the world; nor did he allow himself to be drawn into the facetious conversation of masked guests. He simply ignored all the jesting remarks, and shook off the attentions of several all too merry couples.

Crossing the big crush-room and escaping from the dancers' farandole that had encircled him awhile, he at last entered the salon mentioned by Christine in her letter. The small room was crammed with people either on their way to supper at the restaurant in the Rotunda or back from raising a glass of champagne.

In the midst of the gay and lively hubbub, Raoul thought that, for their mysterious assignation, Christine must have preferred this crowd to some lonely corner.

He leaned against a door-jamb and waited. He did not have to wait long: a black domino passed him and deftly touched his hand. He understood that it was Christine and followed her.

'Is that you, Christine?' he murmured, barely moving his lips.

The black domino promptly looked back and raised her finger to her lips, no doubt to caution him against uttering her name again. Raoul followed on in silence.

Having found her again in such strange circumstances, he was afraid of losing her. He no longer hated her. However bizarre and inexplicable her conduct might appear, he now believed her to be blameless. He was ready to show any amount of compassion, forgiveness and even submission. He was in love. And, surely, he would soon receive a straightforward explanation for her curious disappearance.

The black domino looked back from time to time to check that the white domino still followed.

As Raoul once more passed through the great crush-room, this time in the wake of his guide, he could not help noticing, among the throng, a crowd gathering . . . or rather among the groups engaged in the wildest revelries, a certain group pressing around a figure whose extraordinary costume, peculiar behaviour and macabre appearance was creating a sensation.

This figure was dressed entirely in scarlet. A huge hat adorned with a plume of feathers crowned his skull-like head and ah, what a splendid imitation of a skull it was! The art students applauded and congratulated him, enquiring which master craftsman, which workshop patronized by Pluto,[3] had designed, made and painted so perfect a head! The Grim Reaper[4] himself must have posed for it. A huge velvet cloak dragged on the floor like a trail of fire as the man in scarlet with the plumed hat and the skeletal head stalked. His cloak bore, embroidered in gold, the words: 'Stand aside! I am the Red Death.'[5]

Someone tried to touch him, but a skeletal hand shot out from one of the crimson sleeves and clutched his wrist; under the sharp, unyielding grip of Death the imprudent reveller uttered a cry of pain and horror. When the Red Death at last released him, he fled like a madman amid the jeers of the masqueraders.

It was at this moment that Raoul crossed the path of the macabre figure that had just turned towards him. He recognized that head: it was the skull of Perros-Guirec. Forgetting Christine, he wanted to rush at him; but the black domino, who also seemed strangely agitated, caught him by the arm and dragged him away from the crush-room and the demented crowd through which the Red Death passed.

Continually looking back, the black domino seemed, on two occasions, to glimpse something terrifying for she quickened her step, hurrying Raoul along as if they were being pursued.

They went up two floors. Here the stairs and corridors were almost deserted. The black domino opened the door of a private box and beckoned the white domino to follow. Closing the door immediately behind him, Christine (for it was she; there was no mistaking her voice) urged him softly to remain at the back of the box and keep out of sight. Raoul took off his mask. Christine kept hers on. And, as he was about to ask her to remove it, he was surprised to see her put her ear to the wall and eagerly listen for sounds from the other side.

Then she opened the door slightly and glanced into the corridor. 'He must be on the next floor up, in the "Box of the Blind",'[6] she whispered, suddenly adding: 'He's coming down again!'

She tried to close the door again, but Raoul prevented her; for he had seen, on the top step of the staircase leading to the floor above, *a red foot*, followed by another. Then slowly, majestically, the whole scarlet costume of the Red Death came into view. Once more, he saw the skull that he had glimpsed at Perros-Guirec.

'Him!' he exclaimed. 'This time, he shall not escape me!'

Raoul was about to rush out when Christine shut the door. He tried to push her aside.

'Him? Whom do you mean?' she asked, in a changed voice. 'Who shall not escape you?'

Raoul tried to force his way out, but Christine pushed him back with unexpected strength. He understood, or thought he understood, and at once lost his temper.

'Whom do I mean?' he seethed. 'Why, him, of course! The man who hides behind that hideous mask of death! The evil spirit of the churchyard at Perros! The Red Death! In a word, mademoiselle, your friend – *your Angel of Music*! But I shall tear off his mask, as I shall tear off my own; and, this time, we shall look each other in the face, he and I, with neither disguise nor pretence. And then I shall know whom you love and who loves you!'

He laughed like a man possessed, while Christine gave a disconsolate moan behind her velvet mask. With a tragic gesture, she flung out her arms, barring his way with her pale flesh.

'In the name of our love, Raoul, you shall not pass!'

He stopped. What had she said? In the name of their love? Never before had she said that she loved him. And there had been opportunities a-plenty. She had seen him unhappy, in tears, begging her for a word of hope that never came! She had seen him ill, brought to death's door after the terror and the bitter cold of that night in the churchyard at Perros. But had she remained by his side when he needed her most? No! She had fled! And now she was saying that she loved him! She spoke in the name of their love. Humbug! What a fraud! She was only trying to gain a few seconds so as to give the Red Death time to escape. Their love? She was lying!

And, filled with childish hatred, he declared: 'You are lying, mademoiselle, for you do not love me and you have never loved me! What a poor wretched soul I must be to let you play games with me and deceive me! During our first meeting at Perros, your whole demeanour, the joy in your eyes, even your silence gave me every reason to hope. Why did you give such hopes to an honest man who believed you were an honest woman, when your sole intention was to make a fool of me! Alas, you have deceived us all! You have even shamefully abused the candid trust of your benefactress, who still believes in your sincerity while you accompany this Red Death at the Opera ball! I despise you!'

And he wept. She let him insult her. Her only thought was to keep him from leaving the box.

'Some day, Raoul, you will beg my pardon for all those cruel words, and when you do I shall forgive you!'

He shook his head. 'No, no, you have driven me mad! To think that I had only one aim in life: to give my name to you, a mere actress.'

'Raoul! How can you?'

'I shall die of shame!'

'No, Raoul, you must live,' said Christine gravely, her voice tense. 'And adieu.'

'Adieu, Christine!'

'Adieu, Raoul!'

The young man stepped forward, unsteadily. He risked one more sardonic remark: 'Will you not allow me to come and applaud you from time to time?'

'I shall never sing again, Raoul!'

'Really?' he replied, still more sarcastically. 'So he is taking you off the stage? Congratulations are in order! Then we shall perhaps meet at the Bois one evening!'

'Neither at the Bois nor anywhere else, Raoul. You shall not see me again.'

'May I at least ask to what mysterious shadows you are returning? To what hell or what paradise?'

'I came to tell you that, but I cannot tell you anything now . . . You would not believe me! You have lost faith in me, Raoul. It is all over between us!'

She spoke with such despair in her voice that Raoul started. Feelings of remorse for his cruelty began to stir in his troubled soul. 'But look here!' he cried. 'Will you not tell me what all this means? You are free and unfettered. You go about town. You put on a domino to come to the ball. Why do you not go home to Mme Valerius? What have you been doing these past two weeks? What is this tale of the Angel of Music, which you told the old lady? Someone may have deceived you, taken advantage of your credulity. I saw it happen myself at Perros, but now you know the truth! You seem to have come to your senses, Christine. You know what you are doing. And Mme

Valerius is still waiting for you, and invoking your "guardian spirit"! Explain yourself, Christine, I beg of you! Anyone could have been mistaken, as I was. What is this farce?'

Christine simply took off her mask and said: 'It is a tragedy, Raoul!'

He now saw her face and could not suppress a cry of surprise and shock. Gone was her fresh, glowing complexion. No longer a reflection of her tranquil disposition and untroubled conscience, her face – so charming and gentle in former days – was deadly pale. How anguished she looked now! Her features were cruelly furrowed by sorrow and her beautiful, limpid eyes – Little Lotte's eyes – had become wells of deep, dark, unfathomable mystery and were bordered with terribly doleful shadows.

'Christine! Christine!' he moaned, holding out his arms. 'You promised to forgive me . . .'

'Perhaps! Some day, perhaps!' she said as she replaced her mask over her face. And then she left, motioning to him not to follow her with a peremptory gesture.

He made to rush after her; but she turned round and repeated her gesture with such sovereign authority that he dared not take another step. He watched her walk away. And then, with an aching heart and throbbing temples, he too went down, hardly knowing what he was doing. Mingling with the crowd, he enquired after the Red Death. 'Whom do you mean?' the revellers asked. 'A man with a skull for a head and a big red cloak,' he replied. They all said that they had seen the Red Death pass in his regal attire, but Raoul could not find him anywhere. And, at two o'clock in the morning, he returned to the corridor leading to Christine Daaé's dressing-room.

He had retraced his steps to where he had first known suffering. He knocked on the door. There was no answer. He entered, as he had done that evening when he was searching everywhere for *the voice*. The dressing-room was empty. One gas lamp was alight, burning low. There was some writing-paper on a little desk. He thought of writing to Christine, but he heard footsteps in the corridor. He just had time to hide in the closet, which was separated from the rest of the room by a mere curtain. The door to the dressing-room opened and Christine came in. He held his breath. He wanted to see! He wanted to know! Something told him that part of the mystery was about to be revealed and that he might perhaps begin to understand.

Christine entered, wearily took off her mask and tossed it on to the table. She sighed and let her beautiful head sink into her hands. What was she thinking? Did she think of Raoul? No, she did not, for he heard her murmur: 'Poor Erik!'

At first he thought he had misheard her for he was convinced that if anyone deserved compassion, it must be he, Raoul. After what had happened between the two of them, he would have expected nothing other than 'Poor Raoul' from her sighing lips. But, shaking her head, she repeated: 'Poor Erik!' What had this Erik to do with Christine and why did his sweet maiden from the North feel compassion for Erik when he, Raoul, was so unhappy?

Christine began to write deliberately, steadily and so calmly that Raoul, who was still shaken by their tragic parting, was both impressed and hurt. 'What a cool head!' he thought. She continued to write, filling two, three, four sheets. Suddenly, she raised her head and hid the sheets of paper in her bodice. She seemed to be listening. Raoul listened too. Whence came that strange sound, that distant rhythm? A faint singing seemed to issue from the walls. Yes, it was as if the walls themselves were singing! The sound became clearer; now he could make out the words. He heard a voice, a very beautiful, soft, enchanting voice; but, for all its softness, there was no mistaking that it was a man's voice. It was getting closer and closer. It came through the wall, entered and was *in the room*, before Christine herself.

She rose and spoke, as if she were addressing someone close by: 'Here I am, Erik. I am ready, but you are late, my friend.'

Raoul, peeping from behind the curtain, could not believe his eyes, for there was nothing to see. Christine's face lit up. A contented smile appeared upon her bloodless lips, the smile of a patient at the first glimpse of hope that her illness might not be fatal.

The disembodied voice resumed singing. Never in his life had Raoul heard a voice combining in one breath such extremes, a voice at once immensely, heroically sweet and triumphantly insidious, subtly powerful and powerfully subtle, in short a voice of irresistible potency. There was, in that singing, something definitive and masterful that must, in itself, inspire every mortal who appreciates, loves and makes music. It was a tranquil and pure fountain of harmony from which the faithful could safely and piously assuage their thirst, secure in the knowledge that they were partaking of musical grace. Having touched the Divine, their art was transfigured.

Listening feverishly to the voice, Raoul began to understand how one evening Christine Daaé, no doubt under the influence of her mysterious and invisible master, was able to perform with unearthly exaltation and a beauty hitherto unknown before the stunned audience of the Opera House. Indeed, as he listened to that extraordinary voice, Raoul understood Christine's phenomenal performance all the better: there was nothing unusual about the melody being sung, rather it was that the commonplace was made sublime. The commonplace words, the facile and almost vulgar melody appeared all the more transfigured by the breath that made them soar and fly up into the heavens on the wings of passion, as this angelic voice glorified earthly love. The voice was singing the Wedding Song from *Roméo et Juliette*.

Raoul saw Christine hold out her arms to the voice as she had held them out to the invisible violin playing *Lazarus* in the churchyard at Perros. And nothing could describe the passion with which it sang:

'Fate has united my heart for aye unto thine!'[7]

Raoul was transfixed. Struggling against the spell that seemed to deprive him of all will, of all energy and of almost all rational thought at the very time when he needed them most, he managed to draw back the curtain that hid him and walked towards Christine. She herself was moving towards the back wall of the room, which was entirely occupied by a large mirror. The glass reflected her image but not his, for he was just behind her and thus completely concealed by her.

'Fate has united my heart for aye unto thine!'

As Christine continued moving closer to the mirror, her image tilted forward towards her. The two Christines – the real one and her reflection – eventually touched and merged. Just as Raoul reached out to seize them both at once, some sort of dazzling miracle made him reel, and he was suddenly thrown backwards by an icy blast that swept over his face. He saw, not two, but four, eight, twenty Christines spin round him, swiftly and mockingly; and then flee so rapidly that he could not touch one of them. And then everything stood still again, and he saw only himself in the mirror. Christine had disappeared.

He rushed up to the mirror. He threw himself at the walls. Nobody! Yet the room still echoed with a distant passionate singing:

'Fate has united my heart for aye unto thine!'

His pressed his hands to his feverish brow, felt his tingling flesh, sought out the lamp in the semi-darkness and turned it back up. He knew that he was not dreaming. He was at the centre of a formidable contest, both physical and mental, whose rules were unknown to him and which might crush him. He felt vaguely like an impetuous fairy-tale prince who, having crossed some forbidden boundary, must be prepared to face the magical powers that he had injudiciously braved and unleashed for the sake of love.

Which way? Which way had Christine gone? Which way would she return? Would she return at all? Alas, had she not told him that it was all over between them? And did the wall not repeat the words: *Fate has united my heart for aye unto thine*? My heart? Whose heart?

Then, exhausted, defeated and barely conscious, he sat in the chair that Christine had occupied but a moment ago. Like her, he let his head sink into his hands. When he raised it, abundant tears were flowing down his youthful cheeks, tears as real and heavy as those of a jealous child, tears born out of a suffering which was in no way imaginary but the common lot of all the lovers in the world, tears that made him ask aloud: 'Who is Erik?'

XI

Forget the Voice and the Name

The day after Christine had vanished before his eyes by some kind of dazzling magic that still made him doubt the evidence of his senses, Viscount Raoul de Chagny called on Mme Valerius in search of information. He came upon an enchanting tableau: the old lady sat up in bed knitting with Christine by her side doing needlepoint. Never had a maiden's face looked more charming, her brow more pure, her gaze more gentle as she pored over her chaste occupation. The colour had returned to the young woman's cheeks. The bluish shadows under her clear eyes had disappeared. Raoul no longer recognized the tragic face of the previous day. Were it not for the melancholy that veiled those adorable features and appeared to him as the last vestiges of the extraordinary drama in which Christine was floundering, he might have believed that she was not its mysterious heroine at all.

As he approached, she rose without showing any emotion and offered him her hand. Raoul's stupefaction was so great that he stood there, stunned, unable to move nor speak.

'Well, M. de Chagny,' exclaimed Mme Valerius, 'don't you know our Christine any more? Her guardian spirit has sent her back to us!'

'Mother!' Christine curtly interrupted, flushing. 'Mother, I thought we agreed that he would never be mentioned again! You know very well that there is no Angel of Music!'

'But, child, he gave you lessons for three months!'

'Mother, I have promised you that I would soon explain everything. I hope to do so, but in turn you have promised me to keep silent and not question me again until that day.'

'I wish you would promise never to leave me again! But have you made me such a promise, Christine?'

'Mother, all this is of no interest to M. de Chagny.'

'On the contrary, mademoiselle!' interposed the young man in a voice that he hoped was self-assured, but still trembled. 'Everything that concerns you interests me greatly, as you will perhaps one day come to appreciate. I am both surprised and happy to find you with your adopted mother. After what happened between us yesterday – after what you said and what I was able to guess – I did not expect to see you here so soon. I should be the first to delight in your return, if you did not persist in keeping a secret that might prove fatal to you. As your long-standing friend, I cannot but be alarmed, as is Mme Valerius, at a most disturbing set of events that might harm you, should they remain shrouded in mystery, and could eventually be your undoing.'

At these words, Mme Valerius grew agitated in her bed. 'What does this mean?' she cried. 'Is Christine in danger?'

'Yes, madame,' Raoul bravely replied despite Christine's gestures to him.

'Oh my God!' gasped the sweet, guileless old lady. 'You must tell me everything, Christine! Why did you try to reassure me? And what is this danger, M. de Chagny?'

'An impostor is taking advantage of her trusting nature.'

'So the Angel of Music is an impostor?'

'She told you herself that there is no Angel of Music.'

'But then what is happening, in Heaven's name?' pleaded the invalid. 'This will be the death of me!'

'We are – you, Christine and I – caught up in the midst of an earthly mystery that is more fearsome than any number of ghosts or spirits!'

With a look of terror in her eyes, Mme Valerius turned to Christine, who had already rushed to her adopted mother and was holding her in her arms.

'Don't believe him, mother dear, don't believe him,' she repeated, as she gently comforted the old lady who was sighing pitifully.

'Then tell me that you'll never leave me again,' implored the widow.

Christine was silent and Raoul resumed: 'This is what you must promise, Christine. Only this will reassure your mother and me. We will undertake never to question you about the past if you, in turn, promise to remain henceforth under our protection.'

'That is an undertaking which I have not demanded of you and a promise which I refuse to make!' declared the young woman haughtily. 'I am mistress of my own actions, M. de Chagny: you have no say over them, and I expect you not to interfere. As to what I have done during the last fortnight, there is only one man in the world who would be entitled to demand the truth: my husband! But I have no husband and intend never to marry!'

She threw out her hands to emphasize her words and Raoul turned pale, not only because of what he had heard, but because he noticed that Christine was wearing a plain gold ring.

'You have no husband and yet you wear a wedding-ring.' He tried to seize her hand, but she swiftly drew it back.

'That's a present!' she said, blushing once more and vainly trying to hide her embarrassment.

'Christine! As you have no husband, that ring can only be a gift from someone who hopes to make you his wife. Why deceive us further? Why torture me still more? That ring represents a pledge; and a pledge you have accepted.'

'That's just what I said to her!' cried the old lady.

'And what did she reply, madame?'

'That's my business!' said Christine, driven to exasperation. 'Don't you think, monsieur, that this cross-examination has lasted long enough? As far as I am concerned . . .'

Raoul, deeply affected, was afraid to let her end the conversation and dismiss him outright. 'Please forgive me for speaking as I did, mademoiselle,' he interrupted. 'You are well aware of the worthy sentiments that lead me to meddle in matters which you, no doubt, think have nothing to do with me. But allow me to tell you what I have seen – and I have seen more than you suspect, Christine – or rather what I thought I saw. For, in truth, I have sometimes been inclined to doubt the evidence of my own eyes.'

'Well, what did you see, monsieur? Or think you saw?'

'I saw your rapturous response to *the sound of his voice*, Christine – the voice that came through the wall, or from a room or an apartment adjoining yours. Yes, I saw *your rapture*! And that's why I am fearful for you. You are under a most dangerous spell. And it seems that you are aware of the deceit since you said just now that *there is no Angel of Music*. If that is so, Christine, why did you follow him again? Why did you stand up, with radiant features, as if you were really hearing angels? Ah, it is a very dangerous voice, Christine; I myself, when I heard it, was so much enthralled by it that you vanished before my eyes without my seeing how it happened! Christine, Christine, in Heaven's name, in the name of your father who is in Heaven now and who loved you so dearly and who loved me too, Christine, tell us, tell your benefactress and me to whom that voice belongs. And then we'll save you in spite of yourself. Come, Christine, the name of the man! The name of the man who had the audacity to put a gold ring on your finger!'

'M. de Chagny,' the young woman replied frostily, 'you shall never know!'

Whereupon, seeing the hostility with which her ward had addressed the Viscount, Mme Valerius suddenly sided with Christine and said sharply: 'If she does love that man, monsieur, it is no business of yours!'

'Alas, madame,' Raoul respectfully replied, unable to hold back his tears, 'alas, I do believe that Christine loves him! Everything she does confirms it. But that is not the only reason for my despair. I am distressed at the thought that the man whom Christine loves may perhaps not be worthy of her love.'

'Let me be the judge of that!' said Christine, staring at Raoul with a look of sovereign irritation.

'When a man,' resumed Raoul, who felt his strength draining away from him, 'adopts such a romantic stratagem to seduce a girl . . .'

'Either he is a villain, or she is a fool?' she interrupted.

'Christine!'

'Raoul, why do you condemn a man whom you have never met, whom no one knows and about whom even you yourself know nothing?'

'I at least know the name that you intended to keep from me for ever. The name of your Angel of Music, mademoiselle, is Erik!'

Christine at once betrayed herself. She turned as white as a sheet and stammered: 'Who told you?'

'You yourself!'

'How?'

'By pitying him the other night – the night of the masked ball. When you went to your dressing-room, did you not say: "*Poor Erik*"? Well, Christine, a poor Raoul overheard you.'

'This is the second time that you have listened behind my door, M. de Chagny!'

'I was not behind the door! I was in your room, in your dressing-closet, mademoiselle.'

'Oh, unfortunate man!' she moaned, showing every sign of unspeakable woe. 'You are dicing with death!'

'Perhaps.'

Raoul uttered this 'perhaps' with so much love and despair in his voice that Christine could not hold back a sob. She took his hands and looked at him with all the genuine tenderness of which she was capable, and under her gaze he felt all his grief appeased.

'Raoul,' she said, 'forget the *Voice* and do not even remember his name. You must never try to fathom the mystery of *the Voice*.'

'Is the mystery so very terrible?'

'There is none more awful on this earth.'

Silence fell between them. Raoul was distraught.

'Swear to me that you will make no attempt to find out,' she insisted. 'Swear to me that you will never come to my dressing-room again, unless I send for you.'

'Then you must promise in turn to send for me sometimes, Christine.'

'I promise.'

'When?'

'Tomorrow.'

'Then I swear to do as you ask.'

Those were their last words that day.

He kissed her hands and went away, cursing Erik while telling himself to be patient.

XII

Above the Traps

The next day he saw her at the Opera. She was still wearing the gold ring. She was gentle and kind. She talked with him about his plans for the future and his career. He told her that the departure of the Polar expedition had been brought forward and that he would be leaving France three weeks hence, or a month at the most. She suggested almost gaily that he should look forward to the forthcoming voyage with joy, as a step towards a glorious future. And when he replied that glory without love held no attraction for him, she fondly rebuked him as one would a child whose sorrows would not last.

'How can you speak so lightly of such serious matters, Christine?' he asked. 'We may never see each other again! I may not survive.'

'Nor I,' she said simply. She spoke without smiling, no longer in jest. A new idea seemed to have occurred to her and her eyes brightened at the thought.

'But what are you thinking, Christine?'

'I think that we shall not see each other again . . .'

'Is that what makes you so radiant?' he interrupted.

'. . . and that, in a month's time, we shall have to part for ever!'

'Unless, Christine, we pledge ourselves to one another now and for ever.'

'Hush, Raoul!' she said, placing her fingers over his lips. 'That is out of the question! We can never be married, we both know that!'

Suddenly she seemed barely able to contain her happiness.

She clapped her hands with childish glee. Raoul stared at her, worried and uncomprehending.

'But . . .' she continued, holding out her two hands to Raoul, or rather suddenly offering them to him as one might a gift. 'But if we cannot be married, we can become engaged! No one but us will know. There have been plenty of secret marriages! Why not a secret betrothal? Let us become engaged, Raoul, for a month! In a month's time, you will sail away and the memory of that month will keep me happy for the rest of my days!' She was overjoyed by this prospect. Then she became serious again and added: 'This happiness *will hurt no one.*'

Raoul understood. He jumped at the suggestion and immediately wanted to act upon it. He bowed to Christine with the utmost humility and said: 'Mademoiselle, might I have the honour of asking for your hand?'

'Why, both my hands are already in yours, my dear fiancé! Oh, Raoul, we shall be so happy, playing at husband-and-wife-to-be!'

How rash of her, thought Raoul. This month will give me time to solve the mystery of the man's voice and make her forget the whole affair. By the end of this month Christine will consent to be my wife. In the meantime, let us pretend.

It was a most beautiful game and they enjoyed it with pure hearts, like children. What wonderful things they said to each other! What eternal vows they exchanged! The idea that at the close of the month they might not be here to honour those vows stirred in them feelings which they relished with excruciating delight. They played the game of love as one might play ball, only it was their two hearts that were being tossed to and fro, and they had to be particularly adroit catchers not to hurt each other's feelings. One day when Raoul felt deeply hurt – they had been playing for a week – he brought the game to a halt.

'I shall not go to the North Pole!' he said wildly.

Christine, in her innocence, had not foreseen such a possibility; the danger of the game suddenly became apparent and she reproached herself bitterly. She did not reply and instead went straight home.

This happened on an afternoon in her dressing-room, where they met every day and dined on three biscuits and two glasses of port, playfully laid out on the table with a posy of violets. She did not sing that evening. Nor did he receive his usual letter, though they had agreed to write to each other every day that month. Next morning, he hurried to Mme Valerius, who told him that Christine had gone away. She had left at five o'clock the day before, saying that she would return two days hence.

Raoul was distraught. He resented Mme Valerius for imparting the news with such surprising calm. He tried to draw out more information from her, but the old lady obviously knew nothing. All she could say in reply to his anxious questioning was: 'That's Christine's secret.' And, as she touchingly uttered the words, she raised one finger to urge discretion, while simultaneously seeking to reassure him.

'Wonderful!' seethed Raoul, as he rushed down the stairs on his way out. 'Clearly, girls are perfectly safe with guardians like Mme Valerius!'

Where could Christine be? Two days . . . Two whole days stolen from their all too brief spell of happiness! And he had only himself to blame! Had they not agreed that he would leave? And if he had every intention of staying, he should not have mentioned it so soon! He chided himself for being so maladroit and was the unhappiest of men for forty-eight hours. Then Christine reappeared.

She made a triumphant return. She repeated the staggering success of her gala performance. Since the misadventure of the 'croak', Carlotta had not sung on the stage. Her heart was filled with terror at the thought that it might happen again and she had lost her nerve. She loathed the place that had witnessed her inexplicable downfall and found a way to cancel her contract. Daaé was invited temporarily to fill the vacancy, and she sang *La Juive* to rapturous applause.

The Viscount was of course present. He was the only one in the house who was distressed by this fresh, resounding triumph, having noticed that Christine still wore her gold ring. A nagging voice whispered in the young man's ear: 'She is wearing the ring again tonight – the ring you did not give her. She gave her soul again tonight – but not to you.' 'If she will not tell you what she has been doing for the past two days,' it persisted, 'if she will not reveal her whereabouts, you should ask Erik!'

Raoul hurried backstage and waited for her. She saw him, for her eyes were searching him out.

'Quick! Quick! Follow me!' she said. And she hastily led him to her dressing-room, ignoring the throng of admirers drawn to her door by her new-found fame, who were left muttering: 'What disgraceful behaviour!'

Raoul immediately threw himself at her feet. He swore to her that he would join the expedition as planned and begged her never again to deny him a single hour of that perfect happiness which she had promised him. She wept and they held each other like two despairing siblings who have suffered a common loss and meet to mourn the dead.

Suddenly she drew away from the young man's soft and timid embrace: she seemed to hear something and swiftly motioned him to the door. When he reached the threshold, she said, so softly that the Viscount guessed rather than heard her words: 'Till tomorrow, my dear fiancé! Be happy, Raoul, for tonight I sang for you!'

He returned to her dressing-room the next day. Alas, those two days apart had broken the charm of their delightful make-believe. They looked at each other in silence and with sadness in their eyes. Raoul refrained from crying out: 'I am so jealous, so terribly jealous!' But she heard him all the same: 'Let us go for a walk, my love,' she suggested. 'The air will do us good.'

Raoul thought that she was proposing a stroll in the country far from the building that he now loathed; to him, it was a prison whose jailer he could feel stalking within – a jailer called Erik. But Christine led him to the stage and invited him to sit on the wooden lip of a fountain, in the unlikely coolness and peace of the first set for the next performance.

On another occasion, she took him by the hand to a deserted garden where they wandered together amid vines whose leaves were cut-outs made by some skilful decorator. It was as if real skies, real flowers, real earth were forbidden her for all time, as if she were doomed to breathe no other air than that of this theatre. Raoul dared not question her: aware that she could provide no answer, he was reluctant to cause her unnecessary suffering. Now and again, a fireman would pass on his rounds, watching over their melancholy idyll from afar. Sometimes she bravely sought to deceive herself and to deceive him with the illusory beauty of this fake world. Her ever-lively imagination painted it in the most striking colours – colours, she said, unlike any that nature could provide. As her excitement grew, Raoul steadfastly held her feverish hand.

'Look, Raoul!' she said. 'These walls, these woods, these bowers, these pictures painted on to the backcloth have witnessed the most sublime idylls, love stories invented by poets who soared ethereal above the common man. Tell me, Raoul, is this not a fitting place for our love, since it too was born out of fancy and is, alas, no more than an illusion?'

Disconsolate, he was unable to reply.

'Love is just too sad, down here,' she would also say. 'Let's take to the skies! See how easily it can be accomplished!'

And she would lead him up above the clouds, to the splendid chaos of the upper flies, where she loved to make him giddy by scampering ahead of him along the flying bridges among a thousand ropes fastened to pulleys, windlasses and drums, amidst a veritable aerial forest of masts and spars. When he hesitated, she said with an adorable pout: 'And you, a sailor!' And then they returned to *terra firma*. A solid and steady passageway led them to the laughter and dancing of the ballet-girls, and admonishing cries of: 'Limber up, girls! Watch those pointes!'[1] These young dancers were between the ages of six and nine or ten; but they already wore décolleté bodices, tutus, white drawers and pink stockings. And they worked and worked their feet to blisters in the hope of joining the quadrilles and becoming coryphées, soloists or even ballerinas decked with diamonds. For the moment, Christine rewarded them with sweets.

Once she took Raoul into an immense room filled with tawdry finery, knights' armour, lances, shields and plumes; and subjected the still and dusty ghosts of past warriors to a thorough inspection. She talked to them kindly and promised them fresh glittering evenings when they would parade in front of the footlights to the sound of brass, cymbals and thunderous applause.

Thus she showed him the whole of her fake but vast empire. It spread from the ground floor to the rooftops, over seventeen storeys peopled by innumerable subjects. She moved among them like a much-loved queen, encouraging them in their labours, sitting down in the store-rooms or giving words of advice to the costumiers whose hands hesitated to cut into the rich fabrics destined to clothe heroes. Hers was a country where every trade was practised. Cobblers, goldsmiths ... all had learned to know and love her, for she took an interest in their troubles as well as their trifles. She knew of old couples who lived tucked away in forgotten corners. She knocked at their doors and introduced Raoul to them as a Prince Charming who had asked for her hand; and the two of them, seated on some worm-eaten stage property, would listen to tales about the Opera as they had listened long ago, in their childhood, to old Breton legends. Forgotten by successive administrations and untouched by palace *coups*, these people had lived in the Opera House for countless years and had no recollection of the world outside. The history of France had moved on unbeknown to them and nobody out there now remembered them.

Thus the few precious days flew by. By feigning excessive interest in other matters, Raoul and Christine did their self-conscious best to hide from each other the sole concern of their hearts. Nevertheless Christine, who until then had shown herself the stronger of the two, suddenly grew anxious beyond words. In the course of their wanderings, she started running for no reason; or else she would stop abruptly and her hand, suddenly turning cold, would pull the young man back. Sometimes her eyes seemed to glimpse imaginary shadows. She cried: 'This way', and then 'This way', and then again 'This way', with a breathless laugh that often led to tears. It was during those moments that Raoul wanted most to speak, to question her in spite of his promises. But she forestalled his questions with a feverish: 'Nothing! I swear it is nothing.'

Once, as they were passing by an open trap on the stage,

Raoul leaned over the dark void and said: 'You have shown me the upper reaches of your domain, Christine, but I have heard some strange stories about the lower regions. Shall we go down?' At these words, she seized him in her arms, as if she feared that he might vanish into the blackness beneath and, in a trembling voice, murmured: 'Never! I forbid you ever to go down there! Besides, none of this is mine. *Everything below belongs to him!*'

Raoul gazed into her eyes questioningly. 'So *he* lives down there, does he?' he said sharply.

'I never said that! Who told you such a thing? Come away! At times I doubt your sanity, Raoul. You're too quick to misinterpret my words! Come! Come this way!'

And she literally dragged him away, for he stubbornly wanted to stay there by the trap that so fascinated him.

Then, all of a sudden, the trap was shut. It happened so quickly that they never even saw the hand that did it, and they stood there bewildered.

'Perhaps *he* was there,' Raoul said at last.

She shrugged her shoulders, but did not seem at all reassured. 'No, no, the "trap-shutters" did it. They have to keep busy. They open and shut the traps for no particular reason. It is like the "door-shutters": they need to pass the time as best they can.'

'But suppose it were *he*, Christine?'

'No, no! *He* has shut himself away, *he* is working.'

'Oh, really! *He* is working, is *he*?'

'Yes, *he* is. And *he* cannot both work and open and shut traps. We are quite safe,' she replied. Yet as she spoke she shivered.

'What is *he* working at?'

'Oh, something fearsome! So we are quite safe. When *he* is working like this, he sees nothing; *he* neither eats, drinks nor stops for days and nights on end. *He* is dead to the world and has no time to play with traps.'

She shivered again and leaned towards the closed trap, listening. Raoul said nothing, for he was afraid that the sound of his voice might interrupt the all too tenuous stream of her revelations.

She had not let go of him. She was still holding him in her arms. 'Suppose it were *he*!' she now moaned.

'Are you afraid of *him*?' Raoul enquired, timidly.

'No, no! Of course not!' she replied.

Without thinking, Raoul responded protectively as one might with an impressionable friend who has just awoken from a bad dream. 'I am here, you know!' he seemed to say. Whereupon Christine stared at him in surprise as if he were a marvel of courage and virtue, and she were taking, in her mind, the true measure of his bold, yet futile bravery. And then she kissed poor Raoul as a sister might to reward, with a show of tenderness, a sibling who clenches his small fist at the potential dangers awaiting her.

Raoul, blushing, understood. He felt just as weak as Christine. 'She claims not to be afraid,' he thought, 'but she trembles and wants to keep us away from the traps.' And that was the truth of the matter. The following day and thereafter, they took their strange, chaste love to the upper storeys of the building, well away from the traps. As time passed, her agitation increased. At last, one afternoon, she arrived very late, with her face so pale and her eyes so red that Raoul felt compelled to resort to extreme measures, telling her that *he would not sail for the North Pole unless she revealed the secret of the Voice.*

'Hush, Raoul! In Heaven's name, hush! Suppose *he* heard you!' And Christine looked wildly about her.

'I will break *his* power over you, Christine. I swear! And you will think of *him* no more!'

'Is that possible?' For a moment she allowed herself to hope that it might be so, while at the same time taking the young man to the top of the theatre, far, far away from the traps.

'I shall hide you in some unknown corner of the world, where *he* can never find you. You will be safe and I shall be able to go away, secure in the knowledge that you will never marry another.'

Christine clasped Raoul's hands, gripping them with intense fervour. But soon her anxiety returned. 'Higher! Higher still!' was all she said as she led him onward.

He could hardly keep up with her. They were soon under the

eaves, in a maze of timber-work. They slipped through the buttresses, the rafters, the braces, the joists and the partitions; they ran from beam to beam as if from tree to tree in a fantastic forest.

And, though she was careful to look back at every moment, she failed to see a shadow who followed her like her own shadow, who stopped when she stopped, who started again when she did, and who made no more noise than would a shadow. As for Raoul, he saw nothing; for, when Christine was with him, he had no interest in what might be happening behind.

XIII

Apollo's Lyre

Thus they reached the roof.

Light and easy, Christine glided over it like a swallow. Their eyes surveyed the open view between the three domes and the triangular pediment. Christine took a long, deep breath as she stood high above the city and gazed down at the busy valleys beneath her. She looked at Raoul confidently. She called him to her side, and together they took a walk along streets made of zinc and avenues cast in iron; they watched their twin reflections in the still water of the huge tanks[1] into which, in the summer months, a score of little boys from the ballet school jumped and learned to swim. The shadow that had followed them still clung to their heels, lying low on the roof, reaching with its black wings over the metal crossroads, stealing by the tanks, skirting silently round the domes; but the trusting young lovers suspected nothing when at last they sat down under the mighty protection of Apollo thrusting his monumental lyre against the crimson sky with bronze grandeur.[2]

It was a beautiful sunset ablaze with the colours of spring. Clouds, lightly clad in gold and purple by the setting sun, drifted slowly by.

'Soon we shall flee far from here, further and faster than the clouds. And then you can leave me,' Christine said to Raoul. 'But, should I refuse to go with you when the time comes, take me away by force if need be.'

The young man was struck by her vehemence, which she seemed to direct towards herself, as she nervously drew closer to him. 'Are you afraid that you might change your mind, Christine?'

'I cannot say,' she said, strangely shaking her head. 'He is a demon!' She shivered and sought refuge in Raoul's arms. 'I am afraid now of going back to stay with him down there, below the ground!' she moaned.

'What makes you go back to him, Christine?'

'If I do not go back, terrible things might happen! But I cannot do it any more! I cannot! I know we ought to take pity on those who live "below the ground"; but there is something horrific about *him*. All the same, time is running out: I have only one day left. If I do not go to him, he will come for me with his voice. He will take me away with him into the depths of the earth and he will go down on his knees to tell me that he loves me! And he will weep! Oh, those tears, Raoul, those tears brimming out from the two black holes in his skull! I cannot bear to see those tears again!'

She wrung her hands in anguish while Raoul, sharing her despair, held her to his breast.

'No, no, you must never again hear him say that he loves you! You shall not see his tears! Let us flee, Christine, at once!' And he tried to take her away, there and then.

But she stopped him. 'No, no,' she cried, shaking her head balefully. 'Not now! It would be too cruel! Let him hear me sing again tomorrow evening, for the last time. Then we will go away. At midnight tomorrow, meet me in my dressing-room – at midnight exactly. At that time, he will be waiting for me in the dining-room of his retreat by the lake. We shall be free and you will take me away – even if I refuse. Promise, Raoul! For I feel that if I go to him again, I might never return.' She added: 'You cannot understand!' And as she sighed she thought she heard, behind her, another sigh. 'Did you hear that?' Her teeth were chattering.

'No,' said Raoul, 'I heard nothing.'

'It is awful to be always trembling like this!' she confided. 'And yet we are safe up here. This is where you and I belong: outside, in the open air, in the light. Above, the sun is blazing; and creatures of the night shun the sunlight. I have never seen *him* by daylight. It must be a terrible sight!' she faltered, her eyes wild. 'Oh, the first time I saw *him*! I thought that *he* would die.'

'Why?' asked Raoul, truly disturbed at the turn their strange conversation had taken and this astounding revelation. 'Why did you think he would die?'

'BECAUSE I HAD SEEN HIM!!!'

....

This time, both Raoul and Christine turned round.

'Someone is in pain, injured perhaps,' said Raoul. 'Did you hear that?'

'I cannot say. Even when he is not here, my ears are full of his sighs. But if you heard something . . .'

They stood up and looked around them. They were quite alone on the vast lead roof.

'Tell me how you came to see him,' Raoul asked as they sat down again.

'I heard him for three months without seeing him. The first time I heard him, I thought, as you did, that the delightful voice suddenly singing *beside* me came from a nearby room. I went out and looked everywhere; but, as you know, Raoul, my dressing-room is quite separate. I could not hear the voice outside my door, whereas inside the singing continued. And not only did the voice sing, it also spoke to me: it answered my questions, like the voice of a real man, with this difference: it was as beautiful as an angel's voice. How could I explain so unbelievable a phenomenon? I still remembered that my father had promised to send me the Angel of Music from Heaven when he died. If I dare mention such childishness to you, Raoul, it is because you knew my father as a little boy and he was fond of you; since you believed in the "Angel of Music" as much as I did at that time, I am quite certain that you will neither smile nor mock me. I retained the loving and trusting soul of Little Lotte and living with Mme Valerius could never alter that. And it was that naive soul that I trustingly presented to the Voice in the belief that I was offering it to the Angel. Here my adopted mother, to whom I told everything, is not altogether blameless, for she was the first to say: "It must be the Angel. But, if you are in doubt, you could always ask."

'When I did, the Voice replied that he was indeed the Angel

whose visit I was expecting as promised by my dying father. From that time onwards we became close and I trusted him absolutely. He explained that he had come down to earth to enable me to discover the supreme joys of eternal art, and asked me to allow him to give me singing lessons every day. I agreed only too readily and never missed a lesson. The Voice would come to my dressing-room early in the day when that part of the Opera House was quite deserted. What can I tell you about those lessons? Even though you have heard him, you simply cannot imagine.'

'No, of course not. How could I?' said Raoul. 'But tell me. What did you do for accompaniment?'

'The music came from behind the wall – an instrument I did not recognize, which was beautifully in tune. The Voice seemed to know precisely where my father's teaching had stopped and the simple methods he had used. What I had learned in the past came back to me – or to my voice, rather – and I could build on my father's lessons as well as gain from my new tutor. Thus I made wonderful progress, such as would have taken years under different circumstances. As you know, Raoul, I am rather delicate and initially my voice had little character: my lower register was naturally quite weak, my upper register rather too bright and my middle range lacked clarity. Those were the limitations which my father combated, with some success for a while, and which the Voice overcame once and for all. Little by little, my own voice became stronger than my past achievements had led me to expect, and my breathing more ample; but above all, I learned how to develop the soprano chest voice. And all this came enveloped in the sacred fire of inspiration as the Voice awoke in me an all-consuming and sublime fervour. He had the ability, when I heard him, to make me rise to his level. He made it possible for me to share his superb flight of song. His spirit entered me and breathed harmony into my throat. Within a few weeks, I could not recognize myself when I sang. It was even frightening. I was afraid for a moment that I might be under some kind of spell; but Mme Valerius reassured me. She said that I was much too innocent a girl to fall prey to the Devil. The Voice insisted that my rapid progress remain a secret known only to him, Mme Valerius and myself. Oddly enough, outside my dressing-room I sang as before and no one was any the wiser. I did what the Voice asked. He said: "Wait and see: we shall astonish Paris!" And I waited. I lived in a kind of ecstatic dream where he ruled. And then I saw you for the first time one evening, in the house. It made me so happy that I never thought of concealing how I felt when I returned to my dressing-room. Unfortunately, the Voice was already there and soon gathered from my expression that something had happened. He questioned me and I saw no reason not to tell him about us and the place that you held in my heart. Then he was silent. I called out to him, but there was no reply; I pleaded, but in vain. I was terrified lest he had gone away for good. Now, Raoul, I wish to God he had! Going home that night, I was desperate. I threw myself into Mme Valerius's arms and said: "The Voice has gone! He might never come back!" She shared my fears and asked me to explain. I told her everything and she said: "Why, of course, the Voice is jealous!" And at that moment, Raoul, I realized that I loved you.'

Christine stopped. She laid her head against Raoul's chest and they sat there for a moment in silence, embracing each other. They were so overcome by their feelings that neither saw nor sensed the stealthy approach, low down over the roof, of great black wings, which drew near, so near that by closing upon the young lovers, they could have smothered them.

'The next day,' resumed Christine, with a deep sigh, 'I returned to my dressing-room in pensive mood. The Voice was already there. Oh, Raoul! He spoke to me with great sadness and told me plainly that if I were to give my heart away on this earth, he would simply return to Heaven. There was so much *human* sorrow in the Voice as he spoke that I should hence-forth have grown suspicious and realized that I was somehow the victim of my own delusions. I associated that voice so closely with the memory of my father that I still kept faith with it. I feared, above all, that I might never hear it again. I thought about my love for you and realized all the useless danger of it: I did not know if you still remembered me; and at all events your position in society prohibited all thought of marriage. So

I swore to the Voice that you were, and would forever be, no more than a brother to me and that my heart was empty of all earthly love. And that was why, Raoul, I looked away when you sought my attention on stage or in the hallways, and why I pretended to neither recognize nor see you! Meanwhile, my lessons with the Voice were hours of divine ecstasy. Never before had the beauty of sound so possessed me. And then, one day, the Voice said: "Now, Christine Daaé, it is time you gave those poor mortals a little of the music of Heaven."

'Why did Carlotta fail to come to the theatre on the evening of the gala performance? Why was I called upon to sing in her stead? I don't know, but I sang. I sang with a rapture such as I had never known before. I felt as if I had been given wings, as if, for a moment, my blazing soul soared above my body!'

'Oh, Christine,' said Raoul with eyes misting at the memory of her performance, 'my heart quickened at every note you sang that evening. I saw the tears streaming down your pale cheeks and I wept with you. How could you at once sing and weep?'

'I felt faint,' said Christine. 'I closed my eyes. And when I opened them, you were by my side. But the Voice was there too, Raoul! I feared for you, and again I feigned not to recognize you; I even began to laugh when you reminded me that you had retrieved my scarf from the sea! Alas, there was no deceiving the Voice! He recognized you and was jealous! He went on dreadfully for the next two days, saying: "You love him. If you did not, you would not avoid him! If he were just an old friend, you would shake hands with him as you would with any other friend. If you did not love him, you would not be afraid of finding yourself alone with him here in my presence. If you did not love him, you would not have sent him away!"

' "Stop this!" I told the Voice at last. "I am going to Perros to visit my father's grave tomorrow, and I shall ask M. Raoul de Chagny to go with me."

' "Do as you please," replied the Voice, "but I too will be in Perros, for I am wherever you are, Christine; and, if you are still worthy of me, if you have not lied to me, I shall play

Lazarus for you by your father's grave and on his violin at the stroke of midnight."

'And that was how I came to send you the letter that brought you to Perros, Raoul. How could I have been so easily fooled? There was something so personal about the Voice's concern for me that I ought to have suspected some deception. Alas, I was no longer in control of my destiny. I belonged to him! And, with the prodigious means at his disposal, fooling a child such as me was not difficult.'

'All the same,' cried Raoul, at this point in Christine's narrative when she was tearfully lamenting her excessive candour and lack of judgement, 'you soon came to know the truth! Why did you not at once break free from that abominable nightmare?'

'Know the truth? Free myself from that nightmare? But, Raoul, the nightmare only began on the day when I learned the truth! Enough, enough of this, please! As we are going to leave this heaven and fall back to earth, pity me, Raoul, pity me! One evening, for example . . . that fateful evening when Carlotta thought that she had become a hideous toad and croaked on stage as if she had spent all her life in a marsh, that evening when the house was suddenly plunged into darkness as the chandelier crashed down, when people were killed, others injured and the whole theatre resounded with anguish . . . Well, that evening, Raoul, when disaster struck, my first thoughts were for you and the Voice, for at that time my heart belonged to both of you in equal measure. As I had seen you in your brother's box, I knew at once that you were not in danger. But the Voice had told me that he would attend the performance and I feared for him. Yes, I truly feared for him as if he were an ordinary person capable of dying. I feared that the chandelier might have crushed him. I nearly ran from the stage into the house to look for him among the dead and injured; but then it came to me that if the Voice was safe, he must already be in my dressing-room, waiting to set my mind at rest. I rushed at once to my room. He was not there. I locked myself in and, with tears in my eyes, begged him, if he were still alive, to make his presence felt.

'The Voice did not reply, but suddenly I heard a long, exquisite lament, which I knew well. It was the plaint of Lazarus when, at the sound of Jesus' voice, he begins to open his eyes and see the light of day. It was my father's violin weeping; I even recognized his bowing stroke. It was the sound that made us, you and me, stop in our tracks as children – the sound that cast its spell over the graveyard that night at Perros. The invisible, triumphant violin played again the joyous cry of Life and at long last I heard the overwhelming, sovereign call of the Voice singing the words: "Come! And believe in me! He that believeth in me, though he were dead, yet shall he live! Come forth! Whosoever liveth and believeth in me shall never die!"[3] I cannot tell you the effect that this music had upon me: it sang of eternal life at the very moment when nearby poor wretches, crushed by the chandelier, breathed their last. I felt as if the Voice commanded me, personally, to come, to rise up and go forth. As he moved away from me, I followed. "Come! And believe in me!" I believed in him and followed . . . and as I moved forward – this was the extraordinary thing – my dressing-room seemed to grow longer, longer . . . It must have been some odd trick of the light, for the mirror was before me . . . And then, suddenly, I found myself somewhere else without knowing how!'

'What! Without knowing how? Come now, Christine, you must have been dreaming!'

'I was not dreaming, Raoul, I found myself somewhere else without knowing how it happened. You, who saw me disappear from my room one evening, may be able to explain it, but I cannot! All I can say is that I walked up to my mirror and then, suddenly, there was no mirror before me; I looked back but the mirror, the dressing-room were gone. I was in a gloomy passageway. I was frightened and screamed.

'It was dark all around me, save for a faint red glow of light further along, against the wall where the passageway turned. My voice rang hollow and filled the empty silence – the music had stopped. And then, all of a sudden in the darkness, a hand was laid on mine . . . or rather something bony, icy, seized my wrist and would not let go. I screamed again. An arm curled tightly around my waist and lifted me off the ground. Terrified, I struggled for a moment; but my fingers, slipping along the dank stone walls, could find no purchase. And then I stopped struggling; I thought that I would die of fright. I was carried off towards the faint red glow and as we reached it I saw that I was being held by a man wrapped in a large cloak who wore a mask covering the whole of his face. I made one last desperate attempt: I stiffened and was about to scream once more when I felt a hand cover my mouth; and that hand against my lips, on my flesh, smelled of death! I fainted!

'I cannot say how long it was before I regained consciousness. When I opened my eyes, we were still – that man and I – surrounded by darkness. But by a dim lantern on the ground I saw running water. It bubbled out of the wall and disappeared almost at once into the ground upon which I was lying with my head resting on the knee of the masked man in the black cloak. My silent companion was bathing my temples with a care, an attention and a delicacy of manner that seemed even more horrible to bear than the brutality of my earlier abduction. However light his touch, his hands smelled of death. I tried to push them away, but I had no strength left. "Who are you?" I moaned. "Where is the Voice?" A sigh was his sole response. Suddenly, I felt a hot breath sweep over my face and, in the darkness, I vaguely made out a white shape beside the black figure. And then, as the man lifted me up on to this white shape, a joyous neighing came to my astounded ears and I murmured "César!" The animal quivered in response. Slumped in the saddle, I recognized the white horse from *Le Prophète*, which I had so often spoilt with treats. I remembered that one evening at the Opera, rumour had it that the horse had disappeared, stolen by the ghost. I believed in the Voice, but had never believed in the ghost. Now, however, I wondered with a shudder whether my abductor could be that ghost. I called upon the Voice for help with all my heart, for I could never imagine that he and the ghost were one and the same. You have heard the rumours of the Phantom of the Opera, Raoul, have you not?'

'Yes, I have. But tell me what happened next when you found yourself on the white horse from *Le Prophète*.'

'I kept still and let myself be carried. Little by little the feelings of anguish and terror brought on by these diabolical events gave way to a strange torpor. The dark figure held me; I made no effort to escape him. A curious peace came over me and I thought that I must be under the soothing influence of some narcotic. My senses were not impaired in the slightest. My eyes became accustomed to the darkness, which was broken every so often by gleams of light. I gathered that we were underground, in a narrow circular gallery probably running all the way around the vast Opera House. I had ventured below stage only once before, and not dared go further down than the third mezzanine. Beneath my feet were another two underground floors large enough to hold a town but I had glimpsed some dark figures and taken fright. Demonic shapes stood in front of furnaces,[4] wielding shovels and pitchforks, stoking up the fires and stirring up the flames; when you drew close, they threatened you by suddenly opening the red mouths of their fiery ovens. Well, while César was calmly carrying me on his back through the nightmarish darkness, those black demons appeared far off in the distance: they looked very small in front of the red fires of their great furnaces as if I were seeing them through the wrong end of a spy-glass. They appeared, disappeared and reappeared as our path twisted and turned. And then finally I saw them no more. The masked figure was still holding me; and César, unguided and sure-footed, walked on. How long did this nocturnal journey last? I have no idea, no idea at all. I can only say that we seemed to be going down in circles, on and on, as if we were descending in a relentless spiral into the entrails of the earth. Perhaps it was simply giddiness, but I think not. No, I was sharply aware of my surroundings. At last, César raised his head, sniffed and quickened his pace a little. The air felt damp. César stopped. The darkness had given way, all around, to a pale blue light. I saw that we were at the edge of a lake, whose leaden waters stretched into the distance, into the night; and on the illuminated shore was a small boat fastened to an iron ring.

'There was nothing supernatural about the underground lake or the boat – I had already heard talk of these. But consider

for a moment, Raoul, the exceptional circumstances by which
I arrived upon that shore! The souls of the dead surely did not
feel greater anguish upon reaching the River Styx, nor did Charon appear more doleful,[5] more silent than the black figure
now carrying me into the boat. Had the effects of the drug
worn off? Or was the coolness of the air enough to revive me?
My torpor was lifting and so my terror returned. My sinister
companion must have noticed my restlessness for he swiftly
sent César back with a single wave of his hand. I watched the
horse vanish into the darkness of the gallery and heard its
hooves ringing up the steps of a staircase while my escort
quickly leaped into the boat and untied it. He took up the oars
and rowed with relentless determination. His eyes, under the
mask, never left me and I felt the weight of his still gaze upon
me. The waters all around us were silent. We glided along in
the pale blue light, and then we were plunged into utter darkness again. The boat bumped against something and, once
more, I felt arms lifting me. Having regained enough strength,
I screamed once more. But then I stopped suddenly, dazed by
the light – the blinding light in the midst of which he had just
set me down. I sprang to my feet, all my strength returned. I
found myself in the middle of a drawing-room, which seemed
to be decorated, adorned and furnished with nothing but
flowers, flowers both magnificent and absurd because they
were tied by silk ribbons to baskets like those sold in the shops
on the boulevards. These stylish arrangements resembled the
ones I used to find in my dressing-room after a first night. And,
in the midst of this all too Parisian setting, stood, with arms
crossed, the dark figure of the man in the mask.

' "Don't be afraid, Christine," he said. "You are in no danger."

'It was the Voice! I was at once both furious and astounded.
I reached for his mask and tried to pull it off so as to see his
face.

' "You are in no danger, so long as you do not touch my
mask," he added.

'He took me gently by the wrists and made me sit down. He
then fell to his knees, but remained silent! In the face of such

humility I felt my courage return; and thanks to the light that threw everything around me into sharp relief, I regained a keen sense of reality. However extraordinary my situation, every-thing around me belonged to the visible, tangible world. The wall hangings, the furniture, the candles, the vases and even those mundane flowers in golden baskets – I could almost tell which florist had made them and how much they cost – confined my imagination to the limits of this drawing-room, which was much the same as any other, save it lay beneath the Paris Opera House.

'I thought that the masked man must surely be some wicked eccentric, who had mysteriously settled down here, just as others lodged – for want of a better place and with the silent complicity of the administration – in the attics of this modern Tower of Babel, this land of intrigue where people sang in all languages and loved in all dialects.[6]

'And now the *Voice* – the *Voice* that the mask could not hide and I had recognized – *was kneeling before me: a man!*

'I gave little thought to the dire situation in which I found myself; I did not even ponder my fate and the obscure, ruth-lessly tyrannical purpose for which I had been taken to this room like a prisoner to a jail, or a slave to a harem. No, no, all I could think was: the Voice is only . . . a man! And I began to weep.

'The man, still kneeling, must have understood the cause of my tears. "As you can see, Christine," he said, "I am neither an Angel, nor a genius, nor a ghost! I am a man and my name is Erik."'

Here Christine interrupted her narrative again for she fan-cied, as did Raoul, that she heard the name 'Erik' echo behind them. How could it be? They both looked about them and real-ized that night had fallen. The young man was about to stand up, but Christine held him back.

'Stay here with me,' she said. 'I must tell you everything *here*!'

'But why here, Christine? I am afraid that you might catch a chill.'

'Because of the traps. Here we are well away from them and

safe. He has forbidden me to see you outside the theatre. Now is not the time to upset him. We must not arouse his suspicion.'

'Christine! Christine! We must not wait until tomorrow night. We ought to run away at once!'

'If Erik does not hear me sing tomorrow, he will be devastated.'

'It can only be thus if you want to escape him for ever.'

'You are right, Raoul. At all events, he will certainly die of grief if I run away . . .' And then she added in a muted voice: 'On the other hand, he could just as easily kill us.'

'Does he love you so much?'

'Yes, he would stop at nothing for me, not even murder.'

'But he lives somewhere and could be found. Since Erik is not a ghost, we could talk to him, reason with him!'

Christine shook her head. 'No, no! Nothing can be done, save run away from him!'

'Then why, when you could escape, did you go back to him?'

'Because I must. You will understand when I tell you how I left him.'

'Oh, how I hate him!' cried Raoul. 'And you, Christine, tell me: do you hate him too? I need to know so that I can listen to the rest of your extraordinary tale with some peace of mind.'

'No, I do not hate him,' said Christine simply.

'Then why waste your time here with me? You clearly love him! Your fears, your terror, all of that is still born of love, and love of the most exquisite kind, the kind that one does not admit even to oneself,' said Raoul bitterly. 'The kind that gives you a thrill when you think of it. No wonder: a mysterious man living in an underground palace!' And he gave a deprecatory laugh.

'Then you want me to go back there?' she asked starkly. 'Beware, Raoul. I told you: I would never come back!'

There was a dreadful silence among the three of them – the two who spoke and the shadow listening nearby.

'Before I answer,' said Raoul at last, very slowly, 'tell me the feelings *he* inspires in you, since you do not hate him.'

'Horror!' she said. And she hurled that single word with so great a force that it drowned the sighs of the night. 'This is my

terrible dilemma,' she added with growing agitation. 'He fills
me with horror and yet I do not hate him. How could I hate
him, Raoul? Picture Erik at my feet, in that subterranean retreat
on the far side of the lake. He railed against himself, he cursed
himself, he begged my forgiveness! He confessed that he had
lied. He loved me! He laid at my feet his immense, tragic love.
It was love that drove him to abduct me, to imprison me with
him underground! But he respected me: he grovelled, he
moaned, he wept! And when I rose to my feet, Raoul, and told
him that I could only despise him if he did not give me back my
freedom then and there, it was incredible: he offered to let me
go. I could leave at once, he was ready to show me the secret
route out. Only . . . only he rose too and I was made to remember that, though he was neither an angel, nor a ghost, nor a
genius, he still was the Voice, for he sang. I listened . . . and
stayed!

'That night, we did not exchange another word. Taking up a
harp, he – the man with the voice of an angel – started singing
Desdemona's "Willow Song".[7] I had sung it myself and felt
ashamed at my memory of it. Music, Raoul, has the power to
make one forget everything save those sounds that touch your
heart. I forgot my extraordinary situation. The Voice was back.
Enthralled, I followed his harmonious lead; I became one of
Orpheus' flock![8] He took me through sorrow and delight,
through martyrdom, despair and bliss, from death to triumphant love. I listened. He sang. He sang pieces unknown to
me, new music that induced in me strange feelings of tenderness, languor and peace . . . music which, having stirred my
soul, soothed it little by little, bringing it to the threshold of
dreams. I fell asleep.

'When I woke up, I was alone, lying on a *chaise longue* in a
simple bedroom hung with calico and furnished with a plain
mahogany bed; a lamp was burning on the marble top of an
old Louis-Philippe chest of drawers.[9] Where was I? I passed my
hand over my eyes as if to dispel a bad dream. Alas, I soon realized that this was no dream. I was a prisoner and the only
outlet from my room led to a well-appointed bathroom with
hot and cold water a-plenty. Returning to the bedroom, I found

a note in red ink on the chest of drawers, which left me in no doubt whatsoever as to my plight and the reality of the situation: "My dear Christine, you need have no concern as regards your fate. You have no better nor more respectful friend in the world than me. At present, you are alone in this, your abode. I am going out to purchase everything that you might possibly need here."

' "I have fallen prey to a madman!" I thought. "What is to become of me? For how long does he intend to hold me prisoner down here?" I ran about my small apartment, frantically looking for a means of escape, but found none. I bitterly reproached myself for being so absurdly gullible, indulging in painful jibes at the sheer naivety with which I had welcomed, through the walls, the Voice of the Genius of Music. Being that foolish, I should not have been surprised at this disastrous turn of events and fully deserved my misfortunes. I violently berated myself, both laughing and crying. Such was my state of mind when Erik returned.

'I heard three sharp knocks and he calmly walked in through a hidden door which I had failed to notice and he now left open. He carried boxes and parcels, which he slowly placed on the bed while I reviled him, insisting that he take off his mask if it covered, as he claimed, the face of an honest man.

'Whereupon he replied with great composure: "You shall never see Erik's face."

'And then he chided me for not being fully dressed so late in the day – he was kind enough to tell me that it was two o'clock in the afternoon. He said that I had half an hour to prepare myself and, as he spoke, carefully wound up my watch and set it for me at the correct time. He then invited me to join him in the dining-room, where a splendid lunch was awaiting us. I was very hungry. I slammed the door in his face and went into the bathroom. But before I took my bath, I placed a magnificently crafted pair of scissors within reach, determined to kill myself should Erik in his madness choose to behave dishonourably. Having bathed, I felt greatly refreshed. I wisely resolved not to antagonize him or hurt his feelings in any way and, if need be, to flatter him so as to regain my freedom as soon as possible. When I joined him, it was Erik who spoke first, saying that he wished to apprise me of his plans for me so that I might feel reassured. He enjoyed my company too much to leave me on my own, as he had done the previous day when confronted with my fear and indignation. Now I must understand, he continued, that there was no reason to be afraid of him. He loved me, but would never tell me so without my consent; the rest of the time would be devoted to music.

' "What do you mean by 'the rest of the time'?" I asked.

' "Five days," he said firmly.

' "And after that, shall I be free?"

' "You shall be free, Christine, for by then you will have learned not to be afraid of me; and henceforth you will come here of your own volition to visit your poor Erik!"

'I was deeply moved by his tone when he uttered these last words. His despair appeared to be so genuine, so pitiable that I looked on his masked face with some tenderness. I was unable to see his eyes behind the mask. This contributed in no small measure to the strange unease I felt; but below his mysterious black silk mask appeared one, two, three, four tears.

'Silently, he waved me to a seat opposite him at a small table which occupied the centre of the room where he had played the harp on the previous day. I sat down, disconcerted. All the same, it was not without appetite that I ate some crayfish and a chicken wing; I also drank half a glass of Tokay which, he said, he had personally brought back from the Konigsberg cellars, once frequented by Falstaff.[10] He himself neither ate nor drank. I asked him from which country he came and if the name Erik denoted Scandinavian ancestry. He replied that he had neither name nor country and that he had been given the name of Erik by accident. I asked him why, since he loved me, he had found no other way to let me know of his feelings than to carry me down here and lock me up.

' "It is difficult," I added, "to inspire love in a tomb."

' "One must create the opportunities one can," he replied oddly.

'Then he rose, saying he wished to show me round his abode, and offered me his hand; but I withdrew mine at once and gave

a cry for his scraggy fingers were clammy, and I remembered
that his hands smelled of death.

' "Oh, forgive me!" he sighed as he went on to open the door
before me. "This is my bedroom," he said. "It is rather unusual.
Would you care to see it?"

'I assented. His manners, his words, his whole attitude
inspired my trust and I felt that there was no reason to be
afraid. I entered a room that resembled a funeral parlour. The
walls were all hung in black, but, instead of the white trim-
mings that usually complete such decoration, I saw enormous
staves bearing the notes of the *Dies Irae*.[11] In the middle of the
room was a canopy, from which hung curtains of coarse red
brocade; under the canopy was an open coffin. I recoiled at the
sight of it.

' "This is where I sleep," said Erik. "One must get used to
everything, even eternity."

'As I looked away, disturbed, my eyes fell on an organ con-
sole which took up an entire wall. On the music stand was a
manuscript book scrawled all over with notes in red. He let me
look at it: the title page read "*Don Juan triomphant*".

' "I compose music sometimes," he said. "I began this work
twenty years ago and when it is complete, I shall take it with
me into this coffin and never wake again."

' "Then you ought to work at it as seldom as you can," I suggested.

' "Once in a while I work at it day and night for two weeks
at a stretch, during which music is my sole sustenance; and
then I let it rest for several years."

' "Will you play me something from your *Don Juan triomphant*?" I asked in an effort to please him despite my revulsion
at being in this death chamber.

' "Never ask me that," he said, darkly. "My *Don Juan* has
not been composed to a libretto by Lorenzo Da Ponte, nor
inspired by wine, wanton love and profligacy doomed to incur
the wrath of God. If you like, I can play you Mozart's version,
so that you may shed your beautiful tears and indulge in pious
thoughts. You see, Christine, my own *Don Juan* is not carried
off to Hell by demons, and yet he burns . . ."[12]

'Having said that, he led me back to the drawing-room. During my visit, I had noticed that there was no mirror anywhere to be seen; I was going to remark upon this, but Erik was already seated at the piano.

' "You see, Christine, there is music that is so formidable that it consumes whoever approaches it. Fortunately you have not yet encountered such music. If you had, you would have lost your fresh complexion and no one would recognize you when you returned to the stage. Let's sing 'opera music', Christine Daaé," he said as if he meant it as an insult.

'I had no time to dwell upon the matter, for we began to sing the duet from *Otello* at once and were already doomed. This time he gave me Desdemona's part, which I sang with a genuine despair and a magnificent terror such as I had never achieved before. Instead of overwhelming me, singing with him was an inspiration. My recent experiences gave me remarkable insights into the verse of the poet and my singing would have dazzled the composer himself. Erik's voice thundered in response to mine, his vindictive soul stalked every note, adding to its dramatic import. Love, jealousy, hatred rang all around us in heart-rending cries. Erik's black mask reminded me of the dark complexion of the Moor of Venice: he was Othello himself. I thought that he would strike at me and that I would collapse under his blows. Yet I made no attempt to escape him or evade his fury as the timid Desdemona had done. On the contrary, I moved closer to him, attracted, fascinated: in the midst of such passion, death itself became appealing ... But before I died I wanted to gaze upon the hidden face that must have been transfigured by eternal art, so as to take this sublime image with me to my grave. I wanted to see the *face of the Voice* and instinctively, for I was no longer mistress of myself, my fingers tore away his mask. Oh! Horror! Horror! Horror!'

Christine stopped, raising her trembling hands to her face as if to protect herself from that vision. Meanwhile, just as the name Erik had echoed a moment ago, now the words 'Horror! Horror! Horror!' resounded in the night. Raoul and Christine, brought closer still by her terrifying tale, raised their eyes to the stars that shone in the clear and peaceful sky.

'How strange, Christine,' commented Raoul, 'that this gentle and peaceful night should be filled with sounds of anguish. As if it were at one with us.'

'When you know the Voice's secret, Raoul,' she replied, 'your ears, like mine, will ring with lamentation.' She took Raoul's protecting hands into her own and shuddered for a moment. 'Were I to live to be a hundred,' she resumed, 'I shall never forget the infernal, howling cry of agony and rage he uttered when I finally uncovered the *thing* that passed for his face. I froze – eyes wide with terror, mouth agape, silent.

'Oh, Raoul, that sight! How can I forget that sight? Will it never leave me? While my ears will forever ring with his wailing, my eyes are forever haunted by his face! How can I erase it from my memory? How can I describe it to you, Raoul? You must have seen skulls, dried and withered by the centuries; and, perhaps, if it were not a dreadful nightmare, you caught sight of *his* skull head at Perros. You also saw the Red Death among the revellers at the masked ball. But all of those skulls were still, and inanimate in their mute horror. But imagine, if you can, the mask of the Red Death suddenly coming to life in order to express – through the holes that were his eyes, his nose and his mouth – the unfettered anger and sovereign fury of a demon; and yet *not the slightest gleam from those eye sockets*, for, as I was to learn later, his burning eyes only shone in the darkest night. Recoiling against the wall, I must have seemed the very embodiment of terror, just as he was hideousness incarnate.

'Then he drew close to me, with grinding teeth and no lips; and as I fell upon my knees, he unleashed his hatred, hissing random words, disconnected phrases, curses, ravings. I know not what!

'"Look!" he cried, leaning over me. "You wanted to see! Then look! Feast your eyes, sate your soul on my cursed ugliness! Stare at Erik's face! Was it not enough for you to hear me, eh? You had to know what I looked like! Oh, you women are so inquisitive!"

'He broke into belligerent, hysterical, terrifying laughter, repeating hoarsely all the while: "Oh, you women are so inquisitive!" Then he said things like: "Well, are you satisfied? Quite a handsome fellow, eh? When a woman has seen me, as you have, she is mine. She loves me for ever. Rather like Don Juan, you see!" He drew himself up to his full height with his hand on his hip, shaking the hideous thing that was his head, and roared: "Look at me! *I am Don Juan triumphant!*" And when I turned my head away from him and begged for mercy, he thrust his dead fingers into my hair and viciously twisted my head back towards him.'

'Enough! Enough!' interrupted Raoul. 'I will kill him. In Heaven's name, Christine, tell me how to reach his secret retreat! He must die!'

'Hush, Raoul, let me continue!'

'Yes, do continue, Christine, I want to know how and why you returned to him. That is the real mystery, the only one. I must know! But whatever the truth of the matter, I will kill him!'

'Oh, Raoul, listen, listen if you want to know. He dragged me by my hair and then . . . and then . . . Oh, this is more horrible still!'

'Well, what? Tell me!' exclaimed Raoul fiercely. 'Tell me, now!'

'Then he hissed at me. "Ah, I frighten you, do I? Yes, quite possibly! Perhaps you think that I have another mask, eh, and that this . . . this, my head, is just another mask? Well," he roared, "why not tear it off as you did the other? Come! Come, try again! I insist! Your hands! Your hands! Give me your hands! And if they cannot do it on their own, I shall lend you mine! And the two of us will try to rip off this second mask." I curled up at his feet, but he grabbed my hands and thrust them into his awful face. And he tore at his horrible dead flesh with my nails!

' "Understand," he bellowed, "understand that I am entirely made of death – from head to foot – and that it is a corpse who loves you, worships you and will never, never leave you! I will have a larger coffin made, Christine, for when our loving days finally come to an end! Look, I am not laughing now, I am weeping, weeping for you, Christine, who have ripped off my mask and therefore can never leave me now! As long as you thought me handsome, you could come back to me! I know you would have come back; but now that you know how hideous I am, you will run away for good! So I shall have to keep you here! But why did you want to see me, when my own father never looked upon me? When my mother, weeping, gave me my first mask so as not to see me!"

'He let go of me at last and was writhing on the floor, choking with awful sobs. And then, crawling like a snake, he dragged himself out of the room, went into his bedroom and shut the door. I found myself alone with my thoughts, fearful but free at last from the sight of him. A prodigious, tomb-like silence followed the storm and I could reflect upon the dire consequences of my rash gesture. The monster's last words were clear enough: I had condemned myself to imprisonment for ever and my curiosity was the cause of all my misfortunes. I had not heeded his warning: he had told me that I was in no danger as long as I did not touch his mask, and I had touched it. I cursed my foolishness and concluded with a shudder that there was logic in the monster's reasoning. Yes, I would have returned to him if I had not seen his face. He had already moved me, arousing my interest and compassion enough with his masked tears, for me to respond to his entreaties. And I was not ungrateful: his impossible demands could not make me forget that he was the Voice and that his genius had inspired me. I would have come back! But now, were I able to escape from these catacombs, I would never return! You do not go back to a tomb and a corpse who loves you.

'His frenzy during that whole scene and the way in which he had fixed upon me, or rather brought the black holes of his invisible eyes close to my face, had given me the full measure of his wild passion. That he had not taken me into his arms at a time when I could offer no resistance must mean that there was something of the angel about the monster. Perhaps, after all, he was still, if only slightly, the Angel of Music and would have embodied it perfectly, had God made him beautiful instead of clothing him in rotten flesh.

'Distraught at the prospect of the destiny awaiting me and

terrified at the thought of seeing the unmasked face of the monster appear at the door to the room with the coffin, I had already slipped into my own apartment and seized the scissors that could free me from my appalling fate when I heard the sound of the organ.

'At that moment, Raoul, I began to understand Erik's surprising dismissal of what he called "opera music". What I now heard was utterly different from the music that had delighted me until then. His *Don Juan triomphant* (for I could not doubt that he had thrown himself into his masterpiece to forget the horror of the moment) seemed to me at first one long, horrendous, magnificent lament into which he had poured all his cursed suffering.

'I pictured the manuscript with the red notes and readily imagined that these had been written in blood. His music took me on a painstaking journey through martyrdom and into the uttermost recesses of the abyss that this *hideous creature* inhabited; it showed me Erik banging his poor, ugly head against the dismal walls of the hell to which he had fled, away from those whom he might otherwise terrify. I listened, gasping for breath, beleaguered and pitifully crushed by those gigantic chords, which made suffering divine: ascending from the abyss, they gathered all of a sudden into a prodigious, threatening swarm soaring into the heavens and circling higher and higher like an eagle towards the sun. Listening to that triumphant symphony which seemed to set the world ablaze, I understood that the work had reached its apotheosis and that Hideousness, soaring on the wings of Love, had dared to face Beauty.

'Enthralled, I went to the door that separated me from Erik and pushed it open. When he heard me he rose to his feet, *but dared not turn round.*

' "Erik," I cried, "show me your face without fear! I swear that you are the most unhappy and sublime of men; and, if I shudder ever again when I look at you, it will be because I am thinking of the splendour of your genius!"

'Then he turned round, for he believed me, and I too, alas, had faith in myself. He raised his skeletal hands to the heavens in a gesture of thanks and fell at my feet, with words of love . . .

words of love in his dead mouth. The music had stopped. He kissed the hem of my dress and did not notice that my eyes were closed.

'What more can I tell you, Raoul? You now know the whole tragedy. It continued thus for two weeks – and throughout that time I deceived him. My lies were as hideous as the monster that had inspired them; but they were the price I had to pay to regain my freedom. I burned his mask; and I feigned so well that, even when he was not singing, he dared to seek my gaze like a timid dog looking up at its master. He behaved like a faithful slave and lavished care on me. Little by little, I inspired such confidence in him that he took me walking along the banks of Lake Avernus[13] and rowed me across its leaden waters. At night, towards the end of my captivity, he even took me through the gate of the underground passage that opens on to the Rue Scribe. There a carriage awaited us and drove us to the lonely Bois.

'Your appearance that night was nearly fatal for me, as he is intensely jealous of you. My only recourse was to tell him of your forthcoming departure. At last, after two horrendous weeks of captivity during which I swayed from extreme pity and enthusiasm to utter despair and horror, he believed me when I said that I would come back.'

'And you went back, Christine,' said Raoul, forlorn.

'Yes, I did, Raoul, but it was not the dreadful threats he proffered when he released me that helped me keep my promise, but his harrowing sobs on the threshold of his tomb. Yes, his sobbing,' she said, sadly shaking her head, 'did more to bind me to the unfortunate man than I thought possible when I left him. Poor Erik! Poor, poor Erik!'

'Christine,' said Raoul, rising, 'you talk of your love for me; but you had been free for only a few hours when you returned to Erik's side! Remember the masked ball!'

'That was part of our agreement. And you, Raoul, must remember that I spent those hours with you, thus putting both our lives in grave danger.'

'Yet I doubted your love for me, during those hours.'

'Do you doubt it still, Raoul? Believe me when I say that

with each of my visits to Erik my horror of him has grown; for, instead of calming him, as I hoped, each of those visits only served to heighten his insane love! And I am afraid of him, so very afraid!'

'You are afraid of him, but do you love me? If Erik were handsome, would you love me, Christine?'

'Why do you raise questions that I have pushed to the back of my mind as if they were sinful?'

She rose too and wrapped her beautiful, trembling arms round the young man.

'Oh, my betrothed, if I did not love you, I would not offer you my lips! Kiss them, for the first and last time.'

He kissed her; but suddenly the darkness around them was rent asunder. They fled as if pursued by a storm and, before they disappeared into the forest of the attic, their eyes, haunted by their fear of Erik, glimpsed high up above them a great nocturnal bird of prey with burning eyes which glared down at them from the strings of Apollo's lyre.

XIV

The Master of the Traps Strikes

Raoul and Christine ran and ran, away from the roof and the burning eyes that only shone in darkest night. They did not stop until they reached the eighth floor on their way back down. There was no performance at the Paris Opera House that evening, so the corridors were deserted.

Suddenly, a bizarre figure stood before them, blocking their path. 'No, not this way!' he said, pointing to another corridor, which led to the wings.

Raoul wanted to stop and ask for an explanation.

'Go on! Go on, quickly!' commanded the vague figure concealed by a large cloak and a peaked hat.

Christine was already pulling Raoul along, forcing him to run again.

'But who is he? Who is that man?' he asked.

'That was the *Persian*,' Christine replied.

'What's he doing at the Opera?'

'Nobody knows. He is always here.'

'You are making me behave like a coward, Christine,' said Raoul, visibly upset. 'For the first time in my life, I am running away.'

'Could it be,' suggested Christine, calming down a little, 'that we have simply fled an imagined shadow?'

'If it were Erik, I should have pinned him to Apollo's lyre, just as Breton farmers nail owls to the walls of their houses; and we could have forgotten about him for ever.'

'Sweet Raoul, you would first have had to climb up to Apollo's lyre – which would be quite a feat in itself.'

'Those burning eyes got up there!'

'You see him everywhere now, just like me! But thinking back, perhaps I simply mistook the golden points of a couple of stars, watching the city through the strings of the lyre, for his burning eyes.'

Christine then went down another floor and Raoul followed her.

'Since you are resolved to leave, Christine, it would be better to go at once. Why wait until tomorrow? He may have over-heard us tonight!'

'No, no! As I have told you, he is working at his *Don Juan triomphant* and so is not concerned with us at the moment.'

'But you have so little faith in what you say that you keep looking behind you!'

'Come, let's go to my dressing-room.'

'I would rather we met outside the Opera.'

'Never! Not until the very moment we leave. If I were to break my promise, it would bring bad luck. I have given him my word that I would only see you here.'

'How fortunate for me that he allowed you that! It was very brave of you,' said Raoul bitterly, 'to let us play at being engaged!'

'Why, dear Raoul, he knows all about it! He said: "I trust you, Christine. M. de Chagny is in love with you and will soon be leaving. Before he goes, let him be as unhappy as I am."'

'What does that mean?'

'I should be the one to ask that question. Are people always unhappy when they're in love?'

'Yes, Christine, they are unhappy when they love but are unsure of being loved in return.'

'Are you speaking for Erik, here?'

'For Erik and for myself,' said the young man shaking his head, thoughtful and forlorn.

As they reached Christine's dressing-room, he asked: 'Why do you feel safer in this room than in any other part of the the-atre? If you could hear him through the walls, he can hear us too.'

'No. Erik gave me his word that he would not lurk behind the walls of my dressing-room again and I trust him. This room and my apartment in the *lake-side retreat* are my own, exclusively, and he respects that.'

'How could you have been spirited out of this room and into the dark passage, Christine? Shall we try to remember and repeat your every movement that evening?'

'It is dangerous, Raoul, for the mirror might spirit me away again; and, instead of fleeing, I would have to go all the way down the secret passage leading to the lake and call for Erik.'

'Would he hear you?'

'Erik will hear me whenever I call him. He told me so. He is curiously gifted. Raoul, you must not think that he is just a man who chose to live beneath the ground for his own amusement. What he does, no other man could do; and what he knows is unknown to the living world.'

'Beware, Christine, you are speaking of him again as if he were a ghost!'

'No, he is not a ghost; he is simply a man of Heaven and earth.'

'"Simply a man of Heaven and earth." How well you speak of him! Are you still resolved to flee from him?'

'Yes, tomorrow.'

'Let me tell you why I would like to see you leave tonight.'

'Yes, tell me, Raoul.'

'Because tomorrow, all your resolve will be gone!'

'Then, Raoul, you must *take* me away. Are we not agreed on that?'

'Yes, we are. Tomorrow at midnight, I shall be here in your dressing-room,' said the young man sombrely. 'I shall keep my word whatever happens. Did you say that he would attend the performance and then wait for you to join him in the dining-room of his retreat?'

'Yes, that is where we were to meet.'

'And how were you to get there, Christine, if you don't know how to leave your room by way of the mirror?'

'Why, by going straight to the edge of the lake.'

'All the way down there? Down the stairs and along the passageways where the machinists and other workers would have seen you? No, you could never have kept this route secret until now! Christine Daaé would have been followed by a whole crowd all the way down to the lake.'

Christine brought out a box, from which she took out a very large key.

'What is this?' he asked.

'This is the key to the gate of the underground passage that opens on to the Rue Scribe.'

'I understand now! So the passage leads straight to the lake. Give it to me, Christine.'

'Never!' she said, briskly. 'That would be a betrayal!'

Suddenly Christine's face changed colour: she turned deathly pale. 'Oh, my God!' she cried. 'Erik! Erik! Have mercy on me!'

'Hush!' said Raoul. 'Just now you told me that he can hear you!'

The singer's demeanour became more and more perplexing. She felt her fingers, repeating distractedly: 'Oh, my God! Oh, my God!'

'But what is it? What is it?' pleaded Raoul.

'The ring!'

'What ring? Please, Christine, collect yourself!'

'The gold ring he gave me.'

'So it was Erik who gave you that ring!'

'You know he did, Raoul! But what you don't know is that, when he gave it to me, he said: "I am letting you go, Christine, on condition that you wear this ring at all times. As long as you do, you will be safe and Erik will remain your friend. But woe betide you, Christine, if you ever part with it, for Erik will take his revenge!" Raoul, Raoul, the ring is gone! We are lost!'

They looked about them, but the ring was nowhere to be found and Christine would not calm down.

'It was when I gave you that kiss, up there, under Apollo's lyre,' she sought to explain, trembling. 'The ring must have slipped off my finger and dropped down to the city below! How can we find it? And what misfortunes are awaiting us now! Oh! to run away for ever!'

'Let us leave at once,' Raoul insisted.

She wavered. For a moment, he thought that she was going to agree; but then her bright eyes clouded over and she said:

'No, tomorrow!' And she hurried away in complete disarray, still feeling her fingers as if she hoped that the ring might miraculously reappear. As for Raoul, he went home, greatly disturbed by all he had heard.

'If I don't save her from the clutches of that charlatan,' he exclaimed as he went to bed, 'she is lost; but I will save her.' He put out his light and, lying in the dark, had an urge to insult Erik. 'Charlatan! Charlatan! Charlatan!' he cried out loud.

Then suddenly he raised himself, cold sweat running down the sides of his face. Two eyes like burning coals had appeared at the foot of his bed. Unblinking, they stared at him defiantly in the darkness. Raoul was not a coward yet he trembled. Tentatively, he reached out his hand towards his bedside table. And then, having found the matches, he struck a light. The eyes disappeared instantly.

He was not at all reassured by this: 'She told me that *his* eyes only shone in the dark. Although his eyes have disappeared with the light, *he* may still be here,' he thought. He rose and cautiously searched the room. He looked under his bed, like a child, and thought himself ridiculous. 'What should I believe or not believe in this fantastic tale? Where does reality end, where does fantasy begin? What was it she saw? What was it she thought she saw?' he said out loud. 'And what did I, myself, see?' he added, shuddering. 'Did I see those smouldering eyes just now? Or did they only appear in my imagination? I am unsure of everything! And, as for those eyes, I could not swear I really saw them!' He got back into bed again and blew out his light. The eyes reappeared.

'Oh,' gasped Raoul. He sat up and stared back at them with all the courage he could muster. And after a moment's silence, he cried: 'Is that you, Erik? Man, genius or ghost, is that you?' He then reflected: 'If it's him, he must be on the balcony!' Whereupon Raoul ran in his night shirt to a small cabinet, in which he felt for and found a pistol. Thus armed, he opened the French windows. It was a particularly cool night. He gave only a brief, cursory glance around the empty balcony before going back in and closing the windows. He climbed into bed again, shivering, and kept the revolver within his reach, by his bedside. He blew out his candle once again: the eyes were still there, at the foot of his bed.

Were they between the bed and the glass of the French windows, or outside looking in from the balcony? He wished he knew. And did those eyes belong to a human being? He wanted to know. Then, patiently, deliberately, without disturbing the night around him, he picked up his pistol and took aim. He aimed at the two still, golden stars strangely glowering at him, and then at a little above the two stars. Surely, if these were eyes, if above was a forehead, and if Raoul was not too bad a shot . . .

The silence of the slumbering house shattered. Footsteps came hurrying along the corridors, while Raoul sat up in his bed, with outstretched arm ready to fire again, staring. This time the two stars had disappeared.

Instead there were lights, servants and Count Philippe, exceedingly anxious: 'What is it, Raoul?'

'I think I have been dreaming,' replied the young man. 'I fired at two stars that kept me from sleeping.'

'You are raving! Are you ill? Please, Raoul, answer me! What happened?' cried the Count, snatching up the pistol.

'No, no, I am not raving. Besides, we shall soon find out.' He got out of bed, put on his dressing-gown and slippers, took a light from the hands of a servant and, opening the French windows, stepped out on to the balcony. While the Count inspected the glass, which had been shot through at a man's height, Raoul bent down with his candle. 'Ah!' he said. 'Blood! Blood! Here . . . there . . . more blood! Good! A ghost who bleeds is not much of a ghost!' he snorted.

'Raoul! Raoul! Raoul!' The Count was shaking him as if he were trying to rouse a sleep-walker from dangerous slumber.

'I'm not asleep, brother!' Raoul protested impatiently. 'You can see the blood for yourself. I thought that in my dream I had fired at two stars. But those were Erik's eyes, and here is his blood! Yet, after all,' he added, suddenly anxious, 'perhaps I was wrong to shoot; and Christine might well not forgive me for it. None of this would have happened if I had simply drawn the curtains before going to bed.'

'Raoul, have you gone mad? Wake up!'

'Not again, please! You would do better, brother, to help me find Erik for, after all, if the ghost is bleeding we can follow his trail.'

'There is definitely blood on the balcony!' confirmed the Count's man-servant.

Another servant brought a lamp so that they could thoroughly examine the balcony. The trail of blood followed the hand-rail and ran up a drain-pipe.

'My dear fellow,' said Count Philippe, 'you have shot a cat.'

'Unfortunately,' said Raoul, with a laugh which rang painfully in the Count's ears, 'this is quite possible. With Erik, you can't tell. Was it Erik? Was it a cat? Was it a ghost? Was it flesh and blood, or a mere shadow? With Erik, you simply can't tell!'

Raoul continued with remarks such as these, which related directly and inextricably to his own concerns and naturally sprang from Christine Daaé's revelations, whether real or fantastic. These apparent ramblings contributed in no small measure to the impression that the young man had lost his mind. The Count himself was convinced of it and later the examining magistrate, having read Inspector Mifroid's report, came to the same conclusion.

'Who is Erik?' asked the Count as he squeezed his brother's hand.

'He is my rival. And if he's not dead, it's a pity!'

He waved the servants away. They closed the door of the bedroom on the brothers; but as they lingered in the corridor the Count's butler distinctly heard Raoul emphatically cry: 'I shall take Christine Daaé away tonight!'

His words were later repeated to M. Faure, the examining magistrate. However, no one ever knew exactly what passed between the two brothers during their conversation that night. According to the servants, this was not the first time they had quarrelled behind closed doors. Shouts were heard through the walls, which all seemed to be about an actress called Christine Daaé.

The next morning, as the Count was being served breakfast

as usual in his study, he sent for his brother. Raoul arrived, silent and gloomy, and the meeting was brief.

PHILIPPE: Read this!
(*He holds out a copy of the newspaper* L'Époque *and points to a particular item in the society column.*)
RAOUL (*reading disdainfully*): The latest story in the Faubourg is that Mlle Christine Daaé, the opera-singer, and Viscount Raoul de Chagny are engaged to be married. Rumour has it that Count Philippe, his elder brother, is very much averse to this union and has warned that, for the first time in the history of his family, the pledge would not be honoured. But since love conquers all – particularly at the Opera – how can Count Philippe succeed in preventing the Viscount from leading 'the new Marguerite' to the altar? The two brothers are said to be very close; but the Count is surely misguided in thinking that brotherly love will triumph over romantic love.
PHILIPPE (*sadly*): You see, Raoul, you are making us a laughing stock! That girl has completely turned your head with her ghost-stories.
(*Obviously the Viscount must have repeated Christine's tale to his brother.*)
RAOUL: Adieu, Philippe.
PHILIPPE: So you have made up your mind? And you are leaving tonight? (*No reply from the Viscount.*) With her? Can you not see that this is madness? (*Still no reply.*) Well, I intend to prevent it!
RAOUL: Adieu, Philippe!
(*He leaves.*)

This scene was described to the examining magistrate by the Count himself, who only saw Raoul again that evening at the Opera a few minutes before Christine's disappearance.

Raoul had spent the whole day preparing for their flight. The horses, the carriage, the coachman, the provisions, the luggage, the money required for the journey, the route to be taken – they would not travel by train so as to throw the Phantom off their trail – all this occupied him until nine o'clock in the evening.

At nine o'clock, a closed carriage with the curtains pulled across and the doors locked took its place in the rank outside the Opera House on the Rotunda side. It was drawn by two sturdy horses, driven by a coachman whose face was concealed in the long folds of a muffler. Three broughams stood in front of it. It was revealed later that these belonged respectively to Carlotta, who had suddenly returned to Paris, to Sorelli and, the one at the head of the rank, to Count Philippe de Chagny. No one left the closed carriage. The coachman remained seated on his box, as did the other three coachmen.

A shadow in a long black cloak and a soft black felt hat passed along the pavement between the Rotunda and the carriages. His attention seemed to focus on the fourth carriage. He drew close to the horses and to the coachman before moving away without saying a word. The examining magistrate would later conclude that this shadowy figure was Raoul de Chagny, but I do not believe this; for that evening, as usual, the Viscount was wearing a top hat, which was subsequently found. I am more inclined to think that the shadow was the Phantom, who knew all about the affair as the reader will soon discover.

By coincidence, it was *Faust* that was being performed that evening before a highly distinguished house. In those days, the subscribers did not lend nor rent their boxes to bankers, merchants and foreigners, whose company they shunned. But no longer: today the box of the Earl of X – which is still known as the Earl of X's box since the said Earl is its contractual owner – may well be occupied by a pork merchant who is perfectly entitled to lounge there with his family since he has paid the Earl for the privilege. This would have been practically unheard of in former times. Then Opera boxes were rather like salons where one could generally expect to meet or see fine society, some of whose members happened to be music lovers.

These fashionable patrons all knew each other: without being necessarily on visiting terms, they could put a name to every face; and the Count de Chagny was recognized by all. The story published that morning in *L'Époque* must have already had an effect, for all eyes were turned towards the box in which Count Philippe sat alone, nonchalant and ostensibly unmoved. The female members of the illustrious assembly appeared to be intrigued by it all, while the Viscount's absence gave rise to a thousand whispers behind fans.

Christine Daaé met with a rather cold reception. This distinguished gathering could not forgive her for having aimed so high. The singer sensed their hostility and was naturally upset by it. The regular patrons who claimed to know all about the Viscount's affairs of the heart smiled knowingly during certain of Marguerite's scenes. Thus they conspicuously turned to Philippe de Chagny in his box when Christine sang:

> 'I wish I could but know who was he
> That addressed me,
> If he was noble, or, at least, what his name is.'[1]

Seemingly indifferent to this show of interest, the Count simply sat there with his chin resting in his hand. He kept his eyes on the stage; but was he really watching? He appeared to be lost in thought.

Meanwhile Christine's self-assurance was gradually deserting her. She trembled. Disaster loomed. Carolus Fonta thought she might be ill and wondered if she would be able to hold the stage until the end of the garden act. The audience remembered that Carlotta's unfortunate 'croaks', which had so dramatically interrupted her Parisian career, had occurred at the end of this particular act.

Just then, Carlotta made her entrance in a box facing the stage, and created a sensation. Poor Christine noticed this fresh disturbance and recognized Carlotta. She thought she saw a sneer on her rival's lips; and that saved her. She cleared her mind and thus triumphed once more. From that moment, she sang with all her heart and soul. She tried to surpass all that she had achieved until then, and succeeded. In the last act, when she launched into the invocation to the angels and began to ascend, she set the whole audience a-quiver and carried them with her, making them feel as if they too had wings.

Responding to her unearthly call, a man in the audience rose to his feet and remained standing there facing the stage, uplifted. It was Raoul.

'Holy angel, in Heaven blessed . . .
Holy angel, in Heaven blessed . . .'[2]

Framed in the glory of her hair cascading over her bare shoulders, Christine, arms outstretched and throat ablaze, now intoned her sacred plea:

'My spirit longs with thee to rest!'[3]

. . . .

Suddenly the stage was plunged into darkness. But it was over so quickly that the spectators barely had time to cry out in surprise before light returned.

But Christine Daaé was no longer there! What had become of her? What miracle was this? The audience was aghast, and the excitement at once rose to a climax. The tension was no less high on the stage itself. Men rushed from the wings to the spot where Christine had been singing only moments ago and the commotion was such that the performance had to be interrupted.

Where, but where had Christine gone? By what magic had she been stolen from the thousands of eager spectators and from the arms of Carolus Fonta himself? In truth it was as if the angels had responded to her impassioned plea, and carried her up, body and soul, to rest in Heaven.

Raoul, still standing in the middle of the theatre, had cried out. Count Philippe had sprung to his feet in his box. Everyone in the house looked in turn to the stage, to the Count and to Raoul; they wondered if this curious event and the story in that morning's paper were somehow related. Then Raoul hurriedly left the house, the Count disappeared from his box, and the subscribers made a dash for the door leading to the wings, as the curtain was lowered. The rest of the audience awaited an announcement in an indescribable hubbub. Everyone spoke at once. Everyone tried to explain how it had happened. For some, Christine had fallen through a trap; for others, she had been lifted up into the flies, a victim of some failed stage effect pioneered by the new directors. Still others suggested foul play – surely the coincidence between her disappearance and the sudden darkness must mean something.

At last, the curtain slowly rose and Carolus Fonta stepped towards the conductor's podium.

'Ladies and gentlemen,' he announced in sad, grave tones, 'an unprecedented and deeply alarming incident has just occurred: our fellow-artist, Christine Daaé, has vanished before our very eyes and we know not how!'

XV

The Curious Incident of the Safety-pin

The stage became a scene of chaos beyond description. Artists, machinists, dancers, figurantes, supernumeraries, chorus singers, subscribers, all were asking questions, shouting, jostling.

'What happened to her?'

'She was abducted!'

'By the Viscount de Chagny, of course!'

'No, by the Count!'

'Ah, here comes Carlotta! She's behind it all!'

'No, it's the ghost! He did it.'

Some laughed, especially now that a careful examination of the traps and stage floor had ruled out the possibility of an accident.

Standing apart from this noisy throng, three men were conferring in low tones, with helpless gesticulations. They were: Gabriel, the chorus-master; Mercier, the administrator; and Rémy, the secretary. Having withdrawn to a corner of the lobby, between the stage and the large corridor leading to the Ballet Room, they were engaged in conversation behind some bulky stage properties.

'I knocked on the door. But there was no answer. They might not have been in the office. But we can't be sure as they have the keys.'

Thus spoke Rémy, who was evidently referring to the directors. During the last interval, they had intimated that they were not to be disturbed by anybody, whatever the reason.

'All the same,' insisted Gabriel, 'a singer who disappears from the stage during a performance is hardly a daily occurrence!'

'Did you explain it to them through the door?' asked Mercier, impatiently.

'I'll go back to them,' said Rémy, rushing off.

Thereupon the stage manager arrived. 'We need you, M. Mercier. What are you doing here?' he exclaimed. 'Come along!'

'I shall neither move, do, nor say anything before the inspector arrives,' replied Mercier. 'I have sent for Mifroid. When he arrives, we shall see!'

'But you ought to go down to the organ at once.'

'Not before the inspector arrives.'

'I've already been down there myself.'

'So, what did you see?'

'There was no one there! Do you realize what this means?'

'What do you expect me to do about it?'

'Why, nothing!' said the stage manager, frantically raking his fingers through his unruly hair. 'Nothing! All the same, if someone had been there, that person might have been able to tell us why the stage was suddenly plunged into darkness and how it happened. But Mauclair cannot be found.'

Mauclair was the chief gas-man and so controlled the stage lighting.

'Mauclair cannot be found?' repeated Mercier, shaken. 'What about his assistants?'

'Neither Mauclair nor his assistants can be found! There's no one at the lights, I'm telling you!' roared the stage manager. 'Obviously the girl didn't disappear all by herself! Someone else must have been involved. And now we've lost the directors! I gave orders that no one should be allowed to go down there and posted a fireman in front of the organ. Was that right?'

'Yes, yes, quite right. Now we must wait for the inspector.'

As the stage manager walked off, raging, he shrugged his shoulders and muttered something unflattering about those 'softies' who did nothing but cower in a corner while the whole theatre was 'turned upside down'.

Gabriel and Mercier would have liked to do something. Only they had received explicit orders that impeded them: on no account whatsoever were the managers to be disturbed. Rémy had contravened that order, but without success.

He returned from his latest attempt, looking bewildered and at a loss.

'Well, have you talked to them?' asked Mercier.

'Moncharmin finally opened the door this time. He glared at me and, for a moment, I thought he meant to hit me. I couldn't get a word in and – you'll never believe this – he yelled at me: "Do you have a safety-pin? No? Well, then, go away!" I tried to explain the situation to him, but he kept shouting: "A safety-pin! Someone, bring me a safety-pin! Now!" A clerk who had heard him – he made such a racket – ran up with a safety-pin and gave it to him. Whereupon Moncharmin slammed the door in my face. And that was that!'

'Did you not tell him that Christine Daaé . . . ?'

'You couldn't have done any better! He was seething. He could think of nothing but his safety-pin. And if he had not been given one there and then, I think he would have had a fit! There's definitely something wrong: our directors are going mad!'

The secretary was peeved and he let it be known: 'This can't go on! I will not be treated like this!'

Then suddenly Gabriel whispered: 'This is another of P. of the O.'s tricks!'

Rémy guffawed. Mercier sighed and seemed about to say something, when he noticed Gabriel motioning him to say nothing and checked himself, but, feeling the burden of responsibility weigh heavier and heavier on his shoulders as the minutes passed and the managers failed to show up, he eventually burst out: 'Right, I'll go and talk to them myself!'

Gabriel, suddenly sombre and grave, held him back. 'Beware, Mercier! If they're staying in their office, it may be because they have to! P. of the O. has more than one trick up his sleeve!'

But Mercier shook his head. 'No matter! I'm going! If people had listened to me, the police would have been informed of all this long ago.' And he left.

'What does he mean by "all this"? *All this* what?' asked Rémy. 'What is there to tell the police? Answer me, Gabriel. You know something! What's going on? You had better come clean if you don't want me to tell the world that you're all going mad. Yes, quite mad!'

Gabriel rolled up his eyes and pretended not to understand the private secretary's unseemly outburst. 'What "something" am I supposed to know?' he murmured. 'Tell me.'

Rémy became exasperated: 'Tonight, in this very house, Richard and Moncharmin were behaving like lunatics during the interval.'

'I never noticed that,' muttered Gabriel, glumly.

'Then you're the only one! Do you think I didn't see them? Do you think that M. Parabise, the director of the Crédit Central, didn't notice anything? And that M. de La Borderie, the ambassador, is blind? All the subscribers were pointing at our directors. You must have seen them!'

'But what did our directors do exactly?' asked Gabriel with an innocent air.

'What did they do? You know better than anyone what they were doing! You were there! You were watching them, and you and Mercier were the only two who didn't laugh.'

'I don't understand!' Unmoved and tight-lipped, Gabriel raised his arms and let them drop to his sides, in a gesture obviously meant to convey that the matter was of no interest whatever to him.

'Explain it to me!' Rémy insisted. '*Why won't they let anyone come near them?*'

'What? *They won't let anyone come near them?*'

'No. *They're keeping everyone at arm's length!*'

'Really? You actually saw this? I admit that *is* odd!'

'Oh, so you agree! At last! And another thing: *they walk backwards!*'

'Backwards? You have seen our managers walk backwards? Why, I thought that only crayfish walked backwards!'

'Don't laugh, Gabriel! This is no laughing matter!'

'I'm not laughing,' protested Gabriel, looking as solemn as a judge.

'Perhaps you can tell me this, Gabriel, since you are such an intimate friend of the directors: when I saw Richard outside the Ballet Room during the interval after the garden act and went up to him to shake his hand, why did Moncharmin urge me in a whisper to keep away? "Keep your distance!" he said.

"Whatever you do, do not touch the director!" Anyone would have thought I had the plague!'

'Incredible!'

'And, moments later, when the ambassador went up to Richard, did you not see Moncharmin hastily step between them and hear him say: "Monsieur, I beg you, please do not touch the director"?'

'It's beyond belief! And what about Richard? What was he doing?'

'What was he doing? Why, you saw him! He turned aside and bowed – though there was no one there – before withdrawing *backwards*.'

'Backwards?'

'And Moncharmin, following Richard's example, also turned on his heels and walked away *backwards*! And they kept on *like that* until they reached the staircase leading to the directors' office: *backwards, backwards, and backwards!* If they haven't lost their minds, could you please explain to me what all this means?'

'Perhaps they were rehearsing the steps of a ballet,' suggested Gabriel, with little conviction in his voice.

Rémy was furious. How could he joke like this at such a moment? He frowned, pursed his lips and then, leaning over, whispered to Gabriel: 'Stop pretending! There are things going on, for which you and Mercier might be held partly responsible.'

'What do you mean?' asked Gabriel.

'Christine Daaé is not the only one who vanished tonight.'

'Oh, nonsense!'

'Not at all! Perhaps you can tell me why, when Mme Giry came down to the Ballet Room just now, Mercier took her by the hand and quickly led her away?'

'Really?' said Gabriel. 'I didn't notice.'

'Oh yes, you did, Gabriel, for you followed Mercier and Mme Giry all the way to Mercier's office. And since then, while you and Mercier are still about, Mme Giry is nowhere to be seen.'

'What? Do you think we ate her?'

'No, you locked her up in Mercier's office; and anyone passing can hear her yelling: "Oh, the scoundrels! The villains!" '

At this point in the bizarre conversation, Mercier arrived, quite out of breath. 'Well, this is just going too far!' he said in a despondent voice. 'I shouted: "It is a serious matter! Open the door! It is I, Mercier." I heard footsteps. The door opened and Moncharmin appeared. He was very pale. He said: "What do you want?" I answered: "Christine Daaé has disappeared." And what do you think he replied? "Good for her!" And just before he shut the door, he put this in my hand.'

Mercier opened his hand. Rémy and Gabriel looked.

'The safety-pin!' cried the secretary.

'Strange! Very strange!' muttered Gabriel, who could not help shuddering.

Suddenly a voice made the three of them turn round: 'I beg your pardon, gentlemen. Could you tell me where I can find Christine Daaé?'

The question seemed so absurd that they would, no doubt, have burst out laughing despite the gravity of the situation, had they not found themselves staring at a face so grief-stricken that they were seized with pity at once. It was the face of Viscount Raoul de Chagny.

XVI

'Christine! Christine!'

Raoul's first thought, after Christine Daaé's extraordinary disappearance, was to suspect Erik. He no longer doubted the almost supernatural powers of the Angel of Music in those regions of the Opera House that had fallen under his diabolical rule. Frantic with love and despair, the young man rushed on to the stage.

'Christine! Christine!' he wailed, calling to her as she must now be calling to him from the depths of the dark abyss into which the monster had carried her like a prey, still quivering with sacred exaltation and shrouded in the white robe that she wore when she offered herself to the angels in Heaven.

'Christine! Christine!' repeated Raoul, who thought he could hear her screams through the tenuous boards that separated her from him. He held his head to one side, listening, as he distractedly wandered about the stage. Ah, how he longed to descend into that pit of darkness whose entrances were now all closed to him!

The trap doors, which normally slid open so easily to reveal the abyss he yearned to reach – those boards that creaked underfoot and sounded hollow under his weight because of the vast emptiness beneath – would not move tonight. More than that, it was as if they were fixed in place, as if they had never opened before. And now there were instructions barring anyone from using the stairs that led below stage!

'Christine! Christine!'

People jostled the pitiful young man, laughing. They mocked him, thinking that he had lost his mind.

In what frenzy and through which dark and mysterious passages, known to him alone, had Erik carried that innocent child to his odious lair and the Louis-Philippe room by the infernal lake?

'Christine! Christine! Answer me! Are you still alive? Or have you already expired under the searing breath of the monster in a moment of insurmountable horror?' Hideous thoughts flashed through Raoul's agitated mind. Of course, Erik had discovered their secret and found out that Christine had betrayed his trust. And now he was taking his revenge! The Angel of Music would stop at nothing after such a blow to his overweening pride. Trapped in the powerful embrace of the monster, Christine was lost!

Raoul recalled the golden stars that had lurked on his balcony the night before. If only he could have shot them out of existence! Some people have eyes which dilate in the dark and shine like stars or cats' eyes; some albinos even have rabbits' eyes by day and cats' eyes at night. Yes, yes, it must have been Erik on the balcony that night. If only he had killed him! The monster had climbed up the drain-pipe like a cat or a criminal, who need little more to make good their escape. At that time, Erik must have been planning some decisive move against Raoul, but, once wounded, he had fled and turned, instead, against poor Christine.

Such were Raoul's harrowing thoughts as he ran to the singer's dressing-room.

'Christine! Christine!' At the sight of the clothes, spread out over the furniture, which his beautiful fiancée had meant to wear at the hour of their flight, the young man wept bitter, scalding tears. Oh, why had she refused to leave earlier? Why had she waited? Why had she tempted fate and indulged the monster's feelings? Why had she, in an act of supreme pity and as a final offering to him, sung her celestial plea:

> 'Holy angel, in Heaven blessed,
> My spirit longs with thee to rest!'

Sobs mingled with oaths and insults as Raoul ran his hands tentatively over the large mirror that he had seen open one night to take Christine through to the shadowy world beyond. He pushed, pressed and fumbled about; but the mirror seemed to obey only Erik. Perhaps no action was required with such a mirror. Perhaps it was enough to utter certain words. As a young boy, he had heard that some objects obeyed a spoken command.

Suddenly, Raoul recalled mention of a gate in the Rue Scribe and an underground passage running straight from the street to the lake. Yes, Christine had told him about that. And, although the key was no longer in the box where she kept it, Raoul hastened to the Rue Scribe. Once in the street, he passed his trembling hands over the huge stones that made up the walls of the Opera House, feeling for openings. He came upon iron bars. Were these the right ones? Or these? Or could this be that air-vent? He peered through the bars, but could see nothing. It was so dark in there! He listened, but all was silence! He walked round the building and came to even bigger bars, huge gates opening on to the courtyard of the administrative wing.

Raoul ran to the concierge's lodge. 'Excuse me, madame, could you please tell me where to find a gate, a door with bars – iron bars – leading from the Rue Scribe to the lake? The lake! You know, the underground lake beneath the Opera House.'

'Yes, I know there is a lake under the Opera House, monsieur, but I don't know which door leads to it. I've never been there!' the woman replied.

'And the Rue Scribe? I suppose you have never been there either?'

The woman laughed. She burst into laughter! Raoul fled, raging. He ran up some stairs, down others, through the whole of the administrative wing and finally found himself once more under the bright stage lights. He came to a halt, panting, with his heart pounding in his chest: perhaps Christine had been found! He saw a small crowd gathered there, and asked: 'Messieurs, have you, by any chance, seen Christine Daaé?'

Some of them laughed. The stage was buzzing with a new rumour and, amidst the throng of black coats, all talking and gesticulating together, appeared a man who, by constrast, seemed very calm. He had a pink, chubby, thoroughly pleasant countenance, framed with curly hair and lit up with a pair of wonderfully serene blue eyes.

'This is the gentleman to whom you should put that question, monsieur. Let me introduce Inspector Mifroid,' said Mercier, pointing out the newcomer to Raoul.

'Ah, M. de Chagny! Delighted to meet you!' said the inspector. 'Would you be so good as to follow me? And now where are the directors? Where are they?'

Seeing that Mercier remained silent, Rémy, the secretary, volunteered the information that the directors had locked themselves in their office and as yet knew nothing of the recent event.

'Is that possible? Let us go there!' And Mifroid, followed by a growing crowd, made his way to the administrative wing. (Mercier took advantage of the confusion to slip a key into Gabriel's hand: 'This is all going very badly,' he whispered. 'You had best let Mme Giry out.' Whereupon Gabriel left.)

They soon came to the directors' door, which remained firmly shut despite Mercier's entreaties.

'Open up in the name of the law!' commanded Inspector Mifroid, in a loud, somewhat concerned voice. At last the door opened. The inspector entered the room and everyone rushed in after him.

Raoul was last, but as he was about to cross the threshold, a hand was laid on his shoulder and he heard these words whispered into his ear: '*Erik's secrets are his, and his alone!*' He turned around, stifling a cry. The hand resting on his shoulder was now raised to the lips of a man with ebony skin and eyes of jade, wearing an astrakhan hat: the Persian! The stranger repeated his gesture urging silence and then, just as the astonished Viscount was about to ask the reason for this mysterious intervention, the man bowed and disappeared.

XVII

*Mme Giry's Astonishing Revelations as to Her
Knowledge of the Phantom of the Opera*

Before we follow Inspector Mifroid into the directors' office
the reader must allow me to relate certain extraordinary events,
which had just taken place in the room to which Rémy and
Mercier had vainly tried to gain access. Messrs Richard and
Moncharmin had locked themselves in for a purpose, as yet
unknown, but which it is my duty, as a chronicler, to reveal
without further ado.

I have previously had occasion to say that the directors'
mood had taken a disagreeable turn, and have suggested that
this might not have been solely caused by the fall of the chandelier.

Reader, let me tell you now what the directors would rather
have kept for ever a secret: some time before the fateful night
of Christine's disappearance, the Phantom of the Opera had
been quietly paid his first twenty thousand francs. Oh, there
had been some wailing and gnashing of teeth! All the same, the
delivery had taken place in the simplest possible manner.

One morning the directors found on their table an envelope
addressed to 'P. of the O. *(private)*' with a note from the Phantom himself:

> The time has come for you to fulfil one of your obligations under
> the terms of my memorandum. Please put twenty notes of a thou-
> sand francs each into this envelope, seal it with your personal
> stamp and hand it to Mme Giry, who will do what is necessary.

The directors responded at once, without wasting any time
pondering how this diabolical note had found its way into a

room they always kept carefully locked. They saw this as an opportunity to catch the mysterious blackmailer. So, after disclosing everything, under a pledge of secrecy, to Gabriel and Mercier, they put the twenty thousand francs into the envelope and, without questioning her, handed it to Mme Giry, who had been reinstated in her functions. She showed no surprise but, needless to say, she was closely watched. She went straight to the Phantom's box and placed the precious envelope on the little shelf under the ledge. The two directors, together with Gabriel and Mercier, concealed themselves so as to keep sight of the envelope at all times during the performance and afterwards. As the envelope did not move, neither did they; and they were still at their post long after the theatre had emptied and Mme Giry had gone home. Tired of waiting, and having ascertained that the seals had not been broken, they finally opened the envelope.

At first, Richard and Moncharmin thought that their notes were still there. They soon realized, however, that this was not the case: the twenty genuine notes were gone and had been replaced with twenty fake ones, each with a 'promise to pay the bearer' from the 'Bank of Farce'! The directors were furious, and frightened too.

'Robert-Houdin himself could not have done better,'[1] cried Gabriel.

'No doubt, but he would have cost us less!' rejoined Richard.

Moncharmin wanted to send for the police, but Richard disagreed. He must have had a plan, for he said: 'Let's not make fools of ourselves! We'd be a laughing stock. The Phantom has won the first round: we'll win the second.' He was obviously thinking of the next monthly instalment.

All the same, they had been so thoroughly duped that they could not help feeling somewhat dejected during the following weeks, and understandably so. The reason why the directors did not call the police was that deep down they still entertained the idea that this whole situation, strange as it might appear, was no more than a vile practical joke undoubtedly visited upon them by their predecessors. Thus they felt that it was better to keep it to themselves for the time being. Besides, Mon-charmin had the faint suspicion that Richard himself, who was occasionally given to whimsical pranks, might have a hand in it. So, bracing themselves for all contingencies, they awaited further events. They had arranged to keep Mme Giry under close watch, but at Richard's insistence she was told nothing.

'If she's an accomplice,' he said, 'the notes went long ago. But, in my opinion, she's just an idiot.'

'She is not the only idiot in this affair,' added Moncharmin pensively.

'No one could have foreseen any of this!' said Richard mis-erably. 'But have no fear: next time, I'll have taken all necessary precautions.'

And the next time fell on the very day of Christine Daaé's dramatic disappearance.

In the morning, they received a note from the Phantom kindly reminding them that a fresh instalment was due: 'Do just as you did last time. *It went very well.* Put the twenty thou-sand francs in the envelope and hand it to the trusty Mme Giry.' The note was accompanied as before by a self-addressed envelope. All they had to do was put the money inside. This was to be carried out that very evening, just half an hour before the curtain rose on the first act of *Faust.* And it is at this junc-ture, half an hour before the beginning of that all too memorable performance, that we join the directors in their office.

Richard showed the envelope to Moncharmin, counted the twenty thousand franc notes and slipped them into the enve-lope, but without sealing it.

'And now,' he said, 'call Mme Giry.'

She entered, dropping a deep curtsey. She still sported her black taffeta dress, now worn to shades of rust and lilac, and her dingy hat with the feathers. She appeared to be in a good mood.

'Good evening, gentlemen!' she said. 'You have called me in to deliver the envelope, I presume.'

'Yes, Mme Giry,' said Richard, most amicably, 'the envelope and something else besides.'

'At your service, M. Richard, at your service! And what is this "something else", pray?'

'First of all, Mme Giry, I have a little question to ask.'

'By all means, M. Richard. Mme Giry is here and ready to answer any question.'

'Are you still on good terms with the Phantom?'

'Couldn't be better, monsieur. Couldn't be better!'

'Ah, we are delighted to hear it. Now Mme Giry,' said Richard in a most confiding tone. 'Between ourselves, there is no need to pretend. You are no fool!'

'Why, monsieur!' she exclaimed, at which point the gentle swaying of the black feathers on her dingy hat ceased. 'No one has ever doubted that, I assure you!'

'Of course not, which is why we'll understand each other. Now, all this about the Phantom is nothing more than a trick, isn't it? And, between ourselves, it's wearing thin.'

The attendant looked at the directors as if they were talking nonsense. She walked up to Richard's desk and asked, rather anxiously: 'What do you mean? I don't understand.'

'Oh yes, you do. You understand very well! And now you're going to tell us the truth. First of all, what's his name?'

'Whose name?'

'The name of whoever has made you his accomplice, Mme Giry!'

'Me, the Phantom's accomplice? His accomplice in what, pray?'

'You do all his bidding.'

'Oh! He's no trouble, you know.'

'And does he still leave you tips?'

'I can't complain.'

'How much do you get for bringing him the envelope?'

'Ten francs.'

'Upon my word! That's cheap!'

'Why?'

'I'll tell you presently, Mme Giry. But first of all tell us why on earth you have given yourself over, body and soul, to this ghost. Surely Mme Giry's friendship and loyalty are worth more than five or ten francs.'

'Quite true. And there's no shame in it, I can tell you! On the contrary!'

'We believe you, Mme Giry.'

'Well, it's like this . . . Only . . . the Phantom doesn't like me to talk about his business.'

'Indeed!' sneered Richard.

'But since this particular matter concerns only me, I'll tell you. One evening, in Box Five, I found a letter addressed to me – a kind of note written in red ink. I know it by heart, and shall never forget it, even if I live to be a hundred!'

Upon which Mme Giry, straightening herself, recited the letter to Richard and Moncharmin with touching eloquence:

MADAME, – In 1825, Mlle Ménétrier, leader of the ballet, became the Marchioness of Cussy. – In 1832, Mlle Marie Taglioni, a dancer, married Count Gilbert des Voisins. – In 1846, Sota, a dancer, married one of the brothers of the King of Spain. – In 1847, Lola Montez, a dancer, became the morganatic wife of King Louis of Bavaria and Countess of Landsfeld. – In 1848, Mlle Maria, a dancer, became the Baroness of Hermeville. – In 1870, Thérèse Hessler, a dancer, married Don Fernando, brother to the King of Portugal . . .[2]

As she listed these illustrious nuptials, the attendant became more animated; she drew herself up with some defiance and, like an inspired sibyl, finally launched into the last sentence of the prophetic letter in a voice bursting with pride: 'In 1885, Meg Giry shall become Empress!'[3]

Then, exhausted by this supreme effort, she dropped into a chair.

'Gentlemen,' she added, 'the note was signed: "The Phantom of the Opera". I had heard of the ghost before that, but only half believed in him. However, from the day he declared that my little Meg, my own flesh and blood, the fruit of my womb, would become Empress, I believed in him wholeheartedly.'

There was no need to scrutinize further Mme Giry's elated expression to realize what wonders the two words 'Phantom' and 'Empress' could work on her fine intellect. But who held the strings of this absurd puppet? That was the question.

'So you've never seen him, he speaks to you and you believe all he says. Is that it?' asked Moncharmin.

'Yes. First, he's the one I have to thank for my little Meg's promotion to leader of a row. I said to him: "If she's going to be Empress in 1885, there's no time to lose;[4] she must become leader at once."

'He agreed and only had to say a few words to M. Poligny and it was done.'

'So M. Poligny saw him!'

'No, no more than I did; but he heard him. The Phantom spoke in his ear – you know, that evening when he left Box Five looking so dreadfully pale.'

Moncharmin let out a sigh.

'What a story . . .' he groaned.

'Oh,' added Mme Giry, 'I always thought there were secrets between M. Poligny and the Phantom. He did everything the Phantom asked of him. He would not refuse him anything.'

'You hear, Richard? Poligny would not refuse the Phantom anything.'

'Yes, yes, I hear!' said Richard. 'M. Poligny is a friend of the Phantom; and Mme Giry is a friend of M. Poligny, so what?' he rasped. 'I am not interested in Poligny. At this moment, the only person whose fate is of real concern to me is Mme Giry. Mme Giry, do you know what is in this envelope?'

'Why, of course not,' she said.

'Well, have a look!'

As she peered into the envelope her baffled countenance suddenly lit up. 'Thousand-franc notes!' she cried.

'Yes, Mme Giry, thousand-franc notes! And you knew it!'

'Me, monsieur? Me? I swear . . .'

'Don't swear, Mme Giry! Now I'll tell you the second reason why I sent for you: I am going to have you arrested.'

The two black feathers on her dingy hat, which were usually in the shape of question marks, turned instantly into exclamation marks; as for the hat itself, it wobbled menacingly atop her quivering bun. In surprise, indignation, protest and alarm, Little Meg's mother turned and, performing an extraordinary pirouette – half leap, half gliding step – brought her offended righteousness to within inches of Richard's nose; he could not but recoil.

'Have me arrested!' The mouth that spoke these words seemed ready to spit its three remaining teeth into Richard's face.

He conducted himself like a hero: he retreated no further. 'I am going to have you arrested, Mme Giry, as a thief!' he said, pointing an accusing finger at her as if before an imaginary court.

'Say that again!' snapped Mme Giry. Whereupon she delivered an almighty slap to the director's face before Moncharmin had time to intervene. What avenging wrath! But it was not the wrinkled hand of the outraged attendant that landed on the directorial cheek but the envelope itself – the magic envelope, the cause of all the trouble. At that moment it tore open, thus releasing the bank-notes, which fluttered and whirled about the room like a fantastic flight of giant butterflies.

The two directors yelped and, the same thought having driven them both to their knees, they feverishly picked up the precious notes and hastened to examine them.

'*Are they still the real ones*, Moncharmin?'

'*Are they still the real ones*, Richard?'

'Yes, they are still the real ones!'

Towering above them, Mme Giry's three teeth chattered with vile interjections. But all that could be clearly heard was this leitmotiv: 'Me, a thief! A thief, me?'

She choked, she screamed: 'This is just too much!' And, suddenly, she drew up to Richard again. 'Anyway, M. Richard,' she barked, '*you surely know better than me what became of the twenty thousand francs!*'

'I?' asked Richard, astounded. 'Why should I know?'

A stern, alarmed Moncharmin at once demanded that the good lady explain herself. 'What do you mean, Mme Giry?' he asked. 'Why do you claim that M. Richard surely knows *better than you* what became of the twenty thousand francs?'

At this, Richard, who felt himself flushing under Moncharmin's glare, took Mme Giry's arm and shook it violently. His voice rumbled, roared and cracked like thunder. 'Why should I know better than you what became of the twenty thousand francs? Why? Answer me!'

'Because they went into your pocket!' she gasped, staring at him as if he were the Devil incarnate.

Now it was Richard's turn to be under attack: Mme Giry's unexpected retort, and his co-director's increasingly suspicious looks, struck him like a bolt from the blue. Unfortunately, instead of mustering his arguments to defend himself from so despicable an accusation, he lashed out.

So it is that a perfectly innocent man at peace with his conscience may appear guilty when taken aback by an unwarranted charge. Under the blow, he turns pale, flushes, reels, rises or sinks – keeping silent when he ought to speak, speaking when he ought to say nothing, remaining cool when he ought to break into a sweat, and sweating when he ought to stay cool.

Stepping forward, Moncharmin opportunely stayed the hand of the innocent Richard and hastened calmly to resume questioning Mme Giry. 'How can you suspect my partner, M. Richard, of putting twenty thousand francs in his pocket?' he asked encouragingly.

'I never said that, since it was me who put the twenty thousand francs into M. Richard's pocket,' declared Mme Giry, adding to herself: 'Too late! I've said it! May the Phantom forgive me!'

Richard began to yell at her again, but Moncharmin ordered him, in no uncertain manner, to be quiet. 'Please! Let the woman explain herself. Let me question her. Why are you behaving so strangely? The mystery is about to be resolved, why should you be furious? Personally I find all this most amusing.'

Mme Giry raised her head, martyr-like, her face radiant with belief in her own innocence. 'You tell me there were twenty thousand francs in the envelope I put into M. Richard's pocket; but, as I have said, I didn't know! Neither did M. Richard, for that matter!'

'Aha!' said Richard, whose sudden bravado grated upon Moncharmin. 'So, I didn't know either! You put twenty thousand francs in my pocket and I knew nothing about it! I am pleased to hear it, Mme Giry!'

'True,' the formidable lady continued, 'neither of us knew anything about it. But later you must have found that money in your pocket!'

At this Richard would certainly have assaulted the attendant, had Moncharmin not been there. But Moncharmin protected her and quickly resumed his questioning.

'What kind of envelope did you put in M. Richard's pocket? It cannot have been the one we gave you – the one with the twenty thousand francs that we saw you take to Box Five.'

'I beg your pardon. The envelope that monsieur gave me was indeed the one that I slipped into monsieur's pocket,' explained Mme Giry. 'The one I took to the Phantom's box was another envelope just like it, which the Phantom had given me beforehand and which I hid up my sleeve.' With these words, Mme Giry took from her sleeve a ready-prepared envelope, identical – down to the addressee – to that containing the twenty thousand francs.

The directors snatched it from her and, as they examined it, noticed that it bore their own stamp. They broke the seals and found that the envelope contained twenty notes from the Bank of Farce, like the ones that had so surprised them the previous month.

'How simple!' said Richard.

'How simple!' Moncharmin echoed, solemnly.

'The simple tricks are always the best,' exclaimed Richard. 'All you need is an accomplice.'

'Mme Giry, for instance,' added Moncharmin in a toneless voice. 'So,' he continued, with his eyes fixed upon the attendant as if to mesmerize her, 'it was the Phantom who gave you this envelope and told you to substitute it for the one we gave you? And it was the Phantom again who told you to put our envelope into M. Richard's pocket?'

'Yes, it was the Phantom!'

'Then, Mme Giry, would you be so good as to demonstrate for us your deft hands at work? Here is the envelope. Act as if we knew nothing.'

'As you please, gentlemen.' Mme Giry took the envelope containing the twenty notes and made for the door.

She was about to leave the room when the two directors rushed forward to stop her: 'Oh, no! Oh, no! You've already fooled us once!'

'I beg your pardon, gentlemen,' she apologized, 'but you told me to act as if you knew nothing. Well, if you knew nothing, you'd let me leave with the envelope!'

'But then how could you slip it into my pocket?' questioned Richard, whom Moncharmin was observing with his left eye, while his right eye was busy watching Mme Giry – a cause of considerable strain, but Moncharmin would go to any length to discover the truth.

'I am to slip it into your pocket when you least expect it, monsieur. As you know, I always take a walk backstage during the evening, and I often go with my daughter to the Ballet Room, which I am entitled to do as her mother. I carry her shoes for the *divertissement*,[5] and even her little watering-can. In fact, I come and go as I please. So do the subscribers, and so do you, monsieur. There are many people about. So while passing behind you, I slipped the envelope into the back-pocket of your coat. It was quite simple! There was no magic involved at all!'

'No magic?' roared Richard, rolling his eyes like a thundering Jove. 'No magic? You're lying and I've just caught you out, you wretched hag!'

The honourable lady was less sensitive to the insult than to the assault on her honesty. She bristled, baring her three teeth: 'What?'

'You're lying, because I spent the entire evening watching Box Five, where you had left the fake envelope. I never went to the Ballet Room.'

'Quite right, monsieur, but I didn't give you the envelope that evening. I slipped it into your pocket at the next performance, on the evening when the under-secretary of state for Fine Arts . . .'

At these words, Richard suddenly interrupted her: 'Yes! Oh yes, I remember now! The under-secretary came backstage, asking for me. I went to the Ballet Room and stood for a moment on the steps – the under-secretary and his chief clerk were down in the room itself. I suddenly felt someone brushing against me. So I turned around, and there was no one behind me but you, Mme Giry. Oh, I can see it now!'

'Yes, I'd just done it. That pocket of yours, monsieur, is very handy!' To demonstrate, Mme Giry now passed behind Richard and slipped the envelope into one of his back-pockets so deftly that Moncharmin himself – who had both eyes on her this time – was impressed.

'Of course!' exclaimed Richard, looking a little pale. 'How clever of the Phantom. By going about it this way, his only quandary was how to avail himself of our money without involving anyone else. His solution was to come and take the envelope from my pocket since I would not notice it, having no idea that it was there. Admirable!'

'Oh, undoubtedly!' Moncharmin agreed. 'Only, you forget, Richard, that I provided ten thousand of the twenty thousand francs but nobody put anything in my pocket!'

XVIII

*Continuation of 'The Curious
Incident of the Safety-pin'*

Moncharmin's last statement had made his suspicions of his
partner so abundantly clear that a stormy confrontation ensued,
with the result that Richard agreed to all Moncharmin's wishes
so as to discover the villain who was making fools of them.

This brings us back to the interval following the garden act,
when Rémy – who never missed anything – observed with
interest the singular behaviour of the directors. Now we should
have no difficulty in understanding why they behaved in so
extravagant and undignified a manner, clearly at odds with
what one would expect of directors of the Opera House.

Their conduct had been dictated by the box attendant's
recent revelations: 1. Richard was to repeat exactly what he
had done on the night of the disappearance of the first twenty
thousand francs; 2. Moncharmin was to keep constant watch
over the pocket into which Mme Giry was to slip the second
twenty thousand francs.

Richard went and stood on the very spot where he had
bowed to the under-secretary for Fine Arts, and Moncharmin
took up a position a few steps behind him. Mme Giry brushed
past Richard and delivered the twenty thousand francs into the
back-pocket of his tail-coat. Whereupon she disappeared, or
rather was spirited away.

A few moments earlier, Moncharmin had instructed Mercier
to take the good lady to the administrator's office and lock her
in so as to make it impossible for her to communicate with the
Phantom. Mercier carried out his instructions and Mme Giry
was easily led away. The threat of exposure had had its effect:
now she looked like a poor, haggard, dishevelled bird, fearfully

rolling her beady eyes as she fancied she already heard the foot-steps of a police inspector in the corridor outside; and her sighs were such as would have reduced even the marble columns of the grand staircase to tears.

Meanwhile, Richard was bobbing, bowing and walking backwards, as if greeting that all-powerful government official, the under-secretary for Fine Arts. Whereas this show of civility would have seemed quite in order had the under-secretary of state actually been present, it was, in his absence, so unwar-ranted as to provoke considerable astonishment – understandably so. Richard greeted empty space, bowed to no one, and backed away from nothing. A few steps behind, Moncharmin, re-enacting his own movements, pushed aside Rémy, his secretary, and begged both the ambassador and the director of the Crédit Central not to 'touch M. Richard'.

Moncharmin, who had his suspicions, wanted to ensure that his colleague could not later claim, should the twenty thousand francs disappear again, that the ambassador or the director of the Crédit Central, or even Rémy himself, might be to blame. All the more so since Richard, by his own account, had not met anyone after Mme Giry had brushed past him on the evening of the first instalment. This being so, why should he meet anyone on the way back to the directorial office on the day of the re-enactment? I ask you! All the same, having begun by walking backwards in order to bow, Richard continued to do so for the sake of caution until he reached the corridor of the administra-tive wing. Thus his back was constantly under Moncharmin's scrutiny while he himself kept an eye on anyone approaching from the front.

This novel gait, as practised backstage by the directors of our National Academy of Music, did not go unnoticed; but for-tunately for those two gentlemen, most of the ballet-girls were in their dressing-rooms at the time. Otherwise there would have been no end of laughter and amusement.

But the directors thought only of their twenty thousand francs.

Upon reaching the gloomy corridor of the administrative wing, Richard turned to Moncharmin and whispered: 'I am sure that nobody has touched me. Why not keep at some distance from me now and discreetly watch me until I reach the office, so as to be able to see what happens without arousing suspicion?'

'No, Richard, no! You walk on ahead and I'll keep *right* behind you!' Moncharmin replied.

'But that way,' exclaimed Richard, 'our twenty thousand francs will never get stolen!'

'I should hope not!' declared Moncharmin.

'Then, what we're doing is absurd!'

'We are doing exactly what we did last time. Last time, I joined you as you were leaving the stage and followed close *behind you* down this corridor.'

'That's true,' Richard meekly agreed. He shook his head and did as he was told.

Two minutes later the two directors locked themselves in their office and Moncharmin pocketed the key.

'We both stayed here in this room, that night,' he said, 'until you left the Opera to go home.'

'Yes. And were we disturbed by anyone?'

'No, we were not.'

'Then,' said Richard, thinking back, 'then surely I must have been robbed on my way home from the Opera.'

'No,' said Moncharmin, growing increasingly unsympathetic, 'that's impossible since I took you home myself. The twenty thousand francs *must have disappeared when you got home*: I am absolutely sure of that.'

'I can't believe it!' protested Richard. 'I'm sure of my servants and if one of them had done it, he would have disappeared by now.'

Moncharmin shrugged his shoulders as if to say that such details were of no concern to him. Richard was beginning to find Moncharmin's attitude insufferable.

'Moncharmin, I've had enough of this!'

'Richard, I've had too much of it!'

'You suspect me?'

'Yes, I suspect you of a stupid practical joke.'

'One doesn't joke with twenty thousand francs.'

'I couldn't agree more,' declared Moncharmin, unfolding a newspaper and ostentatiously leafing through it.

'What are you doing?' asked Richard. 'You're going to read the paper now, are you?'

'Yes, Richard, until I take you home.'

'Like last time?'

'Yes, like last time.'

Richard snatched the paper from Moncharmin, who rose with palpable irritation, only to find himself confronted by an exasperated Richard standing there with his arms folded across his chest in an age-old gesture of defiance. 'Listen!' he said. 'Suppose that, having spent the evening alone with you and then been taken home by you, I noticed, as you bade me good-night, that the twenty thousand francs had disappeared from my coat-pocket, like last time. *Do you know what I might think?*'

'No, what might you think?' asked Moncharmin, flushing crimson.

'Well, since you never left me and you were, at your own insistence, the only one who could approach me, like last time, I might think that, if the money was no longer in my pocket, it was probably in yours!'

Moncharmin flinched at the suggestion. '*Oh,*' he shouted, '*but for a safety-pin!*'

'What do you want with a safety-pin?'

'To pin you! I need a safety-pin!'

'You want to "pin" me?'

'Yes, to pin the twenty thousand francs in your pocket! Then, whether it happens here, on the drive to your home or there, you will feel the hand that pulls at your pocket and you will see for yourself that it's not mine! To think that you suspect me!' Then Moncharmin opened the door and shouted down the corridor: 'A safety-pin! Someone, bring me a safety-pin! Now!'

It was at that moment, as you may remember, that Rémy, who had no safety-pin, was rebuked by Moncharmin, while a junior clerk provided the pin that was so urgently needed.

Having locked the door again, Moncharmin went down on

his knees to check the back-pocket of Richard's tail-coat. 'I hope,' he said, 'that the twenty thousand francs are still there.'

'So do I,' said Richard.

'I mean the real ones, not the fake ones!' added Moncharmin, intent on not being fooled again.

'Look for yourself,' said Richard. 'I myself will not touch them.'

With a trembling hand Moncharmin took the envelope from Richard's pocket and quickly pulled out its contents – this time it was neither sealed nor glued down to allow for frequent checking. He was reassured: the bank-notes were all there and quite genuine. He returned them to Richard's pocket and pinned them there with great care. Then he sat down behind Richard and did not take his eyes off him while the latter, sitting at his desk, did not stir.

'Be patient, Richard,' said Moncharmin. 'Only a few minutes to go before the clock strikes midnight. Last time, we left at the twelfth stroke of midnight.'

'Oh, I shall be as patient as need be!'

The time passed – slow, heavy, mysterious, stifling. Richard tried to make light of it.

'I could almost believe in the Phantom's all-powerful presence. Just now, for instance, there is something uncomfortable, disquieting, even frightening about the atmosphere in this room, do you not sense it?'

'Oh, I do!' replied Moncharmin, genuinely overwhelmed.

'The Phantom . . .' resumed Richard, in a low voice, lest invisible ears should overhear him. 'The Phantom . . . Suppose for a moment that he were truly a ghost and it was he who knocked three times on this table, as we clearly heard just now, he who placed the trick envelopes here, he who spoke in Box Five, killed Joseph Buquet, unhooked the chandelier and is now robbing us! For, after all, there is no one here save you and I. And if the notes disappear without either you or I having anything to do with it, well then we shall have to believe in the ghost.'

At that moment, the clock on the mantelpiece clicked and the first stroke of midnight chimed. The two directors shuddered.

They were overcome by a feeling of anguish, the cause of which they could not ascertain. They tried to fight against it but in vain: drops of perspiration appeared on their foreheads. The twelfth stroke rang strangely in their ears.

When all was silent again, they gave a sigh and rose from their chairs.

'I think we can go now,' said Moncharmin.

'I think so too,' Richard agreed.

'Before we go, may I check your pocket?'

'Oh! yes, Moncharmin, please do!'

Moncharmin felt the pocket.

'Well?'

'I can feel the pin.'

'Of course. As you said, now we can't be robbed without my feeling it.'

But Moncharmin, whose hands were still busy with the pocket, cried out: '*I can feel the pin, but I can't feel the notes!*'

'Come, Moncharmin, do not jest! This is hardly the time for it.'

'Well, feel for yourself.'

Richard tore off his coat and the two directors turned the pocket inside out: it was *empty*. Yet, curiously, the safety-pin was still in place. Richard and Moncharmin turned pale: supernatural powers were undoubtedly at work here.

'The Phantom . . .' murmured Moncharmin.

But Richard suddenly threw himself at his partner. 'No one but you has touched my pocket! I want the twenty thousand francs back! Give them back to me!'

'Upon my soul!' sighed Moncharmin, as if about to swoon, 'I swear that I didn't take the money!'

Just then there was a knock at the door and Moncharmin, in a daze, went to answer it. He hardly seemed to recognize Mercier: he exchanged a few words with him without really understanding what was being said and unwittingly dropped the safety-pin, for which he had no further use, into the hands of the loyal administrator, who was by now utterly bewildered.

XIX

The Inspector, the Viscount and the Persian

On entering the directors' office, Inspector Mifroid began by asking after the missing singer: 'Is Christine Daaé here?'

As I have already said, a small crowd had followed him.

'Christine Daaé? Here?' echoed Richard. 'No. Why?'

Moncharmin did not have the strength to utter a word. His anguish was far more severe than Richard's, for Richard could still suspect Moncharmin, whereas Moncharmin found himself facing the mystery that has haunted mankind since the dawn of time: the Great Unknown.

The small crowd now gathered round the inspector and the directors kept an impressive silence.

'Why do you ask me if Christine Daaé is here, inspector?' continued Richard.

'Because we are searching for her,' the inspector gravely declared.

'What do you mean? Why are you searching for her? Has she disappeared?'

'Yes, and in the middle of her performance!'

'In the middle of her performance? How astounding!'

'It is indeed. And what is equally astounding is that the directors of the National Academy of Music should first hear of it from me!'

'That's true,' conceded Richard, sinking his head into his hands and muttering: 'What now? This is enough to make a man resign his position!' Absent-mindedly plucking a few hairs out of his moustache, he then added as if in a dream: 'So she disappeared in the middle of her performance?'

'Yes, she vanished during the prison act, just as she was

invoking the help of the Angels in Heaven; but I doubt if she was carried off by an angel!'

'No, I am certain of it!'

Everybody looked round. A young man, pale and trembling with emotion, repeated: 'Quite certain!'

'Certain of what?' asked Mifroid.

'That Christine Daaé was abducted by an angel, inspector, and I can even tell you his name.'

'Aha! So, Viscount, you claim that Christine Daaé has been abducted by an angel: an angel from the Opera, I presume?'

Raoul looked about him, visibly searching for someone. At the very moment when he needed to secure the help of the police to find his fiancée, he would have been glad of the presence of that mysterious man who, a moment ago, urged secrecy. But the stranger was nowhere to be seen. All the same, Raoul must speak, but not with so many people staring at him. 'Yes, by an angel from the Opera,' came his answer, 'and I will tell you where he lives, but in private.'

'Of course, Viscount.' And the inspector, inviting Raoul to take a chair, turned everyone out save for the directors, who seemed utterly lost to the world and would have all too willingly left the room.

Then Raoul spoke: 'Inspector, Erik is your man. He lives here, in this very building, and is the *Angel of Music*!'

'*The Angel of Music!* Really! How very curious! *The Angel of Music!*' And, turning to the directors, Inspector Mifroid asked: 'Do you have an Angel of Music on these premises, gentlemen?'

Richard and Moncharmin shook their heads, without even a smile.

'But,' said the Viscount, 'these gentlemen have definitely heard of the Phantom of the Opera. And I can tell them for sure that the Phantom and the Angel of Music are one and the same person; his real name is Erik.'

Inspector Mifroid rose and looked intently at Raoul: 'I beg your pardon, Viscount, is it your intention to make fun of the law?'

'Not at all!' protested Raoul. 'Here is another who will not listen to me!' he thought, pained.

'Then, what is all this about the Phantom of the Opera?'

'These gentlemen have certainly heard of him.'

'Messieurs, it appears that you know the Phantom of the Opera?' enquired Mifroid.

Richard rose, having finally plucked out the remaining hairs of his moustache. 'No, inspector, we don't know him. But we wish we did, for this very evening he robbed us of twenty thousand francs!' And he gave Moncharmin a terrible look, as if to say: 'Return the twenty thousand francs, or else I shall reveal all.'

Moncharmin, understanding him only too well, responded with a despairing gesture: 'Oh, tell it! Tell it all!'

Mifroid looked in turn at the directors and at Raoul, wondering for a moment whether he might have strayed into a lunatic asylum. 'A phantom,' he said, passing his hand through his hair, 'who, on the same evening, abducts an opera-singer and steals twenty thousand francs? He has been busy! Pray, let us take one mystery at a time: first the singer, and then the twenty thousand francs. So, Viscount, you believe that Mlle Christine Daaé has been abducted by an individual called Erik? How do you know of him? Have you seen him?'

'Yes.'

'Where?'

'In a churchyard.'

Mifroid gave a start. 'Of course, where else!' he said, again gazing intently at Raoul. 'Churchyards are their usual haunts! And what were you doing in this churchyard?'

'Inspector,' said Raoul, 'I appreciate how absurd my replies must appear to you. But, please believe me, I am perfectly sane. Christine Daaé is the only person dearer to me than my beloved brother Philippe, and she is in grave peril. I should like to be brief, for time is pressing and every minute counts; but if I do not tell you the whole story – one of the strangest there ever was – you will not believe me. I will tell you all I know, inspector. But, alas, all I know about the Phantom of the Opera really amounts to very little.'

'Never mind, go on, go on!' cried Richard and Moncharmin, suddenly showing great interest. Sadly any hope of gaining useful information that might put them on the trail of their blackmailer was soon dashed. They quickly reached the inescapable conclusion that Viscount Raoul de Chagny was completely mad: his account of Perros-Guirec, skulls and magic fiddles could only arise from the disturbed and feverish mind of a youth infatuated with love.

It was clear that Inspector Mifroid was gradually coming to the same conclusion. He would certainly have interrupted Raoul's confused story – a story with which the reader has already been acquainted – had circumstances not conspired to cut it short.

At that moment the door opened and a man strangely dressed in a large frock-coat, with a top hat worn to a shine coming down to his ears, entered. He went up to the inspector and spoke to him in a whisper. He was undoubtedly a detective come to deliver an important message.

During their conversation, Mifroid did not take his eyes off Raoul. At last addressing him, the inspector said: 'Viscount, I have heard enough about the Phantom. If you have no objections, I should like to know a little more about you. Did you not plan to elope with Mlle Christine Daaé tonight?'

'Yes, inspector.'

'After the performance?'

'Yes, inspector.'

'You had made all the necessary arrangements?'

'Yes, inspector.'

'The carriage that brought you here was to take you both away. The driver knew all about it. You had planned a particular route. There were even fresh horses waiting in readiness at every stage of the journey.'

'That is correct, inspector.'

'Yet your carriage still awaits your orders outside the Opera House on the Rotunda side, is that not so?'

'Yes, inspector.'

'Did you notice that there were three other carriages standing there?'

'I did not.'

'These carriages belonged to Mlle Sorelli – as there was no vacant stand inside the courtyard – Carlotta, and your brother the Count.'

'Possibly.'

'What is quite certain is that, though your carriage, Sorelli's and Carlotta's are still standing there, the Count's carriage has gone.'

'This has nothing to do with . . .'

'I beg your pardon. Was the Count not opposed to your marriage with Christine Daaé?'

'This is purely a family matter.'

'You have answered my question: he was opposed to it and that was why you were running away with Christine Daaé. You were running away from your own brother. Well, Viscount, let me tell you that your brother was quicker than you! He is the one who abducted Christine Daaé!'

'Oh!' moaned Raoul, pressing his hand to his heart. 'I cannot believe this . . . Are you sure?'

'Immediately after the singer's abduction, which was achieved by means yet to be established, he rushed to his carriage and crossed Paris at a furious pace.'

'Crossed Paris?' groaned poor Raoul. 'What do you mean?'

'Crossed and left Paris.'

'Left Paris! By which road?'

'The road to Brussels.'

'Oh,' cried the young man, 'I shall catch up with them, I swear!' And he dashed out of the office.

'And bring her back to us!' the inspector shouted cheerfully after him, adding quietly: 'I have sent him on a wild-goose chase that is worthy of his Angel of Music story!'

Then, turning to his puzzled companions, Mifroid delivered an elementary but in no way puerile speech on police methods: 'I have no idea whether the Count de Chagny has abducted Christine Daaé or not, but I need to know; and, just now, there is no one more anxious to help me than the Viscount his brother. At this very moment he is in hot pursuit! He is my right-hand man! Such is the allegedly complex art of police investigation, gentlemen, which turns out to be much simpler when you know that it is all about getting the work done by people who are not members of the police force.'

Inspector Mifroid would not have been quite so pleased

with himself, however, had he known that his speedy agent had been stopped in his pursuit as soon as he entered the next corridor. The gaping crowd, which had gathered there earlier on, had now been dispersed and the corridor appeared deserted.

Suddenly a tall, shadowy figure blocked Raoul's way.

'Where are you going so fast, Viscount de Chagny?' asked the figure.

Looking up impatiently, Raoul recognized the astrakhan hat he had seen but an hour ago, and stopped. 'You again!' he cried breathlessly. 'You know Erik's secrets, yet want me to keep quiet. Who are you?'

'You know very well who I am! I am the Persian!'

XX

The Viscount and the Persian

Raoul recalled that his brother had once pointed out this mysterious character, of whom nothing was known save that he was Persian and lived in a small shabby apartment in the Rue de Rivoli.

The man with ebony skin and jade-green eyes wearing the astrakhan hat leaned closer. 'I hope, M. de Chagny, that you have not betrayed Erik's secret.'

'And why should I hesitate to betray that monster?' Raoul retorted haughtily, trying to escape the man's unwelcome attention. 'Am I to understand that he is your friend?'

'I hope that you did not breathe a word about Erik, simply because Erik's secret is also Christine Daaé's, and to talk about one is to talk about the other!'

'You seem to know of much that is of concern to me,' said Raoul, growing increasingly impatient. 'But I have no time to listen to you!'

'Again, M. de Chagny, where are you going in such haste?'

'To Christine Daaé's assistance, of course!'

'Then stay here, for she is here!'

'With Erik?'

'With Erik.'

'How do you know?'

'I was at the performance and no one save Erik could ever have devised and engineered such an audacious abduction! Oh,' he said, with a deep sigh, 'I immediately recognized the touch of that monstrous fiend!'

'You know him, then?'

The Persian made no reply, but sighed again.

'Monsieur,' said Raoul, 'I do not know your intentions, but is there anything you can do to help me, and, in so doing, help Christine Daaé?'

'I think so, which is why I approached you.'

'Then what can you do?'

'I can try to take you to her . . . and to him.'

'I myself have tried and failed. But if you can do me this service, I would forever be in your debt! The inspector has just informed me that Mlle Daaé has been abducted by my brother, Count Philippe.'

'I do not believe a word of it, M. de Chagny.'

'Neither do I. How could it be possible?'

'I don't know whether it is possible or not; but there are many ways of abducting people; and Count Philippe is not, as far as I am aware, *adept in the art of stage effects*.'

'Your arguments are compelling, monsieur, and I am a fool! Oh, we must hurry! I place myself entirely in your hands! How can I not believe you, when you are the only one who believes me, when you are the only one who does not scoff in disbelief when I speak of Erik?'

And with burning hands the young man spontaneously grasped the Persian's. They were ice-cold.

'Quiet!' said the Persian, stopping and listening to distant sounds from the theatre and the slightest creaks from the walls and corridors nearby. 'We must not mention his name here. We must say "he" and "him" so as not to attract his attention.'

'Do you think that he is nearby?'

'It is quite possible, unless he is *in his lair* with his victim at this very moment.'

'Ah! So you know of his secret retreat too?'

'If he is not there, he may be here. This wall, this floor, this ceiling might conceal him! There's no knowing where he might be. Just now, he may have an eye to this keyhole, an ear to this beam.' And the Persian, asking Raoul to tread quietly, led him down passageways that he had never seen before, even when Christine had taken him on rambles through this labyrinth.

'Oh, I hope,' said the Persian, 'that Darius has come!'

'Who is Darius?'

'Darius is my servant.'

They now stood in the centre of a vast, dimly lit room that resembled an empty town square. The Persian stopped Raoul and turned to him. 'What did you say to the inspector?' he asked, his voice dropping so low that Raoul could hardly hear him.

'I said that Christine Daaé's abductor was the Angel of Music, also known as the Phantom of the Opera, and that his real name was . . .'

'Hush! And the inspector believed you?'

'No, he didn't.'

'So what you said was of no interest to him?'

'None whatsoever!'

'And he took you for some sort of madman?'

'Yes.'

'That's good,' said the Persian, relieved.

And on they went. After ascending and descending several flights of stairs unknown to Raoul, the two men found themselves outside a door that the Persian opened with a master-key drawn from his waistcoat. Of course, the Persian and Raoul were still in dress-clothes; but, whereas Raoul wore a top hat, the Persian wore the astrakhan hat that I have already mentioned. This was a breach of the Opera dress code, which demanded that a top hat be worn backstage; save that in France foreigners may do as they please: the Englishman may keep his travelling-cap and the Persian his astrakhan hat.

'Viscount,' said the Persian, 'your top hat will hinder you: you would do well to leave it in the dressing-room.'

'Whose dressing-room?' asked Raoul.

'Christine Daaé's.' With these words, the Persian let Raoul through the door that he had just unlocked and pointed to the singer's room across the corridor. Raoul had no idea that Christine's room could be reached by a route other than the one he was wont to use – he normally came from the far end of the long corridor in which they now stood.

'You know the Opera well!'

'Not so well as *he* does!' said the Persian modestly. And he pushed the young man into Christine's dressing-room, which was as Raoul had left it earlier. Closing the door behind him, the Persian went to a thin partition that separated the dressing-room from a large adjoining store-room. He listened and then coughed loudly. Whereupon they heard movement in that room; a few seconds later, there was a knock on Christine's door.

'Come in,' said the Persian.

A man dressed in a long overcoat entered. He too wore an astrakhan hat. He bowed, drew a richly carved case from under his coat, which he put down on the dressing-table, bowed again and went to the door.

'Did anyone see you come in, Darius?'

'No, master.'

'Let no one see you leave.'

The servant glanced down the corridor and swiftly disappeared.

'Monsieur,' said Raoul, 'it occurs to me that someone might come upon us here. It will not be long before the inspector decides to search this room.'

'The inspector is not the one we should fear.'

The Persian opened the case. It contained two long pistols, superbly designed and magnificently decorated.

'When Christine Daaé disappeared, I sent word to my servant to bring me these pistols. I have had them for a long time and they are most reliable.'

'Do you mean to fight a duel?' asked the young man, taken aback by the sudden appearance of the weapons.

'Yes. We are indeed about to fight a duel,' replied the other, checking the priming of his pistols. 'And what a duel!' Handing one of his pistols to Raoul, he added: 'The two of us will be fighting against only one; but you need to be ready for anything. I must warn you that we shall face the most formidable adversary imaginable. But you are fighting for love, are you not?'

'How can you doubt it! But you, who do not love her, why are you so ready to endanger your life? It must be that you hate Erik.'

'No,' said the Persian sadly, 'I do not hate him. If I had hated him, he would have ceased his mischief long ago.'

'Have you suffered at his hand?'

'If I have, I forgave him long ago.'

'I am baffled to hear you speak of him thus: you call him a fiend, you talk of his crimes, you say that he has harmed you, and yet I see in you the same extraordinary pity that drove me to despair when Christine spoke of him!'

The Persian did not reply. He fetched a stool and placed it against the wall opposite the large mirror. Climbing on the stool, he put his face to the wall as if looking for something.

'Come,' cried Raoul, burning with impatience. 'We must not tarry! Let's go!'

'Where to?' replied the other, without turning round.

'To confront the monster! You told me that you knew the way.'

'I am looking for it now,' the Persian replied with his face to the wall, still searching. 'Ah,' he cried suddenly. 'Here it is!' And, feeling above his head, he pressed against an angle in the pattern of the wallpaper. Then he turned round and jumped off the stool. 'In a few moments,' he added, 'we shall be *on his trail*!' Then, crossing the dressing-room, he pressed his hands against the mirror, muttering: 'It is not moving yet.'

'So we shall leave this room by the mirror,' said Raoul, 'like Christine.'

'Then you know that she went through the mirror?'

'She did so before my very eyes! I was hiding here, behind the curtain of her closet, and saw it happen: but she did not so much pass through the mirror as melt into it!'

'And what did you do?'

'I thought that my eyes had deceived me! or that I was losing my mind! or that it was all a dream!'

'Or some new trick from the Phantom!' added the Persian with a knowing laugh. 'Ah, if only we were dealing with a ghost,' he continued, with one hand still against the mirror, 'then we could leave our pistols in their case! Now Viscount, take off your hat and hide your shirt as much as you can with your coat; like this: turn your lapels inwards and your collar up. We must try to make ourselves invisible.'

He paused briefly and then, still bearing against the mirror, added: 'It takes some time for the counterweight to be released when the mechanism is activated from this room; but not so from the other side of the wall, where you can release the counterweight itself. Then the mirror turns in an instant and at great speed.'

'What counterweight?' asked Raoul.

'Why, the counterweight that raises this whole section of wall on to its pivot. Surely you do not expect it to move of itself like magic!' With one hand the Persian drew Raoul close to him, while with the other (still holding the pistol) he pressed against the mirror. 'Watch carefully and you will presently see the mirror rise very slightly and shift to the right, again ever so slightly, to move on to its pivot. Then it will swivel open. Oh, the wonders of the counterweight! It can allow a child to make a whole house spin on the tip of one finger. A section of wall such as this, heavy as it is, does not weigh more than a spinning top on its axis when properly balanced on a pivot with a counterweight.'

'But it's not moving!' cried Raoul impatiently.

'Oh, wait! It might take some time! The mechanism is obviously rusty, or else the spring is weak. Unless it is something else,' added the Persian, frowning in alarm.

'What?'

'He may have simply cut the rope of the counterweight and immobilized the whole mechanism.'

'Why? He does not know that we are coming this way!'

'He might suspect it. He knows that I understand how this system works.'

'Did he show it to you?'

'No! I wanted to discover how he could come and go at will so mysteriously and I found out for myself. He uses a very simple system of secret doors, as old as the sacred palaces of Thebes with their hundred doors, or the throne room of Hagmatana, or the chamber in which the Delphic Pythia[1] delivered her oracles.'

'But it's not moving! And Christine! What of Christine?'

'We shall do all that is humanly possible to reach her,' the Persian said calmly. 'But he may foil us from the outset!'

'Then are these walls his to command?'

'He has power over the walls, the doors and the traps. In my country, he was even known as the *Master of the Traps*.'

'Christine spoke of him thus. She too talked mysteriously of his formidable power. But all this seems so extraordinary! Why should the walls obey him. He did not build them.'

'Ah, but he did!'

Raoul stared at him, astounded, but the Persian motioned him to be quiet and pointed to the mirror. Their reflections seemed to quiver. Their images rippled as though reflected in water, and then came to rest again.

'Look, it's not working. There must be another way!'

'Tonight, there's no other way!' declared the Persian, in a singularly ominous voice. 'Now, watch out! And be ready to fire.'

Facing the mirror, he raised his pistol before him. Raoul did the same. With his free arm, the Persian drew the young man close to him and suddenly the mirror pivoted open in a dazzling, dizzying burst of reflected light. Turning like one of those revolving doors that have lately begun to appear on the threshold of public buildings, it opened with an irresistible movement which took Raoul and the Persian out of the light and plunged them into deepest darkness.

XXI

Below the Stage

'Keep your hand raised, ready to fire!' Raoul's companion repeated hurriedly.

Having completed its rotation, the wall closed behind them. The two men stood still for a moment, holding their breath. Around them, all was dark, still and silent.

At last the Persian moved: Raoul heard him shuffle around on the floor, feeling for something in the dark. Suddenly the young man saw the faint, tentative glow of a bull's eye lantern[1] in front of him. He instinctively stepped back as if to escape the scrutiny of some unknown enemy; but he soon realized that the light belonged to the Persian and watched the little red disc glide over the walls, and then along the floor and the ceiling, as the Persian painstakingly inspected all about him. The wall on the right was of solid construction and the partition on the left was made of boards; the ceiling and the floor were wooden too. Christine must have passed through here, thought Raoul, when she followed the voice of the *Angel of Music*; and this must be the route Erik would have taken when he wanted to surprise and intrigue the trusting, innocent girl, casting his spell over her through the walls. Raoul, recalling his conversation with the Persian, assumed that this passage had been secretly built by the Phantom himself. In fact, he would later learn that Erik had found it ready made and for a long time was the only one who knew of its existence. It had been built at the time of the Paris Commune to allow the insurgents to take their prisoners straight down to the dungeon in the basement. The Opera House had been occupied from the first day of the uprising, on 18 March 1871: the lower part of the building became a prison and the rooftops were used to fly the hot-air balloons that carried revolutionary proclamations out to the rest of the country.[2]

The Persian was on his knees again, with the lantern by his side. He seemed to be busy working at something on the floor. And then suddenly he shuttered the lamp. In the dark Raoul heard a faint click and saw a pale square of light appear in the floor of the passageway like a window. It opened on to one of the mezzanine floors below the stage where light still shone. Raoul could no longer see the Persian, but he suddenly felt his presence by his side and heard him whisper: 'Follow me and do exactly as I do.'

Raoul advanced towards the square of light and watched as the Persian went on to his knees again, gripped the frame of the trap and slipped down to the floor below with his pistol between his teeth. Strangely, the young man had total confidence in the Persian. Though he knew nothing about him, and his enigmatic remarks had only added to the mystery of their present undertaking, Raoul did not doubt for a moment that the Persian was on his side and against Erik at this decisive hour. When the Persian called the Phantom a 'fiend', he seemed quite sincere; and his interest in Raoul's plight appeared genuine. Had he been scheming against Raoul, he would not have given him a pistol. Besides, Christine had to be reached at all cost. Raoul had no choice but to trust him. Had he wavered in his purpose out of diffidence, the young man would have thought himself the worst of cowards. He therefore knelt down too, and holding on to the frame of the trap with both hands, lowered himself through the opening.

'Let go!' he heard from below. Whereupon he dropped into the arms of the Persian, who told him to lie down at once. His companion, having shut the trap above them – Raoul knew not how – then came to lie beside him. The young man was about to speak when the Persian placed his hand over his mouth: a voice, which he recognized as that of Inspector Mifroid, could be heard.

They were now behind a lattice screen, which entirely concealed them from view. Beyond, a narrow staircase went up to the next mezzanine floor, where the inspector must be pacing back and forth, asking questions – they could both hear the sound of his footsteps and his voice.

Light was scant but, having just left the dense blackness of the secret passage, Raoul could see into the shadow. He let out a startled cry as he made out three dead bodies. The first body lay on the narrow landing of the staircase leading to the door behind which the inspector was talking; the other two had rolled to the bottom of the steps and lay there with their arms flung wide. They were so close that Raoul could have touched one of the poor wretches simply by slipping his fingers through the latticework.

'Quiet!' the Persian whispered. He too had seen the bodies and his explanation was brief and simple: '*He* did it!'

Mifroid had raised his voice. He demanded explanations about the lighting system, which the stage manager readily provided. The inspector must therefore be next to the organ or nearby.

One might assume, especially in connection with an opera-house, that the aforementioned 'organ' served a musical purpose;[3] yet this was not so. At that time, electricity was employed only for a few very particular theatrical effects and for the curtain bell. The vast building and the stage itself were still lit by gas; using hydrogen, the lighting of a particular set was controlled and adjusted with special machinery consisting of a whole array of valves and pipes, known as the organ. The chief gas-man had his own box next to that of the prompter and sat there throughout the performance, directing the work of his assistants and overseeing the result. But tonight Mauclair was not at his post, and neither were his assistants.

'Mauclair! Mauclair!' boomed the stage manager, his voice resounding hollowly. There was no reply.

As I have already said, the narrow staircase led to a door. The inspector now tried to open it from inside the room, but without success. 'H'm! This door seems to be stuck and will not open. Is it always thus?'

The stage manager forced it open with his shoulder. As he did so, he found a body in the way and recognized it at once. 'Mauclair!' he exclaimed.

The small crowd who had accompanied the inspector on his visit down to the pipe organ stepped forward in alarm.

'The poor devil is dead,' said the stage manager, gloomily.

But Inspector Mifroid, unperturbed as ever, was already bent over the large, inert body. 'No, he's dead-drunk, which is not quite the same thing,' he observed.

'It has never happened before,' said the stage manager.

'Then, quite possibly, someone gave him a narcotic.' Mifroid straightened up and took another few steps. 'Look!' he cried.

By the red light of a little lantern, they saw another two bodies lying at the foot of the stairs. The stage manager recognized Mauclair's assistants.

Mifroid went down to check their breathing. 'They're both fast asleep,' he concluded. 'Very strange! Evidently someone has been interfering with the lighting. And that someone must, of course, be working for the abductor. But why abduct a singer from the stage during her performance? A daring feat, if ever I saw one. Please send for the house doctor.' And he repeated: 'Strange, very strange . . .' Then he turned towards the little room and people that Raoul and the Persian were unable to see, asking: 'What do you think of all this, gentlemen? You are the only ones who have said nothing so far. Tell me, you must have some opinion on the matter.'

At that moment Raoul and the Persian saw the bewildered faces of the directors appear on the landing – the rest of their bodies remained out of sight. 'There are things happening here, inspector, which we simply cannot explain,' declared Moncharmin, nervously. And the two faces disappeared.

'Thank you for that, gentlemen,' scoffed Mifroid.

'But wait! This is not the first time that Mauclair has fallen asleep on the job,' broke in the stage manager, resting his chin in the hollow of his right hand – a sure sign of one deep in thought. 'I remember finding him once snoring at his post with his snuff-box beside him.'

'When was this?' asked Mifroid, carefully wiping his spectacles – he was short-sighted as those with the most beautiful eyes often are.

'Not long ago!' replied the stage manager. 'Let me think! It

was the night . . . Yes, I remember now: it was the night when
Carlotta famously "croaked".'

'Really? That very night?' noted Mifroid. He replaced his
gleaming pince-nez on his nose and stared pointedly at the
stage manager as if to divine his thoughts. 'So Mauclair takes
snuff, does he?' he asked nonchalantly.

'Yes, he does, inspector. Look, here is his snuff-box on this
little shelf. Oh, he loves his snuff!'

'So do I,' said Mifroid, pocketing the snuff-box.

Still unobserved, Raoul and the Persian watched as the three
bodies were carried away. The inspector and everyone else followed, the sound of their footsteps ringing on the stage above
for a few moments. When they were alone, the Persian motioned
Raoul to get to his feet. Raoul obeyed, but without holding up
his pistol in readiness, as the Persian himself had done. At this,
he remonstrated with the Viscount, insisting that he hold his
pistol at eye level and keep it thus, come what may.

'But it tires my arm needlessly,' whispered Raoul. 'And if I
have to fire, my aim will be unsteady.'

'Then hold your pistol with your other hand,' suggested the
Persian.

'But I can't shoot with my left hand.'

The Persian's reply to this was most curious and dispelled
neither the uncertainties of their present situation nor the
young man's distress: '*It's not a matter of shooting with the
right hand or the left; it's a matter of keeping your arm bent
upwards and holding one of your hands as if you were going to
pull the trigger of a pistol. As for the pistol itself, you may as
well put it in your pocket!*' And he added: 'Do exactly as I say,
or I can't answer for your safety. It's a matter of life and death.
Now, Viscount, not a word! Follow me!'

They were down on the second mezzanine floor. By the faint,
still glow of a few scattered lights encased in glass, Raoul could
glimpse but a tiny part of the fantastic, labyrinthine depths that
lay below the stage. These could be awesome, yet also charming –
as delightful as a child's puppet theatre and as horrifying as a
vast cavern.

The below-stage area was five floors deep and each level or 'mezzanine' replicated the lay-out of the stage itself with its traps and slider cuts for scenery; only the chariot slits in the stage floor were replaced by rails.[4] These traps and cuts were supported by cross-joists. Posts rising from cast iron or stone dies and connected at the top to wall-plates or bars formed a series of trusses which allowed for the free passage of heavy stage machines such as the Paradiso; when necessary, these appliances were coupled together by connecting irons for added stability. Windlasses, drums and counterweights were everywhere; they served to manoeuvre bulky scenery and change scenes during performances, as well as conjure away the performers for spectacular effect. It was in the mezzanines, wrote Messrs X., Y. and Z. in their fascinating study of Garnier's architectural masterpiece,[5] that sallow dyspeptics were turned into beautiful knights, and hideous witches into radiant, youthful fairies. It was from those depths that Satan himself would rise, and into them that he sank once more. It was where the fires of Hell smouldered, the chorus of the demons lodged . . . and ghosts freely roamed.

Convinced that the Persian was his only hope, Raoul followed him and did exactly as instructed without trying to reason why. What would he have done without his companion in this extraordinary maze? He would have been impeded at every step by the profuse jumble of beams and ropes, and might have been unable to extricate himself from this gigantic web. And even if he had managed to make his way through the tangle of lines and counterweights constantly appearing before him as he proceeded, he might have fallen into one of those holes that opened here and there beneath his feet into unfathomable darkness.

Down they went, forever downwards.

Now they were on the third mezzanine. Distant lamps still guided them. The further down they went, the more precautions the Persian seemed to take. Although his pistol was in his pocket, he still had his hand raised as if ready to fire and constantly turned round to check that Raoul followed his example.

Suddenly, a loud, booming voice brought them to a halt. Above, someone shouted: 'All door-shutters to the stage! The inspector wants to talk to you!' They heard footsteps, glimpsed shadows gliding past in the dark and retreated behind a flat. Stooping old men, their backs bowed by years of carrying heavy scenery, shuffled past them on their way up. Some could barely drag themselves along; others, from sheer habit, bent forward with outstretched hands as if fumbling for doors to close. These door-shutters were worn-out machinists, on whom a charitable management had taken pity, giving them the task of shutting doors above and below the stage. They would continually come and go, closing one door after another, and were known in those days – they are undoubtedly all dead by now – as the 'draught-stoppers'; for any draught is very bad for the voice.*

The Persian and Raoul were pleased to be rid of these unwelcome witnesses. From idleness or necessity some of those door-shutters, who had nothing else to do and practically no home of their own, often stayed at the Opera and spent their nights there. The two men might have stumbled over them sleeping in the darkness, woken them and aroused their curiosity. For the moment, Inspector Mifroid's inquiry saved them from any such disagreeable encounter. But they did not enjoy their solitude for long. Other shadows now came down the route by which the door-shutters had left. They carried small lanterns, which they swung back and forth, up and down, inspecting everything around them as if they were looking for something or someone.

'Hell!' muttered the Persian. 'I don't know what they are seeking, but they might just find us. Quick, let's go! Keep your hand up, monsieur, ready to fire! With your arm bent further, like this. Keep your hand at eye level, as if you were fighting a duel and waiting for the word to fire. Leave your pistol in your pocket! Quick, come along, down the stairs.' (He led Raoul down to the fourth floor.) 'Hand at eye level ... matter of life

---

* M. Pedro Gailhard, the former director of the Opera House, told me himself that he had created several such posts for old machinists whom he was unwilling to dismiss.

or death . . . this way . . . these stairs!' (They were nearing the lowest floor.) 'Oh, what a duel!'

Having now reached the stage cellar, the Persian breathed more easily. He seemed to feel somewhat safer than when they had stopped on the floor above, but he kept his arm raised as before. Raoul puzzled once more over this but refrained from making any comment. Now was not the time to question the Persian's extraordinary notion of self-defence that consisted in keeping one's pistol in one's pocket while holding oneself ready to fire.

All the same, thinking back to the Persian's earlier remark on the reliability of his pistols, Raoul could not help asking himself: 'What is the good of having trusty pistols if he does not mean to use them?'

But the Persian left him little time for reflection. Instructing him to keep still, he briefly ran back up the stairs they had just descended. Returning, he whispered: 'How stupid of us! Those shadows with their lanterns will soon be gone. They are firemen on their rounds.'*

The two men waited for five long minutes. Then they started retracing their steps towards the stairs when suddenly the Persian, who was leading the way, motioned Raoul to stop: something moved in the darkness ahead. 'Lie down!' he whispered.

They both lay flat on the floor. Just in time: a shadow carrying no light, a shadow in the shadows, passed by. It passed within touching distance and they felt a waft of warm air upon their faces. They could just make out a figure wrapped from head to foot in a cloak with a soft felt hat. He moved away, keeping close to the walls and occasionally prodding hidden corners with his foot. The Persian heaved a sigh of relief: 'That was a narrow escape! He knows me and has twice marched me to the directors' office.'

* In those days, the firemen were still entrusted with the safety of the whole Opera House at all times; whereas now they are on duty only during the performances. When I asked the reason for this, M. Pedro Gailhard replied: 'It was because the management feared that, in their utter inexperience of the lowest floors, *the firemen might accidentally set fire to the building!*'

'Is he a policeman on duty at the Opera?' asked Raoul.

'No, he's much worse!' replied the Persian, without giving any further explanation.*

'Was that *him*?'

'*Him?* No. As long as *he* does not approach us from behind, his shining eyes will give him away! In this sense, darkness favours us. But should *he* creep upon us from behind, we are dead men unless we keep one hand up at eye level as if about to fire!'

The Persian had no time to explain further for there appeared before them a fantastic sight: it was a face ... a head, not just two eyes shining in the dark! Yes, a luminous head was coming towards them, a head of fire, at a man's height from the ground, but with *no body* attached. It was ablaze and, in the darkness, looked like a flame with the features of a man.

'What!' the Persian muttered between his teeth. 'I have never seen this before! Papin, the fireman, was not mad after all, when he said he had seen it! What can it be? It is not *him*, but *he* may have sent it! Be on your guard! Your hand, in Heaven's name, keep your hand raised.'

The blazing head seemed an apparition from Hell, the face of a fiery demon; it floated at a man's height threateningly towards them.

'Perhaps *he* is confronting us with this so as to steal upon us from behind or from the side. With *him* you can never tell! I have seen many of his tricks, but not this one. No, this is quite new to me. Better to flee ... yes, come along ... hand at eye level!'

Together they fled down the long underground passage

---

* Like the Persian, I shall not expatiate upon this particular shadow. While everything else in this true story will be explained in due course, however peculiar the events recounted might seem at first, I cannot expand on what the Persian meant by 'He's much worse' (than a policeman)! The reader must try to guess for himself, for I promised M. Pedro Gailhard to keep his secret as regards the exceedingly interesting and useful personality of the cloaked shadow. Forever wandering beneath the Opera House, this mysterious character has rendered untold services to those who, on gala evenings for instance, venture *below stage*. Suffice to say, these are matters of national security and I am bound to secrecy.

ahead of them. After a few seconds, which seemed like several long minutes, they stopped.

'*He* seldom comes this way,' said the Persian. 'This part is of no interest to him. It does not lead to the lake, nor to his retreat; but perhaps he knows that we are coming *after him* ... although I did promise to leave him alone and never interfere again!'

Then he turned round, as did Raoul. The head of fire was right behind them. It had followed. And it must have moved at speed, faster than them, for it now appeared closer. At the same time, they began to notice a peculiar sound, which they were unable to identify. It seemed to be moving with the face-like flame and getting closer. It was a sharp, screeching, excruciating sound like the grating of a piece of chalk, with a tiny stone inside, on a blackboard, or that of a thousand fingernails raking across it.

The two men continued to retreat from the flame-like face, but it kept coming at them, getting closer. They could see its features clearly now: beady staring eyes, a little crooked nose and a large curved mouth, which resembled the eyes, nose and mouth of the moon when it is red – blood red. But how could that red moon-like face glide through the darkness, at a man's height, with apparently nothing, no body to support it? How could it come straight at them so fast with those eyes, those staring eyes? And then that rasping, grating, screeching sound, what was it?

The Persian and Raoul could retreat no further. They flattened themselves against the wall, not knowing what would become of them. The mysterious head of fire was still moving towards them, as did the sound – an increasingly loud, teeming, living sound; a sound consisting of hundreds of smaller sounds, which stirred in the darkness beneath the blazing head. It was moving closer, closer still. And then it was upon them.

Their backs pressed to the wall, the two companions felt their hair stand on end, for they recognized it. It came in waves, scampering along in the dark in small, countless hurrying waves faster than the surf that runs on to the sands with the oncoming tide – a nocturnal surge ruffling under the moon, under the head of fire that was itself like a moon. And as the onrushing waves flooded over their feet and climbed their legs, Raoul and the Persian could no longer suppress their cries of horror, dismay and pain. Nor could they keep their hands raised like duellists ready to fire: instead they used them to repel the glossy tide of creatures with feet, claws and sharp teeth.

Raoul and the Persian were about to faint as Papin the fireman had done when, in answer to their cries, the head of fire stopped and spoke: 'Stay where you are! Whatever you do, do not follow me! I am the rat-catcher! Let me pass with my rats!'

And then he was gone. His flaming head melted into the night as the passage lit up in front of him. For, instead of shining his bull's eye lantern on to his own face as he had done before, so as not to scare off the rats at his feet, he had turned it round to illuminate the darkness ahead and hasten away. He strode on, taking along with him the deafening tide of scampering, screeching rats.*

Raoul and the Persian, though still trembling, breathed a sigh of relief.

'Erik mentioned the rat-catcher to me, but I had quite forgotten,' said the Persian. 'And he never described him. How odd that I should never have encountered him before.' Then he added with a sigh: 'For a moment, I thought that this was yet

---

* When M. Pedro Gailhard and I met at Cap d'Ail as Mme Pierre Wolff's guests,[6] he told me that a plague of rats had caused extensive damage to the building underground until the administration hired – at considerable expense – the services of a man who claimed that he could rid them of this scourge by patrolling the cellars once a fortnight.

Since then, the only scampering feet heard at the Opera House are those of the ballet-girls.[7] M. Gailhard thought that the man in question had discovered a secret scent to which the rats were highly attracted, just as fish are attracted to the bait with which fishermen sometimes smear their legs. The intoxicated rats could thus be lured along to some watery pit into which they fell and promptly drowned. We know from M. Gailhard that the chief fireman had seen a fiery head which had terrified him to the point of fainting; I myself am convinced that this apparition and the one that so cruelly disturbed the Viscount and the Persian, as described in the latter's papers, were one and the same.

another of his fiendish tricks. But, of course, *he* never comes to this side of the building.'

'Do you mean to say that the lake is still some way off?' asked Raoul. 'Just how far away? Take me there! Take me there at once! When we reach the lake, we will call out to Christine, shake the walls, and shout! Christine will hear us! *He* will hear us, too! And, since you know him, we can reason with him!'

'Your naivety is touching!' said the Persian. 'We shall never gain access to his retreat from the lake itself!'

'Why is that?'

'Because all his defences are mustered there. I myself have never been able to cross the lake and reach the other side. The lake is particularly well guarded. I suspect that several of the men who have vanished, never to be seen again – former machinists, old door-shutters – merely sought to cross that lake. What a terrible fate! I myself would have died if the evil freak had not recognized me in time. Believe me, monsieur: keep away from the lake! And, above all, should you ever hear the *voice under the water*, the siren's voice, sing out to you, be sure to close your ears to it!'[8]

'What are we doing here?' raged a feverish and impatient Raoul. 'Perhaps you can do nothing for Christine, but at least I can die for her!'

The Persian tried to calm the young man. 'Believe me, there is only one way of saving Christine Daaé, which is to enter *his* retreat unbeknown to *him*.'

'And is there any hope of that, monsieur?'

'If I had no such hope, I would not have approached you!'

'Then how can we enter it without crossing the lake?'

'From the third mezzanine floor. We unfortunately had to flee from it earlier, but we shall now return there. I know the exact spot,' said the Persian, with a sudden change in his voice. 'It is between a flat and a discarded cloth from *Le Roi de Lahore*, just where Joseph Buquet met his untimely death.'

'Buquet, the chief machinist who was found hanging?'

'Yes, the hanged man whose rope could not be found,' the Persian replied in a peculiar tone. 'Come, Viscount, be of stout heart! Follow me! And keep your arm raised as before! Now where are we?' The Persian unshuttered his bull's eye lantern and shone it down two huge galleries which crossed each other at right angles and whose vaulted roofs stretched far into the distance. 'This must be where the waterworks[9] are housed,' he said. 'I see no furnaces.' Walking just ahead of Raoul, he tried to find his bearings and stopped abruptly whenever he feared that their path might cross that of some 'water-man'. At one point, they had to avoid the light cast by an underground forge, whose fire was being extinguished by figures that Raoul recognized as the 'demons' glimpsed by Christine during her first abduction.

Thus, they made their way from the sides back to the area just underneath the vast mezzanines. They were standing right at the bottom of the 'tank' and at an exceedingly great depth. When the Opera House was originally built, the earth had to be dug out to *fifty feet below the level of the river* that ran under that district of Paris. All the water had to be pumped out. The volume of water that had to be removed would have filled a reservoir as large as the esplanade of the Louvre Palace and as deep as one and a half times the towers of Notre-Dame Cathedral.[10] Eventually a lake was allowed to form outside the 'tank'.

The Persian tapped a wall and said: 'If I am not mistaken, this could well be part of *his* retreat.' He was tapping one of the walls of the 'tank', and perhaps it would be as well for the reader to know how the bottom and the walls of the tank were built. In order to prevent the water surrounding the edifice from coming into direct contact with the walls supporting the entire stage machinery, whose woodwork, metalwork and painted cloth needed protection from the damp, *the architect lined the excavation with a double shell*. It took a whole year to build, and consisted of a dam, then a brick wall, then a dense layer of cement, and finally another wall several yards in thickness.[11] It was this inner wall that the Persian had tapped. To anyone who understands the architecture of the Opera House, his accompanying remark to Raoul would indicate that *Erik had built his secret retreat within the fabric of the double shell*.

At the Persian's words, Raoul threw himself against the wall and listened eagerly. But he heard nothing, nothing at all, save for the sound of distant footsteps on wooden floors in the upper parts of the theatre.

The Persian shuttered his lantern again. 'Look out!' he said. 'Keep your arm up! And be quiet! For we are now going to find a way into his lair.' And he led Raoul to the small staircase by which they had descended earlier.

They went up slowly, stopping at each step, peering into the darkness, listening into the silence, until they came to the third mezzanine. Here the Persian motioned Raoul to kneel down; and, in this way, crawling on both knees and one hand – the other hand still raised as before – they reached the end wall. A large painted cloth that had once been used for a production of *Le Roi de Lahore* was hanging along this wall. Close by was a flat. And between this flat and the discarded backdrop there was just room for a body, a body which one day had been found hanging there: Joseph Buquet's body.

The Persian, still on his knees, stopped and listened. For a moment, he seemed to hesitate. He glanced at Raoul and then upwards, towards the floor above: the faint glow of a lamp, showing through a small gap between two floor-boards, clearly troubled the Persian. At last, he nodded and seemed to come to a decision. He slipped between the flat and the set from *Le Roi de Lahore*, Raoul following close behind. With his free hand, the Persian felt the wall. Raoul saw him bear heavily upon it as he had pressed against the wall in Christine's dressing-room. Then a stone gave way and a hole appeared. This time the Persian took his pistol from his pocket, motioning Raoul to do the same, and cocked it.

Still on his knees, he crawled purposefully into the opening that had appeared in the wall. Raoul, who had wished to go first, could but follow. This passage was very narrow. The Persian stopped almost at once. Raoul heard him feeling the stone around him. Then the Persian took up his bull's eye lantern, stretched forward to examine something and shuttered the light at once. Raoul heard him whisper: 'We shall have to drop a few yards down, without making a noise. Take off your boots.' And, taking off his own, the Persian handed them to Raoul.

'Leave them behind,' he said. 'We'll find them on our return.'*

Then he shuffled slightly forward on his knees before turning round to face Raoul. 'Holding on to the edge, I am going to lower myself down and drop *into his lair*,' he said. 'You must do exactly the same. Don't be afraid. I will catch you.'

Raoul soon heard a thud as the Persian landed in the room below, and shuddered at the thought that this sound might betray their presence. But even more unnerving was the absence of any other sound. How could that be? According to the Persian, they were within the walls of the Phantom's retreat; yet he could hear no cry, no call, no plaint from Christine. Heavens above! Were they already too late? Scraping his knees against the stone, he lowered himself down nervously, and let go.

The Persian caught him and urged silence. They stood motionless, listening. Never had the darkness around them been so intense, nor the silence so heavy, so terrible. Raoul bit his lips to prevent himself from shouting: 'Christine! I'm here! I've come for you! Christine, tell me you're still alive!' Taking up his bull's eye lantern again, the Persian shone it above their heads, looking for the opening through which they had come; but it was no longer there. 'Hell and damnation!' he said. 'The stone is back in place!' His light swept briefly across the wall and down to the floor. He bent down and picked up something, some sort of rope, which he examined for a second and then tossed away in horror. '*The Punjab cord!*'[12] he muttered.

'What is it?' asked Raoul.

'This,' replied the Persian with a shudder, 'might well be the noose that killed Buquet. It was never found.' Suddenly seized with fresh anxiety, he shone the red disc of his lantern over the walls. Curiously the trunk of a tree appeared, a living tree with leaves and branches growing all the way up the walls and into the ceiling. The small beam of the lantern made it difficult for them to take in their surroundings: they saw the fork of a

---

* These two pairs of boots, which were placed, according to the Persian's papers, between the flat and the scene from *Le Roi de Lahore*, exactly where Joseph Buquet had been found hanging, were never discovered. One can only assume that some machinist or door-shutter took them.

branch, a leaf, another leaf, and then nothing, nothing at all save a reflection of their own light.

Raoul passed his hand over the wall and felt nothing. 'How strange!' he said. 'This wall is a mirror!'

'Yes, a mirror!' said the Persian, in utter dismay. Still holding the pistol, he wiped his perspiring brow with the back of his hand and added: 'We have fallen into the torture chamber!'

XXII

The Interesting and Instructive Trials and Tribulations of a Persian Below Stage at the Opera

The Persian himself wrote an account of how he had vainly sought to enter Erik's retreat from the lake; how he had discovered the secret entrance from the third mezzanine below the stage; and how he and the Viscount de Chagny found themselves pitted against the Phantom's diabolical inventions in the *torture chamber.*

This account – written in circumstances which shall later be explained – is reproduced here verbatim, for I see no reason to leave out any part of the Daroga's* own account of his misadventures on the lake, before he finally entered Erik's lair with Raoul. Although the early and most interesting part of his narrative may appear to lead us astray, away from the torture chamber, it will soon take us back there; by which time much of importance, notably aspects of his character and manners which the reader may have thought outlandish, will have been explained.

The Persian's narrative

I had never entered the lake-side retreat before, though I had often begged the *Master of the Traps*, as we used to call Erik in my country, to open its mysterious doors to me. He had always refused. I was well placed to know many of his secrets and tricks, and yet I had vainly sought to gain access to it by stealth. Since I had first learned that he had taken up his permanent abode at the Opera, I had frequently spied on him both back-

---

* *Daroga* is the Persian word for 'chief of police'.

stage and below stage. I had secretly followed him to the lake
and watched him row to the other side; but light was always
scant and I was unable to see how he passed through the retaining wall to reach his lair. Curiosity, as well as a terrible
foreboding prompted by some of the freak's remarks, led me
one day, when I thought myself unobserved, to step into the
boat and row towards that part of the wall through which I
had seen him disappear. It was then that I heard the siren who
guarded the approach to his retreat and whose singing very
nearly proved fatal to me.

No sooner had I left the shore than the deep silence was,
little by little, disturbed by a sort of whispered singing all
around me – half sigh, half music. It rose softly from the waters
of the lake. I was surrounded by it, but knew not how. It followed me, moved with me and was so gentle that I felt no fear.
On the contrary, I yearned to be closer to the source of that
sweet, beguiling harmony. I leaned out of the boat over the
water, for there was no doubt in my mind that the singing came
from the water itself. I was in the boat in the middle of the lake,
alone with this voice – for now it was distinctly a voice – beside
me, on the water. I leaned out further. The lake was perfectly
still and, although some moonlight filtered from the Rue Scribe
through an air-vent, I could see absolutely nothing on its sur-
face, which was smooth and black as ink. I shook my head a
little lest it were a ringing in my ears; but quickly realized that
no such ringing could have compared with the sweet sighing
that had followed me and now drew me to the water.

Had I been superstitious or susceptible to fanciful tales, I
should have certainly thought that I had fallen under the spell
of some siren, here to confuse the traveller brave enough to
venture on the waters of the lake. Fortunately, I come from a
country where we are too fond of the fantastical not to have
gained considerable insight into it. Having studied it myself at
length, I knew that in the hands of an expert the simplest tricks
could work wonders on a man's imagination.

I had no doubt that the voice on the lake was yet another
one of Erik's inventions. But it was so perfect that, as I leaned
out of the boat, I was driven by a desire not so much to discover

the trick as to savour its charm. I leaned out, further, further . . . until I almost capsized the boat.

Suddenly, two monstrous arms issued from the depths of the lake, seized me by the neck and dragged me down into the watery abyss with irresistible force. I should certainly have been lost if I had not had time to utter a cry. Hearing it, Erik – for it was he – recognized me. Instead of drowning me, as was certainly his first intention, he swam all the way to the shore pulling me in his wake, and gently laid me there.

'How foolhardy of you!' he said, as he stood before me with that hellish water streaming down his body. 'Why did you try to enter my abode? I never invited you! I want neither you nor anyone else there! Did you save my life only to make it not worth living? Beware! Some day Erik might forget the great service you rendered him; and as you know, no one can stop Erik, not even Erik himself.'

I let him speak, but I had only one wish now: to know what I already called *the trick of the siren*. My curiosity was soon satisfied, for while Erik is a fiend – such is my opinion of him, having had, alas, occasion to see him at work in Persia – there is also something of the arrogant, vain youth in him. Thus, having created a sensation, he loves nothing more than to reveal the truly prodigious ingenuity of his mind.

He laughed and showed me a long reed. 'It's the simplest trick you ever saw,' he said, 'but it's very useful for breathing and singing in the water. I taught it to the Tonkinese pirates, who are now able to hide under water in rivers for hours on end.'*

'Your trick nearly killed me! And it may have proved fatal to others too!' I sternly remonstrated.

He made no answer, but rose before me with an expression of childish threat that I knew only too well.

I would not be intimidated. 'Erik, you promised me!' I insisted. 'No more murders!'

'Me, a murderer?' he asked, amiably.

* An official report from Tongking, received in Paris at the end of July 1909, relates how the famous Dê Tham and his men were tracked down by our soldiers; and how every one of these pirates made a successful escape,[1] thanks to this trick with the reeds.

'You, wretched man!' I cried. 'Have you forgotten the *Rosy Hours of Mazenderan*?'[2]

'No,' he replied, suddenly gloomy, 'though I would rather not be reminded of that time. But, all the same, I did make the young sultana laugh!'

'Let's not talk about the past, but the present,' I said. 'You are answerable to me for your actions now! Because if it were not for me, you would not be here at all. Remember that, Erik: I saved your life!'

And I took advantage of this turn in the conversation to mention something that had long been on my mind. 'Erik,' I asked, 'Erik, promise me that . . .'

'What?' he retorted. 'You know that I never keep my promises. Promises are for fools.'

'Tell me . . . at least you can tell me, of all people . . .'

'What?'

'The chandelier, Erik . . .'

'What about the chandelier?'

'You know what I mean.'

'Oh,' he sniggered, 'I don't mind telling you about the chandelier! *I did nothing!* The fittings were old and weak.' When Erik laughed, he was particularly terrifying. He climbed into the boat with such a sinister chuckling that I could not help trembling. 'Old and weak, my dear Daroga! The chandelier fell of its own accord! Just crashed down! And now, take my advice: go and dry yourself, or you'll catch a head cold! Never set foot in my boat again! And above all, never try to gain entry to my retreat: I am not always here, Daroga! And I should be sorry to have to dedicate my *Requiem Mass* to you!'

Still chuckling, he stood at the stern of his boat and sculled away, grotesquely swaying to and fro. I imagined him guarding his retreat like some perilous reef, save that his eyes shone above it. Soon I could see only his eyes and then finally they too vanished into the night.

Henceforth I relinquished all thought of reaching his lair from the lake. That route was obviously too well guarded, especially now that he knew that I was aware of it. But I felt that there must be another way into it, for on more than one occasion when I was spying on him below stage, I noticed that Erik was suddenly able to disappear from the third mezzanine. Yet I knew not how.

I must repeat that ever since I had discovered that Erik had settled in the Opera House, I lived in perpetual terror of his devastating whims, not so much for my own sake as for that of others.* Whenever some accident, some fatal event occurred, I would ask myself: 'Did Erik do this?' while the others cried: 'The ghost did it!' – often enough with a smile on their faces! Poor devils! Had they known that their ghost was made of flesh and blood, and far more terrible than the vain shadow of their imagination, their smiles would have quickly faded. If only they had known to what extremes Erik could go, especially in an arena such as the Paris Opera House! Or had any inkling of the appalling fears that troubled me!

Erik had earnestly announced to me that he had changed, and had become the most virtuous of men since *he was now loved for himself*. This phrase disturbed me greatly – I could not help shuddering at the very thought of it. His ghastly, unique and repulsive ugliness had put him beyond the pale of humanity; I had gathered the impression that it had freed him from any obligations towards mankind. The tone of his voice when he boasted of his newly found love only served to further my anxiety: having heard it before, I dreaded that it might foreshadow new and more appalling atrocities. I knew to what sublime and disastrous climax Erik's despair could rise and the words he had spoken – vague intimations of impending disaster – left me in constant dread.

Besides, I had witnessed the curious exchanges between him and Christine Daaé. Hiding in the store-room that adjoined the singer's dressing-room, I had listened to wonderful musical dis-

---

* Here the Persian might have admitted to being not altogether disinterested, for payment of his modest pension as former Daroga would undoubtedly have ceased, had the Tehran government learned that Erik was still alive. It is only fair, however, to add that the Persian had a noble and generous heart. I do not doubt for a moment that the anticipation of possible disaster and its attendant consequences for others weighed heavily on his mind. His conduct throughout this affair clearly proved it and is beyond praise.

plays which evidently sent Christine into rapture; but, all the same, it was inconceivable to me that the power and beauty of his voice – which sounded at will like thunder or the whisper of an angel – should make her blind to his ugliness. It all became clear when I realized that Christine had not yet seen him! I secretly inspected her dressing-room as soon as the opportunity presented itself and, remembering what Erik had taught me, I soon discovered the device by which the wall supporting the mirror could be made to pivot. I found out that he had used hollow bricks as a conduit for his voice, so that Christine could hear him as if he were beside her. I also discovered the passage that led to the spring bubbling out of the wall and to the Communards' dungeon as well as the trap that gave Erik direct access down to the mezzanines.

To my utter amazement, a few days later, I saw for myself that Christine and the awe-inspiring monster had met. I came upon them at the end of the Communards' passage: she had fainted and he was leaning down, bathing her temples with the water from the little spring. A white horse, the horse from *Le Prophète*, which had disappeared from the stables under the Opera House, quietly stood nearby. I approached them. Erik's reaction was terrible: his yellow eyes flashed at me and, before I could say a word, he punched my head and knocked me out. By the time I came to, Erik, Christine and the white horse were gone. Now I knew for certain that the poor girl was held prisoner in the lake-side retreat. Without hesitation or thought of the danger to myself, I rushed forthwith to the shore. I lay in hiding on the black strand for a full twenty-four hours, waiting for him to appear, for I assumed that he would need to go out for provisions. (Here I must report that when he ventured on to the streets or dared show himself in public, he wore a papier-mâché nose, with a fake moustache attached, to conceal the hideous absence of his nose. This did not altogether dispel his macabre appearance – passers-by could be heard saying: 'He looks as if he's just returned from the grave!' – but it made him almost, and I stress the word 'almost', acceptable.)

So it was that I kept watch patiently from the shore of the lake – his 'Lake Avernus', as I had heard him call it several times, sneeringly. After waiting for many long, weary hours, I began to suspect that he had taken the secret passage on the third mezzanine, when I heard a gentle splashing in the darkness. I saw Erik's yellow eyes shining over the water and soon his boat touched the shore. He jumped out and walked up to me.

'You've been here for twenty-four hours,' he said, 'and you're in my way. I am warning you: your recklessness will have dire consequences. And you'll only have yourself to blame. I have been extraordinarily patient with you. You think you have been following me, you great clod, whereas in fact *I* have been following you; and you cannot conceal anything from me. *The Communards' passage is mine and mine alone.* Yesterday, I spared you. But I am telling you: don't ever let me catch you there again! Do you hear me?'

He was so furious at the time that I did not venture to interrupt him. He snorted and carried on, thereby confirming my worst fear: 'Do you hear me? I am warning you once and for all – once and for all, understood? You must stop your recklessness! The man with the soft felt hat has already arrested you in the cellar on two occasions. He did not find out what you were doing down there; and when he marched you to the directors' office, they took you to be some eccentric Persian curious about the stage and its machinery. (I heard it myself. I was there, in that office. You know I'm everywhere.) Your recklessness will eventually make them wonder what you are after down here, then they will find out that you are after Erik; and then they will be after Erik themselves and they will discover my retreat. And if they do, my dear Daroga, all Hell will break loose! Nothing will stop me! Nothing!' He snorted again. 'If Erik's secrets are no longer his own, all Hell will break loose and *many of the human race will suffer*! That's all I have to say, and unless you are a greater clod than I thought you were, that should be warning enough!'

He had returned to the boat and now sat in the stern, tapping his heel as he waited to hear my answer.

'It's not Erik I'm after here!' I simply said.

'Who, then?'

'Christine Daaé, as you very well know,' I replied.

'I have every right to invite her to my own home,' he retorted. 'She loves me for myself.'

'That's not true,' I said. 'You abducted her and are keeping her under lock and key.'

'Listen,' he said. 'Will you promise not to meddle in my affairs again, if I prove to you that she loves me for myself?'

'Yes, I promise you,' I replied, without hesitation, for I was convinced that he would never be able to prove anything of the sort.

'Well, then, it's quite simple. Christine Daaé will leave this place and later come back of her own accord! Yes, she will return to me because she wishes to do so, she will return because she loves me for myself!'

'Oh, I doubt that she will come back! But you must let her go.'

'You are mistaken, you great clod! I don't have to do it, but I am only too happy to let her go! And she will return, for she loves me! And one day we shall be married ... married at the Madeleine Church![3] Do you believe me now? I'm telling you: my Wedding Mass is already written. Wait until you hear the *Kyrie*!' Beating time with his heel, he sang softly: '*Kyrie! Kyrie! Kyrie eleison!*'[4] and then added: 'Just wait until you hear that Mass!'

'Look here,' I replied. 'I shall believe you if I see Christine Daaé come out of your retreat and later go back to it of her own free will.'

'And you won't meddle in my affairs any more?'

'No.'

'Very well, you shall see for yourself. Come to the masked ball. Christine and I will be attending it briefly. Go and hide in the store-room and when Christine comes back to her dressing-room, you shall see that she is only too ready to take the Communards' passage and join me.'

'I'll be there!'

If I saw her go to him of her own accord, I would have to accept the facts. Surely a beautiful woman has the right to love a hideous monster, especially when he can seduce her with music and she happens to be a distinguished opera singer.

'Now be off, for I must fetch some provisions!'

So I left. I still feared for Christine Daaé, and was especially troubled by his words of warning, which had sharply reawakened my deep sense of dread. 'How will it all end?' I brooded. Although I am rather fatalistic by nature, I could not rid myself of a vague, indefinable anguish. By sparing the life of that knave, who now threatened *many of the human race*, I had taken on a huge responsibility!

To my utter astonishment, everything happened as Erik had predicted. Christine Daaé left the retreat and apparently returned to it of her own free will on several occasions. I tried to forget about this mysterious love affair, but my apprehensions made it difficult for me to put Erik out of my mind. All the same, caution prevailed and I did not make the mistake of going back to the shore of the lake, or the Communards' passage. But the thought of a secret entrance on the third mezzanine never left me; and I repeatedly went down there in the daytime when it was generally deserted. I spent many hours waiting, hidden behind a backdrop from *Le Roi de Lahore*, which had been left there for reasons unknown since this opera was seldom performed. At last my patience was rewarded. One day, I saw Erik coming towards me, on all fours. I was certain that he could not see me. He passed between the scene concealing me and a flat; and, facing the wall, pressed on a spring that caused a stone to move and a passage to appear. He went through the opening, and the stone closed behind him. Now I knew his secret, a secret that would allow me access to his retreat whenever I chose.

Wanting to confirm this, I waited for at least half an hour and then pressed the spring myself. Everything happened as I had seen. But I was careful not to venture into the opening, for I knew that the monster was in his lair. My fear of being caught brought to mind the death of Joseph Buquet. I had no wish to compromise the advantage of a discovery that might benefit a great many people, *many of the human race*, as Erik had put it. So, having carefully worked the stone shut by a method that I knew from Erik's days in Persia, I left the third mezzanine.

As you may imagine, my interest in the relationship between Erik and Christine Daaé persisted, not from morbid curiosity, but, as I have explained, because of the terrible sense of dread that haunted me. 'If he discovers that she does not love him, then anything could happen,' I thought. I continued to wander – as cautiously as I could – about the Opera House and soon learned the sad truth about the story of their love: Erik inspired Christine with terror and the sweet child's heart belonged wholly to Raoul de Chagny. While they played their innocent game of husband-and-wife-to-be, and roamed through the upper regions of the Opera House to escape Erik's attention, little did they suspect that someone was watching over them. I would stop at nothing: I would even kill the monster myself if necessary, and then report to the police. But he did not show himself – which did not reassure me in the least.

I had a plan. I thought that jealousy would draw him out of his retreat, thus enabling me to enter it safely from the third mezzanine. It was important, for everyone's sake, that I should explore the place itself. One day, tired of waiting for an opportunity, I worked the stone and immediately heard the strains of sublime music: Erik was working at his *Don Juan triomphant*, with the internal doors wide open. I knew that he regarded it as his masterpiece. I stayed within the dark opening and listened, careful not to make the slightest movement. He stopped playing for a moment and began pacing to and fro like a madman. Then I heard him say, his voice resounding: 'I have to finish it *first*! Finish it completely!'

This did nothing to reassure me either and, when the music resumed, I gently worked the stone shut again. But I could still hear the faint, distant music rising from the depths of the earth, just as the siren's voice had risen from the depths of the lake. And I recalled the machinists' claim, jokingly dismissed at the time, that on finding Joseph Buquet's hanged body they had heard 'something that sounded like music for the Dead'.

On the evening of Christine Daaé's abduction, I arrived at the theatre rather late, fearful of bad news. In that morning's paper I had read of the forthcoming marriage of Christine and the Viscount de Chagny, and I had spent the remainder of that day anxiously pondering whether, after all, I should not *denounce that monstrous fiend*. But finally I reasoned that such a course of action might only serve to precipitate a catastrophe.

When my cab set me down outside the Opera House, I looked at the building and was almost surprised to see it *still standing*! But, like all Orientals, I am something of a fatalist, so I went in, *ready for anything*.

Christine Daaé's abduction during the prison act, which inevitably stunned everybody, found me prepared. I was quite certain that Erik, that great illusionist, had conjured her away. I thought that Christine's fate was sealed and that *many more were perhaps doomed* too. I even considered urging those who were still lingering in the theatre to run for their lives. But I contained myself, for surely they would take me for a madman. Besides I knew that if I were to shout 'Fire!', for instance, so as to make them leave, the ensuing stampede and frantic struggle for the exits could prove even more catastrophic.

So I decided to act independently without delay. The moment seemed propitious for Erik was probably preoccupied with his captive, leaving me with the advantage. Now was the time to enter his retreat by stealth from the third mezzanine. Needing assistance in this undertaking, I approached the poor desperate Viscount, who agreed on the spot with a show of trust that deeply touched me. I had sent Darius, my servant, for the pistols; and when he joined us in the singer's dressing-room, I gave one to the Viscount, advising him to hold himself, as I myself did, ready to fire. After all, Erik might be waiting for us behind the wall. We were to go along the Communards' passage and then through the trap into the mezzanines.

On seeing my pistols, the young Viscount asked me if we were going to fight a duel. 'Yes,' I replied, 'and what a duel!' But, of course, I had no time to explain anything to him and the brave young man knew practically nothing about his adversary. So much the better! I thought.

Fighting a duel with the most reckless desperado was nothing compared to battling with one of the world's greatest illusionists! I myself was daunted by the prospect of fighting a man who was only visible when he so wished, but saw everything while you yourself remained in the dark – a man whose uncanny science, cleverness, imagination and skill enabled him to draw upon all the resources of nature to deceive your eyes

and ears, and lure you to your death – and all this beneath the
stage of the Paris Opera House, the very home of phantasma-
goria! How could one contemplate such a prospect without
trembling to the core? Imagine pitting yourself against someone as talented as Robert-Houdin, but who mocks and hates
by turns – empties pockets one minute only to kill the next – in
a theatre with no fewer than five levels under the stage and
twenty-five above![5] I was about to fight the Master of the
Traps! I remembered all those pivoting trap doors – so effect-
ive, so deadly – he had installed in the palaces of Persia. And
now it was in a world of traps that I was to confront the Master of the Traps!

While I hoped that he was still in the lake-side retreat with
Christine Daaé, having probably carried her there unconscious,
my greatest fear was that he might be close by, ready to use his
strangling cord.

No one knew better than he how to throw the Punjab cord:
if he were a king among illusionists, then he was a prince
among stranglers too. He had lived in India and acquired
exceptional skills in the art of strangulation. Later, during the
Rosy Hours of Mazenderan, the young sultana, whom Erik
was employed to amuse, demanded new thrills, and he had
introduced the sport of the Punjab cord for her entertainment.
In an enclosure, he would face an adversary – usually a man
condemned to death – armed with a long pike and a broad
sword; Erik's only weapon was the cord; and, just when his
opponent seemed about to kill him with a tremendous blow,
the cord would hiss through the air. With a flick of the wrist,
Erik would tighten its grip round the poor wretch's neck and
drag his body before the young sultana and her female companions, who watched from a window and applauded. The
sultana herself learned to wield the cord, killing several of her
companions – and even a few visiting friends.

But I would rather not dwell on the painful events of the
Rosy Hours of Mazenderan. I only mention all this to explain
my concern with the ever-present threat, once the Viscount and
I had reached the mezzanines, of death by strangulation. Down
there, my pistols were of little use. Since Erik had not opposed

us when we entered the Communards' passage by the mirror, I was quite certain that henceforth he would not allow himself to be seen. All the same, he could still strangle us. I had no time to explain any of this to the Viscount; and I must confess that, had time permitted, I would have probably refrained from telling him that a Punjab cord, ready for use, might be lurking somewhere in the shadows. It would have merely complicated matters. I simply instructed the Viscount to follow my example and keep his hand at eye level, with his arm bent. This way we were sure to protect our necks, for even the most adroit wielder would have caught us around the hand or arm too, and the deadly weapon would have been rendered harmless.

Having avoided the inspector, several door-shutters and the firemen, later faced the rat-catcher and then escaped the attention of the shadowy figure in the felt hat, the Viscount and I reached the third mezzanine without further mishap and slipped unnoticed between the flat and the scene from *Le Roi de Lahore*. I worked the stone, and we jumped into the retreat that Erik had fashioned for himself in the double shell of the foundation walls of the Opera House. (*This had been easily achieved, for he was one of the chief contractors hired by the architect Charles Garnier to build the Paris Opera House. He continued building, secretly and by himself, when the works were officially suspended at the time of the war with Prussia, the siege of Paris and the Commune.*)

I knew Erik too well to presume that I had discovered all the new tricks he might have devised in recent years; so I did not feel at all safe when I jumped into his lair. I knew that in Mazenderan, he had transformed a simple, straightforward residence into a diabolical palace, where no word could be uttered without being overheard or repeated through echo. How many family scenes, how many bloody tragedies had the evil freak and his traps thus provoked? To add to the confusion, one lost all one's bearings once inside the buildings he had transformed. He created amazing devices, the most curious, cruel and dangerous of which was the so-called *torture chamber*. The poor wretches led to that chamber were prisoners condemned to death, save for a few instances when the young sultana amused herself by tormenting some innocent merchant. It was, to my mind, the most horrendous invention of the *Rosy Hours of Mazenderan*. When the victims could take no more, they could always put an end to their suffering by hanging themselves – a Punjab cord or bowstring was left for that purpose at the foot of the iron tree.

Imagine my alarm, therefore, when I realized that the room into which the Viscount and I had dropped was an exact replica of the torture chamber of the *Rosy Hours of Mazenderan*.

At our feet, I found the strangling cord that I had been dreading all evening. I was convinced that this rope had been responsible for Joseph Buquet's death. Like me, the machinist must have seen Erik work the stone, and tried it for himself. Having reached the end of the passage, he had probably fallen into the torture chamber; and, with the stone closed, death by hanging had proved his only way out. I could imagine Erik dragging the body up and hanging it next to the scene from *Le Roi de Lahore* as an example to others or *to fuel superstitious rumours, thus guarding his retreat against potential intruders*! Later he had gone back to fetch his Punjab cord lest this distinctive rope, made out of catgut, arouse the suspicions of some astute examining magistrate. This was how I explained its disappearance.

And here was that self-same rope, at our feet, in the torture chamber! I am no coward, but I broke into a cold sweat and trembled as the little red disc of my lantern glided over the walls. The Viscount noticed it and asked: 'What's the matter?' I frantically motioned him to be silent, for I still entertained the hope that we might have reached the torture chamber unbeknown to Erik.

But even this would not necessarily save us, for I could readily imagine that the torture chamber was designed so as to automatically *ward off intruders*. Yes, the torture might begin *automatically*, and we had no idea which of our movements might set it off.

I urged my companion to keep absolutely still. A heavy silence weighed upon us. The red glow of my lantern was still gliding around the torture chamber. Oh, it was all too familiar!

XXIII

In the Torture Chamber

Continuation of the Persian's narrative

We were in the centre of a small, hexagonal room. All six walls were lined with mirrors from top to bottom. The corners showed joins in the glass, where sections of mirror mounted on winding drums could turn. I recognized these and I recognized too, in one of the corners, the iron tree . . . the iron tree with the iron branch from which one might hang oneself. I seized my companion's arm: the Viscount was quivering in his eagerness to let Christine know that help was at hand. I feared lest he might cry out to her.

Suddenly, we heard some noise to our left. It sounded at first like a door opening and shutting in an adjoining room, followed by an indistinct moan. I gripped the Viscount's arm more tightly, and then we distinctly heard these words: 'Make your choice: *the Wedding Mass or the Requiem Mass!*'

I recognized the voice.

There was another moan, and then a long silence. Now I was convinced that Erik was unaware of our presence, for otherwise he would have ensured that we could not hear him. For that, he only had to shut the small, hidden peep window that looked down into the chamber. Besides, if *he* had known of our presence, the torture would certainly have already begun. This meant that we had the advantage over Erik: unbeknown to him, we were close. And it had to remain thus. I feared nothing so much as the impulsiveness of the Viscount, who wanted to break through the walls to Christine Daaé, whose moans we assumed we had heard.

'The Requiem Mass is not very cheerful,' came Erik's voice, 'whereas the wedding Mass – believe me – is magnificent! Make up your mind and let me know which you have chosen! I just can't go on living like this, buried like a mole under the ground! *Don Juan triomphant* is finally finished, and now I want to lead a normal life. I want to have a wife like any normal man and take her out on Sundays. I have made a new mask that makes me inconspicuous. People will not turn and stare at me in the streets. You will be the happiest of women. We shall sing for ourselves and no one else, in rapturous bliss. But you're crying! You're afraid of me! And yet, deep down, I am not a bad man. Love me and you'll see! *To be good, all I ever needed was to be loved for myself.* If you loved me, I would be as gentle as a lamb; and you could do with me as you pleased.'

Soon the moans that punctuated this litany of love grew in intensity. Never in my life had I heard such despair. The Viscount and I then realized that this terrible lament came from Erik himself. As for Christine, she must have been simply standing there – perhaps on the other side of the wall in front of us – dumbstruck, with the hideous freak pleading at her feet. His lament would by turns rise, roar and die down like the waves of some vast ocean, and thrice he raucously bewailed his fate: 'You don't love me! You don't love me! You don't love me!' Then, relenting, he asked more gently: 'Why are you crying? You know that it breaks my heart to see you cry!'

A silence ensued.

Each silence gave us fresh hope: we thought that perhaps Christine was now alone behind the wall. Our quandary was how we might let her know we were there without alerting her captor. We could not leave the torture chamber unless she herself let us out – we could only help her if she herself helped us first – for no door was visible to us.

Then an electric bell disturbed the silence and there was a sudden brusque movement on the other side of the wall.

'Someone is at the door! Come in, come in!' Erik thundered. 'Who could it be at this hour? Wait for me here *while I tell the siren to open the door*,' he said with an ominous chuckle. His steps died away and a door closed. I had no time to stop and consider what new, heinous crime he might be about to perpetrate. I had but one thought in my mind: Christine Daaé was alone behind the wall!

The Viscount was already calling to her: 'Christine! Christine!'

Since we were able to hear what was said in the adjoining room, there was no reason to believe that she herself could not hear us. Even so, the Viscount repeatedly called her in vain.

At last, a faint voice reached us: 'I must be dreaming . . .'

'Christine, Christine, it is I, Raoul!'

Silence.

'Answer me, Christine! In Heaven's name, if you are alone, answer me!'

Then Christine's voice whispered Raoul's name.

'Yes! Yes! It is I! You are not dreaming! Christine, trust me! We are here to save you. But be careful! You must tell us if the monster returns!'

'Raoul! Raoul!'

She had him repeat time and again that this was no dream and that he had come to her rescue with the help of a devoted friend who knew of the secret retreat. But Christine's fleeting joy soon gave way to a greater fear. She urged Raoul to flee at once. She feared that Erik might discover where the young man was hiding, for the monster would kill him without hesitation. She hurriedly told us that love had driven Erik insane and that he was ready to *kill everyone as well as himself* if she did not consent to become his wife before God and man at the Madeleine Church. He had given her until eleven o'clock the next evening to make up her mind. He would brook no stay; he said that she must choose between the Wedding Mass and the Requiem Mass. And Erik had added these words, which Christine did not quite understand: 'Yes or no? If your answer is no, everybody will soon be *dead* and *buried*!'

I grasped their meaning only too well, for they echoed my own forebodings, terrifyingly. 'Where is Erik?' I asked.

She replied that he must have gone out.

'Can you make sure?'

'No, I am bound hand and foot.'

Upon hearing this, the Viscount could not suppress a cry of helpless rage. Our safety, the safety of all three of us, depended on Christine's freedom of movement. Yet how could we reach her and untie her?

'Where are you?' she asked. 'There are only two doors in this room – the Louis-Philippe room that I once described to you, Raoul. One is the door through which Erik comes and goes; but I have never seen him open the other one. And he has forbidden me ever to use it, saying that it leads to great danger . . . that it leads to the torture chamber!'

'Christine, we are on the other side of that door.'

'You are in the torture chamber?'

'Yes, but we can see no door.'

'Oh, if I could but drag myself that far and knock on it, then you would know where it is.'

'Does the door have a lock?' I enquired.

'Yes, it does.'

I guessed that it opened with a key like any other door from her side, but that on our side it would be activated by a spring and a counterweight. Finding that spring would be very difficult!

'Mademoiselle,' I said, 'you must open that door for us!'

'But how?' she asked, tearfully.

We heard her straining to free herself from the bonds holding her.

'It seems that our only hope of escape is by subterfuge,' I said. 'You must get the key to this door.'

'I know where the key is,' she gasped, as if exhausted by the effort she had just made. 'But these bonds are so tight. Oh, the monster!'

We heard a sob.

'Where is the key?' I asked, commanding the Viscount to be silent lest he interpose, for time was pressing.

'He keeps it with another bronze key inside a small leather pouch, near the organ, in another room. He calls them his *keys of life and death* and has forbidden me to ever touch them. Raoul! Raoul! You must flee! Everything seems so strange and terrible here! Soon Erik will have lost his mind completely . . .

And you, in the torture chamber! Go back the way you came. If it is indeed a torture chamber, I fear the worst for you!'

'Christine,' said the young man, 'we'll leave together or together we'll die here!'

'There must be some way out of here. We must keep our nerve and find it,' I whispered. 'Why did he tie you up, mademoiselle? You cannot escape; and he knows it!'

'I tried to kill myself. Last night, after carrying me here half unconscious from chloroform, he went out to see his *banker*, or so he said! When he returned he found me with my face covered in blood. I had tried to kill myself by smashing my head against the walls.'

'Christine!' groaned Raoul, and he began to sob.

'That's why he bound me. He will not let me die until eleven o'clock tomorrow evening.'

Our exchanges through the wall were much more cautious and fitful than I could ever render in this account. Often we would stop mid-sentence, thinking that we had heard a creak, the sound of footsteps or some other suspicious movement. She would say: 'No, no, it's not him! He went out. I'm sure he went out! I heard the passage to the lake close behind him.'

'Mademoiselle,' I suggested, 'Erik bound you and he will unbind you if you can persuade him to do so. Coax him! Remember, he loves you!'

'Alas, how could I ever forget?'

'Smile at him, plead with him, tell him that your bonds hurt.'

Just then Christine Daaé whispered: 'Hush! I can hear noise from the passage to the lake! It's him! You must go now!'

'We cannot leave, even if we wanted to,' I said as emphatically as I could. 'We are trapped! Trapped in the torture chamber!'

'Hush!' whispered Christine again.

The three of us fell silent.

From behind the wall we heard the sound of heavy, trailing footsteps. There was a pause and then the floor creaked once more. Next came a tremendous sigh, followed by a cry of horror from Christine.

'Forgive me for letting you see me like this!' Erik said. 'I am in a fine state, don't you think? But it's *the man's* fault! Why did he come? I mind my own business, and steer clear of other people's affairs! Well, he shan't meddle again! It's the siren's fault . . .' He let out another deeper, more awful sigh, which seemed to rise from the very abyss of his soul. 'Why did you cry out, Christine?'

'Because these ropes hurt, Erik.'

'I thought I had frightened you.'

'Erik, loosen my bonds. Am I not at your mercy?'

'But you want to die.'

'No, I shall wait until eleven o'clock tomorrow evening for that, Erik.'

Again we heard shuffling footsteps.

'Come to think of it . . . since we are to die together . . . and I am just as eager as you are to end it all . . . I too have had enough of this life, you know. Wait, don't move, I'll release you. Just say "no" to me and it will all be over, *for everyone*! After all . . . why wait until eleven o'clock tomorrow? True, it would have been grander, finer . . . I've always had a weakness for dramatic gestures. But it's childish! We should only think of ourselves . . . prepare for death . . . nothing else matters . . .

'*You're staring at me! Is that because I am wet through?* Oh, my love, I should not have gone out. It's raining cats and dogs out there! And I think I am seeing things . . . You know, Christine, the man who came just now and was met by the siren – now he'll mind his own business at the bottom of the lake – I thought he looked like . . . There, turn round. Are you satisfied? You're free now . . . Oh, my poor Christine, look at your wrists: I hurt you . . .! I deserve death for this alone. Talking of death, *I must sing my Requiem for him!*'

Upon hearing this, I was gripped by a terrible anguish . . . I too had once tried to reach Erik's retreat from the lake and had unwittingly set off some warning signal. I remembered the two arms that had emerged from the inky waters. What poor wretch had, like me, strayed on to that lake?

The thought of his fate tempered my response to the success of Christine's subterfuge as the Viscount murmured into my ear the magic word 'free!' But who was that man whose requiem we now heard?

Ah, what sublime and tormented music! The building roared with it . . . and the entrails of the earth shuddered. Having put our ears against the mirror-lined wall to follow Christine's efforts on our behalf more closely, we now could hear nothing save his music for the Dead, or rather music of the Damned . . . strains to which demons might cavort in the bowels of the earth. Erik's *Dies Irae* raged all around us like a storm. We were surrounded by thunder and lightning. I remembered having heard it once at the palace of Mazenderan, where the stony voices of the human-headed bulls on the ramparts seemed to be singing with him. Never before, though, had I heard him sound like this. He sounded like the god of Thunder.

But then the organ and the voice stopped, and so abruptly that the Viscount and I drew back from the wall. In a changed, distorted voice, we distinctly heard Erik rasp: '*What's happened to my keys? Where are they?*'

XXIV

The Torture Begins

Continuation of the Persian's narrative

The voice repeated angrily: 'What's happened to my keys? You've taken them! Is that why you asked me to release you?' We heard hurried footsteps: Christine must be running back to the Louis-Philippe room, as if to seek refuge nearer to us.

'Why are you running away from me?' asked the furious voice, following her. 'Return those keys to me! I've told you, they are the keys of life and death!'

'Listen to me, Erik,' sighed the girl. 'Since it's settled that we are to live here together, why can I not have them? All that belongs to you now also belongs to me.'

The trembling in her voice as she spoke was poignant. The poor girl must have summoned all that was left of her strength to overcome her terror. But the fiend would not be deceived by her naive ploy and faltering tone.

'What do you want with these two keys?' he demanded.

'I should like to enter the room that you have yet to show me. Women are naturally inquisitive!' she said in a way that she hoped would sound playful, but seemed in fact so contrived that it must have further aroused his suspicion.

'I don't like inquisitive women,' he retorted, 'and you would do well to remember the story of Bluebeard.[1] Come now, give me those keys! Return them to me, you inquisitive little minx!'

And we heard him laugh as Christine yelped in pain. Erik must have retrieved the keys from her.

At this, the Viscount could contain himself no longer and I

could not quite muffle his cry of impotent rage by covering his mouth with my hand.

'What's that?' said Erik. 'Did you hear, Christine?'

'No, no,' replied the poor girl. 'I heard nothing.'

'I thought I heard a cry.'

'A cry! Are you mad? Who but I would cry down here? It was I who cried when you hurt me! And no one else.'

'I don't like the way you said that! You're trembling. You're nervous. You're lying! I heard a cry, I definitely heard a cry! There is someone in the torture chamber! Ah, now I understand!'

'There's no one there, Erik!'

'Now I see!'

'No one!'

'The man you wish to marry, perhaps?'

'I mean to marry no one, you know that.'

He gave another nasty chuckle. 'Well, we'll soon find out. Christine, my love, we need not open the door to see what's happening in the torture chamber. Let me show you. Look! If someone is really in there, light will shine through the small window hidden at the top of the wall. To check we need only draw back the black curtain covering it and put out the light in here. All done! You're surely not afraid of the dark with your dear husband by your side!'

'But I am frightened! I am afraid of the dark!' came Christine's agonized voice. 'I no longer wish to see this room. Why are you always trying to frighten me, as if I were a child, with your torture chamber? You're right, I should not have been so inquisitive. But now, please believe me: I have no wish to see the room, none at all!'

And then what I had feared above all began, *automatically*. The room was suddenly illuminated by a blazing explosion of light. The Viscount was so shaken by it that he reeled.

An angry voice roared on the other side of the wall: 'I told you there was someone in there! Look! There's light coming from the window now! Whoever is behind the wall can't see that window! But you can, and now you're going to climb up this ladder – you've often asked why I keep it here, now you know – and peep into the torture chamber, you inquisitive little minx!'

'Torture? What torture? Who is being tortured? Erik, please say that you're only trying to frighten me! Say it, for love's sake, Erik! Tell me that it's only make-believe!'

'Go up to the window and see for yourself, my love!'

I do not know if the Viscount heard the young woman's agonized plea, for he was distracted by the dazzling display that now appeared before his eyes. As for me, I had seen that sight only too often, through the peep-window, at the time of the *Rosy Hours of Mazenderan*; I concentrated on the conversation between Christine and Erik in the adjoining room, hoping that it might strengthen my resolve and suggest some course of action.

'Go and peep through the little window! And then tell me: *does he have a handsome face?*'

We heard the ladder being raised against the wall.

'Up you go! No, wait! I'll go first, dearest!'

'No, no! I will. Let me!'

'Oh, my love! You're so sweet! How kind of you to spare me the effort at my age! Now tell me how he looks! Does he have a handsome face with a handsome nose? If only people knew how fortunate they are to have a face with a nose of their very own! Then they would never come sniffing round my torture chamber!'

At that moment, we distinctly heard these words above our heads: '*There is no one there, dear.*'

'No one? Are you sure there's no one?'

'No one at all.'

'I'm pleased to hear it. But what's the matter, Christine? Come, come, you're not going to faint, are you? Why would you if there's no one there? Come, collect yourself! *Now, how do you like the view?*'

'Oh, I like it very much!'

'Good! Very good! You feel better now, don't you? That's good! No more excitement! And how strange that a place like this should have such a splendid view!'

'Yes, it's like the waxworks in the Musée Grévin.[2] But, tell me, Erik, I can see no instruments of torture! You gave me such a fright!'

'But why, if there's no one there?'

'Did you design the room yourself? It's very beautiful. You are a great artist, Erik.'

'A great artist indeed, in my own way.'

'But, Erik, why do you call this room the torture chamber?'

'Oh, it's very simple. I'll explain. But first, tell me, what did you see?'

'I saw a forest.'

'And what is in a forest?'

'Trees.'

'And what is in a tree?'

'Birds.'

'Did you see any birds?'

'No, I did not see any.'

'Well, what did you see? Think! You saw branches! And one particular branch is . . .' he said ominously, '. . . a *gibbet*! That's why my forest is called the torture chamber! You see, it's my little joke. I don't express myself like other people. I don't do anything like other people. But I am very tired of it! Tired of having a forest and a torture chamber in my home! Sick of living like a mountebank, in a house full of tricks! Yes, I am sick and tired of it all! I want a nice, quiet apartment like everyone else, with ordinary doors and windows, and a proper wife. You should be able to understand that, Christine. Do I have to repeat myself? I want a wife whom I can love, take out on Sundays and keep amused the rest of the week. Oh, you would never be bored with me! I know lots of tricks, card tricks for instance. Here, shall I show you some? That will help us to pass the time until eleven o'clock tomorrow evening . . . My dear little Christine! Are you listening to me? You seem to feel more comfortable with me . . . perhaps even love me . . . No, of course, you don't love me! But no matter: you will! At first, you couldn't look at my mask because you knew what it concealed. And now you don't mind looking at it and have forgotten what's behind! You don't push me away any longer. One can become used to anything: when there's a will ... Plenty of people who marry without love, later come to adore each other. Oh, I'm deceiving myself! But you would have lots of fun with me. I'm unique, I swear! I swear to the God who will bless our marriage – when you come to your senses. I'm unique. For instance, I'm the greatest ventriloquist that ever lived! You're laughing ... Perhaps you don't believe me? Listen.'

I realized that the evil freak, who really was the greatest ventriloquist that ever lived, was trying to divert Christine's attention from the torture chamber; but to no avail, for she could think only of us!

She repeatedly pleaded with him, gently pressing him: 'Do put out the light! Erik, put out the light that shines from that little window!' She assumed that this light, which had suddenly appeared and of which he had spoken threateningly, must serve some terrible purpose. Yet at the same time she must have felt reassured, for she had seen the two of us behind the wall, bathed in that same resplendent light, alive and well. Even so, she would have certainly rested easier without the light.

Meanwhile, Erik was already displaying his skills as a ventriloquist. 'Here,' he said, 'let me raise my mask a little ... Oh, just a little! So that you can see my lips, such lips as I have. Look: they're not moving. My mouth is closed – such a mouth as I have – and yet you hear my voice. I'm speaking with my stomach. No tricks, it's completely natural! It's called ventriloquism. It's well known. Listen to my voice. Where shall I throw it? In your left ear? In your right ear? From the table? From those little ebony caskets on the mantelpiece? Do you want to hear it distant? close by? loud? shrill? nasal? My voice can be anywhere and everywhere! Listen to it, my love, coming from inside the little casket to the right of the mantelpiece. What does it say? *I am the scorpion, will you turn me round?* And now, quick! What does it say from inside the little casket on the left? *I am the grasshopper, will you turn me round?* And now, quick again! Here it is, inside the little leather pouch. What can you hear? *I am the keys of life and death!* And now it's coming from Carlotta, Carlotta's fine, precious throat, I swear! What does it say? It says: It's me, Mr Toad, it's me singing: *And a*

deep languid charm . . . croak! I feel without alarm . . . croak!
With its . . . croak! And upsy-daisy! It's on a chair in the Phantom's box and it says: "*Her singing tonight is enough to bring
down the chandelier!*" And now? Aha! Where is Erik's voice
now? Listen, Christine, my love! Listen! It's on the other side of
the forbidden door! Listen! I am now in the torture chamber!
And what do I say? I say: "Woe betide those who have a nose,
a proper nose of their own, and come sniffing round my torture
chamber!" Ha, ha, ha!'

The cursed voice of the ventriloquist was everywhere. It was
extraordinary. It passed through the hidden peep-window and
through the walls. It ran around us and between us. Erik was
next to us, speaking to us! We made a move as if to pounce
upon him. But Erik's voice, swifter and more fleeting than an
echo, had bounced back to the other side of the wall!

And then, although we could hear nothing more, this is what
happened, I later learned:

'Erik! Erik!' said Christine. 'Enough of this, please. Stop!
What's happening in here? It's very hot all of a sudden.'

'Oh, yes,' Erik replied, 'it's becoming unbearably hot!'

'But what is it? What's happening here? This wall is so
hot . . . burning hot!'

'Let me explain, Christine, my love: it's because of the forest
in the next room.'

'The forest? What do you mean?'

'Why, did you not notice? *It is a forest from the Congo,*' he
bellowed, with a cruel laugh that drowned the sound of Christine's eager pleading.

The Viscount shouted, banging the walls with his fists like a
madman. I could not restrain him. For a while, we could hear
nothing save Erik's resounding laughter, and he himself could
probably also hear little else. Then came the sound of a struggle, of a body falling to the floor and being dragged. A door
slammed, and then nothing, nothing more save the scorching
silence and midday heat of an African forest!

XXV

'Barrels! Barrels! Any Old Barrels!
Any Old Barrels to Sell?'

Continuation of the Persian's narrative

I have already said that the Viscount and I were trapped in a hexagonal room, regular in shape and lined with mirrors from top to bottom. Since then, many rooms have been designed on this model; they are mainly exhibited at fairgrounds and variously called 'the hall of mirrors', 'the palace of illusions' or some such name. But the author of this invention was none other than Erik himself. I saw him build the first room of this kind at the time of the *Rosy Hours of Mazenderan*. A single decorative feature placed in one corner, such as a column, was enough to create instantaneously a hall with a thousand columns; for, thanks to the mirrors, the real room was multiplied by six, each reflection being, in its turn, multiplied endlessly. To amuse the young sultana, Erik had designed a room that could thus become 'an infinite temple', but she soon tired of this trifling illusion, whereupon Erik turned the room into a torture chamber. An iron tree with painted leaves replaced the architectural motif in the corner. This tree was absolutely life-like but made of iron so as to withstand any assault from the 'patient' imprisoned in the chamber. The resulting view could, as we shall later see, change instantaneously through the use of automatically rotating winding-drums with varying painted motifs that fitted neatly into the angles of the mirrors. These allowed three different sets of decorative features to appear in sequence.

The walls of this strange room offered no purchase whatsoever, because, apart from the one solid item in the corner, the room contained nothing but mirrors, strong enough to resist

any raging onslaught from the poor wretch who had been
thrown into the chamber barefoot and empty-handed. There
was no furniture; light shone from the ceiling; and an ingenious
system of electric heating, which has since been used elsewhere,
allowed the temperature of the walls and hence of the room to
be raised at will.

Erik had relied entirely on simple physical phenomena to
produce, with a few painted branches, the magical illusion of
an Equatorial forest under the blazing midday sun. Reader, I
am offering here a detailed description of it so that you may
not doubt the balance of my mind or suggest that I am a liar or
a charlatan.*

If my account of what happened had merely read as: 'Having
reached the cellar, we came across an Equatorial forest under the
blazing midday sun', the effect upon the reader would have been
one of stunned incomprehension, but this is not what I wish to
achieve. My purpose here is to relate as accurately as possible the
ordeal the Viscount and I endured in the course of the terrible
events that were investigated by the French police for a time.

I shall now resume my story where I left off.

When the ceiling lit up and the forest became visible around
us, the Viscount was shocked beyond all expectations. The
sight of that impenetrable forest, with its countless trunks and
branches, threw him into a dreadful stupor. He raised his hands
to his face in a vain attempt to dispel this nightmarish vision,
blinked as if he had just abruptly woken up and, for a moment,
forgot to *listen*.

I have already said that the sight of the forest did not surprise me; I was therefore able to listen – for the two of us – to
what happened in the adjoining room as well as look about me.
My attention focused not so much on the scene before us as on
the mirrors that created it. The glass *was damaged* here and
there: I could see scratch marks and it was even scarred in
places despite its thickness – which proved to me that the

* One must understand that, at the time when he wrote his account, the Persian could not but make every effort to forestall objections from incredulous
readers. Nowadays, when this sort of curiosity has become rather commonplace, such a level of detail would be unnecessary.

torture chamber in which we now found ourselves *had been used already*.

Yes, some wretch, less barefoot and empty-handed than the victims of the *Rosy Hours of Mazenderan*, had already fallen into this deadly mirage. Enraged and maddened, he had struck at those mirrors, which, despite the slight damage inflicted upon them, continued to reflect his agony. And the branch of the tree from which he had finally put an end to his suffering was arranged in such a way that, at the moment of dying, he had – as a bitter consolation – seen a thousand hanged men kick about with him in unison.

Yes, poor Joseph Buquet had undoubtedly suffered here! Were we to die as he had done? I did not think so, for I knew that we had a few hours before us and that I would employ them to better purpose than Joseph Buquet ever could. After all, I was thoroughly acquainted with most of Erik's 'tricks'; and if ever I were to act on that knowledge, now was the time.

First, I gave up all thought of leaving this accursed chamber by the route that had led us here. I dismissed the possibility of working the stone that sealed the passage for the simple reason that it would have been impossible to reach up to it: we had dropped into the torture chamber from too great a height. There was no furniture in the room and nothing could be achieved either by climbing the iron tree or by one of us standing on the other's shoulders.

There was only one possible outlet, the door into the Louis-Philippe room. But, though this outlet looked like an ordinary door on Christine's side, it was absolutely invisible to us. We therefore had to try to open it without knowing where it was – which would be quite a challenge.

Having given up all hope of being released by Christine and heard that cruel monster drag the poor girl out of the Louis-Philippe room *lest she should interfere*, I resolved to set to work at once.

But first I had to calm the Viscount, who was already wandering about the room and raving like one demented. The snatches of conversation between Christine and her abductor, which he had earlier overheard despite his agitation, had greatly disturbed him; add to that the shock of the magical forest and the oppressive heat which now caused perspiration to run down the side of his face, and you will have no difficulty in understanding his state of mind. Despite my best efforts, the young man was unable to contain himself.

He paced back and forth aimlessly and threw himself into illusive space trying to follow a path that led into the distance, only to knock his forehead, a few steps on, against the reflection that had created the forest.

All the while, he shouted Christine's name, brandished his pistol, called out to the Phantom, challenged the Angel of Music to fight to the death, and swore profanities at the illusory forest. In short, the torture was beginning to affect his unprepared mind. I tried as best I could to combat it by reasoning with the poor fellow as calmly as possible. I made him touch the mirrors, the iron tree and the branches on rotating panels, explaining to him the optical laws that made all this possible and telling him that we could not allow ourselves to be deluded by the luminous images surrounding us like ordinary, ignorant folk.

'We are in a room, a small room – that's what you must keep saying to yourself. And we shall leave the room as soon as we have found the door. Now I must look for it!' And I promised him that, if he let me act without disturbing me with his shouts and frantic movements, I would discover the trick of the door within the hour.

Then he lay flat on the floor, as one might in a wood, and declared that he would wait until I found the door out of the forest, since he had nothing better to do! And he added that, from where he was, 'the view was splendid!' (Clearly the torture was working on him despite my explanations.)

As for myself, ignoring the forest, I set about my task of feeling the nearest mirror panel all over. *I searched for the weak point* that must be pressed so as to open the door, assuming that it was designed like all Erik's secret doors and traps. Sometimes the weak point felt only like a blemish on the glass, no larger than a pea, under which the spring lay hidden. I ran my hands over the glass endlessly as high as my arms could reach on the assumption that Erik, who was about my height, would not have placed the spring higher than he himself could stretch – this was my only hope, yet still a mere hypothesis. I had decided to inspect each of the six mirror panels in turn systematically, and then scrutinize the floor just as painstakingly.

I ran my fingers over the successive panels with great care, but also with great speed, for I was already suffering from the heat. There was not a minute to spare – we were literally roasting in that blazing forest.

I had been working like this for half an hour and had gone over three panels, when I was disturbed by a muttered exclamation from the Viscount and unfortunately turned round to face him.

'I am stifling from the infernal heat reflected by the mirrors,' he said. 'When will you find that damned spring? If you take much longer, we'll be roasted alive!'

I was not sorry to hear him speak thus. He had not referred to the forest, which gave me hope that his reason might still hold out against the torture for a time. But he added: 'What consoles me is that Christine has until eleven o'clock tomorrow evening. If we can't get out of here and save her, at least we'll be dead before her! Then Erik's Mass will serve for all of us!' He took in a deep breath of hot air and almost fainted.

As I did not share my companion's desperation or willingness to die, I gave him a few words of encouragement and returned to my panel; but I had made the mistake of taking a few steps while talking to him and, in the tangle of the illusive forest, I could not be sure that I was facing the same panel as before. I had to begin all over again.

I could not hide my dismay and the Viscount was quick to realize its cause. This came as a fresh blow to him. 'We'll never get out of this forest,' he groaned. His despair grew and, as it grew, made him increasingly forget that he was only dealing with mirrors. He became all the more convinced that he was in a real forest.

Meanwhile, I had begun again to search, to feel. Now the fever gripped me too for I could find nothing, absolutely nothing. No sound came from the adjoining room. There was no way out, we were quite lost in the forest, without a compass, guide or help of any kind. Oh, I knew what awaited us if no one came to our assistance, or if I did not find the spring! But, seek as I might, I saw nothing but branches, beautiful branches reaching straight up before me, or gracefully arching over my head. But they gave no shade, which was to be expected since we were in the midst of an Equatorial jungle, in the Congo, with the midday sun beating down upon us.

The Viscount and I had repeatedly taken off our coats and then put them back on again, finding at times that they increased the sensation of heat and at others that they protected us from it. I still retained some fighting spirit, but the Viscount seemed to me to be quite 'gone'. He claimed that he had been walking in the forest continuously for three days and nights in search of Christine Daaé! Now and then, he thought he saw her behind the trunk of a tree, or slipping through the branches, and his pleading brought tears to my eyes: 'Christine!' he cried, 'why are you running away from me? Don't you love me any more? Are we not engaged to be married? Christine, wait for me! Can't you see how exhausted I am? Christine, have pity on me! I don't want to die here, alone, in this forest!'

And then, at last, he said deliriously: 'Oh, I am so thirsty!'

I too was thirsty. My throat was on fire.

Yet, squatting on the floor now, I went on searching, searching tirelessly for the spring to the hidden door. I knew that it was dangerous to remain in the forest as evening drew nigh. Already dark shadows were gathering around us. Then suddenly it was night: near the Equator, it falls rapidly with hardly any twilight.

The Equatorial forest is always a place of danger at night, particularly when, as was the case with us, there were no means to light a fire to frighten off wild animals and keep them at bay. I did indeed try for a moment to break off some branches, with the intention of setting them alight with my lantern, but I bumped into the glass and then remembered that these branches were but images.

The heat had not subsided with the onset of night; on the contrary, it was even hotter in the blue moonlight. I urged the

Viscount to hold both pistols ready to fire and not to stray from camp, while I went on looking for the spring.

Suddenly, the roar of a lion tore through our ears.

'It's quite close,' whispered the Viscount. 'Can't you see it? Look! There! Through the trees, in that thicket! If it roars again, I'll shoot it!'

It roared again, louder than before, and the Viscount fired. I doubt that he shot the lion; though he hit a mirror, as I saw the next morning, at dawn. We must have covered some considerable distance during the night, for we suddenly found ourselves at the edge of a desert, a vast desert of sand and stone. There was little point in leaving the forest only to wander in a desert. I wearily lay down beside the Viscount, exhausted by my vain search for the elusive spring.

I was rather surprised – and I said as much to the Viscount – that we had encountered no other dangerous animals during the night. Usually, after the lion came the leopard and sometimes the sound of the tsetse fly.[1] These effects were easily produced. As I explained to the Viscount, while we rested before attempting to cross the desert, Erik imitated the roar of a lion by means of a long, narrow drum with a piece of ass's skin stretched over one end. A band of catgut lay across the drum head and was attached in the middle to a catgut string passing down the whole length of the interior of the drum.[2] Erik rubbed this string up and down with a glove smeared with resin and, depending on the rubbing motion, imitated to perfection the sound of the lion or the leopard, and even that of the tsetse fly.

The idea that Erik was probably in the adjoining room, working this trick, made me suddenly resolve to talk to him, for we had now abandoned all thought of taking him by surprise. By this time he must know the identity of the occupants of his torture chamber. I called out to him across the desert as loudly as I could: 'Erik! Erik!' But there was no reply. We were surrounded by silence and the barren expanse of that *stony* desert. What would become of us in the midst of this fearsome solitude? We were literally dying of heat, hunger and thirst – especially thirst. At last, the Viscount raised himself on one elbow and pointed to the horizon. He had just glimpsed the oasis.

Yes, over there, far in the distance was an oasis, an oasis with limpid water that shimmered like a mirror and reflected the iron tree! Yes, this was the mirage scene. I recognized it at once. It was the most terrible of the three! No one had been able to withstand it, no one. I did my utmost not to lose my head, *not to yearn for the water*, because I knew that if one yearned for that water, the water that reflected the iron tree, and if yearning for it, one came up against the mirror, then the next step, the only step was to hang oneself from the iron tree!

So I cried out to the Viscount: 'It's a mirage! Don't be deceived! There is no water! It's another trick!'

He told me outright to shut up; he was sick of my tricks, my springs, my hidden doors and my hall of mirrors! He turned upon me, declaring angrily that I must be either blind or mad to imagine that all that water flowing over there, among those splendid, countless trees, was not real! The desert was real too! And so was the forest! It was no use trying to deceive him! He was a seasoned traveller, he had sailed round the world!

'Water! Water!' he cried as he dragged himself along with his mouth open in readiness to drink.

My own mouth was open too . . .

For not only did we see the water, but we also *heard it*! We heard it flow, we heard it *lap*! You understand that word 'lap', do you not? It is a word that you can *hear with your tongue*! Thus you stretch out your tongue to hear it better!

Lastly – and this was the most excruciating torment of all – we heard rain. But it was not raining! It was yet another diabolical invention. I knew well enough how Erik had created that effect! He put small pebbles into a long, hollow tube that was closed at both ends and lined with a series of protruding wooden or metal pins. When the narrow tube was upended, the falling pebbles hit the pins and bounced off one another, making a sound that imitated perfectly the patter of heavy rain.[3]

Reader, try to imagine us dragging ourselves towards the lapping water with hanging tongues! *Our eyes and ears were full of water, but our tongues were parched!* When we came up against the mirror, the Viscount put his tongue to it and I too licked the glass: it was burning hot! Then we rolled about on the floor with cries of agony and despair. The Viscount put the one pistol that was still loaded to his temple; and I stared at the Punjab cord at my feet. Now I knew why the iron tree was still there in the third and final scene! The iron tree was waiting for me!

But, as I stared at the Punjab cord, I saw something which caused me to start so violently that the Viscount stopped in his tracks even as he murmured: 'Adieu, Christine ...' I grabbed his arm, took the pistol from him, and then crawled towards what I had seen.

I had just discovered, near the Punjab cord, within a groove in the floor, a black-headed nail whose purpose I instantly guessed. At last I had discovered the spring, the spring that would activate the door, liberate us and deliver Erik into our hands.

Smiling at the Viscount, I placed a finger upon the nail and pushed: it yielded to my pressure, yet it was not a door that we saw appear in the wall, but a trap opening in the floor. Cool air came up from below. We leaned over that square of darkness as if over a clear spring: dipping our chins into the cool shadow beneath, we drank it in.

We leaned further and further. What could be down there, in that cellar whose door had mysteriously opened before us? Water, perhaps! Drinking water! I thrust my arm into the darkness and felt a stone and then another. There was a staircase, a dark staircase leading down into a cellar.

The Viscount would have plunged into it at once without thinking, for even if no water was to be found, at least we could escape the searing heat of the abominable hall of mirrors. But, fearing another of Erik's monstrous tricks, I stopped him. I turned up my lantern and went down first.

The winding staircase descended into deepest darkness and felt deliciously cool. All this cool air must have come not so much from any ventilation system installed by Erik, as from the freshness of the ground itself, which must have been saturated with water at such depth – the lake could not be far.

We soon reached the bottom of the staircase. As our eyes became accustomed to the dark, we could make out shapes around us, round shapes upon which I shone my lantern.

Barrels! We were in Erik's cellar, where he kept his wine and perhaps his drinking water. I knew that Erik appreciated good wine, and there was certainly plenty to drink here! The Viscount patted the vessels, repeating: 'Barrels! Barrels! So many barrels!' There were quite a number of them, symmetrically arranged in two rows, on either side of us. They were quite small barrels, which must have facilitated their transport all the way down here.

We examined each barrel, one after another, hoping to find a tap indicating that the contents had already been sampled; but none of the barrels had been opened. We grabbed one, lifting it up slightly to check that it was full. Then I went down on my knees and, with my small pocket knife, set to work on the bung.

Thereupon I heard, seemingly from afar, a strangely monotonous call, which I recognized as one of the street cries of Paris: 'Barrels! Barrels! Any old barrels! Any old barrels to sell?'

I paused. The Viscount had heard it too: 'That's odd! It's as if the voice came from the barrel itself!'

The call was repeated, but more distantly: 'Barrels! Barrels! Any old barrels! Any old barrels to sell?'

'I could swear,' said the Viscount, 'that although more distant now, it still comes from *inside* the barrel!'

We rose to our feet and looked behind it.

'It was coming from inside,' said the Viscount. 'I'm absolutely sure!'

But we heard nothing more. We put it down to our frayed, troubled senses and returned to work on the bung. When I finally succeeded in extracting it, the Viscount cupped his hands underneath the hole.

'This is not water! What is it?' he cried at once, bringing his hands closer to my lantern. I leaned forward to look but what I saw caused me to pull back the lantern so brusquely that it broke and went out, leaving us in utter darkness.

What I had just seen in his hands was ... gunpowder!

XXVI

The Scorpion or the Grasshopper?

Final part of the Persian's narrative

Thus, what we had found down in Erik's cellar confirmed my darkest fears. He had not misled me with his vague threats against 'many of the human race'. Cast beyond the pale of humanity, he had built a secret underground lair to hide his monstrous ugliness; and, should those who lived above the ground track him down to this sanctuary, he had determined to end it all with a catastrophic explosion.

Our discovery threw us into a state of extreme agitation. Only moments ago we had been contemplating suicide; but, as the full horror of the present situation dawned upon us, our past difficulties and current physical deprivations were forgotten. At last we understood the full meaning of Erik's terrible ultimatum to Christine Daaé: '*Yes or no? If your answer is no, everybody will soon be dead and buried!*' Buried in the ruins of the Paris Opera House! Could anyone imagine a more heinous, destructive way to leave this world? The diabolical plan this monstrous creature – the worst that ever stalked the earth – had hatched to safeguard his retreat, would now serve to avenge his tragic, unrequited love. Christine had been given until tomorrow evening at eleven o'clock. The timing had not been chosen at random! There would be crowds of people,[1] 'many of the human race', up there, in Garnier's magnificent palace of music. Erik could not have hoped to die in finer company: he would go to his death surrounded by the most beautiful women of the day, bedecked in their finest jewellery for the occasion. Tomorrow evening at eleven o'clock! Were

Christine Daaé to say 'no', we would all be blown to smithereens at the height of the evening performance. Tomorrow evening at eleven o'clock! Yet what else could Christine say but no? She would surely prefer to espouse death itself rather than marry a living corpse! How could she know that her decision would determine the fate of 'many of the human race'? Tomorrow evening at eleven o'clock!

We fumbled our way towards the staircase, and away from the gunpowder. The light from the hall of mirrors, shining above through the open trap door, had gone out. We kept repeating to ourselves: 'Tomorrow evening at eleven o'clock!' At last, I found the staircase. But as I set foot on the first step, I suddenly stopped. An agonized thought burned through my mind: '*What time is it now?*'

What was the time? For all we knew, 'tomorrow evening at eleven o'clock' might already be upon us, or due in the next few moments! Who could tell us the time? We seemed to have been trapped in this hell for days, for years, since the beginning of time itself. At any minute now, we could all be blown to pieces!

'What's that? I heard something! Viscount, did you hear it? Over there, in the corner. Good heavens! It sounds like the ticking of a mechanical device! There it is again! Why is it so dark in here? It might be coming from a detonator! Can't you hear it? Are you deaf?'

We became frantic and, spurred on by fear, stumbled up the stairs. What if the trap door had been shut? That would explain the darkness! Oh, we must escape from this darkness, even if it meant returning to the deadly light of the hall of mirrors!

When we reached the top of the stairs we found the trap door still open, but it was now as dark in the torture chamber as it had been down in the cellar. We climbed through the trap and crawled along the floor – the floor that separated us from the gunpowder store. What was the time? We shouted, we called out: the Viscount to Christine and I to Erik, reminding him that I had once saved his life. But nothing came of it, save more despair and frenzy on our part: what was the time? We argued. We tried to calculate how long had elapsed since we had entered the torture chamber, but we were utterly confused and at our wits' end. If only we could find out what the time was! My pocket watch had stopped but the Viscount's was still going. He remembered that he had wound it up before dressing for the Opera, which suggested that the fatal hour might still be some way off.

The slightest sound rising through the trap we had vainly tried to shut brought fresh anxiety. What time was it? We had no matches, yet we had to know! The Viscount came up with the idea of breaking the glass of his watch, so as to feel the position of the two hands. We fell silent as his probing fingertips touched the dial, using the winding mechanism at the top as a point of reference. Judging by the space between the hands, he thought it might actually be eleven o'clock!

But perhaps it was not that eleven o'clock which we so dreaded. It might even be past eleven o'clock, in which case we still had another twelve hours ahead of us . . .

'Hush!' I suddenly whispered, for I thought that I heard footsteps in the adjoining room.

Yes, there came the sound of doors opening and shutting, and then hurried footsteps. Someone tapped against the wall. It was Christine Daaé: 'Raoul! Raoul!' she cried.

We all began talking at once, on either side of the wall. Christine sobbed; she had feared that the Viscount was dead. Erik had been impossible, raving insanely for her to give him the consent she denied him. And although she had promised to agree if he would only allow her to enter the torture chamber, he had obstinately refused, and instead uttered vile threats against the whole of mankind! Finally, after tormenting her thus for hours and hours, he had gone out, leaving her alone to reflect one last time.

Hours and hours?

'What's the time now, Christine? What's the time?'

'Nearly eleven. Five minutes to eleven to be precise.'

'But which eleven?'

'The hour that will decide between life or death! That's what he said just before he left,' Christine replied, in an agonized voice. 'He was terrifying. He raved like a madman, he tore off his mask and his yellow eyes shot flames! He laughed like an intoxicated demon, saying: "Yes or no? I'll give you five minutes to think it over on your own. I wouldn't want to embarrass you at the moment of consent. Forever the gentleman, I will spare you your blushes. See" – he took one of the keys of life and death from his leather pouch – "here is the little bronze key to open the two ebony caskets on the mantelpiece in the Louis-Philippe room. In one of the caskets you will find a scorpion and in the other a grasshopper – both exquisitely rendered in Japanese bronze. These are both mounted on pivots and will tell me your answer. If you choose to turn the scorpion, I shall take it to mean *yes* when I return to this, our engagement chamber. But if, on my return, I find that it is the grasshopper that has been chosen, then I shall it take to mean *no* and this room will become our mausoleum." And once again he laughed diabolically. I continued to beg him for the key to the torture chamber, promising to be his wife if he granted me just that one wish. But he replied that there was no further need for that key and he would throw it into the lake! He left, warning me that he would be back in five minutes' time, and his parting words were: "The grasshopper! Beware of the grasshopper! A grasshopper not only turns: it leaps . . . leaps into the air . . . *straight up into the air.*" '

I have tried here to convey coherently Christine's fitful, delirious speech, for she too must have plumbed the depths of human suffering in the past twenty-four hours . . . and perhaps more even than we had. She repeatedly broke off to enquire if Raoul was hurt and, touching the walls that were now cold, asked why they had been so hot moments ago.

The five minutes had nearly elapsed and the scorpion and the grasshopper were rattling my brain. Nevertheless, I was sufficiently lucid to realize that if the grasshopper were chosen, it would go up and so would everything else too. I was convinced that the grasshopper controlled the electrical device that would blow up the gunpowder store.

On hearing Christine's voice, the Viscount seemed to recover his moral strength. In a few hurried words, he explained to her the formidable threat that Erik posed to us and the whole

Opera House, and urged her *to turn the scorpion* at once. Since Erik so fervently wished that she should choose the scorpion, turning it would surely avert the threatened catastrophe.

'Quick! Go and do it, Christine, my beloved,' commanded Raoul.

Silence.

'Christine, wait!' I cried. 'Where are you?'

'By the scorpion.'

'Don't touch it!'

The idea had suddenly come to me – for I knew Erik only too well – that the poor girl might have been fiendishly deceived once again. Perhaps it was the scorpion that would blow everything up. After all, why had he left her? Where was he now? More than five minutes had passed, and he had not returned. Perhaps he had taken shelter and was waiting for the explosion! Perhaps there was nothing else for him beyond this. He could not realistically hope that Christine would ever consent to sacrifice herself. Why had he not returned? 'Don't touch the scorpion!' I repeated.

'He's coming!' cried Christine. 'I can hear him coming.'

....

And there he was. We heard his approaching footsteps. He joined Christine in the Louis-Philippe room without saying a word.

'Erik!' I called out. 'It's me, the Persian! Don't you recognize my voice?'

He replied at once with extraordinary calm: 'So you're still alive in there, are you? Well, keep your mouths shut.'

I tried to speak, but the coldness of his command chilled me to the bone: 'Not a word, Daroga, or I'll blow us all to pieces. It's mademoiselle's prerogative to speak,' he said, adding: 'Mademoiselle has not touched the scorpion' – his voice was so calm! 'Yet neither has mademoiselle touched the grasshopper' – so cold-blooded! – 'but it is still not too late to make the right choice. There, let me open the caskets for you – you see I have no need for a key since I am the Master of the Traps, and open and shut what I please, when I please. Look at the sweet little creatures inside these delicate ebony caskets, mademoiselle. Don't they look real? Don't they seem harmless? But, as the saying goes, appearances can be deceptive' – he spoke in a flat, monotonous voice. 'Should you choose the grasshopper, mademoiselle, we shall all die. There is enough gunpowder under our feet to blow up an entire district of Paris. But if you choose the scorpion, mademoiselle, the gunpowder store shall be flooded. And thus you will grant the gift of life to several hundred Parisians who are at this very moment applauding a rather mediocre masterpiece by Meyerbeer. With your own fair hands, mademoiselle' – he sounded so weary now – 'you are going to turn the scorpion and then the bells of the Madeleine Church will ring merrily – so merrily – for our wedding day!'

A silence; and then: 'If, in just two minutes' time by my watch – and a splendid watch it is – you have not turned the scorpion, mademoiselle, I shall turn the grasshopper . . . and the grasshopper, remember, *leaps straight up into the air*!'

The silence that ensued was terrifying, worse than any we had experienced before. I knew that when Erik spoke with that quiet, gentle, slightly weary voice, it meant that he had reached the end of his tether: that he was capable of the most abominable crimes or the most selfless devotion; that the slightest irritation might unleash a storm.

Realizing that our fate was out of our hands, the Viscount fell to his knees and prayed. As for me, I pressed both hands to my chest, for my heart was pounding so fiercely that I thought it would burst. We were intensely aware of the excruciating dilemma that Christine Daaé faced in those final seconds. We understood why she hesitated to turn the scorpion. What if the scorpion, rather than the grasshopper, were to set off the explosion? What if Erik was simply intent on destroying everything, regardless?

At last he spoke: 'The two minutes are up,' he said in a soft, angelic voice. 'Goodbye, mademoiselle. Off you go, little grasshopper!'

'Wait, Erik!' cried Christine, who must have clutched at his arm. 'Swear to me . . . swear to me, by your infernal love, that the scorpion is the right choice!'

'Yes, to set off our wedding.'

'Ah, you see! You said "to set off"!'

'Our wedding, sweet, innocent child! The scorpion will open the celebrations. But enough! Since you won't turn the scorpion, I'll turn the grasshopper!'

'Erik!'

'Enough!'

I added my cries to those of Christine while the Viscount remained on his knees, praying.

'Erik! I have turned the scorpion!'

The tension was palpable as we waited in the darkness . . . waited to be blown to smithereens . . . waited for thunder and ruin! For we heard something stirring in the black abyss beneath our feet, something that might herald the triumph of death and destruction: through the gaping trap rose a disturbing hiss which sounded like the fuse of a rocket burning! It was quite faint at first, but grew louder.

Picture us as we listened, with our hands clutching our hearts, expecting to join 'many of the human race' in death any second!

But that was not the hiss of a burning fuse. It sounded more like water.

To the trap! To the trap!

Listen! Listen! That's the sound of water!

To the trap!

Water! Water! All our thirst, which had been forgotten when terror struck, now returned with a vengeance at the sound of water.

To the water!

The water was rising inside the cellar, covering the barrels, the barrels of the gunpowder – 'Barrels! Barrels! Any old barrels?' We rushed down the stairs with parched tongues. Now the water was up to our chins, in our mouths and we drank. We stood in the cellar, drinking the brackish water. And then as we climbed back up the stairs, the rising water followed us in the darkness.

All that gunpowder soaked, wasted! Great work! Erik had certainly not scrimped with the water! And at this rate, the whole lake would soon drain into the cellar.

When would it stop? We were out of the cellar and the water was still rising. It had come up with us and was spilling out on to the floor of the room. If it continued thus, Erik's retreat would soon be completely flooded. We were already splashing about in the pool that was forming in the hall of mirrors. Surely there was more than enough water by now and Erik needed to halt the flow!

'Erik! Erik! There's water enough to soak the gunpowder! Stop the flow now! Turn the scorpion!'

But Erik did not reply. We heard nothing but the sound of the water rising.

'Christine! Christine!' cried the Viscount. 'The water is up to our knees!'

But Christine did not reply. We could hear nothing but the sound of the water rising. Not a sound from the adjoining room! No one there! No one to stop the flow! No one to turn the scorpion! We were alone in the darkness and the brackish water was relentlessly rising, engulfing us and making our blood run cold!

'Erik! Erik!'

'Christine! Christine!'

By now, we were treading water. Lifted off our feet by the irresistible rushing motion, we were carried around, thrown to and fro against the dark mirrors; and, thrusting our heads above the whirlpool, we gave voice to our distress.

Would we die here, would we drown in the torture chamber? I had never witnessed such a death at the time of the *Rosy Hours of Mazenderan*. No, Erik had never shown me anything like this through the peep-window.

'Erik! Erik!' I cried. 'I saved your life! Don't forget! You were sentenced to death! You were going to die! I opened the gates, and let you escape so you might live! Erik!'

We whirled around in the water like wreckage from a storm. Suddenly my desperate hands grabbed the trunk of the iron tree! I called to the Viscount, and we both clung to the hanging branch. The water continued to rise!

'Tell me, how far is it between the branch of the tree and the top of the domed ceiling? Can you remember? Maybe the water will stop rising: it's bound to stop sooner or later! In fact, I think it's stopping now! But no, no, it isn't! Swim! Swim for your life!'

Our arms became entangled as we tried to keep our heads above water; we choked; we struggled in the dark water; already we could hardly breathe but we could hear air escaping from the room through some hidden vent-hole.

'Let the swirling waters take us up to the air-vent, so we might breathe through it!'

But my strength was deserting me. I clutched at the walls, trying to find some purchase from the smooth glass – in vain! We were whirling ever faster! Then we suddenly began to sink! One last attempt! One last cry: 'Erik! Christine!' And then only the sound of the dark rushing water pounding in our ears as we sank deeper! And, before losing all consciousness, I dimly recollect hearing through the incessant din: 'Barrels! Barrels! Any old barrels! Any old barrels to sell?'

Thus ended the written account that the Persian had entrusted to me.

XXVII

The End of the Phantom's Love Story

It was Christine Daaé's sublime selflessness that saved Raoul de Chagny and his companion from the horror of their situation and certain death. I heard the end of the story from the Daroga himself.

When I went to see him, he still occupied the small apartment in the Rue de Rivoli, opposite the Tuileries Gardens, and he was gravely ill. It took all my fervour as a committed reporter and historian to convince him to re-live and recount the final episodes of that tragic story, in the interest of the truth. The Daroga received me at a window overlooking the Tuileries Gardens. He sat in a large armchair and, as he drew himself up, I could see that he must have once cut a very handsome figure. His green eyes were as striking as ever, but he looked exceedingly tired. All the hair on his head, which was usually hidden by his astrakhan hat, was shaved; he was dressed in a long, plain coat with wide sleeves and he absently twirled his thumbs; but his mind had lost none of its sharpness.

He could not recall those past horrors without becoming distressed and agitated, and I had to draw from him the extraordinary ending to this strange story little by little. Sometimes, I had to patiently coax from him answers to my questions; at other times, moved by his recollections, he would, unprompted, conjure up with stunning vividness the awe-inspiring figure of Erik and the long and terrible ordeal that the Viscount de Chagny and he had endured in the Phantom's retreat. He trembled uncontrollably when he described the moment he regained consciousness in the gloomy Louis-Philippe room after he had very nearly drowned.

I shall now recount the final part of this tragic affair as the Persian himself told it to me. This will serve to complete the written account that he kindly gave me.

When he opened his eyes, the *Daroga* found himself lying on a bed with Raoul de Chagny on a sofa, beside a wardrobe. An angel and a demon watched over them.

After the illusions and mirages of the torture chamber, the primness of that sedate little room seemed yet another invention designed to confuse the mind of the poor mortal foolhardy enough to stray into the waking nightmare of Erik's secret retreat. The wooden bedstead, the waxed mahogany chairs, the chest of drawers, those brasses, the small antimacassars carefully placed on the backs of the armchairs, the clock, the harmless-looking ebony caskets placed on either end of the mantelpiece, the whatnot filled with shells, red pin-cushions, mother-of-pearl boats and an enormous ostrich egg ... this whole scene discreetly lit by a shaded lamp standing on a small round table and the touchingly homely, peaceful and respectable ugliness of the furniture gathered there, *right underneath the Opera House*, proved more disconcerting than any of the fantastic events they had previously experienced.

In that conventional, cosy setting, the figure of the masked man seemed all the more remarkable. He leaned towards the Persian and whispered into his ear: 'Are you feeling better, Daroga? I see you're looking at my furniture – that's all I have left from my poor, wretched mother.'

The Phantom said other things which the Persian was unable to recall; but – and this seemed oddly significant – he remembered very clearly that Erik was the only one who spoke in that strangely dated Louis-Philippe room. Christine Daaé did not say a word: she moved about quietly like a sister of charity who had taken a vow of silence. When she brought in a cup of cordial or steaming tea, the man in the mask took it from her and handed it to the Persian.

Meanwhile M. de Chagny slept on.

Erik poured a drop of rum into the Daroga's cup and said, pointing to the Viscount: 'He was conscious long before we could be sure that you would survive, Daroga. He's quite well. He's sleeping. We must not wake him.' And then Erik left the room.

Raising himself on to his elbow, the Persian looked about him and saw the white figure of Christine Daaé sitting by the fireside. He spoke to her, called her, but he was still very weak and quickly fell back on to his pillow. Christine came to him, laid her hand on his forehead, then moved away again; and the Persian remembered that, as she went, she did not give so much as a glance to Raoul – who, it is true, was sleeping peacefully. She simply returned to her chair, quiet as a nun.

Erik came back with some phials, which he placed on the mantelpiece. He then sat down by the Persian and felt his pulse.

'You are both safe now,' he whispered, so as not to wake the Viscount, 'and soon I shall take you up above ground, *to please my wife.*'

Without further explanation, he rose and left the room once more.

The Persian looked at Christine, motionless in the lamplight. She was reading a small book with gilt-edged pages, which reminded him of editions of religious books such as *The Imitation of Christ*.[1] He could not forget the matter-of-fact tone of Erik's voice when he had said 'to please my wife'. The Daroga called to her again, softly; but Christine must have been completely absorbed in her book for she did not respond.

Erik returned and gave the Daroga a potion, telling him to remain silent and not to speak 'to his wife' again *because it would only result in harm for all those concerned*. After that, the Persian could only remember Erik's dark shadow and Christine's white figure gliding silently about the room, and occasionally leaning over M. de Chagny. The Persian was still very weak and the slightest sound – such as the door of the wardrobe creaking open – made his head throb. Eventually, he too fell asleep like the Viscount.

When he woke again he was in his own room, nursed by his faithful servant Darius, who told him that he had been found outside his apartment, propped up against the door, the previous night. Someone must have carried him there, rung the bell and left.

As soon as the Daroga had recovered sufficient strength and wit, he sent enquiries to Count Philippe's house asking after the Viscount's health. He thus learned that Raoul had not been seen and that Count Philippe was dead. His body had been found on the shore of the lake beneath the Opera, on the Rue Scribe side. Remembering the Requiem Mass he had heard from inside the mirrored torture chamber, the Persian realized the Count had been murdered and guessed who had perpetrated the crime. Knowing Erik so well, he could easily imagine the turn of events. Convinced that Christine Daaé had eloped with his brother, Count Philippe had discovered their travel arrangements and vainly dashed off in pursuit of them along the road to Brussels. Then, reconsidering Raoul's strange revelations about his fantastic rival, Count Philippe had decided to hurry back to the Opera. Once there he learned that the Viscount had attempted to gain admittance to the mezzanines and had subsequently disappeared, leaving his hat in the singer's dressing-room, next to an empty pistol-case. By now convinced of his brother's madness, the Count in turn quickly made his way down into that hellish underground labyrinth. This was enough, the Persian felt, to explain the discovery of Philippe de Chagny's corpse on the shore of that deadly lake guarded by the siren, Erik's siren.

Appalled by this fresh crime, and anxious to discover the eventual fate of Christine Daaé and the Viscount, the Persian did not hesitate and went straight to the authorities. The investigation was in the hands of an examining magistrate named Faure. To speak plainly, he was an incredulous, unimaginative and shallow individual, utterly unprepared, as one might imagine, to receive the Persian's revelations. Having heard the Daroga's statement, he treated him like a madman.

Despairing of ever being taken seriously, the Persian began to write his own account of events. The authorities had dismissed his statement, but the press might take it up. Just as he was finishing the last sentence of the account given in the preceding chapters, Darius announced a visitor – a stranger who would neither give his name nor show his face, and simply said he would not leave until he had spoken to the Daroga.

Guessing the identity of this singular visitor, the Persian had him shown in at once: the Phantom of the Opera, Erik, entered! He looked extremely weak and leaned against the wall, as if he were about to collapse. He took off his hat: his forehead was deathly pale and the mask concealed the rest of his hideous face.

The Persian rose to his feet. 'It was you who murdered Count Philippe! What have you done with his brother and Christine Daaé?'

Erik reeled from the fierce accusation and remained silent for a moment. He then staggered to an armchair and sank into it with a deep sigh. He spoke in fits and starts, a few words at a time, gasping: '*Daroga*, I've not come here . . . to talk about Count Philippe . . . He was already dead . . . by the time I went out . . . he was dead . . . before the siren sang . . . It was an accident . . . a most unfortunate accident. He simply fell . . . into the lake . . . I had no hand in it!'

'You're a liar!' shouted the Persian.

Erik bowed his head.

'I am not here . . . to talk about Count Philippe . . . but to tell you that . . . I am dying . . .'

'Where are Raoul de Chagny and Christine Daaé?'

'I am dying.'

'Raoul de Chagny and Christine Daaé?'

'Of love . . . Daroga . . . I am dying . . . of love . . . That's the truth of it . . . Listen . . . I loved her so . . . I love her still . . . and that love is killing me . . . She was so beautiful . . . so *alive* . . . when she let me kiss her . . . It was the first time, Daroga . . . the first time I ever kissed a woman . . . and she was so alive . . . so beautiful . . . as if she were dead!'

The Persian rose, approached Erik and, suddenly overcoming his repugnance, shook him by the arm.

'Is she alive or dead? Tell me!' he cried.

'Why are you shaking me?' asked Erik and, trying to be more cogent, continued: 'You're not listening: I am dying . . . Yes, she was alive when I kissed her . . .'

'And now she's dead?'

'Listen: I kissed her . . . on her forehead . . . and she did not recoil from the touch of my lips! . . . Oh, she is such a sweet child! . . . Is she dead now? I don't think so; but it's out of my hands . . . No, no, she's not dead! I won't let anyone hurt a hair of her head! Such a good, honest girl . . . And she saved your life, Daroga, at a time when I couldn't have cared less whether you lived or died. As a matter of fact, no one cared about you. What were you doing there, with that little fool? You would have died with him! My word, how she pleaded with me to spare the little Viscount! But as I pointed out to her, by turning the scorpion she had become, of her own free will, my fiancée and you can only be engaged to one person at a time. As for you, your fate was unimportant – you might as well have ceased to exist – you were simply going to die with him!

'But as you were both screaming for your lives because of the rising water, Christine came to me. She looked at me with those beautiful blue eyes, and swore to me, as God was her witness, that we would *live* as man and wife! Until then, in the depths of those eyes, all I had seen was the promise of death; it was the first time I saw the *promise of life*. She was sincere. She would not kill herself. We were agreed. Within moments, all the water had drained back into the lake; but I struggled to revive you, Daroga. In fact, I thought you were done for! But you lived! I had agreed to take you back up above ground. And when I was rid of you, I went back to the Louis-Philippe room, alone at last.'

'But what did you do with the Viscount?' interrupted the Persian.

'Well, you see, Daroga, I could not carry him back up there, just like that. I had to keep him hostage. Yet not inside the retreat itself, because of Christine. So I chained him – the Mazenderan ether had left him as limp as a rag – and locked him up, nice and cosy, in the Communards' dungeon, in the most remote part of the Opera vaults, deep down under the mezzanines, where no one would ever find him nor hear him. Then I rejoined Christine, who was waiting for me.'

At this point, the Phantom rose to his feet with such gravity that the Persian, who had returned to his chair, felt impelled to rise too, sensing that the solemnity of the moment demanded such a response. The Persian even took off the astrakhan hat that covered his shaven head as a mark of respect – so he told me.

'Yes, she was waiting for me,' continued Erik, trembling like a leaf with genuine emotion. 'I saw her standing there, alive and radiant like a real, living bride. I took a few timid, faltering steps towards her and she did not turn away. No, no, she stayed, she waited. I even think, Daroga, she leaned forward a little – oh, not much, but a little – as if to offer me her forehead, like a living bride. And . . . and . . . I . . . I kissed her! I did! I kissed her! And she did not die of horror! She stayed beside me – as if it were perfectly natural – after I had kissed her like that, on her forehead. Oh, how good it is, Daroga, to kiss someone! You would not understand! My own poor, unhappy mother, Daroga, never let me kiss her – she recoiled from me and made me cover my face – nor did any other woman! So imagine! I was so happy that I burst into tears. I fell at her feet, crying. I kissed her feet, her lovely feet, crying. And you're crying too, Daroga, as she was. My angel was weeping!'

As he spoke, Erik sobbed and the Persian himself could not hold back his tears in the presence of the masked man who stood before him with shoulders shaking and hands pressed to his chest, moaning with pain and tender love.

'Yes, Daroga, I felt her tears drop on my forehead! They were warm and soft! I felt them run under my mask and they mingled with my own tears. Yes, I felt her tears on my lips, on my tongue. And do you know what I did then, Daroga? I tore off my mask so as not to lose one of those falling tears . . . and she did not turn away! She did not die! She stood there, weeping over me, weeping with me. We cried together! Almighty God, you have granted me all the happiness a man could ever wish for!'

Erik collapsed, choking. 'Let me weep for a moment! I shall not die just yet,' he gasped.

Soon he resumed: 'Listen, Daroga, listen to me! While I lay at her feet, I heard her say, *"Poor, poor unhappy Erik!"* and *she took my hand*! From then on, I was ready to die for her, like a faithful hound, Daroga! In my hand I held the ring, the plain gold ring that I had once given her, the one she had lost, and I had recovered. It was a wedding ring, you know. I pressed it into her small hand and said: "There! Take it! It's for you and the Viscount! It shall be my wedding-present to you, a present from your poor, unhappy Erik. I know you love that young man. Wipe away your tears!" She asked me, very gently, what I meant. I replied that, where she was concerned, I was merely her faithful hound, ready to die for her. She could marry the young man whenever she pleased, because she had granted me her tears! Ah, Daroga, as I spoke those words my heart was torn asunder, but I had been blessed: her tears had mingled with mine and she had said: "Poor, poor unhappy Erik!"'

Erik was choking with emotion and had to ask the Persian to look away, so that he might take off his mask. The Daroga complied by going to the window and opening it. His heart was full of pity, but he took care to keep his eyes fixed on the trees in the Tuileries Gardens, lest he should glimpse that monstrous face.

'I released the young man from the dungeon,' Erik continued, 'took him to Christine and watched them embrace in the Louis-Philippe room. Christine was wearing my ring and had agreed to wear it until I died. I had made her swear that, upon my death, she would return to the lake from the Rue Scribe at night, and bury me in absolute secrecy with that gold ring. I told her where she would find my body and what she was to do with it. At this Christine came up to me and for the very first time kissed me on the forehead – don't look, Daroga! Yes, she kissed me on the forehead and then they were gone. Christine was no longer in tears, but I was weeping, and I wept alone. Daroga, Daroga, if Christine keeps her promise, she will soon return to the lake!'

Erik was silent now and the Persian had no more questions to ask. He was finally reassured of the fate of Raoul de Chagny and Christine Daaé. No one could have doubted that the Phantom in his distress had spoken the truth that night. He put on his mask again and summoned up the strength to leave. He said that, at the approach of death, he would make arrangements for his most precious possessions to be delivered to the Persian, in gratitude for his past kindnesses. The parcel would contain all Christine Daaé's papers – letters written during her time at the retreat, which she had meant for Raoul – as well as a few personal effects, such as two pocket-handkerchiefs, a pair of gloves and a shoe buckle. Finally Erik satisfied the Persian's curiosity by telling him that, at soon as they were free, Christine and Raoul had resolved to find a far-away spot where, with the help of a priest, they could plight their troth; they had boarded a train from the Gare du Nord and made for Northern climes. Lastly, upon receipt of the promised relics and papers, the Persian was to inform the young couple of the Phantom's death by placing an announcement in *L'Époque*.

There was no more to say. The Persian saw Erik to the door of his apartment, and Darius helped him down the stairs to the street. A cab was waiting. Erik stepped in; and the Persian, who had resumed his post by the window, heard him say to the driver: 'To the Opera!'

The cab disappeared into the night, and that was the last time the Persian saw the poor, unfortunate Phantom.

Three weeks later, *L'Époque* published the following announcement: 'ERIK IS DEAD.'

EPILOGUE

Thus ends the story of the Phantom of the Opera.

As I wrote at the beginning of this book, no one can now doubt that Erik existed. Much evidence has come to light, which enables us to unravel and *explain* his motives and actions during the course of events that came to be known as the 'de Chagny case'.

With such tragedy, passion and crime surrounding the romance between Raoul and Christine – the charming singer's abduction, the drug-induced slumber of the three gas-men, Count Philippe de Chagny's mysterious death in extraordinary circumstances and his brother's subsequent disappearance – the case aroused intense interest in the capital: how could that sublime, enigmatic singer vanish without a trace? She came to be regarded as a victim of the rivalry between the two brothers. No one guessed the truth of the matter. Following Raoul and Christine's disappearance, no one imagined that they might simply have eloped together, withdrawing from society to enjoy a happiness which might have proved embarrassing given Count Philippe's unexplained death. One day they boarded a train from the Gare du Nord; and some day I too might embark on such a journey to your lakes, O Norway, O silent Scandinavia, in search of Raoul, Christine and Mme Valerius, who also disappeared at the same time. Some day, perhaps, I shall hear the lonely wilds of the North echo with the singing of one who knew the Angel of Music.

Long after the case was filed as 'unsolved', thanks to the incompetence of M. Faure, the examining magistrate, the press would occasionally revive the story and attempt to solve the mystery of the unexplained death and disappearances: what monstrous hand had been behind it all? One evening newspaper, which was particularly well versed in theatre gossip, wrote: 'This must have been the work of the Phantom of the Opera!' But, of course, the claim was made in jest.

The Persian was the only one who knew the whole truth but, having had his testimony ignored by the authorities, he had made no further attempt to talk to them after Erik's visit. Since receiving the papers and relics promised by the Phantom, he was now in possession of the main evidence, and it fell to me to tie up the loose ends with his assistance.

I kept him informed of my progress day by day and acted upon his suggestions. He had not returned to the Opera for many years, but his recollections of the building were so accurate that I could not have hoped for a better guide to its hidden recesses. He told me where I could gather further information and whom I should question. It was at his insistence that I called on M. Poligny, who was now close to death. I did not know beforehand that he was so gravely ill, and I shall never forget the effect that my questions about the Phantom had upon him. He looked at me as if I were Satan incarnate and answered with only a few brief, disconnected phrases. These confirmed – significantly – that, in his time, P. of the O. had brought disarray to Poligny's life, which was already full of intrigues as he was something of a rake.

When I reported to the Daroga the meagre results of that brief interview, he gave a faint smile: 'Poligny was taken in by that outrageous scoundrel without ever realizing the extent of his deception.' At times the Persian spoke of Erik with overwhelming admiration, and at others as if he were an unscrupulous villain. 'Poligny was superstitious and Erik knew it. He was familiar with the public and private affairs of the Opera. When Poligny heard, as he sat in Box Five, a mysterious voice describe how he had abused his partner's trust and squandered his own life, he lost his head. At first he thought that this was a voice from Heaven and believed himself to be damned. Later, when the directors began to receive demands for money, he realized that he was the victim of a blackmailer, to whom Debienne had also fallen prey. Both of them were, for various reasons, already tired of the business of the Opera House. So they decided to quit without trying to find out more about the mysterious P. of the O. who was imposing such exacting terms upon them. Greatly relieved at the prospect of being free of an affair that neither of them found in the least amusing, they simply passed the problem on to their successors.' Such was the Persian's view of Messrs Debienne and Poligny.

But what of those successors? I was surprised that P. of the O. should be repeatedly mentioned in Part One of Armand Moncharmin's *Memoirs of a Theatre Director* but hardly featured at all in Part Two. The Persian, who knew those *Memoirs* as thoroughly as if he had written them himself, suggested that I give some thought to the few lines devoted to the Phantom in the second half of the book. These (which, incidentally, offer an interesting description of the simple transaction that brought the business of the forty thousand francs to a satisfactory conclusion) ran as follows:

As for P. of the O., some of whose vagaries have been described at the beginning of these *Memoirs*, I will only say that, with one fine gesture, he redeemed all the worry and embarrassment he had caused my dear friend and partner, and indeed myself. He must have felt that, with such considerable sums of money at stake, the practical joke had gone too far, particularly now the police had been informed. For no sooner had we arranged to meet Inspector Mifroid in our office to tell him the whole story – this was a few days after the final disappearance of Christine Daaé – than we found on Richard's table a large envelope inscribed '*With the compliments of P. of the O.*' in red ink. It contained all the money that he had, for his own amusement, successfully extorted from the directorial purse. Richard at once suggested that we should be content with this outcome and drop the matter altogether. I agreed with him. All's well that ends well, P. of the O.!

Of course, Moncharmin continued to believe – especially after the money was returned – that he had been the butt of one of Richard's imaginative pranks; whereas Richard was convinced that Moncharmin had invented the whole charade of the Phantom of the Opera as a playful revenge for former pranks. I asked the Persian to explain how the Phantom had managed to remove the twenty thousand francs from Richard's pocket despite the safety-pin. He replied that he had not investigated this particular trick, but suggested that I inspect the directors' office, for I should certainly find an answer to the mystery there – after all, Erik was known as the Master of the Traps. I promised to do as the Persian suggested when time allowed, but I may as well tell the reader at once that my investigation was fruitful. I confess that I was surprised to find so much concrete evidence that the Phantom had actually performed all those feats attributed to him.

I am proud to say that I made several important discoveries which corroborate the documentary evidence contained in the Persian's papers, Christine Daaé's letters, the statements from Messrs Richard and Moncharmin's former collaborators, from Little Meg (the worthy Mme Giry has, alas, passed away) and from Sorelli (who is now living in retirement at Louveciennes)[1] – all of which I intend to deposit in the archives of the Paris Opera House.

To my dismay, I have been unable to find a way into the lake-side retreat, Erik having closed off all the secret entrances to it; but I remain convinced that one could reach it if only the lake were drained, an undertaking I have repeatedly requested of the Ministry of Fine Arts.* Nevertheless, I have successfully entered the Communards' secret passage, whose wooden side wall has now rotted in places; and I have located the trap through which Raoul and the Persian gained access to the mezzanines below stage. In the Communards' dungeon, I noticed many initials etched on the walls by the poor wretches who must have been imprisoned there; among these were an 'R' and a 'C'. Is that not significant? Perhaps 'R C' for 'Raoul de Chagny'! And these initials are still perfectly legible today. Of course, I did not stop at that. I went down to the first and third

---

* I mentioned this undertaking again to M. Dujardin-Beaumetz, our gracious under-secretary for Fine Arts, only forty-eight hours before the publication of this book, and his response did not cause me to abandon hope completely. I told him that the state had a duty to dispel the legend of the Phantom of the Opera and establish the facts of Erik's existence. But for that we need – and this would be the culmination of my investigation – to gain access to his lair. Musical treasures may still be buried there. That Erik was a gifted composer is now indisputable. And who knows? The legendary score of his *Don Juan triomphant* might yet be recovered from the hidden retreat.

mezzanines and discovered two traps with pivoting doors unknown to the machinists of the Opera House, who only use traps with horizontally sliding doors.

Finally I invite the reader to visit the Paris Opera House in person. Ask permission to wander at your leisure in the playhouse without the escort of some ignorant cicerone. Enter Box Five and tap the enormous pillar that separates that box from the stage box; knock on it with your fist or your stick and listen carefully: you will notice that *the pillar sounds hollow* up to a man's height. Hence my suggestion that the Phantom's voice actually issued from that pillar: inside there is more than enough room to accommodate a man. Should you be amazed that no one before me has ever thought of examining this pillar, bear in mind that it has the appearance of solid marble, and that the voice contained therein seemed to come from the opposite direction (as we know, Erik was an expert ventriloquist and could throw his voice wherever he chose). The pillar is embellished with rich, elaborate ornamentation, and some day I hope to discover the particular motif that can be raised and lowered at will, and through which the Phantom was able to leave instructions to Mme Giry and reward her for her services.

I imagine that the little I have seen, sensed or guessed of the Phantom's work cannot compare with what this prodigious, fantastic character managed to achieve within the vast and mysterious edifice of the Paris Opera House; but I would readily trade all these discoveries for the one I was fortunate to make, in the presence of the administrator himself, inside the directorial office. Within a few inches of the desk-chair, I found a trap, the width of a floor-board and at most the length of a man's forearm, whose door opened like the lid of a casket, and through which I could see in my mind's eye a hand appear and adroitly reach for the back-pocket of a coat. This was how the forty thousand francs were taken, and later returned.

I excitedly reported my discovery to the Persian, adding: 'Since the forty thousand francs were reimbursed, had Erik drawn up his memorandum of terms simply as an idle prank?'

'Don't you believe it,' the Persian replied. 'Erik needed money. And, thinking himself beyond the pale of humanity, was not held back by moral scruples. He employed the extraordinary skills and imagination that nature had bestowed upon him, in compensation for his monstrous ugliness, to prey upon his fellow-man, in ways that were not only sometimes artistically inventive but also often highly profitable. He returned the forty thousand francs because *he no longer needed that money*. He had abandoned his plan to marry Christine Daaé; he had renounced the world and all it offered.'

According to the Persian, Erik had been born in a small town near Rouen and was the son of a builder.[2] His ugliness filled his parents with horror and fear, and he ran away from home at an early age. For a time he was exhibited at fairs, where a showman advertised him as 'the living corpse'. He must have crossed the whole of Europe, going from fair to fair, and completed his unconventional education as an artist and magician at the source of art and magic among the Romani.[3] Little is known of Erik's life during that time. He reappears at the fair of Nijny Novgorod,[4] where he performed in all his hideous glory. He had already developed a unique singing voice; and his displays of ventriloquism and legerdemain[5] were so dazzling that they were a constant topic of conversation among the travellers on their way to Asia. Spreading along the caravan routes, his reputation reached as far as the Mazenderan palace, where the young sultana, the Shah-in-Shah's[6] favourite, was suffering from intense boredom. A fur merchant, on his way to Samarkand[7] from Nijny Novgorod, spoke of the wonders he had seen Erik perform, and was summoned to the palace. There he was questioned by the Daroga of Mazenderan, who instructed him to go back and procure Erik's services. Thus Erik came to Persia and for a while enjoyed great influence at court. Seemingly unable to distinguish between right and wrong, he committed quite a few crimes during this period. He had a hand in a number of cold-blooded political assassinations and put some of his diabolical inventions to use when the Shah waged war against the Emir of Afghanistan.[8]

The Shah took to him and thus began the *Rosy Hours of Mazenderan*, which the Daroga mentioned in his narrative. When the Shah heard of Erik's highly original ideas on the subject of architecture – he conceived of a building as a box of tricks – he asked him to design and construct a new palace. The result was said to be ingenious: His Majesty was able to come and go within the edifice without being seen, and to appear and disappear as if by magic. When he took possession of this gem, he decided to deal with Erik in the same way a certain tsar had treated the brilliant architect of a church on Red Square in Moscow:[9] Erik's yellow eyes would have to be put out. But then he reflected that, even if he were blind, Erik would still be able to design a grand palace on similar lines for another sovereign; and that, as long as Erik lived, someone would know the secret of that wondrous palace. So he ordered that Erik be executed, together with all the men who had worked under him. It fell to the Daroga of Mazenderan to carry out this abominable decree.

Remembering that Erik had rendered him some services and often amused him, the Daroga enabled him to escape, and this generous gesture nearly cost him his life. Fortunately for the Daroga, a corpse, half eaten by birds of prey, happened to be found on the shore of the Caspian Sea; the Daroga's friends dressed it in Erik's clothes and passed it off as the body of the fugitive. The Daroga's life was spared, but his property was confiscated and he was banished for ever. As a member of the royal family, however, he continued to receive from the Persian Treasury a modest pension of a few hundred francs per month, on which he lived when he fled to Paris.

As for Erik, he went to Asia Minor and thence to Constantinople,[10] where he entered the Sultan's employment. To give some idea of the services that he was able to render a ruler who lived in perpetual terror for his life,[11] I need only say that it was Erik who constructed all the legendary traps, secret chambers and mysterious strong-boxes that were found at the Yildiz-Kiosk after the last Turkish revolution.[12] Erik also invented automata that were dressed like the Sultan and resembled him in all respects,* so as to create the illusion that the Sultan was awake in one place, whereas, in reality, he was asleep elsewhere.

Erik had to leave the Sultan's service for the same reasons

---

* See the interview that Mohammed-Ali Bey gave to the special correspondent of *Le Matin*, the day after troops from Salonika marched into Constantinople.[13]

that had made him flee Persia: he knew too much. Tired of his adventurous, extraordinary and monstrous existence, he longed to lead a normal life. He became a contractor, an ordinary contractor, building ordinary houses with ordinary bricks. When the foundation work of the new Paris Opera House was put out to tender, he bid for it and was awarded part of the contract. But when he found himself in the basement of the vast playhouse, his artistic, *illusionist* bent gained the upper hand once more. Besides, he remained as physically repulsive as ever. So he dreamed of creating for himself a secret retreat, where he could forever hide his monstrous appearance from the world.

The reader knows what followed or can guess the rest of this incredible yet true story. Poor, poor unhappy Erik! Should we pity him or should we curse him? He simply longed to be 'someone', someone normal. But his hideous appearance would not allow it! And he had to hide his genius or *squander it on tricks*, whereas, with an ordinary face, he would have risen to greatness among his fellow-men! He had a big heart, large enough to embrace the entire world; but, in the end, he had to confine himself to a dismal cellar. Yes, all in all, the Phantom of the Opera deserves our pity.

As I stood by his remains, I prayed to God to have mercy on him despite his crimes. For it was God who had made him so monstrously ugly.

Yes, I am quite sure those were his mortal remains that they exhumed from the spot where recordings of singers' voices were to be buried for posterity. I did not recognize the skeleton by his hideous head, for all men who have been long dead are the same, but by the plain gold ring that Christine Daaé must have slipped on to his finger when she came back to bury him as she had promised. The skeleton was found lying near the little spring, where the Angel of Music had first held the unconscious Christine in his trembling arms.

And now what should be done with that skeleton? Surely it cannot be thrown into a pauper's grave! I put it to you that the rightful place for the remains of the Phantom of the Opera is the archives of the National Academy of Music. After all, these are no ordinary bones.

Notes

[DEDICATION]

1. *To my good old brother Jo*: The novel is dedicated to Leroux's younger brother Joseph, a *chansonnier*. Despite their ten-year age difference, the brothers were close and collaborated on a number of projects: they co-wrote the musical *Le Turc au Mans* (1897) and Joseph played 'Herr Professor' in his brother's play *Alsace* (1913). Gaston Leroux was at Joseph's bedside when the latter died of diabetes in 1917 at the age of thirty-nine.

PROLOGUE

1. *corps de ballet*: The company of ballet-dancers. Dance sequences were an integral part of French opera and provided a break or diversion from the main plot. They were highly popular and appeared in all productions at the Paris Opera. This meant that foreign composers such as Gioachino Rossini (1792–1868), Gaetano Donizetti (1797–1848), Giuseppe Verdi (1813–1901) and even Richard Wagner (1813–83) had to compose ballets for French adaptations of their works.

2. *National Academy of Music*: The principal opera company of Paris (the Paris Opera), whose official name in the 1870s was Académie Nationale de Musique – Théâtre de l'Opéra. It was founded in 1669, under the reign of Louis XIV, when it was known as the Académie Royale de Musique.

3. *The events in question ... no more than thirty years ago*: The first instalment of *The Phantom of the Opera* appeared in *Le Gaulois* in September 1909 and the novel was published as a book in February 1910, which places the story around 1879–80. In fact, allusions to actual musical and art works suggest 1881.

4. *Ballet Room*: Known in French as *le foyer de la danse*. A studio behind the stage where female dancers practised their steps and warmed up before their performances, and to which wealthy and influential patrons were permitted access. This much-coveted salon was a social institution particular to the Paris Opera and functioned in many respects like a traditional gentleman's club. Given the dancers' often meagre pay, it also served as a room where sexual favours might be negotiated. (See *Le Foyer de la danse*, ed. Martine Kahane, Paris: Éditions de la Réunion des musées nationaux, 1988.)

5. *the underground lake . . . the Rue Scribe*: The street on the western flank of the Paris Opera House is named after the most celebrated librettist of the nineteenth century, Eugène Scribe (1791–1861); many of the operas mentioned in *The Phantom of the Opera* have libretti by Scribe – most notably *La Juive* (1835), *Le Prophète* (1849) and *Les Vêpres siciliennes* (1855). There is no lake underneath the Palais Garnier. However, when the foundations for the deep sub-stage of the Opera House were being dug, water seeping from an underground river (the Grange-Batelière) was discovered on the site. As explained in Chapter XXI ('Below the Stage'), water had to be pumped out for the foundation work to proceed, and the lower part of the building was later flooded to ensure that it was watertight. But this water was eventually pumped out too (see Charles Nuitter, *Le Nouvel Opéra*, Paris: Hachette, 1875, pp. 24–8), and the only water that remains underneath the Opera House today is that contained in three fire cisterns. In Leroux's fiction, the water flowing nearby has become a subterranean lake. Its imaginary, literary nature is highlighted by the fact that it can be reached from the street whose name happens to evoke the craft of the writer or 'scribe'.

6. *examining magistrate*: In the French judicial system, the all-powerful independent investigator who plays a central role in the early stages of the process of prosecution for a crime.

7. *subscribers of the Opera*: The patrons who purchased tickets in advance for the whole season, and usually rented front seats in the stalls or boxes. Those among them who had tickets for all three performances of the week (Mondays, Wednesdays and Fridays) were admitted as of right to the Ballet Room, together with a number of influential men, often politicians, who were also allowed access.

8. *the Faubourg Saint-Germain*: A district in central Paris, situated on the south side (or Left Bank) of the River Seine, where the old nobility had resided since the seventeenth century. In Leroux's

novel, it is implicitly contrasted with the fashionable Boulevard Saint-Honoré on the north side (or Right Bank) of the river, where the *nouveaux riches*, including the singer Carlotta, had their town houses (see Chapter VIII).

9. *phonographic recordings . . . to be buried*: On Christmas Eve 1907, twenty-four gramophone records of the great singers of the day, including sopranos Julia Lindsay, Adelina Patti, Nellie Melba, Emma Calvé and Luisa Tetrazzini as well as tenor Enrico Caruso, were deposited in the vaults of the Paris Opera House inside two vacuum-sealed lead urns bearing instructions that they should remain unopened for one hundred years. In 1989 these time capsules were exhumed, together with later additions, and given to the French National Library for safe-keeping. They were presented to the public in an official ceremony in December 2007 but, for safety reasons (the wrapping of the records contained asbestos), were only opened the following year. The original idea came from Alfred Clark, General Manager of the Compagnie française du Gramophone, a branch of the London-based Gramophone Company that would later become EMI. Copies of these recordings are now commercially available.

10. *the Commune*: Following the defeat of the French army in their war against Prussia and the ensuing siege of Paris (September 1870 to January 1871), the French National Assembly, who had retreated from the capital, signed a punishing peace treaty with the representatives of the newly formed Germany. This disastrous sequence of events provoked such resentment among the Paris workers and the National Guard that civil war broke out on 18 March 1871. Having elected a revolutionary municipal council, the *Commune de Paris*, the insurgents launched a short-lived experiment in self-government. Governmental troops soon entered the city and brutally put down the uprising. During the 'Bloody Week' of 21–28 May 1871, the cornered Communards shot a number of hostages and set fire to many public buildings, but they were eventually defeated: between 25,000 and 30,000 people were killed in the fighting or executed on the spot, and over 40,000 were taken prisoner.

11. *M. Messager*: The French composer and conductor André Messager (1853–1929) was co-director of the Paris Opera House with Leimistin Broussan (1855–1921) from January 1908 to July 1914.

12. *Charles Garnier*: Charles Garnier (1825–98) is the French architect whose neo-Baroque design won the 1860 competition for the new Paris Opera House, which provides the setting for

Leroux's novel. Although the construction of what is known to this day as the Palais Garnier began as early as 1861, it was only completed fourteen years later – the new theatre opened with an orchestral concert on 5 January 1875. Garnier's publications include *Le Théâtre* (1871) and *Le Nouvel Opéra de Paris* (1876–81), a monumental explanation of his work which Leroux clearly used as a source of information.

13. *J.-L. Croze*: Dramatist Joseph Léopold (Marie Louis) Croze (1869–1955) was the author of a number of one-act comedies and wrote the libretto to *Javotte* (1890), a ballet by French composer Camille Saint-Saëns (1835–1921).

I

The Ghost!

1. *Polyeucte*: Opera by French composer Charles Gounod (1818–93), after a play by the great French dramatist Pierre Corneille (1606–84), premiered at the Palais Garnier on 7 October 1878, whose third act included a 'Pagan Dance'.

2. *Opera House in the Rue Le Peletier*: The home of the Paris Opera from 1821 to October 1873, when the building was completely destroyed by fire. Charles Garnier had been commissioned to build his new opera house long before that, for the old theatre had been deemed a security risk for Emperor Napoleon III (1808–73) following a failed assassination attempt on his life as his coach reached the Opera House in the congested Rue Le Peletier on 14 January 1858. However, Napoleon III never saw Garnier's opera house completed. After the defeat of the French army in September 1870, the Emperor was captured by the Prussians and deposed by the French National Assembly; he died in exile in England.

3. *portraits of Vestris, Gardel, Dupont and Bigottini*: It is not clear whose portraits these are, as the four names conjure up several prominent figures in the history of French ballet.

The Vestris family included several generations of dancers and ballet-masters, starting with Maria Francesca Vestris, known as Thérèse Vestris (1726–1808), and her brothers Gaetano (1728–1808), a highly renowned dancer and choreographer, and Angiolo (1730–1809); Gaetano's son Auguste (1760–1842) and his grandson Auguste-Armand (1788–1825) were also dancers. Thérèse Vestris is among the twenty great dancers whose medallion portraits by Gustave Boulanger decorate the Ballet Room of the Palais Garnier (see Gérard Fontaine, *L'Opéra de Charles*

Garnier: Architecture et décor intérieur, Paris: Éditions du Patrimoine, 2004, p. 105).

The Gardels, another family of dancers and ballet-masters, owed their enduring fame to Maximilien Gardel (1741–87), who joined the Paris Opera in the 1750s, and his younger brother Pierre-Gabriel (1758–1840). On death of Maximilien, Pierre-Gabriel took over as ballet-master, a post he held for forty years; under his leadership the Paris Ballet established an international reputation, with dancers such as his wife Marie Gardel (1770–1833), Émilia Bigottini (1784–1858) and Louis-Antoine Duport (1781–1853). 'GARDEL' is one of the four choreographers' names inscribed above the paintings adorning the Ballet Room; Marie Gardel's medallion portrait also features there.

No leading ballet dancer by the name of Du*pont* is mentioned in the various histories of French ballet from the seventeenth to the late nineteenth century. However, there are two dancers by the name of Du*port*: Louis-Antoine Duport, a rival of Auguste Vestris as a dancer and of Pierre-Gabriel Gardel as a choreographer, and his sister, Marie-Adélaïde Duport (also known as Mme Baptiste Petit), who made her debut at the Paris Opera in 1800 and danced various roles in her brother's ballets.

Émilia Bigottini was Napoleon I's favourite ballerina. She studied at the Paris Opera Ballet School and joined the Paris Opera in 1801, where she stayed until 1823. Her portrait features alongside those of Mesdames Vestris and Gardel in the Ballet Room.

4. *cassis*: A syrupy beverage made from blackcurrants; possibly crème de cassis, an alcoholic drink.

5. *the chief stage machinist*: The person who managed the elaborate and complex stage machinery in the theatre, with up to seventy assistants, depending on the demands of the production. (See Christopher Curtis Mead, *Charles Garnier's Paris Opéra: Architectural Empathy and the Renaissance of French Classicism*, New York: The Architectural History Foundation, Cambridge, MA: MIT Press, 1991, p. 173.)

6. *Pedro Gailhard himself, a former director of the Opera House*: Stage name of the French bass Pierre Samson Gailhard (1848–1918). He made his debut in 1871 as Méphistophélès in Gounod's *Faust* at the Paris Opera and later became director of the new Paris Opera House. He assisted Jean-Eugène Ritt (1817–1907) in that role from 1884 to 1891 and in 1893 was appointed co-director with Eugène Bertrand (1843–99); on Bertrand's death, he became sole director until 1906.

7. *deposited a horseshoe*: Ancient and widespread superstition that considers the horseshoe as a symbol of good luck, perhaps due to its material (iron), its crescent shape or its association with the horse.

8. *little coral amulet ... bad luck*: Ancient superstitious belief, prevalent in Mediterranean countries, which endowed coral with protective powers, notably against the 'Evil Eye' (see below).

9. *traced ... a St Andrew's cross on the wooden ring*: A gesture which seemingly combines Christian symbolism (the tracing an X-shaped cross) and superstition (the touching of wood) to invoke protection.

10. *'Evil Eye'*: Refers to the notion, widespread in the Islamic world, that certain individuals with malicious intent can gain ascendancy over other people, animals or things by the sheer power of their gaze.

11. *gesture of the 'horned hand' ... their thumbs*: This gesture, also known by the Latin name of *mano cornuta*, is meant to conjure supernatural power, protecting the person who performs it from the 'Evil Eye'.

12. *fingers his keys*: Another instance of the superstitious belief in the protective power of metal, notably iron.

13. *Pomeranian grenadier*: Pomerania is a region on the southern shore of the Baltic whose borders changed considerably through the centuries; today it is divided between Germany and Poland. Following the annexation of Pomerania by the Prussians in 1815, the Pomeranian grenadier became a symbol of the strong, stoic yet ungainly elite soldier that led Prussia to victory over France in 1871.

14. *on the third mezzanine ... between a flat and a scene*: The substage of the Palais Garnier housing the theatrical machinery consisted of four mezzanine floors above the cellar.
   A flat is a section of flat scenery, usually made of wood or muslin on a wooden frame introduced from the sides or lowered down from above; a scene is a painted hanging set at the back and sides of the stage, and intended to give the illusion of a real view.

15. *Le Roi de Lahore*: Opera in five acts by Jules Massenet (1842–1912), lavishly premiered at the Palais Garnier on 27 April 1877, which is considered the epitome of Romantic Oriental exoticism. Set in eleventh-century India, it tells of the tragic love of King Alim for the virgin priestess Sitâ, who suffers at the hands of the offended gods and of the King's jealous and treacherous minister Scindia. *Le Roi de Lahore* lapsed from the Paris Opera repertoire after fifty-seven performances.

16. *Jacob's ladder*: Nautical term for a rope or chain ladder with wooden steps.

II
The New Marguerite

1. *There was something unique about that gala performance*: It is remarkable that the works performed during this gala evening should foreshadow some of the key events, themes and contrasting moods in the novel. Thus Saint-Saëns's *Danse macabre* ('Dance of Death') heralds the churchyard episode in Chapter VI; Delibes's *Sylvia*, the abduction scene at the end of Chapter XIV (the pivotal middle chapter of the book); and the drinking song from Donizetti's *Lucrezia Borgia*, the episode of Carlotta's downfall in the second half of Chapter VIII. Similarly, Guiraud's *Carnaval* prefigures the Shrovetide masked ball in Chapter X; while Erik's feats as a maker of automata in Istanbul and the whole make-believe world of opera are evoked by Delibes's *Coppélia*. Reyer's *Sigurd* clearly relates to the Nordic threads running through the novel and is in stark contrast to the Oriental elements that pervade much of Leroux's writing, as well as the operatic and musical repertoire of the time, exemplified here by Saint-Saëns's *Rêverie orientale* and Massenet's *Marche hongroise*. For further details, see notes 4–10, below. As for *Roméo et Juliette*, but more importantly *Faust* (and later *La Juive*), whose libretti are quoted at key moments in the narrative, they echo – sometimes ironically – recurrent themes in the novel, notably young love, the Faustian pact, seduction and deceit, self-sacrifice and redemption (see notes 11, 13, 14 16 and 17).

2. *Faure and Krauss sang*: A celebrated French baritone, Jean-Baptiste Faure (1830–1914) made his debut at the Paris Opera in October 1861 and sang in seven of the ten operas staged at the newly built Palais Garnier between January 1875 and May 1876. (See Charles Dupêchez, *Histoire de l'Opéra de Paris*, Paris: Librairie académique Perrin, 1984, pp. 331–3.)

    Gabrielle Krauss (1842–1906), a renowned Viennese soprano, made her debut at the Paris Opera singing Rachel in Halévy's *La Juive* (1835) for the inauguration of the Palais Garnier on 5 January 1875, and remained a member of the Paris Opera company until the end of 1888.

3. *Gounod . . . Marche funèbre d'une marionnette*: Charles-François Gounod (1818–93) composed the light-hearted *Funeral March of*

a Marionette as a piano piece in 1872 in London, and later as an orchestral score (1878–9). Leroux is referring to the latter version.

4. *Reyer, the beautiful overture to Sigurd*: Ernest Reyer is the adopted name of French opera composer Louis-Étienne-Ernest Rey (1823–1909), whose *Sigurd*, begun in the 1860s, was first performed as a complete opera in Brussels in 1884. The opera's plot is an adaptation of *Brot af Sigurdharkvidha* ('Fragment of a Poem about Sigurd') from the 'Poetic Edda', a collection of Scandinavian mythical stories in verse. The name Sigurd is the Nordic equivalent of Siegfried. Unbeknown to Reyer at the time, its subject is close to that of Richard Wagner *The Ring* (1876).

5. *Saint-Saëns . . . Danse macabre and Rêverie orientale*: French composer Camille Saint-Saëns (1835–1921) first composed his *Danse macabre* ('Dance of Death') as a song for voice and piano to the words of French poet Henri Cazalis (1840–1909), and reworked it into a tone poem for orchestra in 1875. In the latter version, he replaced the vocal line with a solo violin which is supposed to summon the dead to rise up and dance on their tombs at midnight.

    Rêverie orientale is the original title of a piece he composed during his first visit to Algeria in 1875. At the time, the Orient as a Western representation of cultural otherness was geographically vague: it stretched from Spain to the Far East and included North Africa as well as South-east and Central Europe.

6. *Massenet, an unpublished Marche hongroise*: French composer Jules Massenet (1842–1912) is best known for his operas. The piece in question is probably a Hungarian march by Ignac Szabadi Frank (1825–after 1879), orchestrated by Massenet and then arranged for piano by Franz Liszt (1811–86) under the title *Marche hongroise de Szabadi* (1879).

7. *Guiraud, his Carnaval*: Composer Ernest Guiraud (1837–92) was born in New Orleans (Louisiana) and studied music at the Paris Conservatoire. He is best remembered today for some of his orchestral music and for completing the work of other opera composers. He wrote the ballet *Carnaval* ('Carnival') as a contribution to his comic opera *Piccolino*, which was first performed in 1876 and never revived.

8. *Delibes, the Valse lente from Sylvia and the pizzicato from Coppélia*: *Sylvia*, a ballet in three acts by French composer Léo Delibes (1836–91), premiered at the Palais Garnier on 14 June 1876. It tells the story of the nymph Sylvia who, having fallen in love with shepherd Aminta, is abducted by the evil Orion who carries her off to his cave; she is eventually saved and reunited

with her lover. The delicate *Valse lente: L'Escarpolette* ('Slow Waltz: The Swing') is from Act I.

Coppélia, ou La Fille aux yeux d'émail, is Delibes's first full-scale ballet and was premiered at the Paris Opera on 25 May 1870. It is based on a tale by German Romantic author E. T. A. Hoffman (1776–1822). The heroine of the story is a village girl named Swanilda, who becomes jealous of Coppélia, a dancing doll created by the mysterious Dr Coppélius: the automaton is so lifelike that Swanilda's beloved Franz has become infatuated with her. Although pizzicato sections feature in several of the movements from Act II, Delibes's most famous pizzicato is found in *Sylvia*, not *Coppélia*. This tends to highlight the significance of *Coppélia* as a thematic rather than a musical reference.

9. *the bolero from Les Vêpres siciliennes*: *Les Vêpres siciliennes* is the original French version of *I vespri siciliani* (*The Sicilian Vespers*) by Italian composer Giuseppe Verdi (1813–1901). This monumental opera, which premiered at the Paris Opera on 13 June 1855, deals with the occupation of thirteenth-century Sicily by the French and a successful Sicilian rebellion. The final act, which begins in joyous fashion with the bolero sung by the soon-to-be married heroine, ends with a bloody massacre.

10. *the drinking song from Lucrezia Borgia*: An opera by Italian composer Gaetano Donizetti (1797–1848), *Lucrezia Borgia* premiered at La Scala, Milan, in 1833. The drinking song mentioned here has tragic overtones since a vengeful Lucrezia, unaware that her own son Gennaro would be among the revellers, has arranged for the wine to be poisoned; she offers him an antidote and when he refuses she also drinks of the poisoned cup.

11. *Gounod's Roméo et Juliette*: Opera in five acts to a French libretto based on the *Tragedy of Romeo and Juliet* by Shakespeare and premiered at the Théâtre Lyrique in 1867.

12. *the Opéra-Comique ... Théâtre Lyrique by Mme Carvalho*: In Paris, different institutions dealt with different aspects of the repertoire: the Opéra-Comique, established in 1714, produced and performed comic operas. These were not necessarily comical works, but rather popular, light and often sentimental operas with some spoken dialogue, as opposed to the lofty, purely musical works performed at the Paris Opera. By the late nineteenth century, the differences in repertoire between these two opera companies were beginning to blur, but they catered for different audiences, the public of the Opéra-Comique being predominantly middle class.

Having made her debut at the Opéra-Comique in 1850,

Caroline Félix-Miolan, known as Miolan-Carvalho (1827–95), one of the greatest sopranos of her time, moved on to the Théâtre Lyrique when her husband, the bass Léon Carvalho (1825–97), became its director. Under Léon Carvalho, the theatre, which offered a venue for untried young composers to premiere new works, produced some of the most memorable operas of the time, including Gounod's *Faust* (1859) and *Mireille* (1864), as well as his *Roméo et Juliette* (1867).

13. *'O Lord! Lord! Lord! Forgive us!'*: Dying words of the two lovers and closing lines of Gounod's *Roméo et Juliette*.

14. *the prison scene and the final trio of Faust*: Gounod's opera became part of the Palais Garnier repertoire in 1875. The prison scene takes place in the fifth and final act, when Marguerite, having been seduced by Faust and condemned to death for the murder of their illegitimate child, ignores her lover's entreaties and rejects Satan's offers of escape from prison and execution. It marks the climax of Gounod's opera and of Chapter XIV.

15. *the Paris Conservatoire*: Unlike the Ballet School of the Paris Opera, the Singing School did not survive, and by the beginning of the nineteenth century all opera singers were trained at the Conservatoire, a national institution acknowledged as a centre of excellence for musical practice and erudition.

16. *like the minstrel Ofterdingen ... the Devil*: In 'Der Kampf der Sänger' ('The Singers' Contest'), published by E. T. A. Hoffmann in 1819 in his collection of fantastic stories *Die Serapionsbrüder* ('The Serapion Brethren'), Heinrich von Ofterdingen, despairing of ever being loved by Mathilde, goes to study singing with the necromancer Klingsohr in order to win her over with song, thus enlisting the aid of the Devil.

17. *Siébel*: In Gounod's *Faust*, Siébel is a young man in love with Marguerite, but she prefers Faust. The part of this secondary male character is written for a soprano, hence Christine being cast in this role.

18. *King Louis X the Stubborn in the fourteenth century*: Louis le Hutin (1289–1316), variously known in English as 'the Stubborn', 'the Headstrong', 'the Quarrelsome' or 'the Quarreller', ruled over France for the last two years of his life. His short reign was plagued by feuds with the nobility.

19. *Brest*: Fortified naval port situated at the western tip of Brittany, which grew in importance in the 1850s under Napoleon III.

20. *Borda*: This famous ship, the largest sailing three-decker ever built, was designed by a certain M. Leroux and launched in

1847. Originally named *Valmy*, it was decommissioned at the end of the Crimean War (1853–6) and from 1864 served as a training ship for the French Naval Academy. It was renamed *Borda* after the French mathematician and naval officer Jean-Charles de Borda (1733–99), who played a significant role in the establishment of the metric system.

21. *official mission to the North Pole . . . for three years*: The *D'Artois* episode recalls – transposed to the North Pole – the fate of the expedition led by Swedish geologist Otto Nordenskjöld, the members of which were stranded in the Antarctic Circle for two years (1902–4) and eventually rescued by the Argentine ship *Uruguay*. Leroux travelled to Madeira to join the survivors on their return journey from Antarctica, and spent six days at sea interviewing them. His detailed account of their adventures was published daily in *Le Matin* from 7 to 22 January 1904 (see *Du capitaine Dreyfus au pôle Sud* ('From the Dreyfus Affair to the South Pole'), ed. Francis Lacassin, Paris: UGE, coll. 10/18, 1985, pp. 23–107).

22. *subscribers' door*: The door that enabled the subscribers to gain access to the stage from the auditorium. Crossing the stage, they could reach the Ballet Room and the corridors leading to the dressing-rooms. This was a particular feature of nineteenth-century French theatres.

23. *supernumeraries . . . figurantes jostling past*: Supernumeraries were performers who did not belong to the regular company; they were often poorly paid workers seeking additional income, some being hired for the season, others recruited at the last minute for the 'crowd' scenes. Figurantes were ballet dancers who took no prominent part in the performance.

24. *a 'practicable'*: A prop or item of scenery – a staircase, door, platform, etc. – constructed by carpenters and used by performers.

25. *parterre boxes*: Boxes on the ground floor of the theatre next to the stalls.

III

In which, for the first time, Messrs Debienne and Poligny disclose in confidence to the new directors of the Opera House, Messrs Armand Moncharmin and Firmin Richard, the true reason for their departure from the National Academy of Music

1. *sloping floor . . . M. Boulanger*: Like the stage of the Palais Garnier, the Ballet Room, where the dancers rehearsed and warmed

up before the performance, had a sloping floor. This 5 per cent slope was in the opposite direction to that of the stage so as to create the illusion of distance when the studio was used as an extension to the stage.

The Ballet Room was decorated with four 290 cm × 170 cm canvases on the theme of dance by Gustave-Rodolphe Boulanger (1824–88). These paintings were *La Danse bachique* ('Bacchic Dance') and *La Danse amoureuse* ('Amorous Dance'), which adorned the eastern wall of the Ballet Room, and *La Danse guerrière* ('Warrior Dance') and *La Danse champêtre* ('Rustic Dance'), which were displayed opposite. Thus the two paintings on the western wall showed respectively three warriors wearing costumes inspired from classical antiquity and three semi-naked female figures holding flower garlands over their heads.

2. *the memorandum of terms of the Opera House*: At the time of the novel, the Paris Opera was run as a business for profit. The directors were entrepreneurs who had to match from their own funds the annual public subsidy granted to the Paris Opera by the State, with whom all profits were shared equally. Their duties and obligations to the State as directors of a national institution were outlined in a Memorandum of Terms (or *Cahier des charges*). In return, the directors paid no rent for the use of the Opera House itself and gas was supplied at a 50 per cent discount.

IV
Box Five

1. *fugitive pieces*: Music concerned with subjects of topical interest or written for a particular occasion.

2. *his Mort d'Hercule*: 'The Death of Hercules' is the title of a number of eighteenth-century pieces, most notably an opera by French composer Marin Marais (1656–1728), and a French cantata by Louis-Nicolas Clérambault (1676–1749). Hercules also features as an additional character in the revised French version of *Alceste* by German composer Christoph Willibald Gluck (1714–87), which was performed at the Académie Royale de Musique in 1776. This would tend to suggest that Richard's compositional style was somewhat antiquated.

3. *His love of Gluck . . . admiring Piccinni*: Allusion to the contest which divided the musical public of Paris into two opposing factions, the Gluckists and the Piccinnists, at the end of the eighteenth century. Gluck, who moved to Paris in 1773, endeav-

oured to make opera more dramatic by placing the emphasis on simplicity of expression as opposed to musical virtuosity. Niccolò Piccinni (1728–1800), a central figure in Italian and French opera, tended to favour musical colour and expansion for its own sake. The Gluckists eventually triumphed.

4.   *bows to Meyerbeer, relishes Cimarosa . . . appreciate[s] Weber*: Giacomo Meyerbeer (1791–1864), originally known as Jakob Meyer Beer, was born in Berlin, studied in Italy and eventually moved to Paris in the 1830s, where he developed his own style of grand Romantic opera, with spectacular stage effects and brilliant orchestration. He became the most successful opera composer and producer of his time, and was famously attacked by his former disciple Richard Wagner (1813–83) in a pamphlet entitled *Das Judenthum in der Musik* (*Judaism in Music*), first published in 1850.

Domenico Cimarosa (1749–1801) and Carl Maria von Weber (1786–1826) belonged to the previous generation of composers and represented respectively the Italian tradition and the nascent German operatic style. Cimarosa was, like his master Piccinni, part of the Neapolitan school. His *Il matrimonio segreto* ('The Secret Marriage'), produced in Vienna in 1792, is considered a masterpiece of light opera.

Weber, an early Romantic German composer, was considered a precursor of Wagner. His most successful work, *Der Freischütz* ('The Marksman' or 'The Freeshooter'), is a three-act opera based on one of the stories compiled by Friedrich Laun (1770–1849) and Johann Apel (1771–1816) for *Das Gespensterbuch* (literally 'the book of ghosts'). The opera, which premiered in Berlin in 1821, tells the story of yet another hero who makes a pact with an evil spirit, this time to win a shooting contest and love.

5.   *As for Wagner . . . understands him*: Wagner's opera *Tannhäuser* was remarkably unsuccessful at the Paris Opera, where it was lavishly produced in March 1861 at the instigation of the wife of the Austrian ambassador. *Tannhäuser*, a partial adaptation of Hoffmann's 'Der Kampf der Sänger', had been premiered in Dresden in 1845. For the Paris Opera production, Wagner was required to have the libretto translated into French and to insert a ballet into the score. He obliged, but chose to include the ballet in Act I, where it made dramatic sense, instead of the traditional Act II, thus thwarting the expectations of the subscribers who were in the habit of arriving at the Opera just in time for the bal-

let in Act II. This, and anti-Austrian feeling, led them to conspire to disrupt the performances to such an extent that Wagner with-drew his opera after the third night.

Firmin Richard's claim to be the only person in France to appreciate Wagner is preposterous since the poet Charles Baudelaire (1821–67) had written a lengthy, spirited defence of Wagner, 'Richard Wagner et *Tannhäuser* à Paris', first published in the *Revue européenne* in April 1861.

6. *the new co-directors*: Richard and Moncharmin share some of the attributes of Hyacinthe Olivier Halanzier (1819–96), who managed the Paris Opera at the Palais Garnier from its opening in 1875 to 1879. Like Richard, he was renowned for his bad temper, and he was famously accused by composer Ernest Reyer of having no knowledge of music, which is also true of Mon-charmin. (See Alain Duault, *L'Opéra de Paris*, Paris: Sand, 1989, pp. 73–7.)

7. *the Théâtre des Ambassadeurs and the Café Jacquin*: By the late nineteenth century cafés had become all the rage in Paris, and the fashionable haunt of artists and writers. The Ambassadeurs was not a theatre as such but a music-hall (or *café-concert*) on the Champs-Elysées, depicted by Impressionist artist Edgar Degas (1834–1917) in several paintings and etchings whose titles men-tion the 'Café des Ambassadeurs'. The Café Jacquin, sited in the grounds of the Palais-Royal, was also a music-hall.

V

Continuation of 'Box Five'

1. '*While you play at sleeping*': From Méphistophélès's serenade in Act IV of *Faust* (Charles Gounod, *Faust*, English version by H. F. Chorley, London: Chappell & Co., 1890).

2. '*Accord the bliss . . . Of a kiss*': Continuation of Méphistophélès's serenade in Act IV of Gounod's *Faust* (English version by H. F. Chorley).

3. *La Juive*: Opera by Jacques-Fromental Lévy, known as Halévy (1799–1862), highly representative of the grand opera genre. Halévy's greatest success, it was premiered at the Paris Opera on 23 February 1835 and was the first opera ever performed at the Palais Garnier (8 January 1875). Its convoluted plot tells of the self-sacrifice of Rachel, the 'Jewess' of the title. She is seduced under false pretences by Léopold, a Christian Prince, who is subsequently condemned to death for consorting with a Jewish

woman. She saves him from execution at the request of his betrothed, only to be herself executed for refusing to recant the Jewish faith on the order of a Cardinal who discovers, too late, that she is in fact his long-lost daughter.

4. '*Close to the one I love . . . Shall not tear us apart*': Rachel's aria in Act II. The only translation into English available when Leroux was writing (by Percy E. Pinkerton, London: S. J. Garraway, 1900) was based on a different version and does not include this passage.

5. '*Let us flee! Let us flee! . . . awaits us both*': Continuation of Act II. Here Prince Léopold enjoins Rachel to elope with him just as Éléazar, the Jewish goldsmith whom she believes to be her father, approaches.

VI
The Magic Fiddle

1. *The Magic Fiddle*: Probably an allusion to *Die Zauberflöte* (*The Magic Flute*), opera composed by Wolfgang Amadeus Mozart (1756–91) the year he died.

2. *Hamlet*: A five-act opera by Ambroise Thomas (1811–96) after Shakespeare. It was premiered at the Paris Opera on 9 March 1868, with Jean-Baptiste Faure (see Chapter II, note 2) as Hamlet and Christine Nilsson (the model for Christine) as Ophélie.

3. *the Queen of the Night in The Magic Flute*: This role is notoriously demanding and beyond the range of many sopranos.

4. *Perros*: Perros-Guirec, small fishing port in the Lannion district of northern Brittany.

5. *Gare Montparnasse*: One of the large terminus stations of Paris, from which trains to western France depart. It was made famous in 1895 when a steam train overran the buffer stop and nosed its way into the street below, where it stood on end.

6. *Auberge du Soleil-Couchant*: 'Inn of the Setting Sun'.

7. *the young Swedish singer*: Christine Daaé's life story echoes that of the famous Swedish soprano Christine Nilsson (1843–1921), who was considered to be the most convincing musical and dramatic embodiment of the idea of Marguerite in Gounod's *Faust*, and whose creation of Ophélie in Thomas's *Hamlet* set the standard for generations to come. The parallels are striking: the daughter of a poor working man, Christine Nilsson was born in Sjöabol, near Växjö, and moved to the village of Skatelöv when her family was forced to leave their cottage. From a very young age, the blonde, blue-eyed girl sang and played the fiddle at local

country fairs. One day at Ljungby Fair, her precocious talent was noticed by the district judge Tornérhielm, who took her to Madame Adelaide Valerius-Leuhusen in Gothenburg, on the south-west coast of Sweden, and provided the means for her education. She sang in Stockholm and Uppsala and then went to Paris where, after four years' study, she made her debut as Violetta in Verdi's *La Traviata* at the Théâtre Lyrique on 27 October 1864.

8. *Andersen's tales ... the Great Runeberg's verse*: Danish writer Hans Christian Andersen (1805–75) was celebrated for his fairy tales, including *The Princess and the Pea* (1835), *The Little Mermaid* (1836), *The Snow Queen* (1844), *The Ugly Duckling* (1844) and *The Little Match Girl* (1848), as well as *The Wind Tells About Valdemar Daae and His Daughters* (1859), from which Leroux may have borrowed Christine's family name, Daaé.

    The Finn Johan Ludvig Runeberg (1804–77) is yet another Scandinavian writer. Although he wrote in Swedish, he is generally considered to be the national poet of Finland. His most famous poetic work, *Fänrik Ståls sägner* ('The Tales of Ensign Stål'), published 1848–60, describes the suffering and the bravery of the Finns enrolled in the Swedish army during the Swedish-Russian war of 1808–9. A prose translation appeared within a collection including several short poems by Runeberg and other Scandinavian poets: *Le roi Fialar, précédé de: Le Porte-enseigne Stôle; La Nuit de Noël; Hanna*; etc. (Paris: Garnier Frères, 1879). Leroux may have heard of Runeberg's poetry during a trip to Sweden in 1900, or later, in 1904, from members of the Nordenskjöld expedition to Antarctica (see Chapter II, note 22), who said that they used to recite his poems to pass the time during the long Antarctic winters (see *Du capitaine Dreyfus au pôle Sud*, p. 60).

9. *'A king sat ... amidst the Norwegian mountains ...'*: The original French ('*Un roi s'était assis ...*') is almost a literal quotation from the opening lines of 'Le Lac de la montagne' ('The Lake in the Mountain') ('*Un soir, j'étais assis ...*'), a poem by Norwegian writer Andreas Munch (1811–84), whose prose translation was included in *Le roi Fialar*, 1879, pp. 263–5. Thus the change from *je* ('I') to '*Un roi*' ('A king') works as an allusion to the title of the book from which Leroux is quoting

10. *'Little Lotte thought of everything ... enjoyed'*: The original French is a literal quotation from 'Le premier chagrin d'un enfant' ('A Child's First Sorrow'), another poem by Andreas

Munch, in which the character of Little Lotte listens lovingly to a small bird that her father has found in the snow. This poem was first published in 1836 under the Norwegian title of 'Den Første Sorg', and its prose translation into French is included in *Le roi Fialar*, pp. 263–5.

11. *the colour of a wild strawberry grown in the shade*: The original French for this unusual simile is a literal quotation from the French translation of Runeberg's *Hanna* included in *Le roi Fialar* (1879, p. 124). This would tend to suggest that in the present chapter similarities between Christine's reunion with Raoul in her father's cottage in Perros-Guirec, and Hanna's first encounter at home with her brother's school friend – the 'delightful and caring' girl's entrance, carrying 'a pot of steaming tea' on a tray, the kiss from the boy and her retiring to seek comfort on a 'bench' (*Le roi Fialar*, p. 143) – are not entirely fortuitous.

12. *Inspector Mifroid*: The perceptive Mifroid appears in three other novels by Leroux: firstly in *La Double Vie de Théophraste Longuet* (1904), published under two different titles in English: *The Double Life* (1909) and *The Man with the Black Feather* (1912); secondly in *Le Crime de Rouletabille* (1922), also published under different titles: *The Slave Bangle* (1925) and *The Phantom Clue* (1926); and finally in *Le Sept de trèfle* (1923), which has never been translated (the title means 'The Seven of Clubs'). For details about the translations into English of Leroux's novels, see 'Further Reading'.

13. *Lazarus*: *Lazarus, oder Die Feier der Auferstehung* (*Lazarus, or The Feast of the Resurrection*), by Franz Schubert (1797–1828), which combined elements of cantata, oratorio and staged drama. Begun in February 1820, it remained unfinished, and was published posthumously in 1865. It breaks off in the second of three planned acts, representing the death, burial and resurrection of the biblical character whose story is told in the New Testament (Gospel of St John 11: 41–4).

VII
A Visit to Box Five

1. *This was the tranquil hour when the machinists went for a drink*: Playful echo of the lines from the poem 'Booz endormi' ('Boaz Asleep') – 'It was the tranquil hour when lions go to drink' – by French poet Victor Hugo (1802–85), published in his epic *Legend of the Ages* (*La Légende des siècles*, 1859–83).

2. *Adamastor, as we all know*: Probably an allusion to the 'Ballade
    d'Adamastor' in *L'Africaine* by Giacomo Meyerbeer, which was
    first performed by the Paris Opera company on 28 April 1865.
    Adamastor is a mythical giant representing the dangers that
    Vasco da Gama had to overcome when he rounded the Cape of
    Good Hope (1497), at the southern tip of Africa, in his search
    for a new route from Europe to India, as recounted in *Os Lusía-
    das* (*The Lusiads*, 1572), an epic poem by Portugal's great
    national poet Luís de Camões (1525–80). Leroux mentions the
    poem in his account of the Nordenskjöld expedition to Antarc-
    tica (see *Du capitaine Dreyfus au pôle Sud*, p. 93).

3. *Lenepveu's copper ceiling*: Jules Eugène Lenepveu Boussaroque
    de Lafont (1819–98), known as Jules Eugène Lenepveu, was a
    French painter whose only claim to lasting fame is *Le Triomphe
    de la Beauté, charmée par la Musique, au milieu des Muses et des
    Heures du jour et de la nuit* ('The Triumph of Beauty, charmed
    by Music amidst the Muses and the Hours of the Day and the
    Night'), the painting that originally adorned the copper ceiling
    of the auditorium.

4. *These figures*: Moulded heads by Messrs Walter and Bourgeois,
    placed at regular intervals in the circular frieze around Lenepveu's
    painted ceiling; they were not part of the ceiling itself but stood
    out against it as one looked up. They were the heads of some of
    the mythical figures drawn from Ancient Greek and Roman lit-
    erature, most notably *Metamorphoses* by Roman poet Ovid (43
    BC–AD 17), whose stories provided the focus of ballets, pastor-
    ales and operas well into the nineteenth century.

5. *Isis . . . Arethusa*: All are mythological characters. Isis, the god-
    dess of maternity and fertility in Ancient Egyptian mythology,
    also features with a similar role in Graeco-Roman mythology.
        In Greek mythology Amphitrite, Thetis, Galatea and Arethusa
    are sea nymphs. Amphitrite is one of the many spouses of Posei-
    don, god of the sea; Thetis, goddess of the waves, conceived
    Achilles, the warrior and a central character in Homer's *Iliad*;
    Galatea is loved by the one-eyed giant Polyphemus, but her pref-
    erence for the young Acis has tragic consequences: unable to bring
    Acis back to life, Galatea turns him into a stream; Arethusa is
    changed into a fountain by the goddess Artemis, so that she can
    escape from the unwanted attentions of the river-god Alpheus.
    Hebe is the goddess of youth; Pandora, the first woman and the
    cause of all man's woes, having unwittingly unleashed all human
    ills into the world when she opened a jar (in later versions, a box)

out of curiosity; Psyche, an allegorical figure representing the soul; Daphne, a virgin huntress pursued by Apollo and saved from capture by being changed into a laurel tree; and Clytie, a nymph loved then abandoned by Apollo, who changes her into a heliotrope, or sunflower, always turning her head towards the sun.

Flora and Pomona are both from Roman mythology: Flora is the goddess of flowering plants and Pomona the goddess of fruit, especially tree-borne fruit such as apples.

6. *even Pandora . . . because of her box*: Allusion to the disastrous reception of *La Boîte de Pandore*, opéra bouffe in three acts by Henry Charles Litolff (1818–91), when it was premiered at the Théâtre des Folies dramatiques on 17 October 1871. (See Félix Clément and Pierre Larousse, *Dictionnaire des opéras*, Paris: Larousse, 1897.)

VIII

In which Firmin Richard and Armand Moncharmin have the audacity to allow Faust *to be performed in a 'cursed' theatre and the terrible events that ensued*

1. *There are several grooms at the Opera*: Charles Nuitter lists, among the staff who file past the concierge's lodge, 'grooms leading horses that will be hoisted onto the stage by means of an elevator' (*Le Nouvel Opéra*, p. 188).

2. *Franconi's stables*: Victor Franconi (1810–97) was famed as a riding master and a circus manager. He came from an equestrian family of Italian descent and in 1845 founded with his father the Hippodrome, which excelled in military spectacles and chariot races; he then went on to manage the Cirque d'Été ('Summer Circus') and the Cirque d'Hiver ('Winter Circus') in Paris.

3. *Lagréné, Scholl and Pertuiset . . . at Tortoni's*: Lagréné is probably Edmond de Lagrené (*sic*), who died on 13 February 1909, at the age of sixty-six. He was a former diplomat and a socialite.

Aurélien Scholl (1833–1902), a French writer, playwright and journalist, was renowned for his wit and his readiness to duel with his detractors. He was editor of *L'Écho de Paris* until he was replaced by Adrien Lefort (1856–1925), also known as Robert Charvay, who gave Leroux his first newspaper column.

Eugène Pertuiset (b. ?1833–d. not known) was a big game hunter, immortalized by Manet in his painting *Portrait of M. Pertuiset, the Lion Hunter*, which was exhibited in May 1881.

Tortoni's was the most celebrated of all the cafés in Paris at the time of the story, frequented by artists, musicians, men of letters and dilettanti. It was a favourite haunt of Édouard Manet.

4.   *Cerberus*: Three-headed dog that guards the entrance to the Underworld in Ancient Greek mythology, permitting spirits to enter, but not leave, the realm of the Dead.

5.   *'Selva opaca'*: 'Dark forest', aria from Act II, Scene II, of *Guglielmo Tell* ('William Tell') by Gioachino Rossini (1792–1868). The opera, premiered in French in Paris in 1829, was rarely produced in Italy.

6.   *'Vain! In vain do I call . . . No single word!'*: From the opening lines of Gounod's *Faust* (English version by H. F. Chorley). Sitting alone at night in the semi-darkness, at a table covered with parchments, Faust mourns the loss of youth, love and faith and contemplates suicide. This is a defining moment, for Méphistophélès soon appears, conjuring up the beguiling vision of Marguerite at her spinning wheel; he offers to grant Faust youth in exchange for his soul and Faust agrees.

7.   *'Red or white liquor . . . we have wine?'*: From the opening lines of the fair scene in Act II of Gounod's *Faust* (English version by H. F. Chorley).

8.   *in her male attire*: This is the scene in Act II in which Marguerite's soldier brother, Valentin, bids farewell and entrusts Marguerite to his friend Siébel, played by Christine Daaé.

9.   *'No, my lord . . . on my way!'*: Marguerite's brief reply to Faust's 'High born and lovely maid . . . / Let me, your willing slave, / Attend you home today,' when he approaches her for the first time at the fair in Act II of Gounod's *Faust* (English version by H. F. Chorley).

10. *the ballad of the King of Thulé*: One of the two major solo arias by Marguerite in Act III of Gounod's *Faust* – the other one being the Jewel Song.

11. *'Gentle flow'rs in the dew, / Be message from me . . .'*: Opening lines of the Flower Song at the very beginning of Act III of Gounod's *Faust*. The scene takes place in Marguerite's garden where Siébel gathers a few flowers to make a nosegay that he will deposit on the threshold of her cottage in the hope that it will tell her of his secret love for her (English version by H. F. Chorley).

12. *'Gentle flow'rs, lie ye there, / And tell her from me . . .'*: Continuation of the Flower Song (English version by H. F. Chorley).

13. *'Would she but deign . . . to cheer me . . .'*: Continuation of the Flower Song (English version by H. F. Chorley).

NOTES

303

14. *'Ah, the joy past compare, / These jewels bright to wear! ...'*: From the Jewel Song, in Act III of Gounod's *Faust*: Marguerite discovers next to Siébel's nosegay a casket left there by Méphistophélès and is charmed by the jewels it contains (English version by H. F. Chorley).

15. *Carmen*: The confident and worldly heroine of *Carmen* by Georges Bizet (1838–75), premiered at the Opéra-Comique on 3 March 1875.

16. *'Let me gaze ... To love thy beauty too!'*: From Act III of Gounod's *Faust*: Faust's entreaty to Marguerite when they meet in Marguerite's garden at the instigation of Méphistophélès (English version by H. F. Chorley).

17. *'Oh, how strange! ... And all my heart subdue'*: Marguerite's aside in response to Faust's entreaty (English version by H. F. Chorley).

18. *as Elvira ... could not quite reach*: Allusion to the Finale of Act I of Mozart's *Don Giovanni* (1787), in which the second soprano (Donna Elvira) and the prima donna (Donna Anna) sing together.

19. *Venus de Milo*: Ancient Greek marble statue supposedly depicting the goddess of love and beauty. It was discovered, with its arms broken off, among the ruins of the ancient city of Milos, and later presented to the king of France, Louis XVIII, in 1821.

20. *The chandelier had crashed ... killed her instantly*: Episode based on the events of 20 May 1896, when one of the eight counterweights of the chandelier – not the chandelier itself – crashed down towards the end of Act I of *Hellé* by Alphonse Duvernoy (1842–1907), killing one person. The victim was 56-year-old Madame Chomette, a concierge (see Alain Duault, *L'Opéra de Paris*, pp. 104–5).

IX
The Mysterious Brougham

1. *the Spirit of Music*: Leroux seems to establish a distinction between Christine Daaé's perception of the Voice as a manifestation of the Angel of Music, and Mme Valerius's conception of it as representing the very genius, or 'Spirit', of Music.

2. *the Bois*: The Bois de Boulogne is situated on the western outskirts of Paris. It was formally established as a park by Napoleon III in 1852 and became a highly fashionable place for promenades.

3. *brougham*: A closed, four-wheeled, horse-drawn carriage having a raised open driver's seat in front.

4. *the race-course at Longchamp*: This famous race-course, which boasted permanent stands, was inaugurated in April 1857. It is located within the Bois de Boulogne.

5. *domino*: A loose, hooded garment, usually worn at masquerades with a plain mask by persons not dressed as a specific character. Masked balls are a recurrent feature in operas and sometimes provide the focus for the plot, as in *Le Domino noir* ('The Black Domino'), a comic opera by Daniel Auber (1782–1871), which premiered at the Opéra-Comique in 1837, and in Verdi's *Un Ballo in maschera* ('A Masked Ball'), first performed in French at the Théâtre Lyrique in 1869.

X
The Masked Ball

1. *The renowned German singer Raff*: Anton Raaf or Raff (1714–97), tenor who trained in Munich and in Bologna. He made his debut in Florence in 1738, returned to Germany in 1742, performed again in Italy in 1750–51 and from 1759 until about 1770 sang on various Italian stages, most notably in Florence, Parma and Venice.

2. *Shrovetide . . . La Courtille*: The Christian festival of Shrovetide generally occurs in late February, but its precise dates vary from year to year; a time of feasting and carnivals, it precedes the fasting season (Lent) leading up to Easter.

   The hilly area of La Courtille, in eastern Paris, was popular among working-class Parisians for its drinking booths and dance halls. At the end of the carnival, thousands of masked revellers would parade down from La Courtille on their return to Paris having spent the night of Shrove Tuesday (*Mardi Gras*) celebrating. The Paris Carnival features prominently in the work of French watercolour and sketch artist Sulpice-Guillaume Chevalier (1804–66), known as Paul Gavarni, as well as in *Le Juif errant*, a novel by Eugene Sue (1804–57), which Leroux used as a source (see Chapter XXI note 12) and whose first edition (1845) was illustrated by Gavarni.

3. *Pluto*: God of the Underworld in Roman mythology.

4. *The Grim Reaper*: The Angel of Death represented as a skeletal figure dressed in a black hooded cloak and holding a scythe.

5. *the Red Death*: Allusion to 'The Mask of the Red Death', a short

story by writer and poet Edgar Allan Poe (1809–49), first published in Philadelphia in May 1842; the French translation, by
Charles Baudelaire, appeared in February 1855. The story takes
place in a fortified abbey where Prince Prospero has retreated with
a thousand friends in order to escape from the deadly disease,
known as the 'Red Death', that is ravaging his country; to entertain his guests, he organizes a lavish masked ball, but the evening
is marred by the appearance of a tall, emaciated figure wearing a
blood-spattered, shroud-like mantle and a skull-like mask; having
confronted the mysterious spectre, Prospero dies on the spot, and
subsequently so does everyone else. Leroux's description of the
Phantom's physical appearance owes much to Poe's creation.

6. *'Box of the Blind'*: Probably a box affording a poor view of the
stage.

7. *'Fate has united my heart for aye unto thine!'*: From the wed-
ding-night duet at the beginning of Act IV of Gounod's *Roméo
et Juliette* (English version by Dr Theo Baker, New York: G.
Schirmer, 1897).

XII
Above the Traps

1. *Watch those pointes!*: The practice of dancing on the tips of the
toes (*pointes*) was introduced around 1814. Marie Taglioni
(1804–84) was its first notable exponent.

XIII
Apollo's Lyre

1. *huge tanks*: Water tanks for fire contingencies.
2. *Apollo ... bronze grandeur*: The central figure of the group
sculpture by Aimé Millet (1819–91), entitled *Apollo, Poetry and
Music*, which stands at the apex of the roof over the stage. The
bronze sculpture is 7.5 metres high from the bottom of the plinth
to the tip of the golden lyre, which also serves as a lighting-rod.
3. *'Come! ... shall never die!'*: Gospel according to St John, 11:
24–6.
4. *furnaces*: At that time the Opera House was heated by fourteen
furnaces installed in the vast cellars; they were coal-fired and
measured over twenty square metres each. (See Nuitter, *Le Nouvel Opéra*, p. 222.)
5. *the River Styx, nor did Charon appear more doleful*: The Styx is

the river that winds around Hades, the Underworld in Greek and Roman mythology, and separates the world of the living from the world of the dead; Charon is the old ferryman who carries the souls of the dead into the Underworld.

6. *Tower of Babel . . . all dialects*: After the Flood men spoke only one language and, in defiance of God's will, attempted to build a tower whose top would reach up to Heaven. In his wrath, God came down to earth and confounded their language so they could no longer understand one another; unable to complete the building, they were scattered across the face of the earth (Genesis 11).

7. *Desdemona's 'Willow Song'*: Aria from the third and final act of *Otello, ossia il moro di Venezia* by Gioachino Rossini to an Italian libretto after Shakespeare, premiered in Naples in 1816. It was first performed in Paris in Italian at the Théâtre Italien on 5 June 1821 and in French at the Théâtre de l'Odéon on 25 July 1825.

8. *I became one of Orpheus' flock!*: For the Ancient Greeks, Orpheus is the epitome of the singer whose song has great power. Having failed to deliver his beloved Eurydice from the Underworld, Orpheus retires to the wilderness where his lamenting song moves animals, trees and rocks alike, before dying at the hands of murderous female creatures.

9. *Louis-Philippe chest of drawers*: French king Louis-Philippe (1773–1850) ruled over France from 1830 to 1848. His liberal monarchy was associated with a rather heavy bourgeois style of architecture, furniture and interior design.

10. *a glass of Tokay . . . Falstaff*: Tokay is a rich, sweet, white wine made in the Tokaj region in Hungary. Falstaff is a wine-loving character who appears in the *Henry IV* plays and *The Merry Wives of Windsor* by Shakespeare.

11. *Dies Irae*: 'Day of wrath', first words and name of a thirteenth-century Latin hymn describing the Last Judgment, which is usually part of the musical setting of the Requiem Mass (a special mass sung for the repose of the souls of the dead).

12. *Don Juan . . . yet he burns*: Allusion to the dissolute life and eventual punishment of Don Juan/Don Giovanni in the opera composed by Mozart (1797). Towards the end the inveterate seducer and reveller is carried off to Hell, a fate regarded as just retribution by the other characters.

13. *Lake Avernus*: Volcanic lake near Naples in southern Italy: the Romans considered it one of the entrances to the Underworld.

XIV
The Master of the Traps Strikes

1. 'I wish I could but know ... his name is': From the garden scene of Act III of Gounod's Faust, in which Marguerite is musing over her encounter with Faust at the fair in the previous act (English version by H. F. Chorley).
2. 'Holy angel ... in Heaven blessed ...': From Marguerite's plea to Heaven in the prison scene in Act V of Gounod's Faust. Marguerite, abandoned by Faust, has killed the child she had by him and is now in prison pending her execution; with Méphistophélès's assistance, Faust has entered the prison to help her escape, but Marguerite refuses to listen and calls for the angels to take her away (English version by H. F. Chorley).
3. 'My spirit longs with thee to rest!': Continuation of Marguerite's plea to Heaven at the end of Act V of Gounod's Faust. The prison walls open and Marguerite's soul rises to Heaven (English version by H. F. Chorley).

XVII
Mme Giry's Astonishing Revelations as to Her Knowledge of the Phantom of the Opera

1. 'Robert-Houdin himself could not have done better': Jean-Eugène Robert-Houdin (1805–71), French magician regarded as the father of modern conjuring. Not to be confused with the American magician and escapologist of Hungarian descent who called himself Harry Houdini (1874–1926) as an homage to his illustrious predecessor.
2. In 1825, Mlle Ménétrier ... the King of Portugal ...: During the summer of 1876, the daily L'Événement published a list of the ladies of the stage (actresses, singers and dancers) who had married wealthy or titled men since the 1680s. This list was reproduced in the second issue (summer 1876) of Analectes du Bibliophile (Brussels: Jules Gay, 1876). Leroux is quoting almost verbatim the first five entries about nineteenth-century dancers. These, however, were only partially correct: Marie Taglioni and Lola Montez married into the aristocracy and so did Maria (Jacob), who became Baroness d'Henneville (not Hermeville), but it was Augusta Le Manessier, not Mlle Ménétrier, who became Marchioness of Cussy. Leroux's last entry departs sig-

nificantly from the 1876 list: 'Thérèse Hessler' is, in terms of spelling and information, a cross between Thérèse Essler (1808–78), who married 'the brother to the King of Prussia' in 1850, and what we know from different sources about Elisa Hensler (1836–1929), who married Ferdinand of Saxe-Coburg-Gotha, former Prince consort of Portugal. Leroux may be quoting from a later publication or is already launching into fiction.

3. 'In 1885, Meg Giry shall become Empress!': The character Little Meg Giry did not become Empress, but she married into the aristocracy, as indicated earlier, in the Prologue. Before the twentieth century, dance was considered neither a calling nor a profession. The young girls who joined the Ballet School and trained for four to six years to become members of the *corps de ballet* were not bound to display any particular disposition for dance. By sending them to the Ballet School, their parents, often impoverished artists or single mothers, knew that their offspring would be looked after and would soon earn a few francs by taking part in the performances; later they might rise to fame and find wealthy protectors, or marry into the bourgeoisie or aristocracy. Unlike singers, who could make a living by performing at private soirées or giving lessons, dancers had to rely on their meagre pay or use their charms and glamorous status for financial gain (*Le Foyer de la danse*, pp. 7–8).

4. *If she's going to be Empress in 1885, there's no time to lose*: An indication that the story probably takes place in the early 1880s.

5. *divertissement*: Another name for the dance sequences that were inserted into operas for the purpose of entertainment without being essential to the plot.

XX
The Viscount and the Persian

1. *Thebes . . . Hagmatana . . . the Delphic Pythia*: Thebes, one of the most celebrated cities of Ancient Egypt, is the site of the temples of Karnak and Luxor, as well as the tombs of the Valley of the Kings.

    Hagmatana was an ancient city (now Hamadan in north-west Iran) where successive rulers built sumptuous summer palaces.

    In Ancient Greece, the Pythia was the priestess who sat on a bronze tripod in the inner chamber of Apollo's temple at Delphi; she was believed to deliver the god's prophecies.

XXI
Below the Stage

1. *bull's eye lantern*: A lantern with a round bulging glass lens on one side and a sliding panel that could be closed to conceal the light. The lens focused the light to some extent and it served the same purpose as a modern flashlight.

2. *used to fly the hot-air balloons . . . rest of the country*: The Commune continued the practice established during the siege of Paris of using balloon mail – together with pigeon post – to communicate with the rest of France.

3. *the aforementioned 'organ' served a musical purpose*: Leroux's description of the 'pipe organ' closely follows the explanations of Nuitter in *Le Nouvel Opéra*, pp. 219–20 and Charles Garnier in *Le Nouvel Opéra de Paris* (Paris: Ducher, 1876–81), vol. 2, pp. 140–41.

4. *The below-stage area . . . replaced by rails*: This accurate description of the sub-stage of the Paris Opera House is very close to that of Edwin O. Sachs and Ernest A. E. Woodrow, in 'Wood-And-Iron Stages: The Stage of the National Opera House, Paris' in their *Modern Opera Houses and Theatres* (New York: Benjamin Blom, 1968), first published 1896–8. Sachs and Woodrow, who seem to have consulted the same sources as Leroux, use 'mezzanine' to refer to each floor, reserving the term 'cellar' for the lowest level.

5. *Messrs X., Y. and Z. . . . Garnier's architectural masterpiece*: X. Y. Z. (pseudonym of T. Faucon) is the author of *Le Nouvel Opéra, monuments, artistes* (Paris: Michel Lévy frères, 1875).

6. *met at Cap d'Ail as Mme Pierre Wolff's guests*: Cap d'Ail is a French seaside resort situated on the Mediterranean coast between Nice and Monaco, which became fashionable at the beginning of the twentieth century. At the time when he was writing the novel, Leroux himself was living on the French Riviera with his family, having moved there in 1907 so that they could enjoy year-round Mediterranean sunshine and he could indulge his passion for gambling.

    Mme Pierre Wolff provides another autobiographical allusion as Pierre Wolff (1865–1944) was a popular French dramatist with whom Leroux wrote *Le Lys*. The play was first performed in Paris at the Théâtre du Vaudeville in December 1908, and its English adaptation (*The Lily*) was produced a year later in Washington, Pittsburgh and New York. It was also made into a silent film, *The Lily* (USA, 1926), directed by Victor Schertzinger.

7. *scampering feet . . . ballet-girls*: In French ballet-school girls

were traditionally called *les petits rats de l'Opéra* ('the Opera's little rats').

8. *siren's voice . . . ears to it*: Allusion to Greek mythology. In Homer's *Odyssey*, the Sirens are the enchantresses who charm the sailors with their song and lure them to their death.

9. *the waterworks*: The apparatus that supplied water to the entire building, as well as for stage displays in ballets such as Delibes's *La Source* ('The Spring'), first performed in 1866.

10. *The volume of . . . Notre-Dame Cathedral*: From both Nuitter, *Le Nouvel Opéra*, p. 25 and Garnier, *Le Nouvel Opéra de Paris*, vol. 2, p. 221.

11. *consisted of a dam . . . in thickness*: Leroux's overall description of the double shell is accurate, except that in reality the inner wall was only one metre – that is just over a yard – thick (see Nuitter, *Le Nouvel Opéra*, p. 27).

12. *'The Punjab cord!'*: This is an allusion to the practice of ritual killing by strangulation with a weighted cord or cloth by members of the Thuggee cult in India, who were suppressed by the British in the 1830s; at the time, the Punjab region, whose main city was Lahore, was part of British India (it is now divided between India and Pakistan). The descriptions of Erik wielding the cord in the next chapter are reminiscent of an episode from *Le Juif errant* by Eugène Sue, serialized in 1844–5: 'Suddenly the slave saw the dark figure of the Strangler rise before him . . . he heard a hissing sound like that of a sling and felt a cord, thrown with equal speed and strength, encircle his neck in a triple chokehold . . . The attack was so sudden and unexpected that Djalma's servant did not utter a single cry, a single groan . . . He stumbled . . . and fell to his knees with his arms flailing' (Chapter I ('The Ajoupa') of Part III ('The Stranglers'), my translation). *Le Juif errant* (The Wandering Jew) was immensely popular as a novel, and inspired a now long-forgotten grand opera by Halévy, premiered at the Paris Opera on 23 April 1852.

XXII
The Interesting and Instructive Trials and Tribulations of a Persian Below Stage at the Opera

1. *the famous Dê Tham . . . escape*: Hoang Hoa Tham (18?–1913) was a revolutionary resistance leader who ran a thirty-year campaign against the French in South-east Asia. Dê Tham and his men were not 'pirates' in the strict sense of the term, but were

described as such by the occupying French, who had extended the notion of piracy to include any disorder and opposition they met on land in Tonkin, the delta of the Red River in Vietnam. Dê Tham's involvement in the unsuccessful attempt to poison a French garrison in 1908 led to an all-out effort to capture him and his men, but they managed to escape arrest. (See Danny J. Whitfield, *Historical and Cultural Dictionary of Vietnam*, Metuchen, NJ: The Scarecrow Press, 1976; and *South-East Asia. A Historical Encyclopedia*, ed. Ooi Keat Gin, Santa Barbara, California: ABC-Clio Inc., 3 vols., 2004.)

2. *Rosy Hours of Mazenderan*: Also spelt Mazendaran or Mazandaran. Mazenderan was a province of northern Persia (Iran), on the mountain slopes leading down to the shore of the Caspian Sea. Unlike the high desert oases of Shiraz and Isfahan, famed for their rose gardens, Mazenderan consisted of largely humid rainforest. Not easily accessible to foreign visitors, it rarely featured in nineteenth-century travel accounts of the region. In Firdawsi's eleventh-century epic poem *Shahnameh*, translated into French as *Le Livre des rois* (*The Book of Kings*) (1838–78), Mazenderan's jungles are the home of witches, sorcerers and demons. The name seems to have held a particular fascination for Rudyard Kipling, whom Leroux greatly admired; Kipling uses it unexpectedly as part of the title of a chapter in *From Sea to Sea – Letters of Travel* (1899) and later as the name of an island in 'How the Rhinoceros Got His Skin' in his *Just So Stories* (1902). Hence the phrase 'the Rosy Hours of Mazenderan', and the whole episode related to it, seem to result from a series of loose associations.

3. *the Madeleine Church!*: A Roman Catholic church close to the Opera House, built to a neo-classical design, with fifty-two monumental columns, and dedicated to St Mary Magdalene. Its lavish decor includes a statue by Charles Marochetti (1805–67) depicting Mary Magdalene being carried up to Heaven by two angels.

4. *'Kyrie! Kyrie! Kyrie eleison!'*: Greek for 'O Lord! O Lord! O Lord, have mercy', the first sung words in the Roman Catholic mass.

5. *five levels . . . twenty-five above!*: There were in fact only seventeen floors in Palais Garnier, five of which were underground.

XXIV
The Torture Begins

1. *the story of Bluebeard*: Legend that inspired many writers and musicians, notably French writer Charles Perrault (1628–1703),

who included it in his *Tales*, and French opera composer André
Ernest Grétry (1741–1813), who wrote his *Raoul Barbebleue* in
1789. The blue-bearded prince of the title forbids his wife to ever
use one of the keys in her trust; when curiosity leads her to open
the door to the forbidden room, she discovers the bodies of her
husband's previous spouses, thus putting her own life in peril.

2. *Musée Grévin*: Internationally famous waxworks museum founded
by Arthur Meyer (1844–1924) and named after its first artistic
director, Alfred Grévin (1827–92), a sculptor, caricaturist and
costume designer. It was Arthur Meyer, as director of the newspaper *Le Gaulois*, who first published *The Phantom of the Opera*.

XXV

'Barrels! Barrels! Any Old Barrels! Any
Old Barrels to Sell?'

1. *the tsetse fly*: A grey-brown insect the size of a honey bee abundant in parts of tropical and southern Africa. Its bite can cause
African trypanosomiasis, commonly called sleeping sickness,
which may be fatal to humans.

2. *a long, narrow drum . . . interior of the drum*: This is the description of a particular type of cuíca drum or 'laughing gourd', a
South American friction drum often used in Brazilian samba
music. To play the cuíca, the musician usually rubs up and down
with one hand the string passing down the interior of the drum,
and uses the other hand to apply pressure to the drum head,
thereby changing the pitch.

3. *a long, hollow tube . . . patter of heavy rain*: This is an accurate
description of the 'rainstick', a traditional South American
instrument, filled with beads, beans or suchlike, used to create
atmospheric sounds or percussive rhythms. It is thought to ori-
ginate from Chile and to have been played in the belief that it
might bring rain.

XXVI

The Scorpion or the Grasshopper?

1. *There would be crowds of people*: Erik's desire to injure as many
people as possible evokes some of the statements made by anarchist Émile Henry during his trial for the explosion at the Terminus
café inside the Gare Saint-Lazare in Paris on 12 February 1894,
and reported by Leroux in *Le Matin* in April 1894. Following a

spate of anarchist attacks in 1893 and 1894, Leroux attended four trials for individual acts of terrorism between January and August 1894; three of the four defendants, Auguste Vaillant, Émile Henry and Santo Geronimo Caserio, were condemned to death. Leroux attended their executions and later wrote against capital punishment. Some aspects of Erik's behaviour and statements owe much to Leroux's observations during these trials. Leroux's literary imagination clearly fed on his experiences as a journalist. (See *Du capitaine Dreyfus au pôle Sud*, pp. 155–286.)

XXVII
The End of the Phantom's Love Story

1. *The Imitation of Christ*: A work of spiritual devotion by Thomas à Kempis (*c.*1380–1471).

EPILOGUE

1. *Louveciennes*: Village to the north-west of Paris, which became popular among Impressionist artists and the upper middle class at the end of the nineteenth century.
2. *Erik had been born . . . the son of a builder*: Gaston Leroux himself was the son of a building contractor and his parents were married in Rouen.
3. *the Romani*: Another name for Gypsies.
4. *the fair of Nijny Novgorod*: One of the liveliest fairs in Russia, which attracted millions of visitors every year. A brief description of this fair was published in *Le Matin* on 13 September 1897 as part of Leroux's coverage of President Faure's state visit to Russia (reprinted in *Du capitaine Dreyfus au pôle Sud*, pp. 150–51).
5. *legerdemain*: Term meaning 'light, or nimble, of hand', which was used to describe conjuring tricks and juggling.
6. *the Shah-in-Shah*: 'King of kings', a title given to the Shah of Persia (Iran).
7. *Samarkand*: An important town (now in Uzbekistan) that occupied a central position on the Silk Road, the major trading route between China and the West. At the time of the story it was still ruled by the emirs of Bukhara.
8. *political assassinations . . . war against the Emir of Afghanistan*: These assassinations probably took place under Nasir al-Din Shah's rule over Persia from 1848 to 1896, who had opponents

tortured and executed, and who brought about the murder of his chief minister Mirza Taqi Khan Amir-i Kabir in 1851.

The Shah's war against the Emir of Afghanistan may refer to the unsuccessful siege of Herat in western Afghanistan in 1856, at the time of the Anglo-Persian war of 1856–7.

9. *in the same way a certain tsar . . . in Moscow*: A Russian legend claims that Ivan IV (the Terrible, 1530–84) blinded the architect of the orthodox Cathedral of St Basil the Blessed, built in the 1550s near the Saviour Gate of the Kremlin in Moscow (Maureen Perrie, *The Image of Ivan the Terrible in Russian Folklore*, Cambridge: CUP, 1987, pp. 96–7). Leroux may have heard this story when he first went to Tsarist Russia during the state visit of President Faure in August 1897 (see *Du capitaine Dreyfus au pôle Sud*, pp. 132–40), or during his year-long stay there to report on the failed Russian revolution of 1905–6. (See *L'Agonie de la Russie blanche* ('The Death Throes of White Russia'), Paris: Privat/Le Rocher, 2008.)

10. *Asia Minor and thence to Constantinople*: Asia Minor (or Anatolia) and Constantinople (now Istanbul) are separated by the waters of the Bosphorus and form respectively the Asian and the European part of modern Turkey. In the late 1870s, they belonged to the Ottoman Empire, which stretched from Bosnia in Eastern Europe across to Persia and part of the Arabian peninsula, and was ruled from Constantinople by a Sultan.

11. *a ruler who lived in perpetual terror for his life*: This piece of information and the reference to the Yildiz-Kiosk point to Abdulhamit II's autocratic rule over the Ottoman Empire from 1876 to 1909, and the Sultan's infamous reputation for secrecy and suspicion. However, Erik could not have been in the service of the Sultan in the 1870s since, as we are about to learn, he was working as a building contractor at the Palais Garnier at the time.

12. *secret chambers . . . the last Turkish revolution*: A palace complex, the Yildiz-Kiosk served as the main residence of Abdulhamit II in Constantinople. When the Sultan was finally deposed in April 1909, a whole series of manikins representing him in all manner of poses and costumes were discovered in a locked room. This curious discovery was reported in *Le Matin* on 6 May 1909, at a time when Leroux was probably finishing his novel.

13. *the interview . . . marched into Constantinople*: The troops from Salonika (known as the 'Young Turks') entered Constantinople in the early hours of 27 April 1909. No such interview appeared in *Le Matin* in the following days.